THE COLONY

Annika Norlin

THE COLONY

*Translated from the Swedish
by Alice E. Olsson*

Europa
editions

Europa Editions
27 Union Square West, Suite 302
New York NY 10003
www.europaeditions.com
info@europaeditions.com

Transltion by Alice E. Olsson
Original title: *Stacken*
Translation copyright © 2025 by Alice E. Olsson

The cost of this translation was supported by a subsidy
from the Swedish Arts Council, gratefully acknowledged.

Library of Congress Cataloging in Publication Data is available
ISBN 979-8-88966-082-8

Norlin, Annika
The Colony

Cover design and illustration by Ginevra Rapisardi

Prepress by Grafica Punto Print – Rome

Printed in Canada

CONTENTS

THE ANT COLONY
1970–1998 - 71

THE ANT COLONY
2003–2008 - 115

THE ANT COLONY
2008–2023 - 177

ABOUT THE AUTHOR - 425

In memory of Åsa Norlin (1946–2023),
who taught me to read.

THE COLONY

There were seven of them in the group. They came from higher up, the main road perhaps. Now they were sauntering down the path, not looking at the ground as they walked, as if the soles of their feet already knew the placement of the roots. They were men and women; some looked young and a few middle aged, or older. Fifty? Sixty? They walked one after another, in a line. Onto the little path they turned, the one that led to the lake.

It was morning.

They wore functional trousers and shirts and T-shirts and old jeans. One of them was wearing a dress with a nineties cut: straight, cotton.

The woman in the dress shouted something. She was tall and strong-looking. She shivered a little, crouched down, got to work on a fire in the firepit. It was situated just up from the water, ringed with stones. They must have visited before, I thought. Maybe they were the ones who had built the firepit in the first place.

They said nothing, but suddenly one of them started singing. At least, the attempt seemed to be song, though the notes were solitary, separate:

Ah—

Several of them—not all—joined in: one note, or several. The song was like a call, I thought; it reminded me of bellowing cows or squawking seagulls. All this was only faintly audible from where I stood. There was no wind—perhaps that's why I could hear anything at all.

All the while, the woman in the dress waited eagerly for the little flame. She blew on it, cheered it on like a forward on a soccer team, leaned over it.

From a bag, they produced an old ice cream tub, containing what appeared to be dough, and formed a circle around the firepit, sharing the space over the flames, standing so close that their bodies almost melded together. Their heads leaned against one another.

A somewhat younger man had previously detached himself from the group, and now he came walking back, carrying a dead bird. He plucked the bird free of feathers, struggling a little with the down on its back and wings. Then, he snapped off the wings and the feet, and roasted the bird slowly over the fire.

Thank you, he called out afterwards.

Thank you.

Thank you.

That's what the others said, too.

When the bird was roasted, they carved it up into parts and divided these into little piles. Some ate with more grace—they picked up each small morsel with their hands, seasoning it, inserting tiny, tiny pieces into their mouths, alternating every bite with a piece of campfire bread.

Others, like the one who had started the fire, brought big chunks to their mouths and smacked their lips. *Thank you. Thank you. Thank you.*

Mosquitoes droned around me, a very low, constant sound.

The group lingered, in an aimless way. Someone lay down, looking up at the sky. Someone else squatted by the water. They seemed to have no internal schedule, all just lazing about in their own worlds. Like a group of kindergarteners, only these were adults.

Why didn't I walk down to them? I longed for people. I suppose I felt afraid. Not because they seemed aggressive in some way—quite the opposite—but this: I didn't understand. My mind was running the gauntlet, trying to piece it all together, find a pattern. Who were they? Why were they so thankful? How did they fit together?

If they had been dressed differently, I thought. In kaftans, perhaps, or yoga tights. Then I could have categorized them, sorting them neatly into a box in my mind, perhaps labeled *New Age*. But they weren't dressed like that. They were too functional. Practical trousers. Jeans. Someone wore a shell jacket. Their bodies like a cross-section of bus passengers, they looked like anyone at all. They might as well have been a group of computer programmers. Could they be a family? Or co-workers?

But no. They didn't fit together, they all had completely different vibes.

A short, middle-aged man with big eyes, a sad face. Later he would throw himself into the water and swim far out and back, very fast. It felt like the lake itself was shocked by his speed.

A small dark-skinned woman with glasses.

An implausibly beautiful, tall man who looked almost Greek, like a movie star.

Perhaps they are shooting a film, I caught myself thinking. He is the star, the others are the crew.

But once again: no. There was something about the way they interacted with each other, no chit-chat, just the stillness and the thanking. Complete silence, and their bodies pressed against one another by the fire, like there was no distance at all between them. A closeness that made me wonder if they had been through something terrible, if they were processing something. No families or co-workers I knew acted so tenderly with each other.

*

One of them sat a little further away. He had walked a few yards behind the others on the way down to the lake. He was the youngest, a rather tall youth who limped slightly as he walked. He seemed fidgety, like his body was bubbling with an energy without direction. His face had fine features, but an aura that was—well, *heavy*. I could see it, from as far away as I stood.

When I was growing up, I had a friend whose mother used to take in stray dogs. Each worse than the last, frightened or deadly, dirty and missing a leg, or an ear, or suffering from an infection. But one of the dogs was worse than the others. My friend called him *Poor Bastard*. He was a large mutt with heavy breathing, gooey eyes, and one paw torn right off. When you met that dog, you felt both heartsick and scared. You had two feelings at once: you wanted to both hug him and run the other way.

Then Poor Bastard bit and killed another stray dog, a frightened dachshund.

My friend explained: "Mama always said that everyone deserves a second chance, but when it came to Poor Bastard she said his best chance was to die. She shot him herself."

Only once the others had finished eating did the young man approach the fire. The tall woman in the dress gave him a piece of dough before walking away along the water's edge, and now he stood alone by the fire, letting the dough be baked by the remaining embers. His head moved back and forth; he was searching, wanting to know where the others were, that they were still around. That's how I interpreted it. When he located a couple of them, he visibly relaxed, now sitting down on a rock and rubbing his face. One foot bobbing up and down. Always some body part in motion.

I hadn't thought of Poor Bastard in fifteen years.

EMELIE
SPRING 2023

You run down the stairs, rush to catch the bus, make it in the nick of time, push through the crowd, no available seats—of course—so you go stand by a pole. You put in your headphones and listen to something that blocks out the noise—a podcast perhaps, about American politics. It's important to learn about the world. The bus lurches as it crosses a bridge and you see the sun rise. It paints the hair of the other passengers in gold. People become beautiful. You stand with your body pressed against someone you have never met. Everyone respectfully closes off their bodies so it won't feel unsettling. They are in their own worlds, heading somewhere important, that's how it feels. There is a direction in every gaze. You are part of the hustle and bustle.

Mornings like these, I was always on my way to some early meeting or interview. I had temporary jobs all over the place, one month here, eleven months there, sometimes a project position for up to two years. Everywhere they said: "There might be a possibility of a permanent job later, if you show initiative." So I did, I showed initiative. I can't tell you how much initiative I showed. "Oh no," they sighed, "Rakel is sick. We need someone to cover the evening shift." They glanced around the room. And I always volunteered. "We can always rely on you," they said. And I relied on myself, too! That's the kind of person I was. There was nothing I couldn't handle. Others might say they had to go home to their children, or they felt a little under the weather today, or they couldn't manage—but not me.

I could manage it all. I had built up an impressive network of contacts; that's what happens when you spend eight years at ten to twelve different jobs. I went out after work, almost every night. First I stayed late, then I went out. I went to football games, to plays, to parties, to the gym. I drank cocktails at bars, went running, joined book clubs. I dipped my toe in that sense of community, for a few hours I dipped. Then I went home, to my apartment that I had bought myself, the walls that I had painted the color *eggshell*. I had too many expenses, the mortgage was large, but I loved every square foot of that apartment, which declared to me that I was autonomous. I was prepared to work myself to death to keep it. I was my own ruler. I was so proud of my life. If someone had stood outside looking in, they might even have thought that I knew what I was doing.

My friends longed to have children, to meet someone, but I always felt that the more you let people in, the greater the risk that they would ruin things. That I would have to compromise myself, wake up one day and realize I was living a life I didn't understand.

"Unfortunately, we're unable to offer you a permanent position," they would say when the temporary one was coming to an end. But that was okay because I had a friend who had got a job at another newspaper, and she told me about an opening for a two-month temporary position that might be extended, maybe even lead to a permanent job—for someone who showed initiative.

You don't reflect on being irritated. You think it's justified. You snap at an old man on an escalator for walking too slowly. You get annoyed with your sister for calling and asking how you are doing; you don't have time to talk, and now you feel guilty on top. You roll your eyes at Mika for not finishing her task—she had to take care of her sick child and didn't have time. *Didn't have time*, you say bitterly. You always stay until the job is done. Imagine if we all said that. But luckily for you, Mika, I finished your work. It was necessary, otherwise we wouldn't have been able to move forward with this meeting, Mika.

You don't understand the palpitations. Suddenly they just come. A feeling of discomfort in your chest, every time you ride your bike, every time you exercise, before you go to sleep. Where did it come from? It feels so unnecessary. Can't I just be rid of it? It doesn't last long, only five to ten minutes of so thoroughly hating being in your own skin. But those five to ten minutes. It's like you are . . . *invaded*, by an emotional state. Is it physical or psychological; what is going on? You don't understand. You would do anything to be rid of it.

Sleeping is the worst. You lie staring at the ceiling, and you know that the less you sleep, the worse you'll function tomorrow. The less energy you'll have.

And the anxiety is there, and the irritation, and together they have a little meeting, and you have nowhere to go, nowhere at all. You are trapped inside yourself, inside your own disgusting body.

You are here because you suspect you're suffering from burnout?"

"It started when I couldn't get out of bed. I was supposed to meet some friends, but I couldn't get up."

"Uh-huh."

(Pause.)

"How long were you lying there?"

"Four days. A neighbor came over with some yogurt and cereal. She fed me."

"How are you feeling now?"

"I . . . I don't know."

"I'm going to ask you to fill out a form here, where you'll assess your various symptoms."

(Pause.)

"You're not filling it out."

"No, I . . . I can't. I'm sorry. What were you saying?"

"Emelie, I'm going to read you the questions instead. Does that sound all right?"

"That sounds . . . fine."

(Pause.)

"I know this sounds strange, but would it be okay if we turned off the fluorescent lights, just while I'm answering the questions?"

One morning, I couldn't get out of bed. It was a Saturday, I had planned to sleep until nine or so, but to my horror I woke up and realized I had slept for eleven and a half hours. I had friends expecting me to meet them for lunch. I knew I had to hurry to catch the bus; if I took the one leaving in fifteen minutes, I would be at most half an hour late. I told my body this, but it wouldn't listen.

Come on, I said. The bus is leaving now.

Okay, my body replied, but didn't move.

You really must get up now if you want to make it in time, I said.

I hear you, my body said, but nothing happened.

I tried to lift one body part at a time. It didn't work.

My texting thumbs were still with me. They never fail! I sent a message to the people I was supposed to meet. They were fairly new friends; I didn't know them all that well. I suppose the worst part was they didn't know each other at all—I was the connecting link. It was really uncool of me not to show up.

I wrote:

On the bus now but realized I have a fever, have to go back home and rest. Sorry about this.

I thought for a moment, then sent another message:

You do whatever you want, of course, if you want to cancel lunch or not—but if you still want to go then Elin is interested in humanitarian issues with a focus on children, and Iwa used to work for UNHCR.

I thought some more, and sent another one:
Also, you both have a parent from Halland.
I really wanted to go to that lunch. The restaurant had these delicious mini sandwiches, with whipped butter sprinkled with sea salt and parmesan. After lunch, I had planned to buy some wine to bring to dinner—Amarone wine, because that's what Roy liked. I had also planned to squeeze in a workout. After working out, I would shower, and shave, and try this new body oil I had bought, with a scent of iris, violet, and cedarwood. I would do my make-up and think about what to wear. Roy was so good-looking. I always had this feeling that he was out of my league, and I needed to work my way up to his level so he wouldn't start questioning the disparity between us.

We had plans to go to a gig. The gig was in a secret location; you weren't allowed to know where. It would probably turn into one of those *you should have been there* nights, where you feel entirely swept up in the music.

Surely I would have time for all of it except the lunch; I could just get up in a few minutes.

Four days later, I still hadn't made it further than the bathroom or the fridge. My mind had now shifted into total apathy: I had accepted the situation, I was neutral, and I was unreachable. My phone was dead, and I didn't care to charge it. When I finally did, I had a hundred new text messages, forty emails, and twenty DMs waiting for me. I posted on Instagram that I would be going on a social-media cleanse, which resulted in sixty comments, mostly red hearts.

When I didn't answer the door, my neighbor finally used her spare key and walked right in. She thought I was dead. I assured her I wasn't, but she still made a fuss when she saw me.

"The *tiny work death*," she said.

It turned out that my neighbor had also suffered from burnout once, but in a more dignified way. She has three children and fights for the rights of her people. Everyone understood why she crashed.

Now her children are grown and moved out, but my neighbor still carries it inside, that caretaking instinct. She transferred it onto me now, and I wasn't one to complain. I should have said no, yet at the same time, as we both lamented how everyone had dumped everything on us, I gladly unloaded my own problems on her. I watched as she took care of me, listened to me, and made me soup. I was so glad to have someone who understood.

My neighbor's name is Ánne Helena and she is Sámi. Ánne Helena is so tired of educating Swedes about the traumas of her people that she could puke, but I guess she has given up on us figuring it out for ourselves. From her, I know about how the state took away the Sámi people's land and culture, and these days the Sámi are just supposed to exist as a colorful, exotic flavor. And how the land available to them keeps shrinking and shrinking. How their way of life is hardly possible anymore.

Even though I wasn't there when the land was stolen the first time, I feel ashamed, so I sometimes cook dinner for Ánne Helena. Unfortunately, I don't feel that my pasta puttanesca adequately compensates for the state's betrayal.

Now that she had ended up cooking dinner for me, my guilt grew even bigger; it piled up.

Ánne Helena told me that during the year of her burnout, she brought her three sons up to Sápmi, the homelands of the Sámi people. There they stayed over the summer. Her sons had to shut down their computers and help the family with the annual reindeer-calf marking. "They deserved it," Ánne Helena laughed and poured some more wine.

"Your family or your sons?" I asked.

"Both," said Ánne Helena.

Meanwhile, she spent time in nature, and breathed. Sat outside and lit fires. A few weeks later she felt distinctly better, and her sons had grown to become reasonable people.

"Do you think the reindeer would like me?" I asked, hopeful.

"Definitely not," said Ánne Helena. "They'd sense your stress from a mile away."

Suddenly, life turns into an obstacle course of sensory stimuli. You walk down the stairs, and your feet clatter against the stone floor. *Bang* when the door slams shut. The lights are mercilessly bright, carving into your eyes. Out into the crowd where two giggly women laugh loudly right as they pass you and your ears. You hop onto a bus, where everyone is jostling each other and talking, talking, talking. The man next to you spots a friend further away, yells: "JONTE! I'll be DAMNED!" A girl starts playing a video clip on her phone—pop music blares into the bus for a second before she hits mute.

The bus reels and every time you bump into someone you inhale their body odor, feel the sharp corners of their bag, blink at the blue light from their phone screen. And the bus crosses a bridge and the sun rises and you feel like a stone troll about to shatter if struck by a ray of light. You cower. The sun's biggest fault is that it's too bright. And someone is on their way out, snapping: "You're in the way!" And you see their angry look, and you feel tears well up. It feels so unfair; I always do my best. Can't she see that, the angry snapping woman. I keep on giving and giving and giving, why can't she see that. And you have no control over your nervous system or your tear ducts anymore, so all you do is cry, cry, cry. You stand in the middle of the bus and cry. At first, you lower your head, hoping no one sees—it's so embarrassing—

but then you realized that everyone is just staring at their phone, so you didn't need to worry about it.

Here's the thing. I don't even like nature. I don't like being outdoors. One of my favorite things about becoming an adult was not having to deal with this never-ending, forced Outdoors. "Now you've been reading long enough, go outside for a while." "Now class is over, all children must go outside." Quietly you put on your jacket and your legs felt heavy as you descended the school steps. I used to imagine the teachers' parallel experience of the same break, sitting in their warm teachers' lounge, drinking coffee. Maybe someone had brought doughnuts. That's how I fantasised.

Meanwhile: me and my friends had a bench. There we sat, blowing warm mouth-air into our hands. Talking about *Harry Potter*. Standing up and jumping around a bit when it got too cold. Sometimes you'd take a ball to the gut. Your feet almost completely numbed. We sat there, waiting for the clock to strike ten past twelve, so we could go back inside. Of course we didn't have snow pants, we weren't losers.

I love the city. I love its pulse, its rhythm. It makes me feel safe. Only once in my life have I been truly scared, and it was when I took a wrong turn on a vacation down south in Skåne, ending up in a field that seemed to go on forever. There was nothing to relate my position to.

Before I got sick, sometimes I would go down to the street from my apartment just to take it all in: the people passing by, the lives lived side by side, the lights, the music. A constant noise, cars driving by, the snowplough, some drunk hollering.

How forgiving it is to blend into a crowd. There is always someone weirder than you, always someone feeling worse. Hundreds of people who are different from you, hundreds you agree with. Anything could happen—that's how it feels. Everywhere, a million little possibilities. All I had to do was go out there and make sure to be in the vicinity when they arose.

My dad comes from a village far up the inland. Sometimes we would go visit Grandma there; last time was over Christmas four years ago, shortly before she got sick and died. I hadn't crashed and burned yet, and Dad was still spry. One thing I remember: the complete silence. At eight o'clock in the evening they turned off the streetlights. Darkness. Twice, the power went out, too. Grandma and I sat at the kitchen table, without lights, phones, or Wi-Fi. We lit candles. Ate sandwiches. Brought the food from the fridge down to the old potato cellar. Peed outside, for when the power went out you couldn't flush.

Without electricity, Grandma came alive. All her old knowledge and stuff—piss pots and gas lanterns—surfaced. I realized how all this had suddenly and cruelly been replaced within the span of just two generations, becoming almost entirely obsolete. Grandma was obsolete in contemporary society. She didn't know how to use Instagram. But in that moment, I saw her— all the competence she had, which we never asked for. We sat across from each other then, Grandma and I, at the kitchen table. I heard nothing at all, except the sound as I flipped the pages of my book and Grandma's wheezing breath. I saw nothing at all outside, barely anything inside either, except the page I was reading and Grandma's face, which turned soft and young in the glow of the kerosene lamp. The moment was neither wonderful nor bad, it just . . . was. Impossible to assign a value to. And slowly it dawned on me that this had recently been normal, this was how we'd once lived. No sounds, barely any light, and I compared it to living in the city, like I do, the shops and the cars and the lights, and the screens, screens, screens.

Ánne Helena showed me an interview with a psychiatrist. The psychiatrist had been asked when the world's struggle with burnout began. "When the lightbulb was invented," she said, because from that moment on people could work even when it was dark. Before, the world had sent a clear message: Now it's light, so you should work. Now it's dark, so you should rest. You're not my master, humanity said, and made sure to fuck that up too, so we could continue our ceaseless quest to work ourselves to death.

Ánne Helena brought me to the forest far outside the city. It would never have occurred to her to go to some public barbecue spot where two hundred parents wearing designer gloves grilled veggie hotdogs. She knew places where no one went. Isolated spots, far out, in the middle of the woods. There, she made fires, and I noticed that suddenly my body was calm. Only here was it calm. We sat in silence, sometimes for hours. It was very boring, but I immediately understood that this was the only place where I could get better again, in the odious Outdoors. Only here did my nervous system stop racing.

Ánne Helena thought I was an idiot; she said that distancing oneself from the Outdoors is like refusing to be in your own body. Well, I would do that, too, if I could.

I used to hate the Outdoors because you always come back inside with a bunch of debris. Mud on your shoes that means you have to clean the floor. An ant in your freezer bag. Smoke in your hair. It's so dirty.

EMELIE
(THE NOTEBOOK, JULY 2023)

After a while, five of them gathered in the lake. Gradually, they ended up there, one after another. Sunlight fell upon the water and they positioned themselves in the brightest spot, which was probably also the warmest. Their bodies glistened.

Now, the remarkable thing happened. The tall woman went first. She immersed herself completely, and the others stood close to her. When she resurfaced, she rinsed her face one more time. Two of the others had a sponge. And now they proceeded to scrub her with long strokes all over her body. There was nothing sexual about the act, it just looked . . . *tender*. So incredibly tender, soft, like they cared for her and were taking their time. One arm, then the other. A shoulder, her back. They were focused. While they washed her, she closed her eyes.

When the woman was clean, she took one of the sponges, and the oldest man—the swimmer—stood in the middle and was washed by the others. And now he closed his eyes, too. The ritual was repeated until all five were completely clean.

I noticed that I had tears in my eyes. A bodily memory of what it was like to be little, and held. I thought of mother cats grooming their kittens.

A gleam of water in the sun on the film star's shoulder when it was his turn, and he closed his eyes.

*

Later they would leave, and I wouldn't see them again for a couple of days. But the image stayed with me; it replayed over and over in my mind. It wasn't until later in the evening that I understood what made the washing feel so unreal, almost dreamlike: it was like they were washing each other without any concept of time, of it being scarce and there always being other things to do. As if they did it without expecting anything in return.

In the moment, as I stood there, I had also noticed that two of them weren't in the water. Poor Bastard, who remained on his rock. And another: the woman with glasses. Not once did he take his eyes off her.

By late spring, I noticed that every day I had to be in the woods and light a fire. It was a physical need that came over me—like sleeping, or eating, or having sex. It was the only place where I felt normal, as if the fire served as both meditation and goal. I suppose deep down in us, there is a lingering knowledge that if there is fire, we will survive, and that brings a certain sense of calm. I lit the fire, feeling accomplished even though I relied on matches, lighter fluid, and firewood from the gas station. And then I sat there, gazing into the flames, and things felt bearable.

I no longer asked Ánne Helena if she wanted to join me; I didn't want her to know how often I was out here.

I started dreaming of sleeping out in the forest. Then I wouldn't have to commute back and forth. I could be here all the time. I wouldn't have to spend any time at all on public transport. I wouldn't have to talk to Dad and Ebba and all the people reaching out saying that they were *thinking of me*.

I hated that they were *thinking of me*, because it meant they thought that they were better than me. I was inadequate, while they were healthy and could sit between meetings and *think of* their friend unable to cope with everyday life. Ánne Helena was the only one I could stand, probably because she described her own burnout in purely carnal terms—how her nervous system had been so wrecked that at one point she was yelling at her own child while simultaneously breaking down in tears and pissing herself. I responded to everyone who texted me as if everything was under control, but said that I would be bad at keeping in touch for a while. I added that I looked forward to seeing them again when I felt a bit better.

They agreed to this alarmingly easily. I knew that I was a person who had built a fort around myself, but surely they could have knocked very hard and tried to get in.

The woods. If only I could sleep there. Then I wouldn't have to risk running into some old acquaintance that I'd have to talk to. They seemed to me like obstacles in a video game; I tried to dodge them in the street, but someone always seemed to spot me—an old boyfriend, someone I met at a party once. I cursed my former social prowess.

"How are things?" they would ask.

And me, I was utterly incapable of lying, always had been, so I told the truth, albeit an abridged version:

"It's all right, could be better. I'm on sick leave for burnout."

Here I would try to look facetious:

"How typical of me, always too many irons in the fire!"

Not without pride.

And then they would pause a little, looking at me for a second longer, yet without the slightest hint of surprise:

"Okay, that's too bad . . . But you're on the road to recovery, right?"

I was supposed to say that I was better now, that I had learned something from the burnout, so that the other person could be free of responsibility, say that they understood, tell me about their own immense fatigue and workload, before ending with: "Good to see you, let's get together sometime! Take care, now!"

And I couldn't bear to disappoint them, so I just said, "I'm getting there," or something along those lines, while at the same time wondering where the hell I had parked my bike and what that acquaintance's name was and where we had met, because I could no longer remember.

Finally, I just did it. I posted on Facebook: *Anyone interested in renting an apartment downtown? Rare find! 15 grand a month. Cash only. Broken shower.*
I had ten responses within half an hour.
I packed a sleeping bag and a tent I had used at a festival ten years ago. I still had my dad's car, which had been parked since he got sick. Now I got in and drove north, to where Grandma used to live, as it was the only area outside the city that I knew. I broke up the journey into three days, as I couldn't handle driving the whole distance at once. I made it to Grandma's village. The house had been sold, to some German who is only here for a week now and then. I parked the car by the side of the road, walked until I found the hill where Grandma and I used to pick berries. It felt strange to be here without either Grandma or Dad. It wasn't an ideal place, but it was okay, and I couldn't bear to think anymore. If it stops being okay, I'll have to find another spot, I guess. I really don't want to make any decisions, my brain gets overloaded. Coming here wasn't a decision, it was more like a lifeline. It was the only thing I could think of.
I thought about how it was a shame I hadn't grown up here. If I had, this could have been a classic homecoming story. According to the movies, a city girl only needs to drive a hundred miles up the country and she'll be swimming in picturesque B&Bs and sexy former classmates.
I don't know anyone at all here.
The first few nights were the hardest. It was so bright outside, hard to settle down. In the daytime I felt even more stressed, as if the absence of stimuli led to a hyperactivity in my own brain. I could feel the thumping of my heart so clearly when everything else was gone, and the lack of stimulation made each minute long. I wondered if I would be able to cope with the mosquitoes, whose presence initially was so intense they couldn't be ignored. For a few days I felt almost depressed, before my mood suddenly shifted and a kind of stillness settled in. I went to a

nearby town and bought a ton of canned food—tins of sweet-corn that I ate with a spoon, ravioli that I heated up over the fire, relishing not having to cook.

I'm even starting to get used to the mosquitoes. Partly, they have waned now that it's towards the end of July; partly, I spray the tent so excessively that it might just kill me before the burn-out does.

I feel like I have gone into hibernation.

* * *

I had been here for a week when I first saw the group, that time they roasted the bird. I noticed now that I had started to wait for them, longing to see them. The way they stood in the water and washed each other. The stillness. The aimlessness. I didn't have much to think about up here, so in the evenings I made it a habit to replay the memories of the day in my head and create stories around them. I fantasised about plausible scenarios. *There is a care home for the mentally ill nearby. One of them runs a wellness retreat. They are forest researchers stationed here over the summer.*

Just when I felt like a story was complete, they would show up again, and they always did something—moved in some way—that shot holes in what I had just made up. That man with the cap, for example, he looks so resourceful. Fishing and building and making fires. He doesn't look sick or deranged. Nor like a scientist. He looks like a regular guy who loves the woods.

For a while I would see them daily, then suddenly a hiatus. These last few days it had been raining, so I'd assumed that's why they withdrew. But today the sun was out again. Then suddenly, I heard voices, and some kind of rhythm. I looked down—I'm on a bit of a hill—and there they came. One was carrying a plastic jar, which he was beating, like a drum. It didn't look planned, more like he just happened to be carrying it. That was my guess. But it sounded quite good when he beat it. They sang again, those peculiar sounds, just various overlapping notes.

They moved closer to the trees just up from the water, and here one of them began to dance, without any music. Some of the others joined in. It was still morning! All they had was the jar, which was put down when the person beating it wanted to dance, too. Then there was total silence! Yet they danced anyway. Two of them stopped after a while, and this also seemed fine.

It was a Wednesday in late July. The sun high in the sky. The dance was primal, their bodies jumping; at one point, someone threw themselves to the ground. I remember watching a documentary once about The Stooges, Iggy Pop's twitchy dance moves. This dance reminded me of Iggy's, but here everyone had their own way of twitching: some softly, others with more force. One of them was doing a ska dance, like they were at an indie club. All together it looked beautiful, and not.

The only other people I have seen since coming here: quad bikers at the nearby gas station, a few Thai berry-pickers, a friendly old man out angling. All a natural part of the inland fauna.

Not like these primal dancers.

I said "What the heck" out loud to myself, for that's the kind of thing I do these days.

It struck me that the smoke from the fire might give away that I was sitting here outside my tent watching them, so I quickly spun around to check that it had gone out.

It had.

I wondered if they were high. Maybe that's what brought them together? My experience in the media industry told me that if illogical combinations of people were hanging out, it was always because they were doing drugs together.

An hour or two later, a couple of them were still dancing. One man had gone to sleep. One of the women was hewing kindling from a larger log with a knife and another piece of wood. Poor Bastard was dancing all by himself, maybe a hundred feet away from the rest of the group. He seemed absorbed in the dance. But it looked so very sad, a teenager dancing alone on a bog with no one caring.

The woman with the glasses squatted by an anthill. She stayed there, just staring. For what felt like an eternity. Like she was watching TV.

Poor Bastard was the last one to stop dancing. The man with the mournful eyes called out to him, so I caught his name roughly. Åke?

He really didn't look like an Åke.

LÅKE
(THE LEGAL PAD, JULY 2023)

W e can feel it in our Bodies, when summer begins to weigh over. There are many little clues around us! Now it's high summer now everything is in bloom. & when it's time we shall feel the call to return to our nest.

Dear Diary you should know that the farm we live on is big. Ersmo's Family used to live here, a long time ago. Now they are all dead. The house is outside the village & away from all the other villages. It's only happened maybe 3 times that someone has come & knocked when we were home.

Once, two Berry Pickers when their car broke down.

That time Ersmo went out & helped them, it was Cool & Impressive to see how quick and skilled his hands & eyes were over the engine. We felt pride. *We can do that too.*

The second time: an American who came by wearing a ballcap & said that his family Originated from the village. He wanted to talk & talk though Aagny & Ersmo they aren't very good at English! But József helped. He had a beautiful, British accent said the others. *We can do that too.*

I think they figured out that Ersmo's grandma had been a cousin to the American's grandpa.

The third time, a surprise visit from Town. They wanted to see for themselves that everything was all right with Ersmo's mum after the accident & all. I think they wanted to Sneak in but there's NO sneaking here, there is only one way to get here by car and for every car that comes we sit and stare out the window, debating who it is. When a car stops here it's like a party

That time we stood there huffing in a bit of a panic at first, but suddenly we heard noises behind us & it was Sara who Quick as a cricket had sat herself in the wheelchair that was from Ersmo's mum. & she said to everyone except Ersmo & Aagny to hide. For they get paid to assist Ersmo & his mum with daily life. "Pretend to be dumb Country Folk," Sara said to Ersmo & Aagny, & they did their Thing. Sara looked all broken in the chair, she moved differently when pretending to be Ersmo's Mum, wearing an old Cap to look older, & Aagny spoke for her, saying that everything was fine & they shouldn't complain, but during the conversation Sara made sure to piss in the chair. The piss snaked down. It smelled disgusting!!! The surprise visitors quickly said their goodbyes!! *We can do that too.*

In summer we often go to Big Spruce & Selberget for example but we also spend a lot of time at the house. We harvest Potatoes & so on gradually. In late summer we move back in & harvest more: Raspberries, Strawberries & Zucchini. We roast Potatoes with Perch from the lake, sometimes we eat it with butter. Of course we say thank you, thank you for all the good things life brings!! We are not barbarians!!!!

EMELIE
(THE NOTEBOOK, AUGUST 2023)

I had brought along my iPhone, but I noticed that I had become afraid of it. I was afraid of the emails, afraid there would be some question that needed answering. Afraid of the text messages. Afraid of social media, all those *READ THIS! When will someone do something? It's time to act!* And if you didn't feel exactly the same way and didn't act immediately without thinking, you were evil.

A hundred years ago, we only knew of the injustices we saw in our own villages. Like: the neighbor had had a bad harvest. Then you could go over there and donate, say, a jug of milk or a pork shoulder. (I'm guessing here.) Problem solved. The neighbor won't starve. You have done your part.

But now: the refugees, the wars, the uprisings, the pandemic, the energy prices, the interest rates, the earthquakes, the shootings, the diseases. Every day something new. All the world's wounds laid bare in real time, the imbalance of power. And here you are, sitting like some kind of English king with a scepter in hand, snacking on grapes to the sound of the Earth's demise. I do nothing at all about this. *Perhaps I should post something!* I think to myself. It's the first thought that pops into my head! Share a link to some article. Write: *Enough is enough!* Get a hundred likes from others who feel exactly the same and also can't be bothered to do anything about it, argue in the comments section with an old colleague, then eat lunch and go home knowing that you have accomplished something important!

In reality, you have done absolutely nothing except distance yourself even further from your old colleague.

Well, after three days in nature, half of which I had spent searching for phone signal on the hill, I felt dramatic. I went down to the lake and threw my iPhone out over the glistening water. I felt like a free woman as I watched it sail away. Then I went in and searched for it, but it was water damaged.

In the end, I bought a Nokia with a prepaid SIM card at the gas station. All you can do on it is make calls, and barely that. God, I regret my actions.

I'm starting to feel bored now. Is that good? In the beginning, all I wanted to do was stare up at the tent ceiling. Now I have begun to long to talk to someone. I most certainly don't want to chit-chat with anyone in the shop in town, and I don't want to call a friend who might tell me about the strides they are making in their career. I probably don't want to call anyone at all, if I'm being honest. I never pick up the phone when it rings, so the person calling is forced to text me instead.

I know who I want to talk to. After observing the Mad Bunch from a distance for ten days, I feel the itch. Apparently, the journalist in me is still there. She is looking for answers. Who are they, is it religious, how are they connected, what has happened to them? She creates a storyline in the back of her mind. *This would get lots of clicks*, I think, before gagging a little.

The group is almost always together, and I can't handle that—meeting them all at once—I don't think I have the courage. Instead, I go for walks in the daytime, long loops, maybe hoping to run into one of them alone, talk a little, without them realising that I sit here and gawk at them all day. But my mouth barely works after three weeks in hibernation. When I try to talk to the teenage attendant at the gas station, what comes out are mostly just vowels.

* * *

A brief account, with which I'm amusing myself:
They seem to be seven people.
A man with a bit of a sad face, around fifty to fifty-five.
The tall woman who looks so strong. She is probably also in her fifties.
A woman in her forties, kind of Indian-looking, glasses.
Another woman in her forties, short, long hair, ample bosom, good posture.
The extremely beautiful man, maybe around forty too. Imagine suddenly seeing Jude Law wandering around the inland, if Jude Law was fifteen years younger and Greek.
A slightly younger man, maybe my age, around thirty. A proper inland appearance, in a Helly Hansen jacket and trucker hat.
And Poor Bastard, of course. How old could he be? Thirteen? Fourteen?
Today, they arrived one or two at a time. Someone went swimming, a few chatted, one jumped over various stumps and stones. To clarify, this was a grown person.
Then two of the men walked a little further away and jerked each other off! As I write this, I realize it's a strange sentence, but since it happened in broad daylight and no one else cared, I didn't find it particularly strange at the time. They didn't walk very far, and it didn't seem to matter if the rest of the group saw.
Then they rejoined the others.
After a while, there was more movement. Three of them walked further along the water, to a small bay, and there they pulled out a rowboat from under a tarpaulin. The beautiful man rowed, and he moved the oars at such a quick and steady pace that the water seemed entirely weightless. In the boat, he sat with the Tall Woman and Helly Hansen. Helly Hansen looked down into the water and signaled, and when the spot was

secured all three of them got out fishing rods and positioned themselves facing different directions. They caught some fish, at least Helly did: he hauled in one after another, quite small. I watched as he pulled the hook from the fish's mouths, as gently as he could. The Tall Woman caught a couple of fish, too, throwing one back into the water, twisting the head off a slightly bigger one, and placing it contentedly in the basket.

I thought to myself that they weren't greedy. They could have stayed longer; the fishing was good. But after just a couple of hours, the beautiful man started moving his arms, propelling the boat back to the beach. Waiting there was a fire and a grill rack, and they salted the fish and smiled at each other, and at the dead fish. When they ate, they were meticulous; even the smallest edible morsel had to be consumed. Then the man with the mournful expression took the grill rack down to the lake and rinsed it off, rinsed the wooden cups they had drunk from. He buried the fish waste in a pit, with care, like a tiny quotidian funeral.

The short woman with good posture went out to the shore, stood there staring out. She was wearing a worn summer dress with pants underneath.

Gradually, all the others came, too, stood beside her. It didn't take long. They leaned on each other, gazing out.

M um," said Låke.
The others had gone swimming, so for once they were alone, and Låke ventured closer.

"Tell me about Dad," Låke said.

Sagne said: "No."

"I'll give you anything you want."

"Will you be completely quiet all day tomorrow," said Sagne. "Not a peep from you."

Låke said yes.

Sagne paused, then she responded:

"He was an Outsider. He took without permission."

"What was his name?"

"That's none of your business."

"What happened next?" said Låke.

"Nothing."

THE ANT COLONY

They preferred to sleep outside. It felt right. With the ground beneath their bodies, under the starry skies, with the warmth from the others. So much air to breathe, it never ran out. Forget, forget soft mattresses and table fans. They barely remembered them anymore.

Everything exists within you. You already contain it all. You need nothing. You have a big spruce tree to sleep under and warm bodies to press up against.

Låke
(The legal pad, August 2023)

József & I we sometimes have nice Moments. He can come to me & say come Låke let's go just you & me. And then we do. We go down to the lake & take a long Stroll & talk. & József can ask such strange Questions. He can say Låke how are you? Låke what do you feel? What do you want? But I don't think I want anything in particular. Then maybe he says, Låke do you know the names of the planets & I say Yes you have taught me before and also I have read about them. Mars Jupiter Saturn & all that. Låke what is 8 times 8? It's 64 I say you have already taught me that. How did people live in the past? Well there was the Stone Age & the Bronze Age & the Iron Age you have taught me that. Låke what are the names of the clouds? Cumulus clouds & Stratus clouds & also Rain clouds.

Låke you do know there is another world out there? Yes & in that world people live only for money & they harm each other.

Yes, that's true . . . too. There is also love & friendship & music out there.

& books?

Yes & books.

Yes & Society wants to keep Track of every little thing you do.

& love.

Okay József I say. Then we walk in silence for quite a while before we get back to the others & go our separate ways. It's not Illegal what we are doing but for some reason we only talk like this when it's just József & me. I don't know, it gets weird otherwise.

Like today we went on one of those Walks where József also told me about Forms of Government & when we got back to the lake & Big Spruce we stayed there for a while. I sat watching the ants scurry around hoping Mum would see me do it & I sang while I did it hoping the others would hear & say Låke that's beautiful.

József I said later when we were alone by the water. There is one thing I want. I wish I could come with Ersmo into town to go Shopping sometime. No that's not possible József said. Why not really I asked but József just shook his head. Once I heard Mum say No what if someone sees him.

So I guess I haven't seen many people & it's because I have never been to town.

Is there nothing else you want asked József then with his soft Eyes.

What do you want? What do you mean what do I want. I want it to be sunny tomorrow, & I want more blueberries to grow.

If I step a little out on the hill, I can see past some of the tallest trees; my eyes reach further. There is a small glade up from the lake where the sun likes to shine. Here, the trees are mixed; they all look different. It's spruces and pines and birches. It's like they stand further apart here than in the rest of the forest, and entirely without logic. It makes you think of the Ents in *The Lord of the Rings*. Hanging everywhere is lots of lichen. It's not very neat and tidy. The trees fall onto each other, sometimes bent, logs and underbrush. It looks like a fairy tale. It also looks very messy. One of the spruce trees is bloody huge.

Sometimes they disappear into this clearing, the Mad Bunch. I have seen them a few times at night, they hide out under that tree. It's still bright almost through the night.

Sometimes Poor Bastard goes walking alone.

The Ant Colony

Mostly they were silent. After all, they spent so much time together, they already knew what the others had to say.

They behaved like the crew of a ship. The Colony was the vessel, and sometimes they could see in each other's faces which way things were headed. Now the ship is about to capsize, someone must go stand on the other side, to restore balance. Now Sagne has grown quiet again. Then József needs to say something nice, something to bring them together. Now the atmosphere is heavy. Then Aagny can do something funny, or Zakaria can lighten the mood just by grinning. Some of them were good at teetering on the edge and nearly causing the ship to tip on its side. Others were good at balancing out.

One thing they often said to each other was how lucky they were, to live like this.

LÅKE
(THE LEGAL PAD, AUGUST 2023)

So I was out for a Walk as usual & I was walking along the water & then you get quite close to another Beach a bit further away which is quite nice. Once or twice they have told me Don't go there Låke but it was such a long time ago. Plus I'm also cautious. I sneaked. & today I hit the Jackpot because there were five people on that other beach. I'm guessing a family, someone old & two parents & then two Children little boys. One of the parents she kept calling out to the boys all the time. Don't run there & not here & do you want a sandwich & oh dear oh dear did you cut yourself on that rock here's a Band-Aid. When the boy started bawling he ran to his mum & she made room for him on her lap & smelled his hair & kissed him on the nose.

THE ANT COLONY
AUGUST 2023

I t was one of those nights they slept under Big Spruce.
Big Spruce. How old might the tree be? Two hundred
years? They kept their sleeping pads and blankets beneath
Big Spruce, and they never got wet or even damp. This spruce,
thought József as he lay squeezed in between Sara and Ersmo,
was perhaps the most comforting embrace he had ever felt. Big
Spruce just kept on giving; you never had to wonder how she
was doing. Whatever you were feeling, no matter how bad you
were, she would accept you and never judge. No fear under Big
Spruce.

József often had trouble sleeping, and so during bright summer nights he found solace in searching for details in the bark
on Big Spruce, maybe an insect, that year's needles. A drop
of sap might appear, a pattern he hadn't noticed before—but
never anything that shocked him. The branches had an interesting shape, the base of the tree resembling a woman lifting
her long skirt with one hand to cross a puddle. You could enter
without needing to crawl, and on the other side of the tree its
branches stretched all the way down, serving as shelter against
the rain and snow.

József knew every line on Big Spruce seen from below; that's
how it felt. Sometimes, it actually happened that he was calm
through and through, in moments like these, when they all lay
gathered beneath the tree. He would notice Sara's body beside

him, so clearly there, not going anywhere, and he would hear the others' quiet snoring. In August, it was still bright almost through the night. He could catch little glimpses of feeling pure—pure all the way through. Today, he hadn't harmed another person, and he hadn't been a burden on nature, or so he hoped. He had done as one should: trodden lightly on the surface of the Earth. And his belly was full and his body tired after a day of being outside. And he knew that when he woke up, it would smell of spruce and rain and water.

Then things would shift, and his mind would begin questioning once more, but for a moment, just this: calm.

Sagne also struggled to sleep. She and József often lay awake while the others slept, and sometimes they would wave to each other. They had talked about allowing the circadian rhythm to be adapted to the individual—that for some reason some people wanted to work in the morning and others in the evening, and it was fine that way. The owls and waders were awake at night, and no one would think to bother them, claiming something else was more ideal.

Not far from the group lay Låke. He slept under Little Spruce, next to Big Spruce. It had simply ended up that way. He slept heavily, he always did, until someone else got up—because then Låke would wake up, too, suddenly restless, alert, as though he thought they might leave without him.

It was Sagne who discovered them first. She was woken up by a mosquito on the tip of her nose. They hadn't been able to sleep outside until now, when there were fewer bugs, but there were still some. It had turned into a bit of a competition between them—not to complain about the mosquitoes.

Sagne crossed her eyes to catch the mosquito with her gaze. She empathised with it, relating its yearning for blood to her own morning hunger. Her body was probably covered in bites, but they no longer itched. The Colony had long been immune to mosquitoes—everyone except Zakaria for some reason. It was as if his body had never fully adapted; he grumbled and scratched in the night.

She got up, went down to the lake, filled her cupped hands with water, splashed it on her face. It was cold but no colder than usual. The weather was overcast but not bad. Usually, Sagne could see any weather for what it was without a value judgement, though sometimes she disappointed herself by feeling a touch sullen over clouds and rain. But the weather—much like humans—simply is, and it's best not to go against it. Those who greet the weather with acceptance are spared a lot of grief.

That's what Sagne thought.

So there she stood, gazing out over the lake,

the stillness and the quiet,

and her gaze moved as it always did, seeking out little companions in everyday life, the sticklebacks and the horseflies.

As she stood there, she heard a sound that indicated

logging machines.

A little later, Låke woke up too. He jumped up from his sleeping pad, instantly alert, searching for the sound, following it.

From a distance, he witnessed them.

A green logging machine, two men in hats. Dressed in orange and safety reflectors, lots of pockets. Ear defenders, and one of them wore sunglasses.

Låke walked along the path that skirted the water, following the sound. The men took turns being inside the machine and stomping around outside it with big strides. One tree at a time, sawing them off, running the arm of the machine down the sides of the trunks, making all the branches and twigs fall off. Whole stands of spruce trees, they took. Anything that protruded from the trunk chopped off, just like that.

He studied their faces; it was difficult to see, but from what he could tell they seemed unperturbed. They looked like Aagny when she was washing potatoes or deboning fish: focused and absent all at once. Doing a thing that had to be done.

They didn't even say *thank you* to the tree.

Then placing the trunk in a pile, neatly. The branches and twigs in another pile. It was like one of the men was teaching the other, making everything overly clear. Instructing and pointing.

Låke needn't have worried about being discovered. The noise from the machine was too loud, and they had ear defenders on. Their focus was entirely on the trees. Låke understood this. He felt brave and dared to move even closer. Now he was hiding under a tree, by a boulder, quite close. He followed the men's movements. He felt sorry for them. They were ordinary Outsiders who didn't know any better. Numb, unthinking, ordinary Outsiders, who thought they were kings over the land and animals!

He wondered why they looked so happy when they took a break, pulling out a thermos and sitting down on the other side of the boulder, their backs towards Låke. They didn't see him, but he saw them, and now he could hear them quite well, too, sitting with their faces towards the sun, chatting and guffawing loudly.

One of them did most of the talking. He was young, appeared to be an apprentice to the older one.

This young one, Låke guessed, wasn't much older than himself. The other spurred him on, asking questions, as he talked and talked.

"I don't know," said the young one. "Thought maybe I'd stay here for another year. Save up money and all that, stay at my grandpop's. Then I guess I should go see the world. Got to get sloshed in Barcelona at least once before Lovisa sinks her claws into me for good. Do you know she's already talking about kids?"

"What!" said the other. "But you guys are only twenty!"

"It's her ma's fault," said the first one. "She had her first kid when she was like eighteen or nineteen, so Lovisa, she thinks it's normal. Oh, Lovisa. What a bloody gem. She's so weird. When we first started sleeping together, I thought: This chick is TOTALLY crazy. There isn't a girl as weird as her in the whole country."

"What do you mean, weird," said the other one.

"I mean like she believes in astrology and shit. Has all these different-colored rocks, arranging them in patterns around the apartment. *What star sign are you* she asked before we started making out."

"What star sign are you?" the other one asked curiously.

"Hell if I know. Beaver?"

He laughed, turned to the side, and opened a small round can of something dark. Pinched some kind of powder between his thumb and forefinger, tucked it under his lip.

"Hey," said the older one, "I think we'll call it a day. We've already done more than we were supposed to. We can get back at it after the weekend. There's not much left. Besides, my head bloody hurts."

They walked over to some kind of small house on wheels a bit further away. Through a dirty window, Låke watched them take off their jackets and ear defenders. They walked out and away. Låke heard the sound of a car driving off.

He looked over at the little house on wheels. The door had been left slightly ajar.

Emelie
(The notebook, August 2023)

Of course.

Out of all the deserted spaces in this landscape, I had to pitch my tent in the one spot where there would be 1) some kind of cult, and now also 2) some bloody tractor or whatever. Ever since my burnout, I couldn't even stand the noise when a neighbor blow-dried their hair, and now: this constant roaring!

I hated pitching this blasted tent, and I liked the spot I had found, so I was hesitant to move. But I still considered it when those two clowns in orange clothes and safety reflectors started revving up that machine—the sound got in everywhere, shaking the hill. I felt upset and angry with someone, though I didn't know who. This was supposed to be My Quiet Place! Why did this always happen to me. Why couldn't I have a bit of luck, for once. I felt the familiar sensation of the corners of my mouth twitching; a crying fit was coming, and I let the tears fall freely down my cheeks.

Just as I started pulling on a tent peg, all but dislocating my arm, the two tractor men—from up here they looked like little LEGO figures—seemed to be leaving. They opened a car door, music blaring from the stereo; it felt like someone had smacked me in the face. But it was Friday, this I knew. So they probably wouldn't be back until Monday. I had a couple more days before I needed to move.

Maybe it was time to return home anyway? I explored the thought. It was the same as always, when I dreamed about it:

easy at first, playful. I imagined my bed, sushi, Ánne Helena, a perfect cappuccino. We would go out, stroll around, a breeze, a warm summer evening, the people, the buzz. Want to grab a glass of wine? Ah, a new place, somewhere we have never been before. Exchange a few words with the bartender, catch sight of someone I used to work with across the room, oh my god, Dino! So great to see you. Where are you headed? Ah, a gig. You can add more names to the list, we'll join you.

But gradually, the thought always morphed into something else. Arriving at the concert, standing in line to check our coats, standing in line to buy beer, the lights from the stage, strobe lights, someone tall standing in front, I can't see, two people behind me start talking, can't concentrate, can't become one with the music. An acquaintance of an acquaintance. Hey Emelie, it's been a while! Have you met my new boyfriend? He works with cutlery. Oh okay, which piece of cutlery is the most popular? The spoon—I should've guessed. What do you do for work, then? Where do you live? How did you get that apartment? Which estate agent did you use? Ah, you called the owners yourself and convinced them to sell, yes, it's good to be proactive.

Trying to get hold of Roy, waiting for him to reply. Sleeping with Roy. A surge of stress just thinking of Roy. To spend the night with him, I would need to go to the gym, lose weight, be sharp.

Roy hadn't reached out at all since my burnout.

He liked to say that health was a choice.

Now I stood outside my building, the cars, the cars, the cars.

I was struck by a feeling of nausea, *fear* almost, and I shut off my mind.

I wasn't ready.

As I'd thought of the city, however, I had worked up a craving for coffee. I was all out, and I really didn't want to go back into town. The thought struck me: What if there was coffee in that trailer? What if there was still some left in the thermos they had just enjoyed? Maybe there was even a coffee maker, so I wouldn't have to make it myself? Boiled coffee was the worst, I never got it right; no matter how much ground coffee I used, I never managed to make it strong enough.

I tied my shoes, started walking down the hill.

Låke
August 2023

Låke's body: thin and tall. His legs knobbly, full of bruises and cuts. Lots of hair, tumbling over his forehead. He looked like a lupine, and he felt like one. No one was happy to see him. He would just be standing there, but they assumed he would ruin everything.

He thought about all this, because inside the house on wheels was a mirror, a narrow crappy mirror, mounted on the door. He wasn't used to seeing his own reflection—they barely even had mirrors at Ersmo's—though he would occupy the small one in Sara and József's cabin when no one else was on the farm. He would walk by the mirror, as though in passing. Then he would glance to the left to see if the mirror had noticed him walking by. He liked seeing his own reflection; it was as if the mirror confirmed something he sometimes questioned, that is: his own existence.

And now: this narrow, dirty, mirror.
He put his face closer to it.
Then he backed away.
Then closer again.

Låke searched the trailer. Every now and then, he glanced out of the window, to make sure the men weren't coming back.
A part of him wished they would come back.

Things he found:

A small bag with the word CHIPS.

Two empty plastic cans labeled LARGE PORTION SNUS.

An empty can that said BEER 3.5. It was wedged under the sofa.

A paperback, SURROUNDED BY IDIOTS.

Two empty bags, PICK-N-MIX.

An old sole.

A hat.

Tucked into the sofa, a magazine, with a half-naked woman on the cover.

A cord of some sort.

He sniffed the bag marked CHIPS. It didn't smell of anything. Peered out the window for a moment. Would he dare? Yes. He tried to find a way to open it, pulling and tugging—it didn't work. Finally, he used his teeth, ripping it right open.

Yellow, ridged, with green spots. Now there was a smell. It wasn't so bad.

He read on the bag. POTATOES it said—that seemed reassuring. What's more: DILL CHIVES GRAPE SUGAR. All things he knew and appreciated that is, chives, dill, and sugar.

He put a small piece into his mouth. Nibbled and smelled some more. The taste spread across his palate. It was salty. A little too salty, Låke thought, yet he immediately had another one.

He noticed that the ways he was used to eating—biting into bird meat, tearing bread apart with his teeth, or holding a blueberry in his mouth and crushing it with his tongue—didn't work.

The crisp wanted to be eaten with force but also with ease. Biting down too hard was of no use. His teeth slammed together.

Now Låke sat down on a chair. Outside, the sun was shining and the wind blowing, but inside it was stuffy and quiet. The chair stood next to a small table and, even better, it was positioned in relation to the window in such a way that Låke could see if the men returned—he wouldn't have time to get out, but he would have time to prepare, to hide the bag of chips. After all, there was a chance it wasn't his for the taking.

He sat there. A sense of calm began to spread over him. Suddenly it felt to Låke as if he had something entirely of his own, something the others didn't know about. His secret, his place.

He felt different, what was this feeling? Like he could do things by himself. He savored and enjoyed it, even better than CHIPS.

EMELIE
(THE NOTEBOOK, AUGUST 2023)

Once again, I wished someone was with me. Everything that happens here is so silly, yet there is no one to laugh with. And then it's like it never happened. I might need to start a podcast when I get back, so I can share everything. I noticed now, for instance, that as I sneaked down towards the trailer, I really *sneaked*, like a ninja, even though there wasn't a bloody soul in sight. The LEGO men were gone, and if they came back I would hear the car coming.

If anyone from the Mad Bunch was nearby, I supposed it didn't really matter. After all, it wasn't their trailer. But I hadn't seen them, either.

I considered how, in the past week, I had started thinking about the animals and the trees as though they had souls. Even the insects. It came gradually. After all, I had no one to talk to. Now, I was thinking that a bird in a tree wanted to tell me something—probably because I so desperately wanted to be spoken to. Maybe, I thought, my mum had been reborn as a bird. Now she sat there, calling out to me. "Tuck in your belly!" she called. "Is that really what you're wearing?" "Why is it that you can never walk three feet without getting filthy." I glared up at the bird and gave it the finger; yet at the same time, I felt strangely moved and realized that I missed the feeling of some-one watching over me and having opinions about me. Even if those opinions weren't accurate, there was a sense of direction in that care, which was exactly what I missed.

Ants were running every which way as I set my feet down,

and I wondered who they were. I pictured my math teacher. He had died of prostate cancer. He used to look just like a confused ant when he walked around the school canteen to get more coffee—I think because he got up and forgot what he was doing. We made fun of him then, but after my burnout I understood him better—I never know what I've got up to do. Grandma. My math teacher. A cousin who was in a car accident. A sibling who died in the womb. Now they had returned to Earth as ants.

That's what I thought as I sneaked towards the trailer, lifting my knees high.

I've seen *Ocean's Eleven*, of course. I sneaked towards the trailer from the side, so I wouldn't be seen from the window.

The magazine with the half-naked lady puzzled Låke. It was entirely focused on the mating ritual, he gathered, but he was shocked by the impact it had on him. The people in the magazine looked crazy, but then again people generally did, especially out in Society. They were naked in ways Låke wasn't accustomed to. Sure, he had seen people mating before—mostly Sara and József. Usually, they would walk away from the group, but he had often seen them, especially as a child—Sara leaning against a rock or lying in the grass, József on top of her, both with new facial expressions that scared him—but they seemed happy afterwards, and loving. Ersmo and Zakaria also did it from time to time, Låke had observed: one joyful, the other more focused.

And above all, everywhere: the animals. Moose were rare to see, but he had glimpsed them once or twice; the others had told him how the bull urinated in a pit and rolled around in it to smell more strongly; sometimes there was a struggle for the female, then the moose couple withdrew—like in a film, Sara would say, humming a song about how her heart would go on—and then the cow would give birth to the calves, she would dote on them, feed them, keep them close, for five or six seasons,

until the cow gave birth to new calves and then completely rejected the old ones, as if she had never carried them, as if they were not her children.

One time, he had met a moose calf's gaze, and for a second

he thought he saw himself, and that sight felt more real than the
reflection in the trailer's mirror.

Låke's focus was twofold now: it was on the magazine and
on his sexual organ, and it throbbed, and he felt compelled to
release his seed—it was one of the advantages of being human,
Aagny had said, you could choose to let go of your seed, let
it spread in the wind like the flowers, that's how he felt now,
where he sat in the trailer, like a flower. And this focus on his
sexual organ and the magazine and the flowers meant he was
completely unaware that, outside, a fully grown woman was
sneaking like a ninja, dressed in jeans and a hoodie and sneakers, and she burst through the door just as he released his seed,
and she witnessed his seed spraying its wonderful nourishment
over the pages of the magazine with the half-naked lady, where
a woman and a man were engaging in a mating ritual naked, but
the woman was wearing high-heeled shoes.

EMELIE
(THE NOTEBOOK, AUGUST 2023)

This is what I see when I open the door: Poor Bastard sitting there jerking off to a porn mag, with a bag of dill-and-chive chips beside him. My spontaneous reaction is to feel embarrassed, but the embarrassment has so many layers: Accidentally opening the door on someone masturbating, stepping into a trailer where I'm not supposed to be. Being in close proximity to another person—I have barely seen anyone in weeks. I wonder if he saw me sneaking and I think how royally ridiculous it must have looked.

It's like all the embarrassment and strange circumstances cancel each other out, making the result almost normal. This feeling is helped by the fact that Poor Bastard behaves so terribly unexpectedly. He stares at me, not shyly but attentively, like he is observing a whole new species, and he makes no effort to hide his dick; it's still out. He just looks friendly and curious. I'm glad I have been observing his group for a few days, dancing on the bog, thanking birds, washing each other—in that context, the dick doesn't seem so strange either.

He sits there, staring. He smiles at me. He says nothing. I notice that he is probably a bit older than I thought—sixteen maybe, or seventeen.

I say: "Sorry—I didn't mean to—I'll—"

I close the door.

I wait a few minutes.

He opens the door, with his trousers on this time. I notice that he has a downy teen moustache. He stops directly in front of me, smiling. It's a way of approaching a new person I have never experienced before. I wonder why I don't feel afraid, all alone with a young man who until recently had his genitals exposed. It's not until later that it occurs to me that he approaches me as one would approach a dog or a baby, with warmth and a complete certainty of the other's inferiority. But I am a thirty-two-year-old woman, I have a degree and an apartment worth several million kronor, and now everything I thought I knew about social interaction goes out the window, and the map is redrawn. I don't know how to behave, but what happens is— and I must make sure to write this down: I turn into a baby or a dog, I follow his instinct.

After a moment, I bow my head, look up at the teenager, and I feel safe with him.

LÅKE

A person came through the door. An unfamiliar person, a female, an Outsider if he ever saw one; he could tell from her whole anxious posture. She looked shocked when she opened the door; it reminded Låke of that time when he needed to use the outhouse at Ersmo's and there was a little bird in the ceiling.

She was quite nice to look at, Låke thought. Fully ripe—in a few years she would be overripe, like berries in late September. He quickly closed the magazine and put his clothes on—it was a bit chilly—and then he went outside, hoping to observe her, her patterns; maybe she could tell him about the Outside.

He pulled open the door, and she was still standing there. He didn't want to scare her any further, so he approached with a friendly expression, trying to look kind.

The female smiled, suddenly seemed soft. Then she shrugged, as if gathering momentum.

"Hi," the female said. "Wow, you don't expect to run into someone here! My name is Emelie."

Her voice sounded peculiar, like the LPs at Ersmo's, Carola and Pernilla Wahlgren. She spoke in an exaggerated manner, smiling as if she didn't really mean it. There was silence.

"What's your name?" the female said then, as though holding back.

"Låke," said Låke. Then he remembered that perhaps this ought to be classified information.

"Or something else," he added.

He paused to think. If she had already seen him, it was probably fine.

"It's Låke," he said again.

THE ANT COLONY
1970–1998

SAGNE
1988–1990

S he watched her mother milk the cows. A rhythm to the milking, her mother's experienced hands. Changing teats without losing the flow. The stuffy air inside the barn. A fly above the bucket. Its wings and sound.
Sagne shifted focus, away from her mother and the cow.

Suddenly.
Little Sagne realized that the tiny fly was its very own individual, with a mind, body, and direction. It wanted things.
The cow swished its tail, wanting to be rid of the nuisance.
Mother clapped her hands together, *bang!* The fly fell to the floor.

Later, in the evening: a spider in the window. It patiently spun its web. One thread at a time. Working towards its goal. It had found a small nook by the window where it lived.
Evening and morning, she checked on it. The web slightly bigger. What do you want, spider?
One day, a mosquito got caught in the web. The vibration woke the spider. Swiftly it dashed out to capture its prey.
Mother cleaned, found the spider-web in the window. She vacuumed up towards the glass. Weeks of work gone.

They watched *Dallas* and *Falcon Crest*. At the same time, Sagne now saw: tens of thousands of dramas unfolding here, in their house, and outside, on the walls and the ground and the paths and down by the lake. Everything that lived and breathed and thrived and happened. All you had to do was choose to see it. Now she saw, and it would never be possible to unsee.

Angela Channing, Richard Channing. Mosquitoes, mosquitoes, mosquitoes. They died all the time. The wasp wanted to get out again but couldn't find the gap in the window where it had come in. Sagne opened it.

One time. Mother went out to pick cloudberries. She thought her youngest daughter was at a birthday party: Lina's, in fifth grade. Instead, she found her by the bog at Jonasvattnet, dressed up in frills, squatting, eyes sparkling. A bit too old for it to look cute.

At first, Sagne was afraid of being scolded, but she couldn't hide her joy.

"But Mother, it could be a *treeline emerald.*"

She pointed.

Mother leaned down and saw: a dragonfly.

So what.

A dragonfly, in Sagne's mother's mind, was a bit like a chair in the kitchen. It was there. Sagne's mother wasn't about to blow off work because she wanted to examine the chair in detail.

Lina in fifth grade, on the other hand. She was currently sitting around a long table covered in streamers. She was the one who needed Sagne's attention.

Sagne's mother harbored a constant, vague worry about her daughter's social prospects. All parents do. She knew that success among other people is best understood as work—a constant, daily chore, just like doing the dishes after a meal. It has to be done. Keeping in touch with relatives, stopping to chat, staying updated. Wondering if someone might have taken offense at a comment and extending an olive branch. If you have dinner at a neighbor's house, you must invite them over within a reasonable timeframe, regardless of whether you like them or not.

It wasn't always what you wanted. But it's what you did.

"Run on home and change shoes now. Then hurry over to Lina's, and you might just make it before they open the presents."

Now she looked to the left and noticed that the pink box with a ribbon had fallen out of Sagne's pocket. The box was slowly getting soaked by the bog.

"Oh, *Sagne.*"

Her mother sighed.

She picked up the box, wiped it on her shirt. There was a lip balm from the Body Shop inside; it wouldn't be damaged, just the box.

"But Mother," Sagne said, pleadingly. "The dragonfly is only here right now."

Her gaze on the dragonfly.

"Tomorrow, I might not be able to see it anymore."

Sagne's mother sighed. She didn't understand. But then it dawned on her:

"Sagne, do you not *want* to go to the party? Is that what this is about?"

She thought she understood now.

"Being eleven is a tricky age . . . things start to happen in your body . . . other kids can express themselves clumsily . . . "

She looked down at her daughter. Saw that her words didn't seem to stick at all.

"I think it's a treeline emerald, I really do."

Sagne looked up at her mother, beaming. Opened a small book in the bag she always carried, took out her magnifying glass, examined the dragonfly closely. Bright-green eyes, a dark-green metallic hue. One cross vein . . .

She sighed. Now she saw it: there were two, not one. It wasn't a treeline emerald; it was an alpine emerald. Those she had seen before.

But still, so beautiful.

She wrote the date and the words: *Alpine emerald*. She took out a pencil, sketched it. She wasn't very good.

Mother kept talking, in a panic, wanting to hold on to the theory she had come up with:

"When I was your age, I was invited to the same party as Biggan Lundmark. She thought she was all that, with a rich dad and everything. Biggan had said some nasty things about me behind my back . . . "

The words faded into the back of the world and Sagne could switch them off; at the forefront was only the dragonfly. She hadn't seen a treeline emerald yet, that was still true, but one of these days it would happen. Every day brought a new opportunity.

Now the dragonfly took to the air and flew away. Sagne gasped.

She picked up the lip balm, said she would rewrap it and hurry to Lina's.

Mother continued picking cloudberries.

Sagne made it to Lina's and sang "Happy Birthday".

She talked about football and disco and Paula Abdul.

All the while thinking about the dragonfly.

JÓZSEF
1970–1985

His name was József, but in school nobody could be bothered to pronounce it, and he couldn't be bothered to spell it out to every new teacher, so usually it became: *Joseph.*

When József was a child, grown-ups would call him *melancholic.* Grown-ups love to describe children, to put labels on them, like spices. Troubled children, sweet children. Melancholic children. Cumin. József looked like a painting of a weeping child, and this would remain true throughout his life.

On the playground, when he was little, it happened that other grown-ups said so to József's parents. "Look at that one, so melancholic! Sitting on the swing looking as if the world is about to end!"

Then they would smile.

József's parents would smile, too—that's what you did. But on the inside, it was different.

They hadn't managed to shield him from the weight. Despite trying every day, they hadn't managed. Everything they had been through, they saw in his eyes. What had happened to them stared back at them every day.

Their love had resulted in a wonderful child.

But he had that gaze.

As if the trauma had materialized and become a face.

They tried harder.

Have more dessert!
They bought a book of jokes about Norway.
Why do Norwegians keep an empty water bottle in the fridge?
In case they are visited by someone who isn't thirsty.

They loved József very much, perhaps too much. They let him sleep in their room every night—for far too long, they did. They let him eat whatever food he wanted; for a long time, he hardly knew that some children had to eat food they didn't find exactly delicious. Homemade cinnamon rolls every day. It always smelled like cinnamon.

They mostly stayed home; maybe they would be safe there. They kept double locks on the door.

They were over forty when they had him. They only had one child; they didn't want to go through another birth. There was something about the vulnerability in being naked in a room, the fluorescent lights
that reminded them of something else.
Besides, if their child were to die, there would be no siblings left behind, who would have to experience their brother's death.

At the dinner table, they talked about light-hearted things.
How's school?
What's on TV tonight?
The neighbor next door, what's he building now? His apartment must be the most renovated in the whole country.

József's parents had grown up during World War II. As Hungarian Jews, they had been taken to a forced labor camp in Austria. These were two facts that József knew. It was not something they talked about. This knowledge floated in the air, like an untethered balloon. The balloon hovered up near the ceiling and, every night at bedtime, you would spot it and know that it had been there all day.

His mother woke up screaming in the night. It was usual. She scratched herself in her sleep. It turned into sores, resembling psoriasis. Sometimes she didn't even wake up, just screamed out loud in her sleep. Sometimes she got out of bed; he would hear her step out onto the balcony, breathing, breathing.

Oh, how József loved his parents. He sensed their struggle, and so he gladly participated in the charade. It was the only thing they asked of him.

Good, thanks!

We did math.

Yes, please! Yummy, ice cream!

He read aloud from the book of jokes. *Why do Norwegians dress up in their finest when there is lightning? They think someone is taking their picture.*

His mother screamed at night. His father drank. It was what it was.

But what it was was also beautiful and good, so beautiful and good. They were a family who truly wanted to be a family, one that appreciated each other, appreciated being alive and healthy. Sometimes they could pause in pure joy over this fact. The parents, thirty years into their marriage, took the time to make little gestures for each other—leaving notes with words of love, stealing a kiss as they passed each other, or a hug, if it was József they passed.

Just think, József, that you get to grow up in freedom. You're so lucky. You must make the most of it.

When József's mother woke herself and the rest of the family up with those screams at night, József's father would hold her until she fell back asleep. He warmed milk, lulled her to sleep, until her eyes closed. In this way, he gave his own sleep to her. When József's father had his drinking days, his mother didn't get angry. She understood that this was something he had to do—some days were like that. And so, his drinking didn't disrupt the family much in their daily lives.

There was an agreement. His father had a special room, which he called the Office, where no office work ever took place. Every now and then, he would lock himself in there, listen to classical music. During quiet string passages, József would hear the clinking of bottles and glasses, and his father sighing, or the sounds of him bumping into things, stumbling. You never knew when; sometimes just one single day in the middle of summer, sometimes three or four weeknights in January. József's father would be in his Office, sighing and stumbling. The next morning, he would always get up early, shower, and go to work.

On the evenings when his father was in the Office, József and his mother would watch TV, very intensely they would watch, with the volume turned up high. Whatever was on, they watched it. Sometimes they would go to the cinema, only light-hearted films, romantic comedies. Films with Goldie Hawn.

It was important to drown out the silence with noise and stimuli, otherwise things could get dangerous.

And: *How was school today?*
He's too funny, that Ted Danson.

József was a child who knew that the world was cruel, but not exactly what that cruelty looked like, or why. Only that there was a pain so great it couldn't be comprehended. So great it would swallow you whole if you got too close.

He slept with one eye open.

* * *

In secondary school, they talked about World War II. At first, József was happy about this—finally, he would get to know more, crack open the lid on that locked box. And it was legitimate to do so, it was part of the school curriculum. His parents couldn't stop it.

But:
An ethnic cleansing of the Jewish population in the Hungarian countryside ensued.
In less than two months, more than 400,000 Jews were deported to the Auschwitz extermination camp.
József read.
Out of Hungary's approximately 825,000 Jews, around 550,000 were murdered.
Then came another feeling: that he absolutely did not want to know more.

He faked having the flu, putting the thermometer on the radiator; his mother worried as he ran a fever for more than a week straight.

Then they were done reading about World War II.

But after followed lessons about the Vietnam War and the Khmer Rouge and the Winter War in Finland and the French Revolutionary Wars and Genghis Khan, and now all the wars had morphed into the same—they all merged into one.
And the Cold War. It was still out there. Waiting for him.

What did you do at school today?
Nothing really.

* * *

He had an annual pass to the indoor swimming pool.

Right next to the high-rise where József and his parents lived, there was an indoor swimming pool, a newly renovated water park with a wave machine and water slides and a hot tub. József went there with his mother and father the first time, and immediately felt that he loved it. It was so colorful, and everywhere there were children and adults and lifeguards and French fries. And he loved that his parents saw it in him, that he loved it. They looked at him when he looked at the fries, and he looked at them when they looked at each other, after they had seen him love the fries.

They wanted so badly for him to love something.

They got him an annual pass.

He could see his mother's eyes light up when he said:

"Mum, I won't be coming home after school today. We're going to the swimming pool."

He said "we" but meant "I". In other words, there was a little lie in there—but the rest of the sentence was true. He was definitely going to the swimming pool. Two, maybe three times a week, he went. There, he would bob around between crawlers and families with young children, red floaties and turquoise tiles. He soaked for a long time in the hot tub. He stared up at the ceiling, learned exactly what it looked like. *There, the paint has peeled. There, there is dust on a lamp that's only visible from below.*

He rode the water slide several times each visit, developing techniques. *If I lie on my belly and lift my legs through this bend.*

He became very fast. For quite some time, he would blend in among the visitors; everyone probably assumed he was there with a parent who was just in the bathroom. But as he turned twelve, thirteen, started growing taller, and got a bit of hair on his chest and above his lip, it gradually seemed more and more strange—a teenager going round and round in the wave machine, with that grave look on his face, a bit like Buster Keaton being shot out of that cannon at the circus as a child.

And so he started swimming, too, lots of laps. Not because it was fun. It was something to do, something a thirteen-year-old was *allowed* to do at the swimming pool. He developed techniques here, too. *If I push off with my foot like this, I'm that much faster.*

He could have had friends, if he'd wanted to. His classmates liked him; they even sought him out. He enjoyed spending time with them at school. It's just that they were so different from him. He felt ten years older. One time, he was invited over to Peter's house, a classmate who had a big family with lots of siblings and toys, and when they were sitting down for an afternoon snack, he ended up on the couch; they sat four in a row, squeezed together, sat there burping in each other's faces and laughing, and József felt the air leave his chest, had he forgotten how to breathe? Did he know how to breathe at all? And finally, he had to shoot up from the couch, push past all the siblings, a pitcher of lemonade went flying off the table, and József felt like they were living in two parallel realities: Peter's family sitting there relaxed, eating cookies and burping, and he, who was so strange and ran away and couldn't breathe.

Best to keep to himself.

There was a woman named Ingalill who worked in the cafeteria at the swimming pool. They started chatting. Ingalill was the one who sold him fries every day he was there, and after a few months she started noticing, that he was always there alone. Ingalill had been a lonely child herself. She could spot someone trying to have fun alone from miles away. The boy didn't seem particularly vulnerable, Ingalill thought. He didn't behave strangely. He looked nice. No one teased him.

One day, as she sold him a small fries with ketchup and a glass of water, she said:

"You know, I've seen you out there. You're very fast in the water."

"Okay," said József.

"On Mondays and Thursdays, there's swim practice for kids your age. Maybe you should join."

There are some people who make decisions based on desire, and others who make decisions based on fear. József didn't actually feel any desire for more swimming, but one thing worried him: one of his classmates' older brothers worked as a lifeguard, and there was a risk that the brother might notice József, and say *one of your classmates, he's at the swimming pool alone several days a week.* It would seem strange—József knew that. No one his age hung out in the water park anymore. It could reach all the way to his parents. Signing up for swim practice suddenly felt like a stroke of genius. He could continue coming to the swimming pool, where there were guards and Ingalill and laughter everywhere.

"Here comes Benny!" said Ingalill, pointing at a muscular man walking towards the cash register.

"Here I am!" said Benny, who had a jocular nature, and was one of those people who became a coach of all kinds of things because it gave them the opportunity to speak all day in front of people who had to listen.

"József here might want to start swim practice," said Ingalill.

"That's right," said József.

"Is that so," Benny replied. "Well, we start in half an hour. Why don't you come along and see if you like it. And if you have what it takes. You have to be willing to give it your all if you want to make the team."

This was a lie. The swim team consisted of ten children:

three uninterested siblings whose mother had once been a district champion, and various friends the siblings had brought along to tough it out. But Benny liked the feeling of leading a stellar team, so that's how he talked about it.

"Okay," said József.

No one on the team paid him any attention when he sat down next to them, on the benches at the bottom of the stands. They were chewing gum and talking about their own stuff. But in the pool, he pushed off with his foot in his own patented way and outswam them all. Benny clapped his hands together in delight, and it was decided that József would now be a part of the team and come to swim practice at least twice a week. And from then on, he could tell his parents, classmates, and Ingalill that he was going to swim practice, and his father was so happy, and József could go to the swimming pool several times a week without there being anything strange about that.

He adopted a determined facial expression that said: *No, I have to swim.* He used it when his classmates talked about some game he didn't want to go to anyway. How relieved everyone was! Both his family and his teachers. Now they understood. That's why he didn't really have a best friend! That's why he never went to anyone's house! That's why he didn't socialize with anyone, why he didn't go to parties! He was a dedicated young swimmer, completely absorbed in his training! A lonely child requires action, and that was burdensome. A dedicated young swimmer could be left to his own devices.

That's probably why he had that sad face.

It wasn't sad, it was *focused*!

A swimming prodigy.

One day, József's father came home with an acoustic guitar and a book of songs. In the afternoons on the days he wasn't swimming, József would take out the guitar. In the beginning, it sounded terrible, but soon he learnt a few chords. He only played when his parents weren't home. He played major chords, but in his hands they sounded minor. Here, he built a little place for himself. It was a unique place in that emotions were allowed to exist there. Sometimes his parents would ask him to play them a song, but as soon as he started, their smiles grew stiff. He couldn't even play "Happy Birthday" without it sounding like a funeral march.

SARA
1992–1997

Long before Sara became a part of the Colony, she had just started secondary school. She reached into her pocket and found there a faintly red ruby, shimmering, sparkling, and smoking. At first, she had only sensed it—something was different. But eventually she had to take it out, hold it, check that it was definitely there. She didn't know if it was beautiful or ugly, but it was certainly new.

A ruby, Sara thought. *I'll be damned.*

She dressed to go outside. It was a warm autumn day that felt more like summer; she wore a tank top and shorts. Sara walked into town from the house on the hill, which was one of the fanciest in town. It was a route she had walked many times before—hundreds, maybe thousands of times—and so she didn't usually reflect on it. Her legs guided her, and it was fine that way.

Often, she would take the same little walk around town—the record shops, the bookshops, a pharmacy where a good-looking guy worked—and then she would top it off with a visit to the corner shop selling licorice sticks for loose change. Usually, she bought two licorice sticks. The first one lasted down to the square, the second halfway home.

Working in the corner shop was the same man as usual: tall, lanky, with greasy hair and a snus. Normally, he would barely react when Sara placed her coin on the plastic tray, just nod vaguely while continuing to follow the horses trotting on TV. This was a routine that had played out a hundred times before. But this day was different. Something had changed.

Sara put her coin on the plastic tray and was about to turn around, when he said:

"Out buying sweets today, are we?"

And as he said it, he smiled, in such a peculiar way. Sara didn't understand what way this was, but she gathered that he didn't recognise her from all the previous times she had come here. Instead, he talked to her as if they had never met.

She said:

"Yes."

He looked at her again and smiled.

"Yum."

And then she walked straight out of the door—or she would have walked straight out of the door, if an old man hadn't lunged forward to hold it open.

Sara walked out. Was it Pay It Forward Day?

In school, things had changed, too. Sara had a best friend, Linda. The two of them often sat at the back of the classroom drawing on a notepad they passed back and forth to each other. They drew horses, they signed petitions against torturous animal testing, put up posters around the school, drew bunnies in cages that bled and cried.

They were children. They said things like:

"On Tuesday, I think I'll get to ride Starry Eyes. I told the instructor, and she said she'd think about it."

"But Lisbet usually rides Starry Eyes."

"Lisbet can ride Lukas. He's good, too."

"Lukas has such pretty eyes."

But suddenly, as Sara walked down the corridors, people would call after her.

Simon in ninth grade called: "Ouch!"

Like he had burned himself!
Sara looked around, searching for who he was calling to—
didn't get it.
She reached into her pocket. The ruby.

And Sara met her dad's co-workers, who just a year ago had
greeted her kindly, cheerfully, and disinterestedly, but suddenly
their faces were different; they backed away, stood upright, as
if they wanted to both stay away and come closer. One evening
when Per Hansson and Per Berglund were on the glass veranda
having a gin and tonic, and Dad was in the kitchen mixing more,
Sara walked by. Per Hansson stopped her, asking something
about school, but at the same time he placed his hand on her
shoulder, then moved it to her waist. Just stood there, holding
her, giving her a little squeeze. She wondered why.
Sara didn't know what to do; it felt unpleasant to have his
hand there, but at the same time, he was just Per Hansson.
Then Per Hansson saw Dad coming from the kitchen, and he
pulled his hand away from her waist, as if it had been on fire.

And Sara entered rooms and everyone seemed to notice the
red ruby, and it was fun; she experimented: how to make it the
most visible, how do people react then, and how do they react
when it isn't visible, and Petter Mattsson invited her for a ride
in his old Volvo, and they drove windingly about town; the evening turned late, and he wanted to stop the car and kiss her,
which she wanted—but then she didn't want it anymore, and
he got upset. He said that if you had a ruby and didn't want to
use it, you should wrap it in several layers of paper, so it doesn't
show.

So she tried that, too, but it was so boring. She wore oversized shirts and pants and kept quiet. She stood with Starry
Eyes and buried her head in the horse's soft muzzle. The horse

nuzzled her. All horses smelled different, she thought—that thick stable aroma had long turned into separate smells, like when you step into a friend's apartment and immediately recognise their family's specific mix of scents.

The riding instructor had explained about horses, that they were herd animals. They needed each other. They needed physical contact, with each other and with humans. They would stand and groom each other's necks—for a long time, they would stand like that.

Sara saw them and thought to herself that she understood. She wanted to stand and have her neck groomed, too. She was a person who was always in motion. But with the horses, she wanted to be still.

Starry Eyes had become unruly, perhaps a touch mad. Lisbet no longer wanted to ride her. Several others refused as well. But Sara didn't think much of it; she got up in the saddle, and Starry Eyes turned gentle as a lamb.

This would be repeated many times.

"You're not very advanced as a rider yet," said the riding instructor, "but you have an unusual authority. The horses understand you, and they see that you love them. Look at Sara, everyone, see how she interacts with the horses."

The others looked and looked and tried to do the same, but it didn't work. Only Sara could do it.

She put away her oversized pants, for Starry Eyes didn't care what kind of pants she wore.

Sara was invited to parties. She would receive cards in her mailbox. What was requested seemed to be for her to attend and bring her faintly red ruby. She could never ignore it, never get rid of it. She was both happy to have it and saddened by the feeling that the ruby was more important than she was— that they fell in love with Sara without knowing Sara. For she remembered that she had existed before she got it. Surely she had been a person then, too.

She came to school and saw it carved into the school bathroom: *Sara = WHORE*.

The more Sara backed away, the more interesting she became. That's how it seemed. She couldn't escape people, couldn't escape them opening up to her or asking her for help or advice. She marvelled at the way other people seemed to be able to ride the bus for an hour and a half without the person next to them, when the bus ride was over, asking for their phone number, a time when they would meet again. She didn't know how not to open up. It was like there was no adjustment period; people felt instantly that they had known her their entire lives, they wanted her close. She jumped ahead in friendship rankings, immediately on a par with those who had known each other for twenty years. "One of my best friends," they all said.

Some people know what they want to do with their lives. They have an interest, a talent, which guides them, and they follow that path. This wasn't the case for Sara. She stood in the middle of a field with no paths at all, oozing potential. She knew that she had potential. Everyone else saw that she had potential. Her humour, and her intelligence, and her charisma, so immense.

They all said: "You should really work with people!"

Sara only knew one thing about her future, and it was that she absolutely did not want to work with people. It felt like they were devouring her. At night, she would dream of big, gaping mouths approaching with gigantic maws. And they talked, talked, talked.

Help me, the mouths cried.

See me, the mouths cried.

Kiss me, the mouths cried.

Often, they belonged to boys—boys who had all seen Sara and concluded that she seemed to be the right person, worthy of sleeping with and maybe even calling their girlfriend, and the mouths in her dreams were paired with long, slinky arms, demanding in their manners, pinning down her neck, and she writhed and writhed, and when she finally broke free, they wept and called her wicked. And she shouted: "It's not me, it's not me—it's the ruby."

JÓZSEF
1985–1990

One day, some members of a free church stood outside the school. They looked cheerful and wore special scarves. They invited everyone for tea that evening. There was a girl József liked whose name was Karin-Malin. Karin-Malin was already a member of the church, as it turned out. She stood there, inviting people. Karin-Malin felt that the evening activity could be a good opportunity for József to talk to God. József felt that it could be a good opportunity to talk to Karin-Malin. And so he said he would come.

"Szilágyi?" another young member of the church read from the list of participants. "Is he a Jew?" The young church member's name was Leif, and he was a chubby disciple—the pastor's son.

"I don't know," said Karin-Malin and thought for a moment. Surely he couldn't be Jewish; if so, then why hadn't he said something? They'd even had a special day about the Holocaust in school just last Thursday.

And then Leif shrugged, and then nothing in particular happened. And then it became evening, and time for *On this October eve, the Eneberg Church invites you for tea.*

It was dark outside. It was rainy and windy, the kind of autumn chill that creeps in underneath your clothes. You feel cold to the bones, shivering, walking with your hands deep in your pockets, your body like a hook.

It was the perfect evening to introduce new people to the

church by means of chocolate cake and tea. As they walked towards the building, white and beautiful, braving the rain along the way, they saw the glow from inside the kitchen. There were lit candles and happy people, they saw. And as they opened the door, they heard not only laughter but also singing. It was a mixed song, both sopranos and basses, and some who really could sing, some who sang out of tune and deviated from the guitar's melody, but also some who sang and held their notes without necessarily having beautiful voices. There was room for everyone, it seemed.

József walked from the cloakroom towards the kitchen. His legs were shy. But immediately, a woman approached him; she was older—not much older, maybe ten or fifteen years. She had a warm face, and she said: "Welcome!" And József got to say his name, surname and everything, and the woman didn't tell him it was unusual or that he didn't fit in.

After József, other kids from school arrived—not many, but three or four. The Ström twins were there, both the normal and the weird one. And Rosa Pettersson, who had a father in prison; and perhaps one other person, too. They glanced at each other, the newcomers, and smiled with ten percent of their mouths.

In the kitchen, they were assigned seats. There was a long table, but they were spaced out with empty chairs in between, like little islands. Those who were already believers got to sit next to the newcomers. József ended up near the normal Ström twin, Karin-Malin, and the woman with the warm face. The woman read to them from the Bible. The story she read was about a man named Jonah, who was on a journey. There was a storm, his ship was about to sink, and what's worse: he was eaten by a gigantic fish. He found himself in the belly of the whale fish for three whole days, and felt very desperate. Later, it would turn out that God was behind the whole thing. He wanted to save Jonah from the storm.

In groups, they began discussing the story, what thoughts it had raised. As soon as someone said something—the twin or Karin-Malin or József—the woman listened carefully, confirmed what had been said, and then asked follow-up questions. "That's a very interesting thought, József. How do you think Jonah felt inside the belly?"

And this, that someone wanted to hear him think his thought to the end! That they talked about the darkness, and darkness was allowed to be present!

Finally, the pastor said that he had heard from Karin-Malin that it was a special day today for someone in the room. And the special thing was that, today, József was turning fifteen. József had almost forgotten about it; in his family, they didn't celebrate birthdays. Why, he didn't know, but he had a hunch. Once, he had overheard his parents talking; his father was in the Office making an unexpected amount of noise, and his mother had to go in and check that everything was all right, and the music was so loud that his parents had to shout, and his father shouted in Hungarian about someone being murdered on their birthday. He didn't know more, but he could imagine that was the reason why they didn't celebrate.

And now, in the church, everyone looked at József, and the woman who had greeted him brought out another cake from the fridge, one with whipped cream and candles, like a real birthday cake. And then they sang for József, several times they sang. And then they thanked God for the cake and for life, and then they ate.

"Dear Jesus," prayed a man in his mid-twenties with a beard and faded jeans. "Thank you for all that you give to us. May you keep us from darkness and evil at bay. May you not give to us more than we can bear."

And József peeked through the candles and looked at everyone in the room, the beard and Karin-Malin and the twins and Rosa Pettersson and the older woman and even Leif, and they all looked at him as if they genuinely cared for him.

He assumed there might be something problematic about participating in Christian activities as a Jew, but no one asked, and he avoided asking the question himself, because he knew: it wasn't the religion he was after.

* * *

How easy it seemed for everyone else. How light their steps were, their voices. How naturally they seemed to make friends, find partners, develop interests, go to restaurants, make small talk. Get drunk, drink wine in parks. Go skiing, try board games.

József was best at the butterfly stroke—a tormented butterfly swimmer. When it was sunny and calm in the outdoor pool, his body looked like it was forging through a hurricane.

He had intended to quit swimming. To his parents, he didn't mention the church. They still thought swimming was his top priority. They attended every swim meet, standing in the audience and clapping as if the local junior championships were the Olympics. Sometimes József won, and then the following happened: his father smiled, genuinely. His whole face took part, his whole body. He was completely swept up in the competitions. He sat up straight, proud. He shouted. *Go, József! Go get 'em!* He didn't hold himself back.

And for this reason, József continued to swim several times a week.

He was tired of swimming. He had a shoulder injury that never quite felt right. He had the church now, people he called friends who sat close to him and accepted him for who he was, who wanted him to be involved, and when he contributed he felt a sense of purpose.

But his father's smile.

So he kept swimming, climbed in the rankings, became a name to reckon with in local swim circles.

A club from Sundsvall was sending their best swimmers. The best swimmers from József's hometown and the visiting team were considered fairly evenly matched. One of the swimmers from Sundsvall was seen as a promising talent. He would amount to something. József was the best on his team.

"A lot is riding on you now, Josse," said the coach, who mistook József's dedication for interest. In the name of good sportsmanship, he thus seized the opportunity to add a few extra pounds to the weight József was already carrying around on his shoulders.

And his father in the audience, and the people cheering.

In the changing room, they shook hands with the other swimmers. Last in line was the Promising Talent. József, with his watchful gaze, immediately recognised the type: narrow, insolent eyes; posture like an emperor. He knew he was standing in front of a bully disguised as a fun guy.

The Promising Talent had a grin like a wolf, utterly irresistible—like Jack Nicholson.

"Look, if it isn't the swimming Jew!" said the Promising Talent, with a friendly grin. "What's up, swimming Jew!" He said it in such a friendly way that there was no room for József to object; he was just joking, where's your sense of humor. He patted József on the shoulder, a friendly pat.

József stared at him.

"Good luck!"

They walked out to the pool.

The opponent turned to him, smiling once more. Then he made a hissing sound while pretending to twist something. József didn't understand what he meant. He turned around and joined his team, when suddenly he figured it out.

He had pretended to turn on the gas.

His father in the audience, raising his thumbs in the air so József could see.

They stood in their places, and they were ready and set and it was GO time.

Never had he swum so fast. Never had he fought so intensely. Never had he been so strong, never worked so hard, never swallowed so much water. Onward, onward, his arms like engines. The water like solid matter.

He swam side by side with the Promising Talent. The audience noticed the Promising Talent smile as he swam; it all seemed effortless. They also saw how hard József Szilágyi was fighting today.

"Go, Jew, go!" shouted a supporter who had heard the opponent's joke and didn't find anything offensive about it. It was just sports banter! If you were fat or short or had an unusual haircut, the spectators would pick up on it—that was part of the fun in sports.

The supporters had long been looking for a good nickname for Szilágyi. He didn't have any distinctive features to banter about; he was handsome, not tall but not short either, neither fat nor skinny, well-groomed hair—it was difficult to find something funny about him. What's more, József Szilágyi was a difficult and cumbersome name to shout. But now, finally!

"Go, Jew, go!" more and more people shouted, their voices chanting. "Come on, Jew!"

Eventually, they simply shouted *Jew! Jew! Jew!*

His father in the audience.

The word reverberating against the walls of the swimming pool—

József, side by side with the Promising Talent, forging through the water—

At first, he didn't hear it. They were shouting something, but what? Was it directed at him?

Then he heard.

His body heard.

He paused. It felt like a noose around his neck. His breathing faltered. He tried to feel. Was he getting any air at all? He paused again. He couldn't breathe! There was a pressure against his chest. He was dying now. He felt it so strongly. It was coming. This feeling usually stayed away during swimming, but now it was here.

By now, the bully from Sundsvall had pulled almost half a length ahead, with the other swimmers close behind.

József lost himself. He couldn't.

His chest was completely void of air.

He started sinking, towards the bottom. It was like he felt stuck, as if the water and the cramping in his chest cancelled each other out, so that he couldn't focus on either. He went into apathy.

The Promising Talent had won. Everyone's eyes were on him. He hung on to the edge of the pool, basking in the audience's applause.

Meanwhile, a short man ran down from the stands, jumped straight into the water, diving down. He wasn't strong, but he pulled his son up with a force he didn't know he possessed. He lifted József's head above the water, pulled him to the side of the pool, waited until his son began to breathe normally. There they stood, father and son, one in Speedos, the other in soaked trousers and a shirt, holding each other in the water. In the background, the loudspeaker blaring the name of the Promising Talent.

József quit the team and started playing the piano. Father and son had walked home side by side, the short distance to their apartment, the father in dripping wet clothes, both completely silent. When he announced that he had quit swimming, neither of his parents said anything at all.

A pause, and then his mother said:

"I'll start making dinner."

A swimming bully. Some shouting teenagers. Why couldn't he handle it? He should have been able to handle it. His parents had survived the Holocaust, fled here, started a new life. They had given him everything. He should be happy. Why couldn't he be happy? He must be the most ungrateful son who ever existed. His father had had to save him. It should have been the other way around. Why wasn't it the other way around?

Why wasn't he happy? From now on, he would always seem happy.

SARA
1997

They met after dark. They stood outside the factory, bolt-cutters and spray cans in hand. They wore hoods, scarves covering their faces. Black clothes.

Someone carried a video camera.

They helped each other over the fence; it was tall, but not too tall to climb over. They wore soft clothes, sweatpants. Now their hearts were racing, as they jumped down from the fence; they were on the other side. They knew where the chickens were kept: inside the large building that was conveniently left unlocked—there was no reason to lock it, no similar incident had ever taken place in the town where they lived.

They had bided their time. One of them had got his first summer job at the factory last year. That's what had turned him into an animal-rights activist.

They had started with a peaceful demonstration outside McDonald's. They had been too few, it looked pathetic, and on the benches outside had sat an entire hockey team, eating nuggets very slowly and laughing at them.

After that, some dropped out, while others went even further. They became vegan. They started a band. They printed T-shirts.

The building was big and tall. A fan humming. Through the walls, faint sounds of birds. And right in front, a container.

"In there are the dead ones," said the one with the summer job, nodding. And the others breathed loudly; they understood that inside the inconspicuous container, heaps of dead birds lay stacked.

Tanja climbed onto the others' backs, filming down into the container.

When she got back down, she vomited.

The one with the summer job went first; Sara followed. Then the others, four or five of them. They were all teenagers. Someone's legs trembled so badly there were sounds coming from their kneecaps.

A smell hit Sara, that of hundreds of chickens. The air, stuffy and dusty. The fans and the sound of metal cages rattling against one another.

The chickens' small faces, all those ticking hearts, all those feet and feathers and eyes, those bodies, wings that didn't have the space to lift.

She noticed the others looking at her, not surprised but *expectant*. They were expecting her to initiate.

She looked at Tanja, and at Ante. Tanja was going to record it, Ante was going to spray the words. *MURDER*, he wrote on the walls. *MURDERERS.*

She went to the far end of the row of cages, looked in through the door. A gaze met hers. Two eyes. A life.

Then: many eyes. Maybe fifteen chickens and thirty eyes in each cage.

A chicken can live for fifteen years, she had read. But in egg factories like this one, they usually lived for one year, or two. Beyond that, they no longer served a purpose. They were sent to be slaughtered. The male chicks didn't serve a purpose either. They were killed as soon as their sex could be determined.

Chickens wanted to live in small flocks, she knew. In the factory, it was impossible to form relationships.

Chickens wanted to sleep on perches, high up, otherwise they felt anxious. Here, the perches were only a few inches above the cage floor.

"Let's open them," she decided.

It wasn't the plan, but now that they were there, they couldn't not open them.

The one with the summer job was the fastest; he knew exactly how it was done, had opened the cages many times before. The others followed his lead. It wasn't ideal. For one, the chickens weren't happy, but scared. At first, they stayed in their cages, but when one chicken got so scared that she jumped out of the cage, others followed. They were confused by the light in the middle of the night. They cackled louder.

Sara threw grains into the cages and on the floor, wanting them to have something yummy before they embarked on their journey to freedom. Ante wrote with big, wobbly, red letters. Tanja filmed the cages that hadn't been opened yet. If people saw, they would understand. Some chickens had made it down onto the floor. Some ran towards the open door. Maria R had cut the fence with the bolt cutters and now they ran out into life, the chickens and the humans—the latter straight and with purpose, the former confused and cackling. The moon shone; it was cold and clear.

Sara turned to the one with the summer job and smiled grimly. They hadn't wanted to have to do this, but they had done it. *Fuck you* to the hockey team. *Fuck you* to the egg-factory owners. New times were coming, times when humans and animals would walk hand in paw towards the future, and they were the young, the brave, who wouldn't accept anything other than the times changing.

Sara exited the building. Before her stood a man in a security guard uniform. He was tall and looked angry. Acting on instinct, she took the spray can from Ante's hand, sprayed the man in the face, kicked him in the shin. Then she ran—ran towards the fence—but she didn't make it over, none of them made it over.

* * *

"Bloody idiots," said the police officer.

She was a round woman, with a southern Skåne dialect, red hair. She chewed gum as if it were a bone. She was angry and fed up. It was one thing to deal with criminals with a troubled background. In this town, everyone knew exactly who was whose kid. Seven out of eight times, you could guess who would commit petty crimes; it was hardly surprising that Bäckström's kids—with a dad like Bäckström—would shoplift some clothes. But having to take witness statements from seven middle-class brats, from families wealthier than hers, with high grades and even higher ideals, was more than she could stand. The police officer had been a teenager once, too; she had been through that phase when you think you know better than everyone else, and she had grown up and realized that as a teenager she had been an idiot. And so she felt annoyed just looking at them, these rich kids with their pins and hoodies over designer jeans.

"Fact one: Chickens don't want to run away. They didn't run into the woods and live it up, as you imagined they would. Almost all of them just ran around in a panic. Fact two: We've found at least five dead so far. And there'll be more. Fact three: The Jonsson family's entire livelihood is at stake here. Damn fools. There are people working in this factory! Someone might lose their job now."

She held up a picture, of the Jonsson family. She pointed at one of the people in the photo.

"This is their youngest son. He has a life-threatening disease—he's in the hospital! You bloody idiots. They have things to deal with! They don't have time to go around catching chickens just because a bunch of kids read some brochure."

She shook her head.

Read some brochure.

Now something stirred in Sara. Her voice sounded clear and calm as she spoke.

"This isn't about some brochure," said Sara. "It's about us, sitting here, not being people who assume that animals are worth less than we are."

The police officer rolled her eyes. Sara dialed up the intensity.

"Do you know how many chickens are crammed into each cage at Jonsson's? Have you seen the pictures? They can't even spread their wings in there."

Here, her voice softened.

"Imagine standing in a room with thirty other police officers all day without being able to lift your arms."

The officer smirked.

"That's not that far from reality," she said.

Sara giggled a little. It was an unusually infectious laugh, which didn't fit the situation at all.

"Yes, I can imagine," she said. "But where do we draw the line for who deserves a good life? Is it only those who can speak for themselves?"

The officer struggled not to join in laughing. But her face had softened. She wasn't angry anymore.

"That's the circle of life," she said. "We eat each other. That's just how it is. That's how all life on Earth has always been lived. You just have to accept it."

"That's how it's been," Sara agreed. "But just because it's always been that way doesn't mean it's optimal. Think about the police, think about the whole legal apparatus. If it didn't exist, maybe the physically strong would always triumph over the weak. It's us as a society who have worked to develop our human instincts. Maybe it's the same with animals."

The officer was about to say something, but couldn't remember what.

"And even if you think it should stay the way it is, what you said about the circle of life," Sara said, "that humans eat cows who eat grass—that whole cycle. Where does it fit to cram fifteen chickens into one tiny cage, barely two feet wide, pump them full of drugs to make them lay bigger eggs, let them live in ways that go against all their instincts? Chickens are social creatures. They want to be in small flocks, move around, get to know each other. Lay their eggs in peace, take care of their chicks."

The officer was silent. This girl was touting exactly the same nonsense she knew she would, yet there was something about *the way she said it*. Suddenly it sounded logical. She felt herself siding with the girl.

She didn't say this, of course.

The officer shook her head. What was happening to her? She loved hotdogs.

"Anyway," she said then. "You're the leader of this movement, is that true?"

"Not at all," said Sara. "We have no leader. Everyone's voice is worth the same."

"Interesting," said the officer. "Because all the others pointed you out as their leader."

One of the participants in Operation Egg Factory was over eighteen. Unfortunately, it was the same person who the others had identified as their leader. It was also the same person who had sprayed a security guard in the eyes with graffiti paint, rendering him unable to work for two weeks. What's more, all of this had been caught on tape.

"Oh, Sara," said Sara's dad with a tired look.

He had previously been on several golf trips with the father in the Jonsson family. Now there would be no more golfing.

He stood powerless as Sara was sentenced to four months in prison. "To set an example," said those who knew.

"That girl had so much potential," people gossiped around town when the story broke in the newspaper.

The son in the hospital reached out to the animal-rights activists and let them know that he agreed with them. He had seen an interview with their leader on local TV.

* * *

They rode in a minibus. Apart from two police officers, it was Sara and a couple of other women. One of the women smelled awful, of many days' sweat. She was older than Sara, maybe just under thirty, quiet, tall, and wide. The police officers called her Aagny.

"Aagny," said the third woman, who went by Sussie. "What the hell kind of a name is that?"

Sussie had a malicious grin and stared at each one of them: the police officers—Sara—the one named Aagny—one at a time, like she was watching a ping-pong match. Her gaze had an agenda. It wanted to keep people in their place.

Sussie was silent for a while.

"What did you do?" she finally asked, turning to Sara—more interested in establishing rank than making small talk.

"I tried to save chickens from a factory," said Sara. "Accidentally sprayed a security guard in the face with graffiti paint. But it wasn't intentional."

Sussie snorted. She wasn't impressed by the crime. It was also clear that she was a seasoned snorter.

"And you?" she asked the one who smelled like sweat, Aagny.

Aagny didn't reply.

"I said, what about you?"

Aagny stared back at her.

"Manslaughter," she said.

An indeterminable dialect.

The bus fell silent. Sussie nodded, impressed.

Sara thought: She would stay far away from Sussie. She would stay even farther away from this Aagny.

Aagny the manslayer continued to stare out the window.

Sussie continued to stare at Sara and Aagny.

"It'll be damn good to see the others again."

"Yeah, what is it now, your third time? Fourth?" one of the police officers asked, interested.

"Third," said Sussie.

Her tone as if they were sitting around a coffee table.

The minibus huffed and puffed its way through the landscape. It was raining. The rain carried a scent of spruce that lingered like a memory when the car doors closed. The link between freedom and fields suddenly felt palpable. How strange it was to know that from now on it wouldn't be possible to stop the car if you wanted to, to swim in a lake, sit by a fire. All this was now forbidden. Sara never used to swim in a lake or sit by a fire, but suddenly lakes and fires felt very important.

A glimpse of sun behind the clouds.

Then the bus suddenly stopped. Walls and brick. Sara thought: It looks like a prison.

Just as they were about to get out, Aagny the manslayer turned to Sara and said:

"I had a dog once. That dog was the most beautiful soul to ever walk this Earth. I'll show you a picture later."

They moved forward, towards a door, led by the police officers. Aagny walked in front of Sara but turned around, gave her a crooked smile, and said: "Sprayed a security guard in the face . . ."

"It all happened so quickly," said Sara.

They smiled at each other.

* * *

During yard time, Sara initially sat alone.

She was afraid of two things.

One was: that they would hate her.

The other was: that they would love her.

She wrote letters to one of her friends from the activist group: *My plan is to be completely blank. I won't make any impression whatsoever. I won't say anything, to anyone.*

She intended to wear oversized trousers and an oversized shirt.

Sara brought a book to the yard, and she read, and read.

The manslayer named Aagny often walked around chatting with various people, joking and messing around, with a caring manner alongside her tough appearance. Sometimes she would sit alone in a corner and enjoy the sunshine when it reached the courtyard. The woman named Sussie sat with her gang, the same gang every time. Half of them looked lethal. They laughed and hollered.

Sara read and read. Kept her head down. She covered the ruby with her hand, trying to hide it.

It was the eighth yard time since Sara had arrived at the women's prison. She was reading her book when suddenly she heard the woman named Sussie talking about her.

"And that one," said Sussie. "Do you know why she's here? She helped some chickens escape!"

She cackled a little into the air.

The gang laughed, wanted to mimic her cackling, too. One of them was quite good.

Sussie looked at Sara, teasingly.

"You love animals, don't you?"

Sara said nothing.

"Cute little animals!"

Sara said nothing.

"Do you know what I love? Chicken drumsticks. Burgers. Hotdogs. Chicken. Fried in butter. Lots of butter."

She roared with laughter.

In her mind, Sara rolled her eyes. So far, prison was a lot like secondary school, and this gang reminded her of the girls in the smoking area.

Outwardly, she continued to read.

Now Sussie pointed at another woman, one in her gang who sat next to her and looked completely lethal. She turned to Sara and asked:

"Do you know what this one over here used to do as a child?"

Sara shook her head.

"Set rabbits on fire. What a sick fuck, huh!"

"It was their ears," the girl made a point of explaining. "I set fire to their ears."

Sara bit her lip, looked down at the ground. She wasn't going to let herself be provoked. She repeated her mantra. *Don't say anything. Don't draw attention. Don't draw people's eyes here.*

She had just started to ponder how to retreat inside, in the hope that they would start to harass someone else instead. Far away across the paved yard, she saw an almost thirty-year-old woman, tall and strong, rising from her corner, wiping her nose on her arm, before walking up to Sussie and her gang, and saying:

"That's vile. You're a psychopath, you are. Ain't like those rabbits went and done anything to you."

Aagny. The manslayer.

A short, dumpy woman with a Spanish accent, who looked as though life had been hard on her, suddenly called out from another table:

"Yeah, hell no. You can't do that. Animals, you stay away from them. Animals and children, you don't touch 'em."

She looked at Sara, stood up, and walked closer:

"Sometimes I think there's nothing waiting for me out there, that it doesn't really matter if I get out again, but then I think about cats. I think that if I just get out, I'll move to the countryside and live alone with horses and cats. And the horses and cats won't care how I've lived my life; they'll see me for who I really am."

The woman's eyes filled with tears.

An older woman sitting at a table nearby exclaimed:

"There's nothing I wouldn't do for my dog. She's waiting for me out there. I know she'll come running the moment I get out."

A blonde with hard eyes said:

"Everything that went wrong in my life started when my cat got run over. He just lay there."

Now everyone was talking at once, in a jumble. Everyone directed their words at Sara when they spoke, like it was her response they were seeking. The chatter reminded Sara of the sounds in the henhouse.

She looked around, and realized she was at the epicenter of the conflict. She hadn't said a word. Yet it had turned out like this anyway. Why did it always turn out like this?

Aagny stared at her. Spat on the ground. But in a friendly way.

She smiled at Sara.

EMELIE
(THE NOTEBOOK, AUGUST 2023)

I had just found out Poor Bastard's real name. *Låke*. That's all I knew. He didn't ask any questions. Instead, he looked at me kindly, in a comforting way. I felt that I had, in record time, ended up in the middle of what I had previously witnessed only from a distance: an interaction not based on words or information. Still looking at me, he sat down close, without making any apologetic movements.

This made me very stressed. I stood up, started circling him, asking questions with an intensity only I can summon.

Do you live here? It's so beautiful! Lots of mosquitoes! Do you get many mosquito bites? Do you fish? Oh, blueberries! So many blueberries!

My gaze searched around frantically, trying to find something to bring up that could lead him to start talking, making the conversation normal—like when you get stuck with someone in an elevator or a train compartment, trying to find the smallest common denominator that isn't loaded.

He looked at me calmly. After a while, he rose to his feet and began walking down towards the water. I thought it meant that he was leaving, but he stood down there, washing his hands in the cold water, while occasionally casting a friendly glance back at me.

Then he came back, and now he said:

"You can relax now. You're no longer out in society. You're safe here with me."

The way he said it was like I had been held hostage for a long time by a drug dealer.

I didn't need to be afraid anymore. That's what he meant.

I thought at first maybe *I* should be afraid of her but then when we talked a bit she was so stressed & strange like when you come across a Squirrel & it scurries up a Tree.

That's when I realized she's the one who has been forced to be out in Society & suffered & I'm the one who needs to be Kind to her.

I saw where she went & she sleeps in a Tent, I'll go there tonight. I wonder if she has books I've read most of the ones at Ersmo's all the Jackie Collins & the *Legend of the Ice People* & the *Flowers in the Attic* books.

THE ANT COLONY
2003–2008

AAGNY
2003

When she was released from prison, there was no one there to pick her up.

She considered reaching out to Sara, who had been there at the beginning of her stay. One of Aagny's best friends, she thought. Actually: Aagny's only friend. The dog was dead, you see.

Ove was dead, too, and that was because Aagny had happened to kill him. But he was never a friend. He was her husband. For a short time, he had been her husband.

Ove hadn't been a handsome man, but a man he had been. When Aagny was young, Ove had shown up at a dance one time. She had been very drunk—and Ove, too, for that matter. Ove was much older than her. It was an advantage. Then they had gone back to his place. It was filthy and disgusting, but there was a bed, a kitchen, and a dog.

The dog had been very unkempt. Its fur was long and dirty.

The first thing Aagny did, after she had shagged Ove—and slept on the couch, as Ove had trouble sleeping next to others—was to shower and groom the dog.

She wasn't great at grooming dogs; its fur turned out patchy and uneven. But it looked neater, and smelled better. It felt like a new dog as it leaped into the yard, basked in the morning sun, barked at a bird up a tree.

"Aagny," said Ove. "What kind of name is that."

"I chose it myself," said Aagny.

Once, Ove was rummaging through her papers, trying to

find some bill or other, and accidentally saw her real Christian name: Öline.

He took the paper and held it up in front of her triumphantly, ready to mock.

"I wanted to come first, for once," said Aagny.

And that was the end of it.

Now she stood there, her time in prison over and done, without a husband, and without a dog. She needed a few things. Those things were:

A job.

A home.

Someone to take care of.

If there was one thing Aagny excelled at, it was this, daily acts of *taking care*. That's how she had grown up, and it had been her currency with Ove, too. How could you leave a woman who was so good at taking care? That's what she had thought. Cooking, laundry, nursing the sick. At the same time: no coddling, never coddling.

Ove's house was empty and sold now. The money had gone to his grown children. Aagny had tried to explain, but they didn't want to hear from her.

She had a little, very little, money in her account. She had a temporary bed, for a few weeks, in a halfway house, arranged by the prison. That would keep her afloat for a while. But she most definitely didn't want to live in a city! Who would want that? She wanted to live as far out as possible. Her personality didn't fit in the city.

Right-foot, left-foot. Right-foot, left-foot, said Aagny as she walked the city's narrow streets on her way to the public employment office.

At the employment office, they initially said they had nothing for her. A manslayer, with no education. She hadn't even finished secondary school.

"I'm sorry," said the woman, smiling with her mouth but not with her eyes.

"I'll do anything," Aagny offered.

"I'm sorry," said the woman.

"I'll work around the clock," Aagny insisted.

"I'm sorry," said the woman.

"Maybe in home care?" Aagny suggested, but then the woman said that unfortunately they couldn't have people convicted of such heinous crimes taking care of the elderly, how would that look.

But perhaps she could study, pursue vocational training? the woman suggested. Find somewhere to belong?

Aagny shook her head.

"I don't study," she said as an explanation.

Aagny was about to walk out of the door when another employee, who'd been sat at the desk next to where she had just been sitting, caught up with her.

"I might have something," he said, in a low voice. "We're not really supposed to do this. But I overheard what you said. You look tough. There's a job no one else wants. I think everyone would be willing to turn a blind eye. Would you consider working day and night for a mean old bitch, living out in the middle of nowhere?"

"When do I start?" said Aagny.

She took three different buses and walked several miles on foot, and the next day she met Ersmo and his mother for the first time. Ersmo's peculiar little face that lit up as he took the first bite of that first crispy pancake. His face turned halfway towards hers, a tentative smile. The way he looked at her as he took a second bite.

ERSMO
2003

It was Ersmo who had grown up here, with his mother. The house was quite far from the village, and in the village there were five families living year-round. The village, in turn, was a little way outside town. He had a four-mile bike ride to school in the mornings, and Ersmo biked it every day, back and forth. Often, he was tired when he got to school. Often, it was dark when he got home.

There was an option of getting picked up, but Ersmo and his mother agreed that it was silly for a perfectly healthy boy to take a taxi.

The biking wasn't something Ersmo thought much about. He liked getting away from home. If he biked, it took a long time. He got to be away from home longer. Which was good.

Ersmo's mother was a strong woman, short and stocky. Shaped like a cube, she was. She drove a snowmobile and worked in the forest, until one day when her body said no and her back caved in completely. So she was put on sick leave, stayed home, and had difficulty moving around. Relatives and friends dropped by occasionally, bringing some cake or a drink, shooting the shit in the kitchen.

"Your father," Ersmo's mother would sometimes say, "was a real limp dick."

Then everyone in the kitchen would laugh, including Ersmo. Sometimes, when his mother was in the forest, he would dig out old photo albums and find pictures where his father had been cut out.

Over time, he learned that *limp dick* meant a man who'd had an affair with Ersmo's mother, and who then didn't have the guts to man up, moving with his wife to Örebro. There, Ermo's father had got sick with cancer and died.

"Dying is a limp-dick thing to do," his mother said.

Gradually, she went from being strong, ill-tempered, and funny to plain mean. It may have been partly due to her new boring life—imagine what it's like for someone who has always been told that their worth is tied to the work they do, and then they aren't able to work anymore—but perhaps even more due to the fall.

She was climbing up on the roof to remove a bird's nest from the chimney. Despite her back. This she did wearing slippers.

Ersmo heard a shriek and through the window he saw his mother fall. For a moment, he thought it didn't look like you would have expected. It happened so quickly, you barely saw it. His mother looked like a rag doll.

She lay there for a while, tried to get up but had to lie back down.

"We should call an ambulance," Ersmo suggested, but she didn't believe in that.

Getting injured from a fall. Like a limp dick.

A week later, she saw a doctor. She needed to buy butter and cereal in town anyway, and then it might be convenient to stop by the doctor's. The nurse sent her to the hospital in the big town, where they informed her that, besides her back, her head was no longer working—that she had suffered a brain injury.

"She'll need help in daily life. We'll have to do an assessment. Is there anyone who could help out at home in the meantime?"

Ersmo nodded, even though there wasn't. He didn't know why.

He drove the car home. He didn't have a driver's license but he supposed he could drive, since it was necessary.

"Put it in fourth," Ersmo's mother yelled, lying with back pain in the back-seat.

Ersmo was fourteen years old.

This thing with the brain injury was information that didn't register in his mother's head, only in Ersmo's. Ersmo's mother didn't inform their relatives and friends about the accident and the brain injury. It was silly to complain, and even sillier to burden others with one's own problems. Now she was on painkillers, taking the snowmobile to visit friends even though the doctor had strictly advised her not to operate a vehicle, driving in the middle of the road or in the wrong lane, getting lost, travelling at the wrong times—in the middle of the night or early morning—scolding people over trivial matters, cutting contact. Crawling naked into someone's bed.

It was such embarrassing things, all of a sudden. It felt awkward.

"How's everything going?" asked a second cousin, who stopped his car, honked, and insisted that Ersmo take five quarts of blueberries.

This thing with the blueberries, the second cousin thought, was a nice gesture showing that he cared, without really having to.

"It's fine," Ersmo said desperately. "Mother is getting some kind of assistant. Some lady coming here to clean and stuff, help out. She's going to live here, I think."

This was the twenty-second day in a row that Ersmo had eaten sandwiches for dinner.

The second cousin exhaled behind the wheel. A personal assistant. That meant someone would be around.

Within just a day or two, the news spread around the village. Someone was coming. Which meant they wouldn't have to deal with it.

One by one, they stopped dropping by, stopped bringing cookies and gossip to the kitchen. The only one who couldn't stop dropping by was Ersmo. He lived there.

Soon he would leave her, she said. Soon he would go away, like everyone else. She who had raised him, and always put food on the table, and given him LIFE, too, goddammit. She had a belt with a touristy print from Majorca, which she used to beat him with so he wouldn't become too big for his boots or think he was better than her just because his body worked and hers didn't. It would have looked comical, if it hadn't been so awful: the crazy old lady sitting in a chair, yelling at the teenager to come over so she could whip him. It never occurred to him not to go stand by the belt; if he didn't, his mother would escalate her bitterness, which was worse than the lashes. Sometimes it was as if beating him made her straight-up cheerful, and it could turn into a rather pleasant evening.

An ad was placed. *Personal assistant/housekeeper wanted.*
They lived outside the village, which was outside of town. The village had a total population of thirteen. It would be a lie to say that applications poured in.

But one person responded to the ad. One whose name was Aagny. No one knew where she was from, but she was a resourceful woman. She was thirty and a few. When Aagny came for the job interview, Ersmo's mother said she had prepared some tests to see if Aagny knew what she was doing.

"Make a pancake," his mother said, and Aagny did, and it was perfectly delicious and crispy (test one) without using too much of the expensive butter (test two).

"Clean the floor," his mother said, and Aagny did, and it was quite clean even in the corners (test one) yet without using too much soap (test two).

She got the job, and immediately moved into the bakehouse on the farmstead. She had very little luggage, said she didn't need to have anything shipped. It was unclear where her actual duties began and ended—cooking? snow shovelling? fishing? household finances?—but Aagny didn't care much about that; she looked after the farm like it was her own.

Ersmo's mother sat there dictating everything Aagny should do, and Aagny did it. Aagny was usually a talkative person, but here she was mostly silent. Overall, Aagny chose the following strategy: not to converse with the mother at all, unless she said something nice, which the mother rarely did. Therefore, they now coexisted in the house at the same time yet kind of in parallel: one silent, the other screaming.

She once tried to hit Aagny with *Majorca*. Aagny looked at her as if she were a child. Took the belt and cut it into pieces. Without a word.

Ersmo, on the other hand, was naturally taciturn. He had learned in school that he would usually embarrass himself if he tried to answer a question. What he was good at were things done with his hands.

So at first, he only said to Aagny:

"Hi."

And:

"Goodbye."

But sometimes he would forget something on the kitchen table: a wooden figure he had carved, a drawing he had made. A small house he had built from matchsticks and glued together.

And when Aagny saw them, she would smile with her whole face and say:

"Ersmo. You know how to do things, don't you!"

And he would smile back.

Ersmo. He loved Aagny. Suddenly there were cinnamon

rolls waiting for him when he got home from school. She asked how his day had been. He didn't answer, but still.

It was as if both of them could sense that they needed each other, and that's why they suddenly felt safe.

They were tied to each other, him and Aagny:

A thirty-four-year-old woman from who knows where, with a dialect you couldn't place. It was Finnish and West Bothnian and North Bothnian, and sometimes a little fancy and sometimes very crude. And she had a sorrow in her eyes and the hands of a worker.

And a fourteen-year-old boy, bloody terrible at school, with dyslexia and dyscalculia and all sorts of stuff.

They built things together. One weekend, they cut down a birch on the farm, and built a treehouse on the stump.

His mother sat screaming inside the house. *Damn it to hell.*

Once or twice, after about a year, Ersmo asked Aagny where she was from, but she always joked away the answer.

"Hell," she said once.

"Sure wasn't Gällivare," she said another time.

He shrugged his shoulders, didn't ask further. She must have had her reasons.

He knew that at least she understood what it was like to hate your mother. She had said so once. Ersmo hadn't responded.

He was ashamed that she had seen it so clearly in him.

"Ersmo," his mother said at one point. "Come here and give Mummy a kiss."

His mother was unhinged. Now when Ersmo dutifully leaned in to give his mother a peck on the cheek, she quickly turned her head and gave Ersmo a snog, tongue and all.

The teenager was stunned. He backed away, his face disgusted. His mother laughed out loud. Aagny saw it. Now she saw Ersmo's sad, befuddled gaze. And it tore her apart.

She stepped forward now, separating Ersmo and his mother.

"You are not to touch that boy anymore," she said. "Do you hear me. You're not capable of raising a child."

"I'll do whatever I want with the boy," his mother said. "It's my son. You're my employee. And I can fire you whenever I want. Yes, I think I will! Hey! You're fired!"

She pointed to a piece of paper on the wall, an information line to call.

"It's Sunday today," said Aagny. "No one is going to answer."

"Tomorrow, I'll call," his mother said.

The day after that, no one saw Ersmo's mother anymore. People probably assumed she stayed indoors, that she was so sick she didn't go out. If a relative ever came and asked about her, Ersmo would say that unfortunately she was sleeping, but he would tell her they had been by. And they didn't really want to see her—no one did—so they said they would come back another day. But they never did.

And everyone agreed it sure was very fortunate that the resourceful housekeeper Aagny was there to take care of Ersmo and his mother. She seemed so capable, Aagny, always assuming the role of the mother, driving Ersmo to school, buying clothes for the boy in town, helping him with his homework.

They kept to themselves.

They continued working on the treehouse.

SAGNE
2006

She worked at the university.

It was a big deal in her family. They were alternately proud, alternately teasing. When she came home with an Italian cheese, they would say *oooh, look at you, so fancy.* When she spoke on the phone with a colleague, they would eavesdrop and say *I didn't understand a word you just said!* But when she couldn't hear them, her parents would tell the neighbors about their daughter, who had always been so interested in bugs and had got good grades, and was now an academic—the first in the family!

"Oh really," the neighbors would say. Then: "But does she have any kids yet?"

"No," they would say. "Not yet."

They placed emphasis on the word *yet.*

Her mother asked if there wasn't usually a party when you finished a dissertation after such a long time? Sagne lied and said no. Then she invited her colleagues and neighbors from the student dorm to the defence and hid from her family that it even took place. They didn't know how these things usually went, so it was easy to lie. The next time she went home, she brought a sandwich cake, and declared that she had completed her dissertation.

It wasn't that she didn't love her family, her mother and father and Jon and Erik and Jon's wife and Erik's wife and all the kids and aunts and Grandma. It was that they were so many, and they were a certain way that the university wasn't. It was that half of Sagne was the university and half was her family, and never the twain shall meet. It was for the best. There would be too much to keep track of, otherwise.

One of her colleagues was named Sharon. She was Brazilian. Sagne liked Sharon: she was chatty without being pushy, and she understood Sagne's work. Plus, she was almost always there. The other entomologists tried to do research that allowed them to be away for long periods, or didn't require them to take daily measurements. But Sagne wanted to be there every day. She had the part of her research that took place in the forest, and she had the part in the lab. And every day, she would observe, take notes.

It felt familiar.

It's what she had done all her life, but suddenly she was getting paid for it.

They started having lunch together every day. Sometimes they went to a concert together, or the cinema. Sagne helped Sharon in the lab, out in the forest, many hours, several nights a week. She liked it. She liked Sharon. She liked not being alone.

Sagne had always longed for something specific. She had been thinking about this thing with ants. Ants were born with different tasks. There was the queen, the workers, the drones. They didn't have to be everything all at once. Sagne longed for this, to be included without being questioned. If you were a certain way, people shouldn't interfere and think you ought to be a little of everything else instead.

It felt a bit like that with Sharon. Sharon accepted her and filled in the gaps herself, being everything Sagne couldn't be. At the same time, she needed Sagne too, often asking for her advice at work. Because Sagne was the best. Everyone said so. No one knew more. No one was more meticulous.

When they were out in the forest, Sharon would smile at the

joy in Sagne's eyes. And she kept talking, Sharon—an endless chatter that Sagne eventually learned to treat like a radio broadcast that she could choose to pay attention to, or not. Sharon didn't love insects the way Sagne did, but she was interested and knew things, she understood what Sagne was talking about. And they became best friends; for the first time, Sagne had a best friend.

It took several months for Sagne to realize that Sharon was flirting with her. And once she realized this, she assumed it was a mistake. No one had ever flirted with Sagne before, you see. Sagne had never flirted with anyone either. It was a first step into a labyrinth she had no interest in reaching the end of.

There was a party at work. A short, neat man researching alternative uses for spider-webs had defended his dissertation, and now the man stood in the break room screaming his joy into a karaoke mic through "Without You" (Mariah Carey's version). As a bit of a lark, some of the partygoers started slow dancing; an exaggerated slow dance; a Russian professor asked the head of finance to dance, the spider researcher's sister asked her father, and so there was no romance in the air, just a lighthearted, drunk mood,

so when Sharon took a bow in front of Sagne, naturally Sagne stood up and they joined the dancing crowd. A disco ball in the corner illuminated the dancers; a doctoral student had fallen asleep in his chair.

I can't liiiive, cried the spider researcher. But his initially theatrical singing softened the further he got into the song; he enjoyed singing now and met the music, which also calmed the dancers, whose movements shifted from exaggerated to relaxed and genuine within a single verse. And when the second chorus came on, Sharon's body softened, too; she pressed herself against Sagne in a different way, caressingly. She rested her head against Sagne's shoulder and started touching Sagne's hand, slowly, stroking it. Then she lifted her head, so that her gaze would meet Sagne's, and she let her red, beautiful lips, soft and warm, meet Sagne's.

Sharon's eyes—

Sharon's scent—

Sagne froze. Just like a spider when it realizes it's being watched. That's how it felt. She panicked, became motionless.

Sagne wasn't used to big emotions. You could say that she avoided big emotions. Whenever they arose, they turned to chaos in her mind. She didn't know what was what. It only caused panic, her head spinning, everything a blur; it was impossible to make quick decisions. She had never longed for Sharon's lips, but never anyone else's either. She liked Sharon so very much. She didn't want to make Sharon sad. She didn't want to stay in this uncomfortable and demanding situation, having to show so clearly how she felt when she didn't know how she felt. So, for a brief moment she kissed Sharon back, the way she thought it was done.

It felt completely unnatural.

Then, fortunately, the spider researcher finished wailing, and the song came to an end. Sagne let go of Sharon, and uttered the most frequent white lie of our time:

"Sorry, I need the ladies'."

After her visit to the bathroom, she fled home through the back door.

It was around this time in her life that she was invited to a wedding at her cousin Ulrika's.

SARA
2006

It was Sara's brother, Albin, who was getting married, to Ulrika, his girlfriend of several years. They had been planning the wedding for some time. The music and the cake, but most of all the seating arrangement—who would sit where to ensure optimal pleasantness, and as little conflict as possible.

Sara had been placed at what they secretly called the Difficult Table. Table 4. This was the first thing they planned.

Seated at the Difficult Table were:

* Two very old relatives, who kept falling asleep, and who might still be alive by the end of the evening.

* A quiet uncle who, after a few units of alcohol, always changed personality to loud and borderline right-wing extremist.

* A very nervous daughter of Ulrika's stepfather who often found herself wondering if everyone else hated her. Every time she said something, a long string of apologies would ensue regarding what had just been said—*I didn't mean—what I wanted to say was—oh, you probably think I'm—*

* Albin's currently depressed best friend, Lukas. Lukas had been dumped two years ago, and ever since he assumed that all women wanted to hurt him. The more alcohol was poured into him, the more the floodgates opened.

Their strategy was obvious: take all the boring and annoying people, and seat them at one table so that everyone else would be spared. Throw Sara into the mix; she would deal with them.

Sara could be thoughtless. She often forgot things. On this day, she had forgotten that she needed to go pick up the dress she intended to wear to the wedding from a friend in a village, and then it turned out that the car was out of gas, and then a neighbor gave her some so she could go to the village and pick up the dress, but the neighbor offered coffee, too, which was nice of her, and in the end it was past seven o'clock when Sara was finally dressed.

By this time, Albin and Ulrika were already married,

the uncle was already drunk and racist,

the nervous stepsister was trying to smooth over the fact that she had jokingly called Lukas serious,

Lukas had taken great offense, and the table fell silent and awkward.

Ulrika watched all of this unfold from where she sat, and couldn't concentrate on being jubilantly happy at all.

She hissed at Albin: *Where is Sara?* And Albin became just as upset. It was like they had called a plumber about a leak, and the plumber didn't show up, and now the water was gushing and flowing every which way.

"It's all China's fault," the uncle hooted and downed another drink.

The nervous stepsister was of Asian origin.

Not until after the starter did Sara slink in. Ulrika's mother had just delivered a completely unintelligible speech with inside jokes that no one understood. Albin's father had given advice for a happy marriage, with a focus on logistics. Ulrika's friends had sung their own version of Madonna's "Like a Virgin," but they held the microphone too far away and the speaker didn't work, so no one really caught the new lyrics—except for one line that went:

We remember when you slept with Roberto in Italia
And came back with duty-free gin and chlamydia

The bridal couple squirmed in their seats.

Wasn't it terribly hot in here?

Now it was time for another speech, apparently. By someone who hadn't signed up with the toastmaster.

Ulrika was bubbling with anger.

But it was Sara. She stood up, spoke loudly and clearly, without needing a microphone:

"I'm the groom's little sister, Sara."

"We know," shouted the wedding guests.

Sara smiled.

"Albin is five years older than me. What many of you may not know about our family is that, when I was born, Mum had pre-eclampsia, and almost died. She was very weak for a long time, and Dad was worried. They both slept poorly."

She nodded towards their father, who was sitting there huffing after giving his logistics speech.

"There was a lot to process," Sara continued. "Mum and Dad have told me that they'd wondered how Albin would take it—getting a baby sister. But when I arrived, it was like Albin immediately understood that Mum and Dad had too much else going on to devote themselves to a new baby. So it was like I partly became Albin's baby for a little while. He was only five years old and had been a very lively kid. Now he sat next to me all day. Reading books—or, rather, making it up as he went. Completely calm the whole time. Mum and Dad were there, but they were given time to heal, because I was safe with my big brother."

Sara's parents closed their eyes. As usual, Sara had shared more private information than they were comfortable with—but, as usual, they nevertheless ended up feeling proud somehow.

Sara looked up, her big eyes glistening now. There was a meditative streak in what she said, no exclamation marks or sentimentality, but warmth, a hint of humor behind the words.

"That was many years ago now, but you know, Albin, I've always felt that way. The way you look at me, like there is always someone there to help me, to watch over me. When our sister died a few years ago, I think I would have—if it weren't for you—"

She looked down at the table, and then continued:

"I know that many here might see you as an amazing professional, logical and clear-minded, but to me you are one big, thumping heart, and a backbone in my life. And when Ulrika came along, I saw right away how she looked at you. She had that same gaze when she looked at *you*, Albin, the same one you had when you looked at me. Unconditional love. She only wanted the best for you. And I saw it in you too, when you looked at Ulrika."

Now everyone was sobbing uncontrollably. Ulrika had begun to let go of her panic over Table 4, and was now focused on the joy of being in a room full of people who loved her. It was the same people, the same room, as half an hour ago, but now, only now, did she *see* it: She loved them all. They all cared for her.

"My big brother. Albin. And Ulrika, my new sister. We are many here who wish that we might someday come close to what you have found in each other. And it's easy to be jealous, but we don't feel that way, we who are here tonight. We are just so genuinely happy to have you in our lives, and to see your respect for each other, and we are grateful to be a part of it and be inspired by it. If it was out there for you, maybe it's out there for us too."

Depressed Lukas looked up. He hadn't thought about it that way.

"A toast to the bride and groom."

Now everyone raised their glasses, and Ulrika clinked hers and cried out in a shrill, emotional voice: "No, I can't help it, Albin, I'm gonna say it now! We're pregnant!"

And everyone rushed up to the bride and groom and hugged them, and when someone tripped over the cord to the speaker it suddenly started working, playing "Close to You" by the Carpenters, and Sara turned to the nervous stepsister and said, as though in passing: "Gosh, that was nerve-wracking. Good thing you were sitting next to me and had such a calming influence. What a beautiful dress you're wearing, by the way."

At the end of another table sat a cousin to Ulrika. She was staring out of the window. Glasses, bangs. Wearing a skirt, but with practical hiking boots.

Was that a European curlew she heard in the summer night?

Yet now her gaze turned indoors. Someone was transforming the room with their mere presence. The cousin saw it in her: that she, too, longed to get away.

Sagne stared at Sara.

JÓZSEF AND SARA
2007–2008

J ózsef at the piano. The choir singing *ah*—
"And one higher," he said, playing a D
The choir sang *ah*—
Playing an E.
The choir sang *ah*—

The rehearsal space next to the church hall smelled of wood
and coffee. Heavy perfume, lipstick. A promise of pastries; you
could see it in Ingabritt's gaze. She was excited to show off the
discipline in which she excelled.

Being the choirmaster of the world's whitest gospel choir
had given József an entirely new view of this group of older
women. Before, his view had been: gentle, caring, sometimes
strict. They lived to serve others. That's what he had thought,
when he saw his friends' mothers, always doing, smoking, fixing, tidying. Perhaps he had thought: A bit daft? Uninterested
in the world? Anchored in the practical?

Here in the choir, people stood out to him—the individuals
in the group. Suddenly freed from their duties, the women
who emerged into view were a rich flora. Many were foul-
mouthed, they argued a lot, they were passionate, some po-
litical, and they were constantly competing with each other.
One of the disciplines they competed in was baking for break
time, and today Ingabritt stood ready, with a facial expression
like it was the world championship and she was waiting for the
starting shot.

Occasionally, he smiled. Here, where all notes were equal and strove towards the same goal.

"Today," he said, "we'll be trying a new song."

The song was called "Until I Found You" and was a modern gospel song. When the choir sang, József felt a certain joy. It sounded truly terrible. The song was written for great gospel singers and now it was being performed by thirty women and two men, most of them pensioners who had never sung in a choir before. He guessed that barely half of the women were Christian. They just wanted to sing.

"Carina, will you do the solo?" he asked, and Carina was pleased and said, just to be safe:

"Oh, not little old me . . . "

And everyone else said: *Yes!*

And, just to be safe, Carina said: *Oh well, oh my goodness*—hiding her face in her palms—

And everyone else: *Yeees.*

And that's when Carina dramatically threw her folder onto the chair and said: *All right then, if you insist!* And then she took a breath, and József played the opening four chords, and then Carina stepped forward with her swelling soprano searching for the notes, uncertain like a swaying compass needle, some notes were beautiful, her whole face formed the letter O regardless of what she was singing, and she rushed forward:

In this world of worriers / Let me be a rock / I was once a searcher, too / until I found You

And that was the precise moment Sara walked through the door.

Another discipline: being the kindest to József. The women in the choir just couldn't stand his sad appearance, so they simply had to fix and coddle! If there was cake, he got the best piece—*for sure* the marzipan rose—the finest pastry; in the break, they would talk about what a won-der-ful choirmaster and cantor József was, and everyone would agree. More and more adjectives were piled on top of each other. He is so musically talented, and hardworking, and nice, and isn't he handsome, too—especially in a button-down shirt.

Today, Ingabritt had baked lemon muffins with lavender blossoms, and József had been given one with his name written in icing. They had stepped into the break room, and now Sara walked in. Suddenly he felt embarrassed sitting there with his infantilising muffin.

He stood up—muffin in hand—and approached her.

"Hello," he said. "József Szilágyi, choirmaster and cantor! Are you interested in joining the choir?"

The woman had a distinctive appearance, he noted—humorous, warm eyes; you couldn't help but instantly like her. She didn't have to say anything, but when she did, her voice was even better, clear until certain words where she sounded raspy. Just from hearing her speaking voice, he knew she could sing.

"Hi! I'm Sara. I've heard a lot of good things about you guys."

That's what she said.

In his quiet mind, József wondered who could have had a lot of good things to say about the choir. Surely no one from the audience.

Here, Sara turned to Ingabritt and said loudly and openly, so that as many people as possible could hear:

"And these muffins! They look amazing. I wish I could bake like that. And the smell! Is that cardamom?" She closed her eyes, as though to emphasize.

Ingabritt, who had stood ready to dislike the younger woman for coming and stealing her spotlight, completely lost the thread now that praise was being served before an open room.

"Yes, it's cardamom. Please—help yourself!"

"Are you sure? I don't want to come here and . . . "

"TAKE ONE!" Ingabritt howled, all but pushing the plate into Sara's face. She smiled now, completely open.

Sara took one, visibly relishing it when she had a bite. She said loudly, once again so it could be heard throughout the room:

"You sing so beautifully. My whole body felt calm. To escape the stress of daily life and be absorbed by the music."

There was a contented clucking in the background and a rising chorus of "No, you're too much".

József, who after a childhood of reading others' emotions had developed a certain sensitivity as to people's social abilities, noted that Sara had taken on the room with absolute finesse. She had stepped into the group, knowing that she could be perceived as a threat, but instead she had showed that she understood and appreciated the existing rules, and had no intention of changing them.

After the break, they continued to sing "Until I Found You". József noticed that the choir sounded better than usual. There was a mezzo-soprano who had come in with a calm, warm voice, which settled like a blanket over the others' spiky attempts to reach the highest notes. Everything sounded softer.

As for Sara, she saw that József took such good care of the group that she didn't need to do anything. No conflicts needed resolving. No one looked upset or offended. No one focused on her at all. Her shoulders dropped.

"Now it's time for the Circle," Ingabritt said expectantly when "Until I Found You" had been rehearsed many times. Here she glared at Sara, eager to see how the newcomer would react. "József says it's important to be open about how you feel, so people don't have to guess!!!" For the choir members' generation, there was something tremendous about this notion.

The choir reconfigured itself, lifting chairs, forming a circle. Going around the room, everyone briefly got to express how they were feeling and how they had experienced the evening. They got a chance to speak up if something didn't feel right.

Solbritt said: "Yes, it was lovely to sing. I've been through a lot lately. You know, with the divorce and all."

Now the choir nodded. The divorce and all. Solbritt had got divorced five or six years ago, but it still gnawed at her, and there were times when the rest of the choir felt like the Circle was Solbritt's private group therapy session.

Sara noticed József's calm when Solbritt started crying, and how Carina glanced at József out of the corner of her eye as she walked up to Solbritt and hugged her. The hug wasn't for Solbritt but for József, so that he would see it, and Carina kept her body turned towards József while hugging Solbritt. Solbritt, too, hugged her back wholeheartedly, with her face towards József. The whole situation gave Sara the urge to giggle. She managed to hold back her laughter, but she looked at József and could see that he, too, was fighting the corners of his mouth. She caught his gaze, very briefly, and they both looked down at the ground, biting their cheeks.

Sara felt all warm because of everything he *didn't* do: he didn't validate Carina, didn't swell with pride at being the king of the group. He just sat there, the same way, looking at the choir with his soft gaze.

Sara also noticed that József had the ability to gently and kindly rebuff Solbritt in the middle of a sentence, so they could move on.

Next up was Sandra, a warm-hearted and short woman who—unlike Solbritt—had a tendency to downplay her pain.

"How's your rheumatism, Sandra?" asked József. "How did you do today?"

"It's fine. It feels better when I get to sing, see other people. You almost forget about the pain."

József nodded, smiling.

When it was Sara's turn, she simply said:

"Thank you. This was wonderful, getting to sing with you all."

Then there was a knock on the door again; it was Sara's boyfriend coming to pick her up. József swallowed his disappointment. The boyfriend was young and handsome, looked fit. József was ten years older with a hunched shoulder. How could he even have thought.

* * *

By now, József's father was dead; his mother lived in a dementia care home. She was growing worse by the day—a subjective truth, for as his mother grew sicker, her gaze became lighter, her mouth happier. She thought that József was her brother, a brother who had never been mentioned before. József guessed that the brother was one of the people who had died in the Holocaust, one of the people who must not be spoken of. But his mother knew nothing of the Holocaust now, as she sang in her room.

"Bela! Mum has made *dobos*," she said, her posture like a child's, her body that of an elderly woman. Every other sentence in Hungarian, every other in Swedish. It was his mother's body but not his mother's posture, his mother's face but not her facial expressions. The same mother but possessed by a different soul. She looked so giggly, expectant.

His mother no longer woke up screaming in the night. He was glad to see her like that, and shocked and sad that he had known her for thirty-five years without ever seeing her like that before: like every day wasn't a struggle. He wondered if he should have done something differently all those years, insisted on therapy, persuaded her to go back to Hungary, anything that could have changed things. He wondered if he should talk to her about his father, bring pictures. It was so strange: two people who had lived as one for so many years, one of them dies, and the other doesn't care—

but it was only occasionally that she remembered his father at all, and why should he impress on her to be sad, when she had already spent her entire life being so?

He indulged her this lightness.

How strange it was, this: he had spent much of his life worrying what would happen when one of his parents died, the loneliness he had thought would follow for the other. Now when it finally happened, it was a non-issue. Life. You can never guess.

His mother didn't recognise him, but she loved him and she said it, too, regardless of who she thought he was.

"I love you, Bela."

She patted him on the head, rubbed his ears. He stopped her when she wanted to blow on his belly. She mentioned as if in passing that she was in love with the shopkeeper's son, that they were meeting that night. She mentioned a name; it wasn't his father's. They ate marzipan cake, not *dobos*. His mother chewed loudly, chocolate all over her face. Her whole life, she had been neat and tidy.

* * *

The day József's mother died, the sky was gray and it was right at the beginning of autumn. The wind blew over the water. József had been at the palliative-care ward, keeping vigil for days. He had been sitting beside her when she drew her last breath, her body small and fragile—yet another new way to see her, as if a third soul had come to live in her body. He didn't know if she recognised him at all—as Bela or anyone else—and he realized she could have been frightened, a stranger by her bedside. But for once he acted selfishly; he needed to touch her, needed to feel her pulse one last time, so he decided to lay his hand on hers anyway,

and when he did, she closed her eyes and drifted away.

For a moment, he thought she couldn't have died, for she didn't usually, but her breathing had ended.

József called for a doctor, who confirmed that the woman in the bed was dead, and, as soon as he said that, József experienced a mix of emotions in his body so intense that he needed to scream. He went into the bathroom, grabbed a paper towel, and screamed into it. Screamed over how much he had loved her,

screamed over who she was and who she had been and what had befallen her,

and screamed over now, finally, being free.

He sat back down in the chair and remembered nothing more until he suddenly found himself outside. He tumbled down the streets, everything a jumble, logistics and questions and familiar feelings and new feelings, away from people, and he walked down to the fields where large blocks of massing birds flew around him just as it seemed in his head, and the leaves, and the leaves, and the wetness of the mud.

There he walked all the way down to the water, leaned against a big rock. The wind splashed water on him where he stood, but he didn't think about that. His body behaved like he had never known it before, it lurched and reeled,

he bent and stepped back,

as if the air was punching him in the gut.

His mind hadn't grasped what had happened yet, but his body had. His body remembered what it was like to be little and sit on her lap; her warm, soft arms; how she had loved him so boundlessly; her gaze on him; that he was the only and most important thing that existed.

When that goes away. The person who thinks you are the most important thing that exists. What that does to a person. He took a deep breath and his throat screamed out the exhalation.

It was a moment in life when he really didn't want to run into someone—
but other people were the last thing on his mind as he stood there now,
breathing in and out—

There was someone there.

The person who was there was a short woman with a warm gaze. She walked straight up to him. She guessed, and she guessed right.

"Sara?" József said. He fixed his hair—how strange that he cared to do this now; he immediately felt ashamed that he cared to fix his hair when his mother had just died.

József and Sara had only met three times, at the choir rehearsals, only exchanged pleasantries.

She said nothing. It was a brave move. What, if she had guessed wrong.

Instead, she approached him, and held him. For a few seconds it felt strange; his body resisted, he didn't want to be held. Then he gave in, and fell into the hug. And he noticed his body starting to jump and wriggle again, but she stood firm, she stood strong. She held him like a pillar. He opened his mouth and wept. And he wept and wept, and she stayed there. She stayed there until his body calmed down. For maybe ten minutes, they stood like that.

Then he had to let go, wipe away the snot with his sleeve.

"My mother," he said then. "She died just now."

He stared down at his feet. He looked like a child now.

Which is exactly what he was. Forever a child, to she who had just passed away.

"It might seem like . . . " he began.

Sara said:

"You don't have to say anything, if you don't want to."

Then she said:

"My sister died when I was younger. I recognised the . . . your body. I remembered how it felt to be so sad that my body made those movements. Before that, I didn't know they existed in me."

Without either of them thinking about it, they sat down on the ground, and held on to each other. It was cold, but they didn't notice. Life-and-death events have an ability to rip people right open. They were wide open now. They dove right in, both of them. And the place where they met was so intensely intimate that it seemed impossible to go back from there; everything was different, nothing else was enough.

If in everyday life, at work, you meet at level 2,

in a close conversation with a trusted friend at level 4,

in a sexual act with someone you love, afterward, you find yourself at level 5—

then Sara and József, in a matter of minutes, had climbed straight up to level 6. It was a level neither of them knew existed. It was as if, together, they became a third individual. It was as if they breathed with the same mouth, and both wanted it. It was difficult to explain afterwards to Sara's boyfriend, who became an ex-boyfriend,

and difficult to describe to oneself or anyone at all,

that you might want to do something like that on the day your mother passed away,

but they went to Sara's place,

and they slept together,

and after that they were completely incapable of ever doing anything else.

It was as if they dug into each other, body and mind, hungrily, selfishly they stood there, each with a shovel, digging and digging—let me come deeper inside, *let me merge with you.*

József would later think that this was the worst day of his life, and the best,
and in hindsight, he would understand that he could never have experienced the best without it being the worst.

That's how life is, and if you think you can take shortcuts, you are mistaken.

József. "Tell me about yourself. Tell me everything."
Sara. "I have two siblings. A sister who died, you already know that. A brother who got married, it was only a few months ago. Your turn."
József. "I have no siblings. I have no family at all now. Tell me more."
Sara. "I've never managed to finish a degree or hold down a job. Tell me more."
József. "I'm not really Christian. I just want to be among people with a faith. Tell me more."
Sara. "I've lived in India and been the mistress of a guru. Before that, I was in prison. Tell me more."
József. "My parents survived the Holocaust, but we've never talked about it. Tell me more."
Sara. "Sometimes I get such bad anxiety, I can't breathe. Tell me more."
József smiled. "Me, too. I can't breathe."

The ruby was in her pocket, and it was like he didn't seek it, nor did he shun it. It wasn't a factor. Not at first.

* * *

Sex can be as many things as a conversation. A game. A bandage. A shrug. A party. Yoga? Violence. Something purely physical, almost like exercise. Bragging. People seeing each other. One seeing the other. If you are lucky: a bond.

All of this is good enough. But sometimes it happens: that a person is lucky enough to sleep with someone who loves her, and whom she loves in return. When the person you love is both secure and wide open, and you are, too. Like a football game where everything works, József thought. All the balls you kick are received. You find the other player instinctively, by being both observant and present but also completely disconnected from your mind, utterly immersed in the flow. You are simultaneously yourself and fully capable of being someone else. You become spiritual. One with the Earth. You are an instrument. Played upon. You swim. Streaks of light in the air. You undress in front of a person and stand there before them and dare to be, and the other does the same.
Surel it's just hormones and neurotransmitters?
Or is it really

If you have ever experienced this, it becomes very difficult to go back to other kinds of sex. If the other person no longer wants to, it's devastating. You live alone for a while. You try to fool around with other people, but it's like it's almost harmful. You were once wide open, are you then supposed to go back to being closed? You try to open up to others, but if they aren't open too, it feels jarring, painful.

And it was as if both Sara and József now realized that: what they had always thought was a burden, that darned sensitivity they both carried, they suddenly understood that: it was a gift, it's what allowed the two of them to be a part of this. Those who were closed off, tough, they would never get to experience this.

That's why József said to Sara: "I'm yours now."
And Sara said: "Yes."
That's where it all began.

* * *

Since they were newly in love, they did things that newly-in-love people do, and reasoned as newly-in-love people reason. When you are newly in love, you don't need to do fun, luxurious things; instead, you do well to take on tasks that are difficult and taxing because the activity itself is insignificant—all that matters is that the other person is present. So when József had to clean out his parents' apartment AND his mother's room at the dementia care home, Sara was there. Through shirts and books and old notes, she got to know József's parents without ever having met them. Pictures of József all over the apartment, at all ages. Bottles and records in the Office. Pill jars in the cabinet, anti-depressants, lots of anti-depressants.

In a box hidden inside another box, hidden in a closet, József found several envelopes with his mother's name on. He instinctively understood that the envelopes were important. When he touched them, it was like they burned his fingers. He put them in his bag, unopened. To Sara, he said nothing.

* * *

They traveled north to visit Sara's parents. On one of the days, they drove straight into the inland. It was late autumn. They wandered around among the bogs, the forest. József gaped. He was in awe.

"There's nothing here!" he said.

"What do you mean nothing here," Sara replied, suddenly a smidge annoyed; she was used to being defensive against southerners who thought everything outside the big cities was exotic and picturesque.

"There's no one here!" he said.

"What do you mean no one here," Sara asked. She pointed at the reindeer droppings on the ground and the moose droppings on the ground and the ants and the crested tit and the woodpecker. "And look there," she said, pointing to a bloody enormous tree that lay felled. "A beaver."

"Yes, but no people!" József said.

He gaped at it all.

"There's no one to have to deal with! No one to keep in a good mood! No one to take care of!"

"I know," Sara said, putting her arm around him.

They slept under the stars; it was cold, but they huddled their bodies together, breathing as one; they marvelled at the way the body was designed, how it thrived next to another, like it was meant to be. Sara thought of the horses grooming each other; she stared up at the sky; József said something about Orion's Belt; Sara thought that inside her there was nothing but calm, for a second, there was calm.

The next morning, when she woke up in the cold tent, she saw him crouching down by the lake. Throwing rocks like a man possessed. He didn't manage to make a single one skip.

He turned around, and smiled.

"Imagine when we're not here," József said. "Then there's no one seeing these trees."

"Maybe it's the other way around," Sara replied. "That when we're not here. Then there are no trees seeing us."

József pondered this.

A Siberian jay approached. It couldn't be very used to

humans, József assumed, but he wasn't surprised when it hopped onto the fallen tree where Sara was sitting and looked at her as if they knew each other. "Do you know what we call Siberian jays?" she said. "Camp robbers. It's because they come begging for food by the fire. And here's this one, doing exactly that. He looks so freaking greedy, do you see it?"

József looked at the Siberian jay's wide-open eyes and couldn't help but laugh.

How typical of Sara, he thought. She sat there just being and of course the camp robber understood that she was the one to be close to; just like people, *I'll stay close to her*. Sara's gravitational pull frightened József. He had never felt this way before. She said the same—that she had never felt for anyone else the way she felt for him—but it was different with Sara; he knew it, they both knew it. He felt anxious about going back to the city where others, not just men, but people in general, would see her, hit on her, want to be close to her.

He looked at the Siberian jay.

Stop staring at her with those googly eyes, he caught himself thinking.

Then he thought: It's official, I'm now jealous of a bird.

It was so painful, this, being newly in love and seeing everything as a threat that could take away your happiness. He longed for it to be two years later, and they would still be together and he would be in love, but not like this.

* * *

In her bag, she had books by Arne Næss and Henry David Thoreau. She was utterly engrossed by these books, even spoke in a heated tone when she talked about them.

"Næss says that everything in nature has an inherent value," she quoted. "Everything in nature has the right to self-realisation."

József nodded. "That sounds reasonable," he said. "Every insect, every flower, every animal, has an agenda— they want something. To grow, or reproduce, or whatever. But in the long run," she said, "the animals and species can't do that if humans continue the way we do, living at the expense of animals and plants. So us humans, we're the ones who need to change."

"I see," said József, who was only listening with half an ear while longing to return to his own book, *The Girl with the Dragon Tattoo* by Stieg Larsson.

"It ties in with Gandhi's concept of *ahimsa*—that we must not use violence, neither against other people, nor any living being."

"Okay."

"We use violence against other species, and so we aren't living according to *ahimsa*."

"Interesting," József said.

Then they talked about something else.

* * *

They were having pizza in town. The autumn sun was warm, so they sat outside on the main street. Sara had a margherita and a Fanta; she had childish taste. József had a Greek salad and mineral water. He didn't dare eat pizza—lest he become both the old and the fat one in their relationship.

They sat there, staring at people, watching kids drive around in their hand-me-down cars, when all of a sudden a woman József's age stopped; tall and robust she was, with a buzz cut and a floral jacket that jarred with the rest of her appearance.

She stared at Sara, then at József, then at Sara again, as if she couldn't believe her eyes.

"Sara!" the woman eventually exclaimed in a perplexing dialect.

"AAGNY!" Sara shouted back. She stood up, knocking over her chair, and threw herself at the woman who, in other news, had some kind of flower brooch attached to her shoe. Now they embraced, the two women, their bodies bobbing and bouncing. Sara was almost two heads shorter, so her face landed in the tall woman's bosom, and a dog on a leash a bit further off started howling; it was quite the commotion. Aagny was crying now, and the dog howled even louder, and in the midst of it all a young man with acne and a trucker hat came walking towards them with a can of Coke in his hand. He stood at a bit of a distance from Aagny without saying hello, but positioned himself in such a way that Sara and József understood that he *belonged*.

"What are you doing here?" both women shrieked simultaneously, which led to even more laughter and tears, and the young man shifted awkwardly where he stood.

"Sit, sit," demanded Sara, and Aagny took a seat at the table next to them.

"I probably oughta buy something if we're gonna sit here," said Aagny. "You want anything, Ersmo?"

The young man looked like he was considering whether or not to sit down next to two strangers, eventually deciding that this was most definitely too scary and following Aagny at the heels into the restaurant.

"Who is she?" mouthed József.

"That's *Aagny*! God, haven't I told you about her."

"Who?" mouthed József.

"We met in prison."

József paled. "What was she in for?"

"Manslaughter," Sara mouthed now, and here came Aagny and her young companion again, with two cans of Coke in tightly clenched fists. They sat down at the next table.

"And who's this?" Sara asked, nodding at the young man who sat there with peculiar posture, looking down at the table.

"This," said Aagny, with pride in her voice, "is Ersmo. He's not mine by birth, but I wish he was. I worked as a housekeeper for a cripple in a village nearby. This is her boy. And . . . well, she's not with us anymore, but by then me and this guy had gotten so acquainted that we decided to keep going together." She smiled warmly at the young man.

"Oh," said Sara. "I knew things would work out for you."

"Sure did," said Aagny. "Ersmo here owns the farm, but I don't mind working on it. It's bloody beautiful now. We have chickens and potato fields and everything."

"And hey," said Aagny. "The chickens, they have a bloody good life with us. Really high perches in the chicken coop, running around as they please. You don't need to worry—no need to come to our house in the middle of the night and spray anything."

Here, she let out a laugh so booming that it first infected Sara, then József, and finally even Ersmo. Now all four of them giggled, loudly.

"So what are you doing here?" Aagny asked. "And who's this?"

"This is József," said Sara. "My fiancé."

Aagny fixed him with her gaze.

"I hope you know that you've landed the very sun itself," she said. "You treat her well, or you'll have me to deal with."

József swallowed three times quickly, but Sara said: "Never been treated better by anyone. Not since you watched over me in the clink, at least."

Another burst of laughter. József felt jealous again, but it quickly faded.

"So, you don't live here now, do you?" Aagny asked interestedly.

"Sadly not," said Sara. "We live in the big city. We're just here visiting."

"Ugh," said Aagny. "What a wasted life."

"It's starting to feel that way," said Sara.

"Well," said Aagny. "Why don't you come to our place and stay for a while? We have plenty of space. You can come anytime. We're almost always home. Drive past the village, then continue down the road for another mile or so. Ours is the only house there, you can't miss it."

She burped, and Ersmo stifled a sound, too. Then they stood up, Aagny turned and waved, and her cheerfulness put even József in a good mood.

As he watched the odd pair disappear around the corner—the big woman and the teenage boy—he heard the word ringing in his head:

Manslaughter

* * *

Sara was in such a good mood after running into Aagny that the next hour turned into a jolly good time. She was an unbeatable storyteller when she put that foot forward.

"So, one night," Sara narrated, "I lay sleeping in my cell.

"I shared it with this demented old lady who seemed all confused.

"They said she was in for fraud, but I doubt it was intentional—I think she had just misplaced the money, kind of like my grandma used to forget where she put her glasses.

"Where is it, where is it? Oh dear, I accidentally transferred it to my own account, how silly.

"Anyway, I had been to the shower room; the old lady was already asleep, or at least it looked that way.

"So I sneak in and get to bed too, creeping in the darkness so as not to wake the old lady. But as I lay there, suddenly I see something moving under the old lady's bed, and it turns out that somehow another inmate, Roger—he was born a woman but that's another story, just so you understand why there was a Roger in a women's prison—Roger has got in there and is now standing by my bedside. And in the bed next to me, I suddenly realize, isn't the confused old lady, but the craziest inmate of them all, Sussie.

"She hated me. *Hated*, do you get it? I don't even know why!

"Still, my first thought is: *What the hell have they done with the old lady? Did they lock her in a shower stall or something?*

"But then I didn't have time to think about that because Sussie comes up to my bed, too, and Roger pulls a knife.

"I must have called for help at some point, but they shushed me, and my throat couldn't make another sound.

"Anyway, so I lie there, so bloody scared, feeling something wet—apparently I had peed myself—"

Sara laughed so loudly at this fact that József had to laugh, too,

"and it turns out they had planned to slash my face, because they were tired of me and my, as they put it, *sanctimonious smirk*.

"But just when they are about to,

"Roger is holding me down while Sussie approaches with the knife,

"then the door opens and in walks Aagny, carrying the Bible,"

here, Sara shrieked with laughter again,

"and she *smacks* Sussie in the head with the Bible, from the side you see, making Sussie lose her thread,

"and that's when Aagny takes the knife from her,

"and she is *completely* calm, József, I swear.

"Roger and Sussie just scurry away,

"and Aagny, she looks DEADLY, so not only do they scamper away but I can tell that they'll never dare to do it again.

"And I'm scared of Aagny too, in that moment! The expression on her face. But then Aagny starts to laugh, sits down, and pats me on the cheek, like a child, because she can see how scared I am.

"And then she helps me remove the wet sheets from the bed,
"and she lies down in the old lady's bed and sleeps until
morning. And then she slips out and crawls into her own bed,
in her own cell."

József was speechless.
"I have three questions," he said eventually.
"That's horrible," he said first, with empathy.
It wasn't a question, but it felt like one.
Sara shrugged:
"I don't see it as horrible—more than anything, I felt like
someone had my back. I will always love Aagny for that. Though
I would have loved Aagny anyway."
"Where was the old lady?" József asked as his second question.
"She was snoring away in Roger's bed. They just pushed her
out when morning came. She didn't even realize she had slept
somewhere else."
"Now for the last question. How poor was the security in
that prison?"
Sara burst out laughing again. "Absolutely horrendous," she
said. "All the guards were men who thought women couldn't
hurt each other, so they didn't even bother locking the doors."
He loved her for painting this picture of prison and guards
for him, of their humanity. The ease with which she navigated
life, everything she had been through; nothing seemed to leave
any lasting scars on her—experiences were always positive, a
good story to tell.
"I think we might need to go visit Aagny. I feel that now. Can
we, József?"
József had been somewhat reassured by the story, but he still
had to know:
"What was the manslaughter she committed?" he asked.
"I don't know the details, but I think her husband assaulted
her, so she had to kill him in self-defence."

József breathed a sigh of relief. He pictured the flowerpot that poor Aagny had grabbed as she was being raped and struck the perpetrator's head with; how it had landed—regrettably—on a blood vessel.

"I want everything you want. Let's go see Aagny."

They bought Oreos, got in the car, drove forty-five minutes to the village and then another mile, to the only house there. It was almost completely hidden from the road; they could see the back of the house, but the rest was shrouded in tall trees and a fence. There was a beautiful treehouse built a little way up on a tall trunk. When they entered the yard, the house was plain but welcoming, like it was cared for. A smaller house, perhaps a bakehouse, was located further down. It looked nice enough.

* * *

Sometimes Sara got such a bad headache that she had to go to bed. That's how it was. The headache would creep up on her, at first just a twinge, barely discernible at all—then a mild throbbing, which grew stronger and stronger. She described it as wandering around in a parallel world, where a filter lay over everything; nothing felt real.

And so, on the first night at Aagny's, this headache came on. She and József lay sleeping, snugly accommodated by Aagny in the bakehouse, which turned out to have a large comfy bed. The window let in a cool breeze from the yard. Sara had wine in her system, and Aagny's pancakes—the only dish Aagny could think to make that was vegetarian. Despite the headache, Sara managed to fall asleep, and she dreamed.

In the dream, she floated around in light. Everything felt warm. In the dream, she was standing up. Next to her: József. Aagny, Ersmo. Anyone else? She looked to the side. There, Aagny was crouching on the ground, delivering a baby. She couldn't see the woman giving birth, only the baby that Aagny pulled forth. She looked the other way. There stood a bear. There was something about it. Around its eye, a bald patch, as if it had been injured.

She looked down at her own feet, found cloven hooves. She was an animal, too? It was so easy to walk. The air was so easy to breathe. *This is the answer.* Everything was worth the same. She was a part of.

She woke up. *This is the answer* said her mind. József woke up, too, having recognised the uneasy sleep from earlier in life. He assumed it was a nightmare, held her and rocked her. He knew exactly how to handle night-time anxiety. But Sara didn't think about his practice from childhood; she was simply struck by the ease of it all—the light, and the room, and the laughter with Aagny in the kitchen, and József holding her like it was completely natural, so that her headache felt approved, and bearable.

This is the answer.

"How do you support yourselves?" József had asked the day before. "If I may ask."

Aagny had glanced at Ersmo. You could tell there was something they weren't saying.

Later, it would come to light that Aagny and Ersmo might not exactly have informed the authorities about the death of Ersmo's mother—she fell from the roof, apparently—and that they continued to receive disability benefits from the state. What's more, Aagny was still paid a salary for her work as Ersmo's mother's assistant.

It wasn't planned, or anything. It was just that money kept coming into their account, and it seemed silly not to accept it.

"Off this and that," Aagny said now, when József asked. "But mostly, you don't actually need much money when you live like this."

She pointed out towards the yard. Here, not much had

changed in the past fifty years. There were potato fields and a chicken coop and fish in the lake. The rifle in the shed meant that the freezer was periodically full of moose meat. They had a toilet and electricity, but even if it went out, they would surely manage. They had a wood-burning stove and a well and an outhouse.

Aagny set the table with eggs and toast and butter and cheese. She sang as she brewed coffee, pouring it into small cups for Sara and József. A chicken hopped onto Sara's lap. They talked prison memories. The hours went by. Ersmo went outside and continued building the new chicken coop.

"Can't you stay a while," Aagny thought.

Sara and József looked at each other. They grinned.

The next morning, the headache was gone. Sara got up and saw József outside, talking to Ersmo. There was something exuberant in the boy's eyes, presumably due to the complete and total attention that only József could bestow on another person. Aagny was painting a fence and cursed a little as she spilled paint on her foot.

This is the answer.

As it happened, Sara didn't show up for work the following week. Neither did József. And not the next week either. József had no family. Sara sent a letter to her parents, saying that she was visiting a friend and would be hard to reach.

They were used to it, her family. She could seldom be reached. Geographically, she was now quite close to them, but they didn't know that.

* * *

Sara told József that he had to live a little, follow his instincts sometimes. As she lay naked in bed, with the sun on her breasts and that infectious laughter in her mouth, it sounded

tempting. And now, when he was taking a break from his duties as a cantor and had sold his parents' home, he realized he was in a state of
total free fall.

He had nothing at all! The framework around him was gone, shattered the moment his mother closed her eyes. Staying here for a while to catch his breath, find solid ground beneath his feet. It wasn't worse than anything else. In the midst of a hurricane, you have no view of the future or the past. And a person who has no goal can't chart a direction either.

He entered the kitchen, where Aagny and Ersmo sat in silence, having breakfast, listening to the radio. They were both lost in their own breakfast worlds, one on the kitchen sofa, the other at the table. Life with them was undemanding—each person responsible for themselves; you could work on the farm as you pleased, go mend a fence or try to grow something. You could be alone or join the others, if you wanted.

"Oh, damn it," said Aagny, who had spilled yogurt on her belly.

Aagny was a relaxing factor in herself. She was so authentically Aagny that everyone else understood it was impossible to be judged in this setting. She voiced everything she felt—that she needed to pee, that she loved Sara, when she thought Ersmo had a grumpy tone and needed to pull himself together. Just days after they met, she walked up to József, licked her thumb, and wiped some jam off his cheek.

Sometimes he would go stand over by the chickens. Most of them were running around, cackling away. But there was one that was shy and sad, ignored by the others, with black feathers and a murky gaze, like she was sick in some way. Ersmo had named her Dr. Snuggles. Just the sight of Dr. Snuggles made József feel strangely moved. He found himself digging for worms to offer to Dr. Snuggles. At first, it led to fighting—the other chickens also felt they were entitled to the tasty worms—so, after a while,

József started to wait for moments when she was alone, only serving the worms then. And he found himself starting to talk to Dr. Snuggles.

"I don't know who I am anymore, Dr. Snuggles," he would say, fumbling for the words.

Then: "You'd think that when your parents die, your focus would be on them as individuals, on how much you miss them."

He hesitated.

"But I've noticed that I mostly think of myself. I've lost my map. I don't understand anymore. And it's like I've been trying for so long to make them happy that I don't know what makes me happy."

He paused.

"I only know one thing. That I want to be with Sara."

He spoke with long pauses, as if he were pouring out everything that came into his mind and listening to it as it came out, like it was the first time.

Dr. Snuggles listened, head cocked to one side.

They gave up their apartments. Later, they could always get a new place, together.

József also resigned from his job at the church, effective immediately. He sent a postcard to the choir. This would inconvenience people, he explained, first to the black-breasted hen, and later to Sara. Each individual in the choir stepped forth in his memory—the loneliness some of them suffered, the purpose he knew that the choir served for them. Solbritt and her divorce, Sandra and her rheumatism . . .

Sara listened, but also laughed a little.

"That's just like you," she said. "You're so kind to think of them. But your parents died. You're grieving, changing. You have to think of József now. Just once, you have to think of József."

He didn't agree with what she said, but he loved that she

said it; he took pleasure in thinking about it, that he would get to prioritize what he wanted. And now he thought that he would think of himself, for her sake. She wanted it so badly, for him to think of himself, and for it to result in him wanting to stay here for a while.

He felt a pang of sadness, wondering what the next cantor would think of Ingabritt's muffins, and then taught Ersmo to sing a harmony from a spiritual. Ersmo sang the song with pride, a bit off-key but focused. The others rumbled on—Sara's voice beautiful and Aagny's out of tune. There was an old guitar. József bought new strings in town and played it as they sang.

He thought it was as good as anything. Here we can stay, he reasoned, for a few weeks, maybe months. Then they would return to the city, buy a place together, start a new life.

In the meantime, he would have her all to himself.

SARA
1998–2000

Sara had always *ended up* in places. It was her thing. Life just worked out that way. She never understood how things worked for others, who didn't *end up*.

She had always needed to go places. She needed to see what was out there.

After prison, she *ended up* in Kristiansund, Norway, where she got a job shucking crabs. There, she accidentally started a trade union. By the time the first meeting was held, she had already moved on.

Then she *ended up* in a bar in London, serving pints to Englishmen and accidentally joining a jazz band. She tried a plethora of drugs, which she would definitely have got addicted to if she hadn't happened to meet two Danish friends, who she then followed on their journey to find themselves. Sara was interested in finding herself, too.

She boarded a plane, and realized she had *ended up* in Kerala, in southern India. To the ashram in Kerala, rich tourists traveled from all over the world to connect with themselves. Here, Sara and the two friends spent their money saved up from shucking crabs and bartending to work, practise yoga, and be silent.

The idea was to mortify one's flesh, but in a luxurious way. They had to be silent until noon. Then, hot water and rice were served. After that, four hours of yoga. For dinner, a feast of fruits and vegetables and dips and teas from a bountiful table. Then followed self-study, which for Sara and the two friends meant going to the bar across the street, getting drunk, picking a fight, making up, and finding a fellow yogi traveller to sleep with. Then they would wake up under a mosquito net, draped in sweat and anguish, silently nursing their hangovers until noon.

Sara was pretty bad at yoga. She never managed to touch her heels to the ground in *downward-facing dog*, never remembered which way her feet should point in *warrior 2*, fell asleep immediately during *yoga nidra*.

The ashram perhaps wasn't the most serious India had to offer. The yoga teachers were mostly Americans overdosed on henna tattoos.

Yet there was something there.

Sara often experienced herself as fluid. Whenever she heard something interesting, saw something interesting, she moved towards it. Nothing could stop her. That's how it felt. But what yoga now provided was this: Sara suddenly saw her own outline. What was her, and what wasn't her. It felt like two completely separate things—the actual practice of yoga and the feeling it brought afterward. The connection between them was unclear to her: first, you stood there, breathing and trying to touch your heels to the ground for an incredibly boring hour and a half.

But afterwards. That's when it happened. The outline. The calm.

Once, an inkling: home. A feeling of home. Apparently, it wasn't out there in the world to search for. It resided within herself. A single flash of that feeling, lasting thirty seconds.

She had that giggle. It was the kind of giggle that put people in a good mood; it was *boisterous*. What is it about some laughs? They cut through everything: age, class, gender, generation, mood. That kind of giggle is an equaliser. It's irresistible. No one talks about the currency of a really good giggle. She struggled to stay quiet until noon, often accidentally saying something, letting her laughter pour out, putting the other tourists in a good mood and making them laugh, too. It only took a couple of days before Sara had made a name for herself at the retreat.

There was a guru. The guru was known as *Siddha*, which roughly translates to the "perfected one". Siddha insisted on living in the middle of the retreat, in an ordinary room, just like the visitors. The rooms were beautiful but a bit dilapidated, gorgeous colors but the paint on the walls was peeling. In Siddha's room there was a fan. He dressed in simple clothes, just like the others. The concept of the resort was clear thanks to the fact that everything revolved around one person. All day, they talked about him; stories circulated.

"A true guru lacks worldly desires," one of the two Danish friends claimed to know. "He is a guru because he has managed to suppress his individuality and has now become like a gaseous form, in direct contact with divinity."

"He gets up at 1.30 am and meditates for three hours every night," said the other Danish friend.

A Frenchman, who had been at the retreat for several months, added:

"I heard that a homeless alcoholic came here, and after spending five minutes with Guru Siddha he got clean and started one of the world's most successful investment companies."

Once a month—if you were lucky—Guru Siddha held a midnight gathering for the tourists. He would sit on a simple mat, outside, in front of the ashram, and each person got to sit down across from him for a short while. You were supposed to look into the Guru's eyes, and through this gain wisdom and come closer to your own consciousness.

The tourists were waiting in line. The first one immediately started crying when she met Guru Siddha's gaze.

"Now I see," she wept. "Now I know."

The second one got a blissful smile on his face.

"I felt what's important in life," he said later, when they all compared notes. "Now it's time for me to go home and be with my children."

Both the first Danish friend and the second also felt that they had immediately identified "what's important" through their encounter with Siddha, and would for the rest of their lives describe this meeting as utterly pivotal. Sara was thus a bit nervous when it was her turn to approach the Guru. Her legs were shaking. She wanted so badly to feel what they felt, to gain a sense of direction, to let something greater than her determine and define her.

She sat down opposite the Guru, looking into his warm, dark eyes. Hoping to find what she was seeking. To encounter something she had never encountered before.

But instead, it turned into this: a competition.

It wasn't what she had expected. But the Guru refused to look away. This was, of course, the whole premise of the meeting. His gaze seemed to trigger her, she noticed, so she didn't want to look away either. His calm demeanour transformed into something else. She understood that he had expected her to be submissive, like the others. And she realized now that she had expected *him* to be submissive, like people usually were when she looked at them.

Now his gaze was steady and calm once more.

This made her feel that she absolutely shouldn't look away.

Her eyes narrowed. She saw the Guru's eyes narrow, too.

A sudden instinct: to part her lips slightly, show her canines. It just came.

He did the same.

She felt her hand clenching, into a fist. She held it at bay. But it clenched.

Time ticked on.

The encounter usually lasted no more than a couple of minutes; then the Guru would put his hands to his chest in a farewell gesture of gratitude, whereupon it was time for the next tourist to meet his gaze. But this? How long would this go on? Sara realized that with each passing second, it became less and less possible to stop. She needed to win. The line shuffled impatiently behind her. An agitated murmur rose, mixed with the intense breathing of people trying to exert control over their own impulses by nose-breathing away their agitated murmur.

Ten minutes—fifteen—

finally, the Guru waved his hand in the air, a gesture of dismissal. He was still looking into Sara's eyes as he whispered something to a man standing next to him, and this man went and stood between Sara and the Guru, bent down, and said to Sara:

"The Guru wants to see you tomorrow."

* * *

It was very early morning. In truth, Sara wasn't comfortable going in to see the Guru alone. She kept her hand over the ruby in her pocket, knowing that men, when they wanted to see you alone, weren't usually interested in discussing inner growth. But it was light out, and there were lots of people circling outside the room. And everyone—not least the Danes—were jealous of her; they also wanted time with the Guru. She had to seize the opportunity.

The Guru's room smelled strongly of incense, and of the Guru's feet. He was sitting on the floor. In the daylight, he looked small, and old. Humorous wrinkles around his eyes.

"How do you like it here?" he asked. His gaze was soft. Sara was surprised. She had assumed the Guru would talk, not listen. She saw that he was making an effort to appear laid-back.

So she made an effort in return. Apparently, the competition was over.

"Fine, just fine," she therefore said.

She fell silent.

"I'm sorry if I've sometimes disturbed the peace. By being too loud."

"Laughter is not a disturbance of peace," said the Guru. "Some others think so. Not I."

A brief pause, which could have led to another competitive situation, Sara recognised; if that were the case, she would keep the silence longer than he did.

But he broke the pause voluntarily.

"Tell me," he said then.

"About what?" Sara replied.

"Only you know," said the Guru.

There was no contrast as big as that between this conversation and the ones that used to take place in her hometown on the Norrland coast. So immense was the difference that it almost came full circle; they started to resemble each other in their brevity.

"I don't know," said Sara.

"You do know," said the Guru.

Then he held his tongue again, but now the silence was kind, as though allowing her to reflect; she need not hurry.

A wave swept over Sara, a kindness, a gratitude. The Guru assumed nothing about her—that's how it felt now—or, *if* he assumed things, he was wise enough to understand the difference between an individual and his own assumptions about her.

She was a blank, clean slate, until she chose to define herself. That's how it felt.

She began to speak, incoherently at first, her English stuttering—but after a while the words fell into place; it was like she needed five minutes initially to find the right thought path in her brain, and once begun, she only had to follow it through to the end.

She spoke about the animals, the people, the crabs, the chickens, the horses. She spoke about getting paid to work in Norway, and paying to work at the retreat. She spoke about her racing mind, about the dreams she had, about the images she sometimes saw in her mind, about her parents' money. About her anxiety.

And the ruby.

The Guru listened. In complete silence, he listened.

He gave her a name, and a mantra, to keep to herself.

Sara tried out the thought. Keeping something to herself, not telling anyone. It suddenly seemed . . . doable.

She felt strong, and straight-backed, as if she had been allowed to show her full self, and in the middle of her initially incoherent speech, she had caught glimpses of herself.

There she stood now. An individual.

"I would like to teach you," he said. "You have a potential within you."

Sara stopped socializing with the Danes and, accepted into the Guru's inner circle, suddenly found herself meditating for several hours a night, watching her thoughts come and go. She learned to listen to her body, to ask it, to search within it.

Previously, if she felt bad, she had let herself be consumed. *Oh, a feeling of discomfort in my body. It must be because both the world and I are so inadequate.*

Now she allowed the feeling to exist—noted it, tried not to add a value judgment.

I feel bad today. Huh, what an interesting thought.

My sister no longer exists. It's unfair. Why did it happen to her, and to me, of all people? Everyone else's sisters are still alive. That's also how the world is made; things come and go. You can't fight it. Just like the flower that blooms today and wilts tomorrow.

There was an energy flowing around the Earth. Like the trees and the animals, she was a part of it, but they were all the same.

Just like the way people ate and drank, moved, conversed, you could also consume each other's bodies. It was natural. The Guru gave her a yogic massage, working his way down the lower part of her abdomen. She barely reacted when he approached her genitals. It happened so gradually, she didn't know how she suddenly lay without clothes and with him inside her. He did the same with others, and so did she. There were no longer any clear boundaries between physical practices; a yogic position could become a meditation, could become a hug, could become sexual. He dissolved all the tension within her, so that her body was completely open and ready for whatever might come. She was hardly in her head at all. Everything was body, body, body.

Sometimes, there is a bafflingly small difference between romance and assault. Was she comfortable in his presence? No. Did she feel that he was different from everyone else she had met? Yes. Did she find him attractive? Absolutely not. Did she learn something? Everything.

Guru Siddha had a technique. He signaled for the others to lie down on the floor. Mattresses. He told the group to breathe in a completely different way than usual, through the mouth. Breathe into your abdomen, breathe into your chest, exhale. Breathe into your abdomen, breathe into your chest, exhale. The breathing was quick and rhythmic.

It was no longer yoga at all; it was something else. Her head was spinning, it was awful, she wanted to leave—

But Siddha signaled for her to continue, and the others kept breathing. She heard them make sounds, almost pained. The strict breathing was demanding on the body; she felt a panic begin to rise.

"Now," he said. "Let go."

And the entire group surrendered to a regular breathing. They let go completely, and it became quiet. Tears began to roll. Anxiety had been exchanged for relaxation, the greatest she had ever felt in her life. From different parts of the floor, she heard people releasing grief from their bodies. She understood that the others were used to it, that the Guru did this with them on a regular basis. First, she thought he was incredible. Later, she realized that it was her body. You only needed to know the commands. He knew them.

Now she knew them, too.

And the group, being there, with people—all different ages and nationalities and backgrounds, but no one pointed out their differences; they just existed there, next to each other, wanting to achieve their shared goal, to dissolve, to become part of the greater whole.

Though Sara noticed that money was a prerequisite for becoming part of the greater whole. Only the seekers with plenty of it could afford to stay long enough. The poorer tourists had to go home. The Indians living in the city never found their way to the retreat.

She got to stay for free.

For five months, she lived in Kerala. One morning she woke up. Now the sun was rising outside. The sound of a car passing by. It was so warm, stifling. Some kind of feeling in her chest—
the wind in her hair, the world outside. Everything she could be, everything she wanted to become. She felt a restlessness in her body, her anxiety unfolding its limbs.

She got up and looked at the Guru lying beside her. He slept with his mouth open, saliva dripping down into his beard. It made things easier.

He would never care about her anxiety; he would argue that she ought to take responsibility for it herself, do more yoga, that it shouldn't be assigned value, should barely be noted; and she knew she needed something else. She wanted to share it with someone, that's the only way it would diminish—if someone saw it and approached it. She wanted to be seen with it, for someone to see it, and say: *I see your anxiety and that you carry it. I want to carry it with you.*

Perhaps that's what it wanted her to say, too.

She grabbed her passport, opened the door, snuck out into the sunrise, direction towards the airport. Curious to see where she would end up next.

EMELIE AND LÅKE
AUGUST 2023

Oh, hello. Here you are, sitting right outside my tent.
That's . . . cute. And perhaps a bit scary.
I was waiting for you.
To think that you and I would bump into each other again!
Who would have thunk?
This place isn't that big.
No, I know. I was joking.
Oh.
Ha-ha-ha. Ha. Soooo, what's up?
Do you have any books?
Books?
Yes, books. I've read all the ones we have.
Okay . . .
So, do you have any?
Let's see, what did I bring? I have three books. I've finished this one, if you want to borrow it? It was terribly good.
There's no one on the cover.
No.
What's it about?
It's like short stories, a woman talking about the slave trade in Ghana, its consequences and stuff. It's dark, but also very easy to read. The woman who's written it is called Yaa Gyasi.
Okay. What's the slave trade?
You don't know about the slave trade?
No.
Have you never . . . well, it's like people in Europe used to

believe they had a right to take people from African countries, and use them as their own slaves.

You're kidding.

Unfortunately not.

The Society you live in is truly awful.

This was a long time ago.

So the slave trade is completely gone now?

Yes, it is. But in some ways, you could say . . .

What?

That it still exists—but in other ways, other hidden ways.

I can't believe my ears. Good thing you fled.

* * *

Oh . . . hello, Låke.

Hi.

I haven't even had breakfast yet.

Okay.

I'll just put some clothes on. Wait here.

Do you have anything to eat?

I have breakfast, I was going to have a sandwich and some coffee.

I've already had a sandwich and coffee today. Don't you have anything else?

Ehrm, yeah, I have some chips here.

Chips, with dill and chives.

No, sour cream and onion.

Okay, I'll have those, I guess. Why are you here anyway? It's not common to camp here.

No, I just . . . I needed to be here, that's all.

Because you're fleeing?

I'm not fleeing! Well, yes, in a way I'm fleeing. But hey. What are *you* doing here? What are all of you doing here?

(Silence.)

Do you have any more chips?

The Ant Colony
September 2023

Outside the farmhouse, a car pulled up. The people inside it wore well-pressed clothes. They joked with each other during the journey, but as soon as the car stopped, they rearranged their faces and made them serious. They had tried to call, but discovered there was no longer a phone number connected to the house. Eventually, they'd had to decide to go straight there and investigate.

THE ANT COLONY
2008–2023

THE ANT COLONY
2008

They had settled into the bakehouse. Aagny showed them how to pull up potatoes, and József got started. His energetic body, used to doing sports, had rested for a long time, and now it rejoiced as it began to rake and harvest and, soon—as autumn turned to winter—to shovel snow.

József had it in him that he needed to always be doing something. That's how it is for those with a brooding mind. For such a person, shovelling snow is perfect. A brooder does well replacing questions like *What is the meaning of it all?*

with more urgent questions like

Why are there so many larvae on this kale?

It was the four of them: Aagny and Ersmo, and Sara and József.

When József and Ersmo went for long wordless walks in the evenings, when all four of them had their hands deep in the potato field, when the chickens laid eggs, when they turned on the TV,

there were moments when József felt like he wasn't quite sure where he began and the other three ended. And it wasn't just the people, he confessed to Sara, but also the chickens, and the trees, even the potatoes.

"And the worst part is I like it—that it's like that," he said. "No one thinks about a potato that it needs to live up to something. You just think that the potato is there. It is the way it is."

"I've started talking to the chickens," he confessed further.

"There's one that I like more than the others, because it feels like she *listens* to me."

Sara already knew this, but she didn't say anything. In the mornings, she could sometimes hear her fiancé walking around inside the chicken coop picking up eggs.

Should I go back, visit their grave more often? I don't know, Dr. Snuggles, I don't know. It's like the thing I've loved most in life is now chasing me in the form of a nightmare. I see all of it together; I hear her wake up and scream, I hear him locked in his office, and the music—pam-pa-paaaam!—and it's like what I see is cross-cut with their smiles, Dad in the stands.

He spent a lot of time staring at animals. He saw how they lived together, the groups. His favorite were the beavers; sometimes he would take morning walks to the lake, wait for them, trying not to make any noise or movements.

Aagny had told him that beaver couples mated for life. They had babies, and the babies stuck around for at least another year or two, helping to take care of next year's babies. They built lodges, sometimes several that they rotated between.

When József looked at the animals, Sara and Aagny looked at József. They saw him with Ersmo. They saw Ersmo grow under the grown man's solemn listening and how József asked Ersmo to teach him things, to build, to sow. That Ersmo got to be the competent one. Slowly, they saw a confidence bloom in him.

SARA
2008

S ara took the car to her hometown to see her brother, who was visiting their parents. It was winter. It was the first time she had been back since they'd moved to Ersmo's. Her parents were getting old.

They sat around a table—Sara, her parents, and her brother and sister-in-law—talking about this and that, while the coffee sputtered in the coffee maker.

Now the doorbell rang. Sara looked at the others. Weren't they all accounted for?

"We're expecting one more," they said. "It's Ulrika's cousin—she happened to be in the neighborhood, so we invited her for coffee."

The woman who now entered the room was small and thin, possibly of Sri Lankan origin? Sara guessed that she had been adopted and raised in Sweden. The woman came across as plain but could probably be cute if she wanted to. She wore big glasses, and behind them a piercing gaze. She immediately walked over to the window and peered down at the water, before taking in the people. When the parents' dog ran up to sniff her, a Finnish hound, she patted her warmly on the head.

"Hello," she said then—to the dog, not the people. "Yes, you're a good girl, aren't you."

She lingered there, by the dog, for quite some time before turning to the people at the coffee table.

"I'm allergic to hazelnuts and almonds," she said and took a seat in an empty chair.

"Oh," said Sara's mum, with rising irritation; this cousin hadn't said a single nice thing. She had been invited over for coffee after all, she could have at least said that the house was nice or that it was good to meet them.

Ulrika blushed.

Sara decided to put on her diplomat's hat, one of the roles she played best. She had hardly needed to do it since meeting József—he possessed it naturally, and she had begun to leave it entirely up to him, which was a relief—but now she noticed how easily she fell into it. Like an old key code she had used often, it was just there, in her body.

"I guess you noticed the light, too," she said to the cousin, nodding towards the window. "It falls so beautifully over the beach here at Mum and Dad's, I've always thought so. When I was little, I could sit here and stare for hours."

Would you look at that—with a single comment she had effectively:
a) included the cousin in the conversation
b) normalised the cousin's staring out the window
c) given her validation-craving mother a compliment
d) saved Ulrika from embarrassment.

The cousin stared at Sara, and looked happy.

"I've always wanted to live by the beach."

"Where do you live now?"

"In the city," said the cousin.

"Sagne works at the university," Ulrika interjected.

"Oh really," said Sara. "What's your field?"

Sagne looked at Sara, the way scientists always do when trying to assess if the person they are talking to will understand anything they are about to say.

"Ants," she said then. "I'm an entomologist, specialising in myrmecology."

Sara stared back questioningly. Sagne sighed, choosing her words.

"The science of ants," she said. "I study how ants build their colonies."

"How interesting," said Sara's mum, in a way that clearly signaled she would now prefer to talk about something else.

"How do they build their colonies?" Sara asked.

Sagne saw in her eyes that the question was sincere, so she made an effort to explain in a way that would be understandable even to a layperson.

"In short, you could say that ants are some of the world's best builders. Their colonies can be miles long, underground networks. They build in efficient ways that even our engineers could never master."

"Hmm," said Sara's dad interestedly; he had worked in construction.

"There's lots to be inspired by when it comes to ants," Sagne said.

Sara raised an eyebrow. This afternoon had taken a very unexpected turn. She had thought they would sit dunking little cookies into their coffee and gossiping about their relatives. Instead, this peculiar woman had showed up and said things that were genuinely interesting. She wished József was there.

"So how are things?" interrupted Ulrika, who after several family gatherings with Sagne knew that myrmecology was neither a party starter nor a social lubricant. "Mmm, what a delicious almond cake. What's your secret?"

"Extra butter and extra eggs," said Sara's mum.

"So when are you going back to work, Sara?" Ulrika asked.

Sara paused for a bit.

"It's unclear," she said. "I need to do some other things."

"Other things?" Ulrika said, smiling.

"As usual for Sara," said Albin.

"József and I realized we really like it in the forest. And we ran into an old friend who has a house in . . . a village. So we've been staying there for a while."

"Where is this village exactly?" Ulrika wondered.

"The cake is truly incredible," said Sara.

"In the village," said the cousin called Sagne. "What's there?"

Sara thought about it.

"Peace and quiet," she said. "There's peace and quiet."

She saw that the new one called Sagne understood.

"The village," said Sagne. "It's the one near Skalnäset, isn't it?"

"Perhaps," Sara replied.

"I have a family house there," said Sagne. "In Skalnäset."

"Not me, though, right?" Ulrika said.

"No, it's on Mum's side."

"But the more time goes by," said Sara, "I've realized that the peace and quiet are deceptive. There are animals and insects and trees. There are lots of things happening if only you pay attention."

Sagne nodded. She really nodded, so vigorously that she almost toppled over.

Albin feigned a snore.

"Sorry," he said in Sagne's direction.

She didn't look upset at all.

"What a cake!" Ulrika said again.

Sara and Sagne looked at each other, and smiled.

SAGNE
2008

It was later that same day. Sagne had long since left the
white-brick house where she had met her boring cousin
and the cousin's charismatic sister-in-law. Afterwards
she had visited her own family, who lived an hour away; now
she was heading back to the university town. Sagne thought
the sister-in-law had been on her side, maybe—as if they were
friends? It was hard to explain, but it felt like she *understood*?
Sagne very rarely felt like anyone else understood, or like she
understood anyone else.

She was driving back; it would take a few hours. But first,
she needed to find somewhere to eat. She pulled up to a road-
side restaurant. *Huckleberry Inn* it said in big glowing letters
over an almost entirely deserted parking lot. Snow hung from
the roof; it looked idyllic. And this is what happened.

WHAT HAPPENED
Sagne sat down in a booth and ordered a burger and Coke.
The burger wasn't very good; it was limp, gelatinous, relating
to the bread like Salvador Dalí's clock. She had another Coke.
She stared out of the window. The sun was setting early now,
and a thick darkness lay before her. She took out a dissertation—a doctoral student's work that Sagne had promised to
look at. Sagne was a meticulous reader, so it took time. She had
brought a pencil, underlined, wrote comments. *Cf. Dockson
1984!!!* she wrote, and *Interesting line of reasoning, missing a
reference though.*

The restaurant smelled of cooking fumes, and something old.

Everything as usual.

Her leg itched, so she scratched it.

She felt lonely.

Now the door was opened by two sixteen-year-old boys. They had driven here in an old pickup and now they stepped inside, megalomania on their faces, with trucker hats and the posture of two people who were both used to physical activity and eating a lot. One of them was tall and straight, the other short and V-shaped.

They hollered loudly. Most likely, they had been drinking. There were never any police around these parts, so it wasn't like they risked getting caught.

"Hey," they shouted from the till. "Hey, could we order now or what!"

One of them burped.

Sagne shrank back. She didn't like loud people, especially not the kind who showed aggression. It was like they oozed a question. They were in the middle of their development. *Are we allowed to behave this way?* was the question. *How far can we push it?*

Sagne hated people in the middle of their development.

The man who worked at the restaurant—brown hair, big eyes, and a mouth with a beautifully arched Cupid's bow— stepped up to the till. His mouth made him look like an angel.

"Simmer down," he said, "and you'll get to order. Maybe you want to take that table over there."

The boys ordered two burgers each, and large Cokes. Immediately, they started throwing fries at each other, and soon also at the man behind the till.

Sagne didn't know how to act. Should she stand up? Say

something? She wasn't used to being a person who stood up. But the situation reminded her of a few occasions in school, when she had dropped her tray in the dining hall. The whistles and the laughter, standing alone in the middle of the floor, chili con carne on her shoes, completely defenseless against the cool kids. She remembered wishing that someone had stood up for her then.

A small lace-webbed spider climbed next to the windowpane. She felt like they made contact and that the spider encouraged her to do something. After all, she was an adult, a scientist. It was her role to step in.

Wherefore she, as she went to pay, took the route past the table where the teenagers were sitting.

"Lay it off," she said. "He's just doing his job."

That last part she said a little louder, so the man at the till would hear that she had his back.

"Oooo," said the teenagers. "Your bodyguard is here, Max! Max! You're just doing your job, Max! Max!"

The man at the till—the one who was apparently named Max—took her payment with a stressed look.

"Do you have a restroom here?" she whispered.

The one named Max replied:

"There's one over there."

He pointed to a restroom located just behind the teenagers' table.

She would have to pass them again to use it.

They looked at each other, in mutual understanding.

"But you can use the staff restroom. I'll take you."

The restaurant was empty except for the teenagers and an old man who had just been served his fourth beer and sat weeping in Finnish in a corner. Soon it would be closing. Sagne followed Max through a surprisingly long kitchen corridor.

"Here," he said, pointing to a door. She nodded gratefully at him.

BUT THEN THIS HAPPENED
The one named Max held the restroom door open for her and pushed her inside. Once inside, he pressed
her up against the wall.
This was when things
stopped being usual. Her body

tensed up and at the same time
became a question,
it wasn't used to

the situation.
"Fucking whore."
That's what he said.
"You think I need some
whore to
come and help ME. I know what I'm
doing. Those kids won't make it
even a DAY, they'll never get a real
job, like
ME."

And she saw it in his eyes, that he
Was high on something and wasn't
A normal person who you could trust to think
Rationally.
It was like he believed he was right

And things were happening
outside Sagne now.
On a theoretical level, she noticed

what was going on. There was a strange
man
who was currently pulling down her pants,
ripping open her

shirt,
searching over her body with cold and
dirty

hands,
he smelled of gravy,
he smelled disgusting,
he was cold and strange and

disgusting,
he took a finger and shoved it up inside her so that she
wanted to scream

but her voice
wasn't there, he grabbed hold of
her and forced himself inside her and slammed her against
the wall,
and yelled, *Do you get it now, whore, do you get it now.*
His mouth so vivid, his *Cupid's bow*. That disgusting mouth

and it was like she could see:
There is a before and an after this
moment.
From this moment on, I no longer trust people.
From this moment on, nothing will be all right again.

Now a bell rang in the restaurant now there was a customer
there.
He struggled to come and when he finally did, he looked

proudly at her with his head held high, slamming her against the wall one more time.

"I know who you are," he said.

Then:

"If you tell anyone it'll be worst for your family."

She didn't think he knew who they were he was probably just making it up but

She saw her mother before her eyes,

worried, defenseless.

For a second, he looked away and she hurried to pull up her pants again, quickly

Then he led her back out, pushing her in front of him, through the restaurant he took her. The teenagers had left. She said nothing, allowed herself to be led. Her legs moved, but it surprised her. The whole thing had taken about ten minutes. There was no blood, but it hurt so badly she didn't know her own name. She shouldn't be broken between her legs. It shouldn't hurt there. It didn't used to. The man leading her thought she could walk as fast as usual

And her legs tricked her and pretended they could. But they wouldn't lift as high in each step. Her feet rolled forward, like wheels

She ended up outside, alone, rolled up to her car, where she collapsed.

She lay there for a while.

The teenagers saw her.

"Look at her," one said to the other.

They were quiet for a moment, exchanging glances.

Then they walked up to her, spoke with small, uncertain voices: "Are you okay?"

She looked back at the restaurant.

She thought of her mother.

"I fell," she said.

"We'll take you to the hospital," they said, and they did.

Now she sat in the front seat of an old pickup, between two tipsy teenage boys listening to Eddie Meduza on the cassette deck, and one of them drove the pickup so carefully, so carefully to the hospital,

where they waited until she could see a doctor.

The doctor had a bored look and said that she could file a report if she wanted to.

Sagne nodded and was without words.

The doctor said that physically she seemed okay, so then she must be?

Why wasn't she?

Animals were raped all the time. Dolphins could rape their females for several days on end. None of them made a fuss about it, as far as she knew. Many—even some scientists!—went so far as to say that, unfortunately, that's how humans function, too. They take what they need for the species to live on, whether it be food or sex. It's natural. That's what they said.

She went back to the city, her apartment, and her job, but noticed that she couldn't focus on her work. Sharon walked around giving her the evil eye. If it had been before the party, she would have told her. Now she no longer dared or wanted to.

Nor could she smooth things over between them; she didn't have it in her.

She didn't have it in her to say anything to anyone.

It was as if her mouth had completely forgotten how to speak.

She stopped going to the break room.

She said she was sick.

She closed the blinds.

She was supposed to give a presentation to a group of visiting researchers from Amsterdam. Normally, she enjoyed these kinds of events—gatherings with other people where all the focus was on their common subject—but now it felt utterly impossible, I mean *utterly*, to stand there in front of others and speak,

to exist at all,

to be expected to take the researchers out for dinner.

Her head stalled, it boiled and buzzed. No clear thoughts made their way out.

There was an empty house she knew of. There was a house where no one would ask anything of her. So she just up and left.

In the big formicarium, the ants died. They took their infrastructure with them to the grave.

SAGNE
2008

Sagne found herself in Skalnäset. It was the house her grandmother's brother had lived in. Now, no one wanted it, and no one was interested in getting rid of it. The monetary value was very low, and there was a risk that selling it might start a family feud. Who would do what when the house needed to be cleaned out, and who would receive what money? Did a cousin who had never been there have the same right to the house as another who had visited every summer? It wasn't worth stirring up conflict for a mere fifty thousand kronor. It was one of three houses in her family with the same situation. Where Sagne was from, houses were sometimes the kind of thing you had a whole bunch of—all laden with guilt because some relative once built the house, and so you don't want to do anything wrong with it. But most of the time, you don't manage to do anything right either. And it's not like you get any money if you sell it. So it just stands there, until it collapses.

Sagne had always liked it at Skalnäset, the few times they visited her great-uncle. The house was built of timber, so it was stable. The bed was small and crooked, but then again so was she. The garden was all overgrown but that didn't matter. Lupins everywhere. She would see to all that in the summer.

Every now and then, she went into town and bought dry goods and matches for the stove.

Sagne wasn't someone who spent a lot of money; her salary

had piled up in her bank account, so she didn't think she would need to change her living arrangements anytime soon.

She wondered if her family had started looking for her. By now, she had been gone for several months without telling anyone. She knew she was hurting people, but she pushed that thought away. If she were to let people know, they would ask so many *whys* that she would have to answer.

For example: why there was a bump on her belly.

It had been a long time before she noticed, and even then, she hadn't been sure. She had always thought she wasn't someone who would have children, and that conviction was so strong that her zip burst before she even guessed what was happening.

She already hated the child in her womb. She wanted to get rid of it, but couldn't find a way to do so. It was too late for an abortion, and since she wasn't someone who would get pregnant, she also wasn't someone who would have an abortion. It felt important to stand up for herself and ignore the child in her belly. The man at Huckleberry Inn may have taken her without asking, but he hadn't taken away her plan for life.

So she postponed it. After all, she wasn't someone who would have children, so the child would probably go away in one way or another, in the womb or after being born.

There were books in the cabin. She read them. They were old-fashioned books that smelled of mold, and the Bible. And she went out during the day, near the house, always with a rifle in case she encountered someone who shouldn't be there, someone who might try to jump her, someone who wanted to take her without asking. She walked around during the day, and when it turned into spring and summer she walked down to the water, saw the fish spawn, watched the ants crawl over the blanket, the mosquitoes and horseflies.

She didn't get lonely.

It was a morning. Aagny was out on her morning walk. She made an effort to pick a new route every day, no matter how small the change. Could she jump over this log instead of going around it? Is it more beautiful on this side of the bog or the other? It was a modest adventure. She walked to the water, was about to sit down and stare for a while, when she heard a strange sound. It was utterly quiet and still, so the sound stood out.

She listened. It sounded like it came from across the water.

Aagny was a curious soul, and she had an immense amount of time at her disposal—especially on a day like this, when it still got bright early, when they had just harvested and stored large quantities of potatoes and herbs and apples and raspberries, and they had pickled and preserved, and now everything lay in the root cellar waiting to be eaten.

She listened again. It was like a *groan*.

At first, Aagny thought it might be some animal being attacked by another, but pretty soon she felt it was probably human. And when she looked closely and squinted, she did indeed see something on the far side of the water, an orange-and-brown speck that appeared to be lying on the ground—she squinted even harder—perhaps leaning against a tree?

Aagny wasted no time. Throughout her life, she had been forced to learn to act quickly, when need be. Without hesitation, she threw herself into the water now and let her strong arms carry her over to the other side. The water was cold but also invigorating—she felt high on adrenaline; this was better than jumping over logs.

It took a few minutes to swim across the lake. When she reached the other side, she was soaking wet and cold, but focused. She listened for sounds. It was quiet now. She waited a little longer.

There, what was that?

Her ear guided her. When she saw the source of the sound, she was both surprised, and not surprised.

There was a small woman with glasses, sitting by what was indeed a tree, looking terrified.

"Don't be afraid," said Aagny, dripping with water. "I heard a sound, thought something might be wrong. How are you?"

Now she saw it: her belly, gigantic.

"Are you about to go and have one," said Aagny.

The woman said nothing. She looked panic-stricken.

Aagny's mother had suffered from postpartum psychosis after giving birth to Aagny's third sibling. It was a phrase she had read later, in the Sunday paper. In Aagny's family, they used the term *gone doolally*. Aagny had also witnessed childbirth number four. She didn't remember much except that her mother had seemed completely insane, and that the midwife had reacted as if this was normal. So Aagny knew what childbirth could do to people.

"What do you need?" Aagny asked.

The woman stared at her questioningly.

"If you're giving birth."

Aagny turned, looked around, as if searching for something nearby that could help, a phone booth or a midwife or a hospital, but surprisingly enough there was none of that.

She swallowed.

"Do you need help?" Aagny said.

The woman shook her head.

"Nonsense," said Aagny, but turned around. Surely it was up to each person to decide for themselves if they needed help or not. She stood up, preparing to go back into the lake.

"Immmmm," the woman groaned in a high falsetto. She sounded like she was in pain.

Aagny thought. She wasn't used to delivering babies, but she was used to stepping in where needed. She had watched not only her mother and the cows give birth, but also cats and the occasional pig. It shouldn't be too far off. She felt mildly concerned about having to glare into someone else's groin, see their bloody placenta, and get splashed with amniotic fluid. But she had mucked out the barn, cleaned up Ove's vomit, and held Ersmo's mother while she peed—and surely that wasn't so far off. The body needed to do certain things, and it was mostly humanity's own fault that in our minds we had turned it into something disgusting. That's what she thought.

"Okay, I'll stay here with you." She spotted an old syrup bottle nearby and concluded that it probably contained water. She handed it to the small woman. "What's your name?"

"Sagne," said the woman, still glassy-eyed and almost speechless, but this she managed to hiss.

"Do you want to lie on this, Sagne?" asked Aagny, taking off her wet shirt. "If it dries a little in the sun first. So you don't get ants up your beaver."

"It's okay," said Sagne.

Three hours later, Sagne was screaming into the air.

The baby came out, head first, and before he started crying it was as if he looked Aagny straight in the eye.

"Goddammit," swore Aagny as she realized there were no scissors at hand, and this mammal wasn't going to bite the umbilical cord herself, so Aagny had to do it.

Then her gaze fell on the child again, and now she paused and witnessed the miracle of life.

"Look here," Aagny said in delight, and shed a few tears. "What a child, what a beautiful, beautiful child!" Aagny was genuinely moved; she usually thought babies this small were rather ugly, but this particular child was remarkably gorgeous, with black tousled hair and olive skin.

She placed the baby against Sagne's breast. When it started sucking eagerly, Sagne felt an urge to vomit, but she was too exhausted to object.

Aagny took off her T-shirt, wiped Sagne down, and then she held the baby, held it while Sagne fell asleep.

* * *

When Sagne woke up, she found herself in a strange room. The smell was new. She shook her head, as if to stabilize her gaze and understand where she was.

"She's awake!" someone said. "She's awake now!"

Several faces approached the bed. She blinked, as if to comprehend.

One of the faces, she realized, was Ulrika's sister-in-law—the one who had been there that day, before the terrible thing happened. The one who had felt like a friend.

"Sagne?" said the woman—Sara, Ulrika's sister-in-law. "Sagne, here, drink!"

She held out a water bottle, and Sagne drank, greedily, guzzling it down.

"Oh, Sagne," said Sara, "you have such a beautiful boy, such a beautiful boy. What a beautiful mouth! The sharpest Cupid's bow I've ever seen."

The newly delivered mother stared. No words came from her mouth.

They held the baby up to her; she looked away. They brought

the baby closer. Sagne shifted slightly, as much as she could with the pain in her lower abdomen. They placed the baby on her chest. Sagne closed her eyes.

The others were in a state of dissolution. An all-but-mute woman and a newborn baby in their home, nestled in Aagny's bed. What should they do, what could they do? They ran around in circles. They stood outside the room and peeked inside. Both mother and child needed to be taken care of. Sagne into the shower. The baby washed with a sponge. Aagny went to the shop and bought diapers—diapers that she changed on the baby several times a day.

They also weren't a combined package; they came separately. Sagne never looked at the baby. The baby cried; Sagne placed a pillow over her ears. Eventually, it was Aagny who shoved Sagne's breast resolutely into the baby's mouth—after all, it was pretty much the same as milking a cow. Sagne looked away as the baby's little mouth sucked and sucked, but she let it continue to nurse. And so it would go on: Aagny listening and reacting, Sagne the machine that produced the food.

"Could you call Ulrika?" József said to Sara after a couple of days, and Sara nodded. They had expected Sagne to rest up for a day or two and then tell them who they should call, where she would go. But two days later, she still showed no signs of having a will—regarding anything at all.

"I'll just talk to her first."

Sara went in to see Sagne.

"Sagne," she said softly. "I don't know if you can hear me, or what's happened to you. But I'm going to call your family now. Everything will be fine. You may have to go to the hospital."

There was silence for a while. Then Sagne suddenly opened her mouth, and sat up in bed. In a clear voice, she said:

"I *don't* want you to call."

She paused, changed her voice to pleading.

"Please. Please, Sara. Don't call them."

"But we think you need . . . " Sara said. "Okay. But what about the father? Who's the father?"

"I'll be on my way. You don't need to worry about me. I'll get dressed and—"

"But what about the baby?"

Sagne looked as if she had been struck down where she lay. The baby. Right.

"We'll be just fine. Just drive us to Skalnäset. That's where my car is."

THE ANT COLONY
2009

S ara remembered that she had dreamed about this. *Aagny delivering a child*. It must mean something. It must mean that there was something special about this child. That it was connected to them in some way.

That's what she thought. But now it was time for Sagne and the child to go.

"If we drive you to Skalnäset," she said. "What will happen then?"

Sagne wasn't a person who lied, but she nodded along when Sara suggested things too speedily.

"Will you contact your family?"

Sagne nodded.

"You should go by the hospital, too."

Sagne nodded.

"Someone needs to look after you. And the baby."

Sagne nodded.

"You need to inform the father."

Sagne nodded.

Sara suddenly felt confused. She couldn't read Sagne. Sagne had pretty much the same expression the whole time, and hardly said anything. Slowly, Sara walked out of the room, shaking her head.

"She wants to be driven to Skalnäset," she told József. "Then she will call her family and go by the hospital. That's what she says."

"All right, then," said József, getting up, a little too quickly. He felt relieved. The air had been too heavy recently. He wanted to escape it. "Are we leaving now? Right away?"

Gently, József and Sara helped Sagne into the car; even more gently, they placed the baby in her arms. Sagne gave Sara driving directions in a metallic voice. Right. Left. In there. Straight ahead. She looked at the road, her head turned away from the baby.

They started a fire for her in the wood-burning stove, left some food. Checked that she did indeed have a car, and told her to be in touch should she need anything.

They kissed the baby on the head.

Closed the door and drove away.

* * *

They drove in silence. For most situations in life, there is a template. At some point you have experienced something, which you can use as a reference when deciding how to handle similar situations. This—dealing with an almost unfamiliar woman with a newborn baby, and deciding whether it was safe to leave them alone in a cabin—was something they had never experienced before. József therefore drove away kind of jerkily, as if questioning himself every other mile or so. When they were almost home, he suddenly slammed on the brakes.

"No. It won't work. She's not well."

He looked at Sara questioningly.

"Women have given birth throughout the ages. It's normal to be a bit shaky at first," said Sara, who as it happened had never before been near a woman who had just given birth.

József continued driving.

They parked the car outside the farmhouse.

"Or," Sara suddenly said. "Are we wrong?"

"Should we call her family anyway?" said József.

"Maybe the hospital?" said Sara.

"Go to Skalnäset, say that we're bringing more food, but really just keep an eye on them?"

They discussed this as they got out of the car, crossed the yard, and entered the kitchen. There stood Aagny, eyes wild, dressed in a nightgown and boots.

"Where are they?" she roared. Her whole body in fight mode.

They felt ashamed.

"She wanted us to leave her at Skalnäset," said Sara. She spoke the sentence as if it ended in a question mark.

"Idiots," Aagny said in her way. "That baby will die."

Aagny had had a crazy mother. She had been responsible for her siblings more than she could remember. Perhaps it was also the fact that she was the one who had delivered the boy? She had seen him at the very moment of birth.

If it weren't for Aagny, the baby might have died!

Perhaps that's why.

"Let's go," said Aagny, throwing on a sweater over her nightgown.

And so it happened that, five minutes later, all four of them were sitting in Ersmo's mother's car, heading towards Skalnäset. Ersmo was driving.

"Faster," hounded Aagny, "faster."

Smoke rose from the tires as they sped along the back roads. Sara showed the way.

* * *

The first thing they noticed was that Sagne's car was gone.

"Damn it," swore Aagny. "Damn it, damn it, damn it."

Sara was already at the house. She knocked, but no one answered. She looked around. The door wasn't locked. She opened it and went inside.

"Sagne," she said. "Sagne? Where are you?"

József and Ersmo walked around the yard, looking everywhere, as if searching for something very small. This—attempting to localize a missing mother and child—also wasn't a situation they had experienced before.

It had rained, and the rain had left mud, which held tracks. In the best of worlds, Aagny thought, Sagne might have come to her senses and gone home to her family, or to the hospital.

But Aagny didn't feel that people usually behaved like in the best of worlds. Nor was there anything in Sagne's recent actions to indicate that she was capable of thinking rationally at all.

In a way, maybe Aagny also hoped she hadn't.

Right-foot, left-foot, Aagny said to herself. *Right-foot, left-foot*.

Now she stepped resolutely into Ersmo's mother's car, taking a seat to the right in the front, calling out to the others to hurry. She saw that the tracks turned left, and shouted at Ersmo to do the same. Into town is where that road went.

Like a detective, Aagny felt, as the car drove faster than the gravel road could handle. Not that she thought about it with more than ten percent of her mind.

Her heart was pounding. She had to make it. She didn't know in time for what exactly, but she had to make it.

"Faster, Ersmo," she said. "Faster."

* * *

In town, it was eerily quiet. The weather was bad; there were hardly any people out. A flag in the square made a flapping sound in the wind.

They only needed to drive around the main street twice before they saw her.

Town hall, newly built in brick. A short woman with glasses who walked in a stilted manner, as you do when you have recently delivered a child and are still in pain. The woman carried a bundle, by the looks of it. But the people in the car knew what it was: a baby, wrapped in cloth. They recognised the cloth. It was a cherry-pink shawl that Ersmo's mother used to wear.

They didn't reach her in time, but they saw it happen: The woman placed the cherry-pink bundle on the town-hall steps. Then she looked to the side several times and snuck away.

Aagny wasn't thinking logically now. Ersmo had stopped the car, and Aagny *heaved* herself out of the passenger seat, rushed to the steps, and scooped up the bundle.

The baby was sleeping. Its little nose was cold.

She held the baby, while József and Ersmo went into the supermarket and made haphazard purchases: a baby bottle, formula, and pacifiers—the smallest size. Ersmo bought himself a Snickers ice cream cone.

The pacifier was tucked into the baby's mouth. It was immediately accepted, as if it had always been there.

The baby recognised Aagny's scent. It fell asleep in Aagny's arms.

Sara had followed Sagne. The latter had plunked herself down on a bench in the square. There she sat, staring into the drizzle.

Sara approached Sagne now. She sat down next to Sagne, leaned her head against Sagne's. Just sat there.

Sagne didn't react.

The others came, too. Aagny on Sagne's other side, whispering so as not to wake the baby. A strain in her voice. It was as if several different films were playing at once, with Sara in the final scene of a warm-hearted comedy, Sagne in a black-and-white

Bergman film, and Aagny in an action flick. It was thus logical that Aagny's voice was stressed and focused when she turned to Sagne.

"You've gone doolally. There's nothing strange about that. The human body is bloody weird sometimes. But unfortunately, you can't decide for yourself right now, because the baby needs your milk. And you'll regret leaving him here. Trust me. You'd regret it. Come back home with us. We'll help you with the baby. If only he gets to drink your milk, we'll take care of the rest."

The others looked at each other.

Aagny had a template. She had taken care of her younger siblings during her mother's psychosis, as well as a couple of calves whose mothers died in childbirth. The mother must be kept, the baby must be cared for. Nothing strange about that.

Sagne looked like she was giving up. She didn't say anything, but she followed Aagny to the car and didn't object when Aagny placed the bundle in her arms.

Aagny said, now from the back seat between József and Sara, while Sagne sat in the passenger seat with the baby:

"They're staying. They can have my room."

She stated this as a truth. There was no space for other suggestions.

Sara said:

"Aagny, I don't know if—"

But not even Sara could see past the look on Aagny's face now. It was determined, completely impassable. She had that expression again, the one hidden deep inside her. The one where she looked deadly.

But she gazed at that child like he was made of the finest crystal.

Aagny said:

"We have to take care of the baby and Sagne until they get

better, until they're ready to try their wings on their own. She will soon start to love it. It's common."

She said this with the confidence of someone who had been close to many expectant mothers. Which she had; it's just that most of them happened to be animals.

József said:

"But wouldn't it be better if we reached out to her family?"

Aagny said:

"She doesn't want that! Didn't you hear? We can't betray her . . . her . . . what's it called?"

"Confidence?"

"Right. We can't betray that."

"We can't betray that," said Sara.

In truth, they all knew why Sagne and the baby had come home with them. It was Aagny, who wanted so badly to be close to the baby. If Sagne left, they would never see each other again. If they approached the authorities or the healthcare system, the situation would be scrutinised, and Aagny might lose everything—she wouldn't be allowed to care for the baby, Social Services would get wind of them, perhaps they would even take Ersmo from her, perhaps she would have to move.

So Aagny thought: They can stay for one more day.

And she thought the same every day after.

"I'll be responsible for the baby," she said to the others. "You don't have to bother."

What the others didn't know was the reason why Sara didn't kick up a fuss. She could have sent Sagne and the baby off to their relatives in a heartbeat, if she'd wanted to. But. She had dreamed of this birth. There must be something special about this child. There must be a reason why they were here. She could feel it.

In the end, the baby would have to fend for itself most of the time. It would crawl around the yard, and if it started calling, Aagny would pick it up, run to Sagne, and lift up her shirt. Sagne would sit there motionless, sensing the peculiar twitching in her breasts that happens when a mother feels the presence of her child, and her body prepares to give its milk. Her body gave its milk. But her mind wasn't there. Aagny would walk away, continue with other things. Then Sagne would leave the baby on the bench by itself, lying there crying until Ersmo or József came and burped it or changed its diaper.

Then it was on its own again. Or a part of the group. Somewhere in between.

Sometimes József saw this. He paused and noticed, brief moments. There were many things that didn't feel quite right about it. That jarred.

But there was no template, and besides, it was only for now, he thought. Soon, Sagne would recover and she and the baby would go somewhere. This was just a life-sustaining measure, for now.

Perhaps he also thought:

If things got bad enough, Sara would intervene.

* * *

Sagne heard their voices as if in a nightmare. Always someone running after her, shouting, always with exclamation marks.

The baby is crying!

The baby needs to eat!

The baby has peed!

He was so loud all the time, the baby. His body was always on her, sticky. He had that Cupid's bow. Evil little eyes, she thought.

He just wanted and wanted and wanted. He fed off her body. They woke her up at night. *The baby needs to eat.* As if that's all that mattered?

Aagny didn't seem to think the baby was evil, Sagne noted. She often doted on it. When they sat talking in the kitchen in the evenings, Aagny would sit there with the baby in her arms, like it was completely normal.

Sagne would take it from her then. She didn't want Aagny to have to suffer for her sake. Have to hold that baby. She put it down a little further away, where it could lie and babble to its heart's content, until Ersmo or József or Aagny put it to bed.

It should have reached a natural end point, it should have. There should have come a time when Sagne had gathered enough strength to want to leave the house on her own, and the others would let her do it. She should have gone to her family.

But Sagne couldn't think that far; all the difficult thoughts about the future stuck together somehow—they were a sticky mass she didn't want to go near. Besides, she noticed that she *liked* it here. She felt safe in this house. They had fun together, in a way she could never have dreamed of. They didn't go to bars or restaurants or gossip. They talked, about vital things, Sagne thought, and made fires, and worked, and worked. Sagne believed that farming should be based on what is best for the vegetation and the pollinators, so she told them, and they listened with gratitude, and together they created a farm where the grass would grow tall all summer long and bees and wasps and bumblebees were invited.

And then there was this: no one asked her to move out.

In the evenings, they asked Sagne to tell them things. And so she told them, everything she knew. And Sara asked and asked. Sagne told them that ants live in communities with each other, where everyone helps out. That everyone has a clear role: workers, soldiers, drones, and queens.

The workers and soldiers are females, said Sagne.

And: the queen mates with the drones.

Everyone has a task for the community, said Sagne.

Everyone is needed.

No one has to know everything.

Sagne told them how ants, if they see another insect—a beetle, for example—how they work together, behaving as a single unit; coordinated, they climb onto it, grabbing its soft parts, biting down until their prey is dead. Then they carry it back to the colony.

And some species take slaves from other colonies. Blood-red ants, for example, they go so far as to enter other ant colonies, imitating the scent of the new colony to avoid drawing attention, killing competing ants, taking the other colony's pupae with them, turning them into slaves in their own home.

* * *

Before things have happened, it always feels impossible that they would. If you had seen from the beginning which way things would go, you would have pumped the brakes from the start. But one day turns into the next and, without much thought, it becomes a life.

And so it happened that Sagne stayed, and so did the baby, who was named Låke. He continued to follow them around. He walked slowly, because he was a child, so he always lagged behind. Later he would trip over a root and come to walk with a hobbling gait.

Låke soon discovered that a strange atmosphere developed in the group if he came too close. Sagne would fall silent and turn sour. But if she didn't have to look at him—if instead he sat a bit further away—then they would talk, and sing. If he was there, but a bit further off. Not too close, and not too far away.

It was like that sweet spot with the clutch when driving stick. Eventually, everyone got used to it. *Låke, he's the kind of person who likes to be on his own.* That's what they told themselves.

* * *

Dr. Snuggles had grown old. They chopped her up and cooked her with sauce.

SARA AND JÓZSEF
2010

One morning, József opened his eyes and realized they had been at the farmhouse for almost two years. He had woken up with a song in his head and started thinking again about the choir, how much he missed it. But there were other things he missed, too: going on vacation, taking a ferry to Gotland, standing on deck and feeling the wind on his face, watching other people, disembarking in Visby and wandering through the alleys . . .

Those were the things he thought about.

"Sara," József therefore said, a little later in the day. The others had walked down to the water, and now he and Sara were alone in the kitchen. "Could we talk about something?"

"Of course," said Sara, taking a bite of a carrot. "What is it?"

Her voice casual. József took a deep breath. He could hear that he sounded dramatic, was ashamed of this, and so he tried to sound more and more light-hearted with every word he spoke.

"Sara, for a long time I have . . . well, I've been thinking about something. We've talked about it before. I mean, we've had a good life here, haven't we? Really good! But now I'm starting to feel that maybe it's . . . now I'm ready to . . . I suppose I'm missing our old life, a little. I was thinking that now . . . well, that maybe now it's time to move away from here? Don't you think?"

He added, trying to look mischievous:

"Do you remember what we said? We said we'd stay for a short while! But it's been two years! Isn't that crazy?"

He chuckled a little.

But Sara looked at József, her gaze soft.

"No," she said. "I don't think so."

Here, he didn't know what to say. After all, they had talked about.

"But . . . I think so," he replied feebly.

She smiled, looking into his eyes.

"But, darling, think about it. What's out there that's so great? You have no family left. The church has hired someone else by now. You don't have an apartment. Do you even remember how difficult it was to get an apartment in the city?"

"Well, I could get a new job," he said.

He corrected himself.

"*We* could get new jobs. And I have money, from when we sold Mum and Dad's apartment. It's enough to buy a new one."

She sat silent.

Then she changed her tone. Her voice was dreamy now. Her face took on a vulnerable streak, like a child's. She looked unsure of whether what she was about to say was fully thought out, like she was testing the idea.

"Do you know what I think every morning," she said. "I wake up and I look over at your side, and there you are, snoring away. And you make these *sounds* in your sleep, not like you aren't feeling well—but *sleep sounds*, like you're telling me about your sleep. And you search for my body in the night, you always keep one body part on me."

She smiled again, turned down her gaze, looking almost shy.

"And when I hear that sound, and feel that hand or leg," she said. "Then it's like every question inside me dies.

"The state of the world?

"Your leg.

"My anxiety?

"Your leg.

"The wars and hatred?

"Your leg.

"Then I get up, and I see the sun settling over the house. And I step into the kitchen, and they're all sitting there. Aagny is sitting there, eating yogurt and slurping it through her cereal, so damn loud. And Sagne is sitting there reading and cutting her sandwich into tiny, tiny pieces before eating it, like little mini sandwiches—I don't know why she does that, but I love it. And Ersmo is tending to the fire in the stove, adding more logs, and the scent of birchwood fills the whole kitchen. And then I sit down at the table, and you come in through the door, because you always wake up when I get out of bed, and your hair is all tousled, and then you sit down next to me. And if I have a question, it answers me again.

"Your leg."

She paused now, rearranging herself.

"I want all of this, József. I want the house and the sun and the fire, and I want your leg. And I want this community, because it has made me suddenly believe in something—that there's a way of living that suits me, that I don't just want to run away from."

She fell silent.

"And I want our children to grow up in this."

It was as if the joy of what she said about his leg and their children washed over him so completely that he forgot what the conversation had originally been about.

He couldn't help but grin, and said:

"Okay. A little while longer."

I suppose we can always move later, he thought. When we've had the children. Then we can move.

ERSMO
2010

It was morning, and the snow was dripping from the roofs. The sun had appeared in the sky and had just started to bring some warmth, and in some places the ground lay bare. A faint scent of spruce trees and roots. The ice had not yet melted, but soon.

Ersmo had been sent to town to do some shopping. He was twenty years old, still without a driver's license, but he drove like he was born to do it; the car was a part of him, the gear stick an extension of his arm. On the back roads, it was slushy and Ersmo drove slowly, but not too slowly, as that could cause the car to get stuck and spin. Sometimes he passed by a vehicle or a farm, and then he raised his arm in greeting; anything else would have been suspicious. That's what you did. He was nothing special. Not worth noticing. He was Ersmo, son of Ingela—poor Ingela who had gone mad with age, and perhaps one really ought to knock on their door and see how things were . . . but another day. Today is no good. And anyway, she is there—that Aagny woman—and she seems a bit scary, not exactly the type you would want to stop by and have coffee with.

That's what the neighbors thought, when Ingela's old Saab drove into town ever so steadily, its driver wearing sneakers, pants with lots of pockets, a T-shirt, a chequered shirt, a hat with a Polaris logo.

Ersmo checked the list, which began:
1 large pack of sugar
1 large pack of salt

1 large pack of flour
1 large pack of ground oats
1 large pack of baking powder . . .
And so it went on.

Some of them wondered aloud: Why don't we buy more when we are in town anyway. We could buy two packs of flour. Otherwise, one batch of waffles is enough to make us run out again. But Sara said: "We mustn't shop in a way that attracts attention. We can't draw people in. Outwardly, we must be as boring as possible."

And this was because Sara would have the Swedish Enforcement Authority chasing her for outstanding payments; it was because Låke's existence mustn't be revealed to the Social Service, and because Sagne wanted to hide; it was because no one must start wondering where Ersmo's mother was.

Ersmo and Aagny were the only ones allowed to be seen, but they had to lead quiet, natural lives that didn't bother anyone. And that's why it was Ersmo who, week after week, drove the Saab to the big supermarket, bought his usual things, said nothing to no one beyond normal greetings, went to the gas station and filled up normally, and went home.

"Nothing else, Ersmo," said Aagny. "It's best if you come straight home."

She didn't know how Ersmo would react to meeting an old classmate, but she knew that—bless his heart—he wouldn't be able to explain their living situation, why he stayed, what he did during the day, why he didn't have a job . . .

But on this day, it was spring-winter—the best season where they lived. It was before the mosquitoes had hatched and when there was still snow on the ground. It was so bright everywhere, both from the snow and the sky, and the sun was warm, and the restaurants had put out reindeer hides in the outdoor seating areas, and it looked so terribly inviting.

Ersmo checked the time. It was early, maybe half past ten.

There wouldn't be a line inside the kebab restaurant, and they were quick in there. He could get a kebab in ten minutes at most—something they never had at home—with two kinds of sauce, and he would drink a Coke with it, a cold Coke with ice cubes, sipped through a straw.

He made the decision, went inside and placed his order, then sat down at one of the tables, on the reindeer hides, felt the sun on his face. Across the street was a hair salon, and when he looked in that direction he saw people coming and going, and he saw one of the hairdressers, standing right by the window, working on someone's highlights. The lady in the chair wore a cap; she looked absolutely insane—that's how you look wearing a white swim cap with strands of hair sticking up— but the hairdresser was incredibly beautiful; she removed the cap and started washing the lady's hair. The hairdresser had a round bottom and breasts, and when she laughed she covered her mouth with her hand, as if she was a little embarrassed. Now she was rinsing the lady's hair and massaging her head at the same time, making pulsating movements with her fingers against the lady's temples, slowly.

Ersmo couldn't help but stare. She was the prettiest thing he had ever seen.

He got his kebab, and he drank his Coke. And he tried not to stare too hard at the hairdresser through the window, and as he sat there, he was overcome with sorrow and eagerness. Perhaps he could go in there? Perhaps he could get a haircut?

He fingered his wallet; he still had some money left. How much could it be?

Maybe he could become handsome, potentially. Aagny liked to tell him he already was.

Maybe the hairdresser could
run her fingers
through his hair.

As he sat there, a young man suddenly passed by on the other side of the street. And Ersmo recognised him, and what's worse: the young man recognised Ersmo. And now he came pelting over.

"Hey there!" exclaimed the young man, who had an energetic manner—it made you happy to see him; Ersmo had always felt that way.

It was Kim, his childhood neighbor. Kim had lived in the village as a child but had eventually moved into town; Ersmo hadn't heard from him since—it is what it is.

"Do you recognise me?" the guy asked, and Ersmo nodded and said yes, well of course I do.

"I had to come say hi when I saw you, I've been thinking about you just this week. Grandma passed away'—he paused, as if waiting for a sympathetic nod, which Ersmo promptly provided—"so we're going through her house. And that's when I started looking in all our old photo albums, and you were in so many pictures. We had a hell of a good time back then."

Ersmo thought back, and a string of memories rose to the surface of his mind—he and Kim sledging at the Johanssons'—he and Kim making blueberry pie in the Johanssons' kitchen—he and Kim watching *The Lion King* on the Johanssons' VCR—and suddenly he remembered that Kim had been a friend, and ever since Kim moved away it hadn't been as much fun to be Ersmo. He had never thought about it before, but now it was suddenly crystal clear to him—that it had been sad, that he had become the only child in the area. Now he remembered sledging down the hill alone, the first day after Kim moved, and realising that the action suddenly lacked meaning. Sledging with a friend, challenging each other to jumps and spins, riding side by side, sharing the same sledge. That was something. But sledging alone, down a hill that's not even very steep. It wasn't anything.

"I heard you still live in the house? That's so nice," Kim said now, and Aagny had been right—Ersmo didn't know what to say, so he just nodded.

"I might stop by some day, before I leave," said Kim. "We could go for a ride," referring to the snowmobile. And then he walked away, before Ersmo could even manage to respond.

"Now I need to pick up my girl for lunch. See you!" And Kim crossed the street, and he walked into the hair salon, and he approached the hairdresser with the bottom and the breasts, and at first she just waved at him, but after taking payment for the highlights, she took Kim aside discreetly. No one at the salon saw it, but Ersmo saw, through the window, how she kissed him, and he saw Kim put his hand around her waist.

Ersmo saw his own face reflected in the window. He looked dreadful, he realized—a little overweight and his hair and beard all over the place and a dirty shirt, and now also garlic sauce dripping down his mouth.

Ersmo grabbed his bags and went home, where he had a second lunch, so that no one would know that he had eaten at the kebab place. He didn't mention Kim.

* * *

It was evening, probably a week since Ersmo had been to town and run into Kim, and he had already forgotten about the encounter. In the house, they sat around the fireplace. Låke was asleep on the kitchen sofa. József had his guitar out and they sang, and closed their eyes, those who wanted sitting close together. Ersmo sat next to Aagny and József's knee rested against his, and he hit a low note, enjoying the feeling as it reverberated in his body, listening to József's gentle strumming and feeling his body ache from chopping wood all day. And Aagny stroked his head, and it wasn't a wonderful moment, but a nice one; they were content with what they had accomplished today.

That's when they heard a sound.

Someone drove into the yard on a snowmobile.

Someone tried the door. It was locked. There was a knock. Ersmo felt both Aagny and József freeze, and he did the same.

"Who is it?" someone whispered—maybe Sagne—and the voice sounded terrified.

"I'll check," said Aagny, one of the people who could check, because she was *supposed* to be there. "Maybe someone got a flat tire."

Aagny tiptoed to the kitchen window, and from there she could see the silhouette of the person now knocking on the door.

"It's a young guy," she said, baffled. "No idea who."

"Keep it closed," said Sara. "Don't answer."

"I think I know who it is," said Ersmo. "I have to answer. He knows this house. He knows when someone is here or not."

Ersmo remembered how he used to ride his bike over to the village, looking for lights in the Johanssons' house, and only when he saw that they were on did he drive into the yard.

So now Ersmo went to the door, and they closed off the living room, hiding the others. Aagny brought a sleeping Låke in from the kitchen; he whimpered.

There he stood now, Kim. He had ruddy cheeks and frost in his stubble, and Ersmo thought how happy he was to see him, that for a brief moment it was just like when they were kids; that he was here now, his friend, and now the whole world was an amusement park; thought about everything they could get up to in the forest and by the lake and with the snowmobile if there were two of them.

"Hey," said Kim. "We're done clearing out the house. I was just about to head home. But I felt like . . . Wanna go for a ride first?"

He pointed to the snowmobile behind him.

Ersmo's head was burning now.

"I'm not sure if—"

It was a lovely evening, he could sense it—still bright out, but the sky tinged with red and orange. Winter was transitioning into spring. In a week or so, the snow would be almost gone, what was left of it mixed with mud.

He heard a sound behind him. Låke whining.

"What was that?" Kim said. "Surely you don't—"

"It's . . . my mum," Ersmo said. "And: I can't," he added. "Sorry. I'm sick. Another time."

He closed the door in Kim's face.

Through the window, he saw his friend move away from the house. Kim walked slowly towards the snowmobile. Then he straddled it and drove off.

"It sounded like you had just seen each other," said Aagny.

"We bumped into each other at the shop," Ersmo replied.

And that was the end of that.

THE ANT COLONY
2011

It was morning. Ersmo and Aagny were in the boat, pulling up nets. József was feeding Låke. Sara suddenly realized that she was craving an oven pancake, but they were all out of butter.

God, she really wanted an oven pancake. Nothing else would do.

She looked at the clock. There should be enough time. It would only take an hour or so. In and out of the shop. She didn't usually go into town, but just this once, surely she could. That's how she felt now.

Sara didn't like being alone. Everyone thinks in different ways. Some by simply *thinking*. Others by writing. Some—like Sara—need to talk to understand their own thoughts, bounce them off someone else, hear them expressed. They sounded good when they came out of her mouth. When she was alone, she sometimes felt blocked up, like her head was full of fruit and her speech was a juicer that allowed the fruit to be used. There was no room for anything new until the old had been squeezed out, in the form of finished thoughts or opinions. Walking around alone was sometimes straight-up uncomfortable, her head in a jumble; she couldn't grasp her thoughts.

And so she grabbed Sagne, who was sitting on the couch next to her, reading.

"Are you coming into town?" she said.

"Is that really—" said Sagne. She was afraid of taking on

town—there were so many risks. There might be someone she knew, someone asking a question, maybe even a relative . . .

"It's not like we'll run into someone we know," said Sara, as if she had read Sagne's mind. "And if we do, we'll make something up."

Sara looked strong today, lively. She couldn't be refused. So Sagne reluctantly got up. Maybe she could stay in the car, while Sara did the shopping. In any case, she knew it was utterly impossible to say no to Sara, so it was better to skip the whole process of refusing and being persuaded.

In the car, Sara went on about cows. Maybe, she thought out loud, they should get a cow after all? That way they could become even more self-sufficient. The cow could live in the old pasture.

"If we have a cow, we'll have to milk it several times a day," Sagne said.

She had grown up with cows.

"And the cow needs at least one companion. It's animal cruelty to keep it alone," she continued. "And you have to muck out every day. It's a lot of work for a little milk."

"Hmm," said Sara. Quite often, it annoyed her that Sagne knew so much, about everything, and that she didn't hesitate to show it. She also had a demeanor that always tended very slightly towards the negative, as if the baseline was -0.1.

"But imagine waking up in the morning, feeling the cow's warm body against yours . . . " Sara dreamed. "Drinking a glass of fresh, foaming milk . . . "

Sagne stifled a yawn.

When they reached the shop, Sagne stayed in the car, pulling up the hood of her sweater to cover her face. She sank down a little in her seat, looking around the parking lot.

It was the car she noticed first. A remarkably beautiful vehicle, red and classic. A Volvo from the sixties, Sagne guessed. It glowed where it stood in the parking lot next to dirty station wagons, a few pickup trucks, a Saab with lurid SpongeBob SquarePants sunshades. A person who knew more about cars could probably have commented on its condition and the work that had gone into it; Sagne could not. But she understood that this was the kind of car that was loved by its owner.

And now, he stepped out of the car, the owner. He was a man of average height, hair cropped short. There was something familiar about his figure.

He turned around, towards the shop, and now Sagne saw his face and gasped. She grew cold, her body reacting before her head could catch up. Vertigo, and once again this: she was no longer present in her body, witnessing herself from the outside.

It was Max. Was it? Yes, it was Max, all right—from the Huckleberry Inn. Those foul legs, those foul arms. That foul pelvis and hands. Most of all: that foul, foul mouth with the sharp Cupid's bow. She felt sick just looking at him. Now she turned to ice where she sat, sinking down into the seat, deep down, so he wouldn't see her.

Why did *she* feel weak, embarrassed? *He* was the one who had committed a crime. Or had he? Should she have acted differently? Should she have spoken up? Would it have changed anything? Should she have filed a report? If so, would he be in prison now instead of walking around the supermarket parking lot?

So why hadn't she done anything? Why, why, why. And why wasn't she doing anything now? She should know what to do. She should have known this could happen.

The man who was Max seemed to realize he had forgotten something. He turned mid-step and ran back to the car before closing the door ever so gently. This was a man who loved his car.

Just then, Sara came back, whistling, with flour and butter

and also milk and apples and a gigantic pack of toilet paper, and she jerked her head and opened the trunk and shoved all the items inside, as if it were just a regular day.

But as soon as she got in the car, she saw it on her friend's face.

"What is it?"

Sagne didn't answer.

"What is it, Sagne?"

"You said we wouldn't run into someone we know."

And now Sara truly looked at Sagne, and with just one glance she could tell. She embraced her friend, whose body was limp in her arms.

"What, is he here, *now*?"

Sagne nodded.

"He's in the supermarket right now. That's his car."

And what happened now was something Sagne would never, ever forget. She watched Sara transform. It was like she slipped into armor. Her back straightened. Her eyes narrowed, shooting daggers. At the same time, so composed, so incredibly composed. Her mouth tightened; her cheekbones became visible.

"That damned creep."

She turned to Sagne.

"We have to do something."

Once again, Sagne didn't reply; she had sunk even deeper into the car seat, and now she breathed, "He's coming out now," and there he was, the hated one, sauntering towards the red car, placing a bag of frozen fries and some wrapped meat in the back seat, reversing, pelvis and Cupid's bow and all.

"We have to follow. Stay low."

That's what Sara said.

Sagne whimpered. She had no desire to follow that car, but what should or shouldn't be done she couldn't say, for her mind was empty and her body in a state of fear. But Sara, completely calm and focused, now also turned out of the parking lot, and started following the beautiful, red Volvo at a distance, a distance of fifty yards—too close for Sagne's liking.

Sagne slouched down, thinking about Sara's facial expression. She thought about how angry Sara was, for Sagne's sake. She was truly *oozing*. Through Sara's eyes, she could see it so clearly—that Max was in the wrong, that he was harmful, that rape shouldn't be considered normal for the mammal known as Homo sapiens. She was furious, Sara. She was her friend. She stood by her side.

They drove only a few miles, in the opposite direction to the farmhouse. Sara increased the distance, but there were hardly any cars on the road; it was easy to see the shiny red Volvo forging ahead, there was power in that car, while Sara struggled with Ersmo's mother's old piece of junk. Then, the red car made a turn, in towards a small house. They drove past the house slowly, saw the owner of the car getting out, fries and meat in his arms, and unlocking the front door.

This must be where he lived.

"We'll go home and think."

That's what Sara said.

* * *

It was the height of summer, in the evening, a light breeze in the air. Max had replaced the windows with bug screens to block out the mosquitoes, and now he enjoyed the cool air, the breeze moving through. He'd had a drink—and a refill—and his body felt light. Finally, he thought, things had started to fall into place in his life. It wasn't like a few years ago, when he was taking steroids and they made him crazy, aggressive, thinking that everyone was after him. He had quit working at the restaurant, had finally got a job at a garage. He liked it much better there. The owner of the garage thought he was doing a good job. And he *was* good at what he did, working fast and skilfully; after a while, he'd had enough for a down payment on a ramshackle house. He liked building on it, didn't mind living in the middle of an ongoing renovation, watching it progress every day. He had started to feel like maybe things would work out for him, too.

He watched an action film, two men involved in money laundering. Max liked to have the volume turned up high when he watched; the bass should tremble when the motorcycles drove off the road, and so it took a while before he heard it. He paused the film. Yes, there was definitely some kind of sound. Where was it coming from? He tried to define it. From outside, in the yard? Was it even—and now he sniffed the air—smoke, didn't he smell smoke?

He got up, his gaze still fixed on the TV, still with the drink in his body, confident there wouldn't actually be anything re-markable waiting for him outside. Maybe someone passing by had popped a tire on the gravel.

But through the window on the door, he saw it.

A fire.

His car was burning.

Now he rushed out through the door, adrenaline in his veins, his head still not fully there, and when he reached the car, staring in a panic, it was already engulfed; for a second, he wondered how the hell it could have happened,

and that's when he saw.

Next to the car, she stood: a tall, broad woman. She looked completely mad, he thought. It was like her eyes were burning; was it the fire reflecting in her pupils—no, it was something else, a fury. She saw him too. And now she *rushed* towards him, and he was frightened. So frightened. It's a woman, he tried to think. Big as a man, but he should be able to face her.

That's how he reasoned.

He rolled up his sleeves.

But just as his head and body caught up with each other and he started trying to break free from the woman's grip, he saw: there were others. A shorter woman with long hair, who seemed to be giving some kind of orders. He couldn't hear what she was saying, but when she said it they all came at him, behind the tall woman. A young man held his feet.

They were all over him now, attacking him at the same time, scratching and clawing, someone *biting*, the tall woman beating, *are they going to devour me*, he thought for a moment, such a strange thought but it came, *are they going to take me with them*

What's going to happen to me

and just as he wondered what was happening and why, a small dark-skinned woman in glasses stepped forward behind the others. She looked vaguely familiar; he didn't know why.

At first, nothing. As if he could no longer make sounds. The words were gone. He wanted to say something, but there was no sound.

The small woman in glasses came all the way up to him. She didn't look at him, but poured something over him, a liquid from some kind of bottle.

It's lighter fluid, he thought. *They're going to set me on fire. Why are they going to set me on fire?*

But it didn't smell like lighter fluid. It smelled sweet.

The tall woman sat down on his leg in a certain way. *Crack* said the bone, and he screamed, straight out he screamed, where he lay next to the burning car, waiting for them to set him on fire, too. He didn't know that his throat could produce such a sound. It was so loud and pitiful and terrified, as if the cry further emphasized how much trouble he was in, and he noticed that he was getting wetter—he had wet himself.

The woman with the long hair said something, and then they suddenly stopped, moving away.

He still didn't understand.

He tried to drag his body further away, further from the fire, but his leg hurt too much, he couldn't. For several hours, he lay there. It started raining, a light rain. The fire didn't reach him. He lay there and watched it slowly die out, the car and all the work he had put into it in vain, all in vain.

He looked down at his body. It was almost morning. Suddenly he noticed that his stomach was completely black. A swarming darkness.

And now he noticed the smell, the other one that wasn't smoke. Sweet and sticky. The liquid on his body was syrup, and on top of him now:

a mountain of black garden ants. They crawled over his face, into his ears, nostrils, under his shirt, into his pants, his underwear.

He thought about it every day. Maybe it was that dangerous Russian he had bought those steroids from a few years ago. Maybe he had done something to upset him, something he wasn't aware of.

He never told anyone.

He bought a new lock, on top of the old one, locking the door twice every night. He couldn't sleep for months.

In the end, he moved.

* * *

In the car, they cheered and hollered. So much had happened in the past twenty-four hours, since Sara and Sagne had seen Max in the supermarket parking lot. They had acted on a feeling, a vague feeling directed by Sara, and by Aagny's dark gaze. "You have to stop when I tell you to," Sara had said and they had agreed, Aagny reluctantly, the others more confused, but it had most definitely been an adventure, and they had carried it out together, each with their own individual task. Of course the man who had done this to Sagne deserved to suffer, they all felt as they drove back home. They had done the right thing. They poured into the house now: Aagny exhilarated, Ersmo pleased that he had managed to pick the lock on the car so smoothly and quietly in order to pour lighter fluid inside. Sara laughed loudly and brought out the booze.

"FUCKING HELL THAT WAS FUN!" she shouted, and they raised their glasses in the air. "He could have had it worse, but it sure was something."

Aagny whistled and sang. Sara put an LP from the house on the record player, and now a disco song played in the kitchen with upbeat strings.

She took a seat at the table, where Sagne sat silent.

"You have your own army, Sagne," said Sara. When the sentence reached the air, it almost sounded like she meant the group draining their glasses, not the tiny black garden ants.

Sagne looked around. She remembered Sara's fury in the parking lot, how her certainty had drawn a line for Sagne, too. What was right and wrong. She saw it through Sara's eyes.

And she saw the others, all fired up, the risks they were willing to take for her.

"I have my own army," she said.

In the next room, Låke lay sleeping with his beautiful mouth.

The others went to bed, but Sagne stayed in the kitchen. She sat there, staring.

József tiptoed in. He had pretended to sleep, but had not had a wink all night.

He sat down across from her.

"How are you?" he said, simply.

Sagne shrugged.

He got up, started baking the morning bread, so used to it

now that his hands poured the ingredients without thinking. He was quiet, waiting for her to speak if she wanted to.

They were in the kitchen in silence; the bread went into the oven and out.

He handed her the knife, so she could cut the first slice.

"I thought it would feel better," she said, finally. "But it only feels worse. It was silly. Stupid. We should have done more. Or nothing at all."

She looked at József.

"When we started talking about what we should do," she said. "We sat shouting different suggestions at each other. But you—you just left. Why did you do that?"

József considered speaking his initial thought, which was, "You were acting like children," but since he understood that this wasn't what Sagne needed now, he spoke his second thought instead:

"I don't believe in revenge," he said. "I believe that if one person hurts another, you have to assume that it's the first person who deserves pity—that they just don't get it. Revenge only means digging a deeper hole, not letting go. You won't feel better because someone else feels worse."

Sagne nodded.

"Ideally, we should have reported him to the police," he said. "But we couldn't. So maybe this was a form of justice after all," he added, when he saw that his words might have brought her down.

"He probably learned a lesson," József tried, though both of them knew he didn't believe his own words.

A pause, where nothing was said.

Then:

"Would you like a hug?"

Sagne nodded.

They sat like that, for a short while, holding each other in the morning light.

Then Sagne chose to take the memory of last night and push it away, like she always did. Everything except Sara's face and the loyalty in the house. Those, she kept.

Låke called from the other room.

When Sagne finally went to bed, and Ersmo, and Sara, they all saw the same thing: Aagny's face, when she'd heard what had happened. When she'd changed before their very eyes. When she'd driven the car to Max's house, completely silent, without saying a word. Ersmo had carried the lighter fluid, picked the lock on Max's beautiful Volvo, lit the flame. Sara had been there to—well, they all knew, but no one said it outright—to fix things somehow, with talking, if something went wrong. Sagne poured the syrup.

But it was Aagny who took it further than they had intended; she was the one who broke his leg, and the worst part was that she seemed to know exactly how to do it, how to break bones.

They thought about this when they fell asleep and when they woke up, but then Aagny sat there eating a sandwich as usual and talking about this and that, and gradually they forgot about the Other Aagny, that she had ever existed. And maybe they had looked the same, where they stood by the burning car, adrenaline in their bodies and the heat of the flames on their faces.

AAGNY
2012

Aagny went for her morning walk. As she walked, she liked to talk to herself, as it was her best way of thinking.

Often, her thoughts revolved around Låke or Ersmo:

Låke took his first steps. I can't believe he is walking now.

Or:

I can't believe Ersmo built those front steps all by himself.

And, a few years later:

I stayed up all night with Låke who had the stomach flu. It was gross when he threw up on me, but also, he looked so weak, poor mite.

She liked walking alone and talking about Låke, because she couldn't quite do it inside the house. When she walked alone out here, she could pretend he was her own.

Recently, though, the talking had been about something else.

It's been one thousand, two hundred and eighty-five days without sex . . .

I brush against the trees.

And:

It's been one thousand, two hundred and eighty-six days without sex. Soon I'll dry up completely. I find myself relating to the potatoes.

And it had been a really bad year for potatoes.

Once a month, Aagny would head into town to go dancing.

She never asked the others if they wanted to come, partly because she had a feeling they probably wouldn't, and partly because she didn't want them to. They knew she went dancing, but sensed that she didn't want to talk about it.

She was there on a mission that didn't concern them.

Before heading into town, she would bathe carefully. On these occasions, she would wear a blouse, with flowers on it, and her skirt—there was just the one.

Oddly enough, Ersmo used to think when he saw Aagny in those clothes, they made her look even more masculine. The sight made him warm inside. He had to hug Aagny, who hugged him back. Her hands felt like bear paws around his back.

Now Aagny stood there in front of them, in her floral blouse and her skirt and her practical ballet flats, with her long strong arms and muscular calves. Her gaze expectant. Her eyes like a child's. Today, she would drive all the way to one of the cities, buy a spare tire while she was there.

"All right, I'm going," Aagny growled, slamming the door shut and jumping into the car.

On the drive, she played "Suspicious Minds" by Elvis.

As was customary, Aagny took a shot in the car—not a big one, just a little something to boost her spirits. She patted her cheeks, breathed, smeared on lipstick.

She looked at herself in the mirror. Often, she thought she looked uglier with lipstick on than without, but it was a ritual that had to be performed.

Perhaps, she dreamed, there will be someone tonight. Perhaps someone who will dance. Perhaps someone who will want to follow me out back, when no one is looking, push me up against the wall so I can feel his breath, so I can feel him against my leg. I will see his face, and I will see that he wants me.

The week before, she had taken a long walk, and the talking had gone something like this:

Living without sex isn't something you MUST do something about.

And it's not like I just want any sex in general, either. Ideally, I want it with someone I like and am actually attracted to.

Men think it's so hard for them. "All a woman has to do is go out and ask for sex, and she'll get it." That's what Ove always said.

But it's like they don't even SEE you if you aren't beautiful! You stand there jumping up and down, but it's like you don't even exist.

And it's not like you can just go up and ask for sex. Men think they like that, but they don't. They feel miffed. The chase is over. Like if the moose walked up and asked to be shot!!!

Here she laughed at herself, for she thought it was well put.

I've been rejected so many times I can't even count.

The look they give you. It's like . . . they're angry with you, because they don't want to have sex with you and they like to believe they always want to have sex. And when they say no, they feel like less of a man.

Plus, now they have to reject you, put you down, and see, men hate that even more, having to be responsible for you, so that makes them even crankier. Often, they don't even respond, you're just left standing there.

Some have said yes, like that guy a few years ago. But he did so without really wanting it. Then you're left standing there with a floppy dick in your hand, feeling guilty for not being prettier. You try and you try. But it's like the dick is almost retracting.

And that makes them even angrier . . .

Aagny had once read that happiness is found in the crowd. If you ask ten times, maybe you'll get one yes, and then those nine nos won't matter.

But no, that doesn't work either. I've tried EVERYTHING. I've tried just standing there, hanging out at the bar, waiting, but nothing happens. I've tried walking up to the ones hanging out at the bar. I've tried walking up to the drunkest ones hanging out at the bar. I've tried being quiet. I've tried talking a lot.

She paused her walk, saying to herself, like a mantra:

Aagny, you must continue to believe that the one-thousand-two-hundred-and-eighty-seventh day will give it to you. It will give it to you. Otherwise, you won't be able to bear it. It's okay to go ONE day without sex, but it's impossible to go on if you think you'll never have sex again in your life.

Even though that's probably where we're headed.

ZAKARIA
2012

I t was at work, a regular evening, or slightly better. Zakaria
had wandered through the streets, the houses and the
cobblestones, a breeze had caught his hair, and it was still
bright out. Women and men had smiled at him as he walked,
such a tall man; he looked like a statue of a warlord, but a giggling statue, excited almost, like he was five years old. His gaze
wide open to the world.

He had entered the building that was the nightclub, changed
into his work clothes, placed himself in the doorway, and
thought that this—this would be a truly great evening. He had
joked a little with the bartender, called his mother and grandmother in Nicosia, had coffee, now he stood talking to the doorman, goofing around almost. Zakaria was a man who played
for both teams; at some point Zakaria had kissed the doorman
and the doorman had kissed him back, but then nothing more
happened, as if they both knew that the connection they occasionally felt only applied in a work setting: the doorman liked
French design magazines and Russian literature, while Zakaria
preferred culture that fell more into the *Eat, Pray, Love* genre—
the kind that made you feel things deeply exactly where it was
intended. But at work they were impressed by each other: the
doorman by Zakaria's physical strength and warm heart, and
Zakaria by the doorman's—for lack of a better word—*know-
how*; all he had to do was glance at someone to see who they
were, that is, not by name but as a being in the world. Who had
the person arrived with, what were they wearing, what words

did they use? To the doorman, these were all clues. Zakaria was also afraid of him for the exact same reason; he knew that if he had shown up alone, he would probably have got in—solely based on his cheekbones—but as soon as he spoke a sentence or introduced his friends, the doorman would have made them wait, and wait, before turning them away at the door. His friends' old jackets and trousers that were the wrong brand, the accents in their voices, hairstyles without reason. They would have had to go to the pub instead.

He had stood there in the doorway. The guests had stumbled on by; early in the evening almost everyone got in, then fewer and fewer as the night went on. And suddenly a thin, blonde guy had stood there in front of him with a face like a weasel and an expensive jacket, doing that thing where you bet everything on one card and walk confidently up to the door, quickly trying to bypass the bouncer and the doorman, hoping they will be so confused by your behavior that they let you in, but the doorman was sharper than that. He pointed at the weasel and said: "Back of the line." Not without satisfaction, Zakaria noted; one slightly unsettling thing about the doorman was that he obviously enjoyed it—the reprimanding. But perhaps he wouldn't be suited for his job if he didn't enjoy the thought of exerting control over someone else.

The weasel face had been sent back in line. Zakaria saw a very mild wave of shame quickly pass over the man's small eyes. But soon it changed, his face; it stabilized. Now his pride needed to be restored—there was no way he would get back in line and wait obediently. Zakaria had seen this sequence of events before; usually the guest would slowly back away, facing the doorman and Zakaria, spitting, shouting swear words and obscenities, to make it clear that he wouldn't come back to the club if they paid him—

but this time, things took a different turn.

The weasel pulled out a knife. A sharp little knife, pointing it at the doorman, and now it was he, the weasel, who was enjoying himself. The people in line gaped, not entirely without glee, both at seeing the arrogant doorman being scared but also at *something happening*, the same kind of mild joy that runs through you when you see an ambulance or a fire engine; something bad has happened, but before your brain has grasped that information, the energy from the adrenaline has taken hold and you find yourself with a faint smile on your lips.

Now everyone was staring at Zakaria, and Zakaria felt the same, that he was staring at himself from the outside. He had warm feelings for the doorman; he had his suspicions about where the man's arrogance came from—growing up gay in a small town perhaps—and therefore Zakaria's only thought now was how scared his co-worker must feel, with a knife under his chin, held by a heterosexual big-city hand.

Zakaria shouted: *Ey!* And the weasel looked away for a second, long enough for Zakaria to grab his wrist and twist it; the knife fell to the ground, and Zakaria snatched hold of the weasel. The doorman squealed and ran into the club. Zakaria led the weasel away. No one thought to call the police, and Zakaria felt no need to further humiliate the weasel; he had just felt his scrawny, trembling body in his hands.

Zakaria returned to his spot. The people in line applauded. A few women and a man swept their eyes over his body. The evening went back to its regular rhythm.

It was a few hours later, and they were about to close. There was hardly anyone going inside anymore, only people pouring out, intoxicated people walking in a zigzag. One girl stumbled out, so drunk that Zakaria had to lift her up—

and just as Zakaria had got the girl onto her feet, he appeared again, the weasel. This time, he wasn't alone. He had three men with him, all broad, one of them holding his hand conspicuously near his pant leg—you understood that he had a weapon concealed there.

"I recognise those guys," the doorman mumbled, and Zakaria nodded; they were part of one of the gangs that used to come here—Zakaria had already thrown one of them out once or twice for selling cocaine in the men's room. These three were cause for concern; they had an organisation behind them. The weasel approached, now confident once more. The doorman fled into the venue again. But it wasn't the doorman they were after this time, it was Zakaria. He took a few steps forward; he found it was usually better to take an offensive, albeit friendly, approach. It had always worked before.

But as he stood there now, facing the three broad men, he realized he no longer had the weasel within his field of vision. He could feel why. The weasel had appeared from behind; Zakaria turned around now, and this time it was he who felt the knife against his throat.

Zakaria very rarely acted on instinct. He had been trained not to; his father, who had been gone for a long time now, had explained to him that if you are tall and strong, you can't allow yourself to act on instinct—your head must always be one step ahead. You must always be kind and polite, say thank you and apologize twice as many times as everyone else. But this time, with a knife pointed at him and three men behind him, he *did* something, without thinking at all. He needed to get away. He acted on muscle memory. And so he lifted the weasel, a lift he had in him from his days practising judo. But the weasel didn't act like a judo opponent. He resisted. He didn't fall softly.

He fell hard,
and when he fell
it was on his own knife

against his throat.
And blood

Now time passed quickly and
slowly all at once. The weasel lay on the ground,
motionless. And it was as if the whole party had stopped
dead in their tracks—the towering men, who surely should
have gone after Zakaria, instead bent down in front of their
friend, all three of them did,
and Zakaria saw the world transpire before him in a haze.
And one of the men said, *What the fuck did you do.*
That's what he said.
Not angrily but *sadly*—he sounded sad. He had pretended
to be a gangster, but suddenly you could see what the man must
have looked like as a child. He loved the weasel; you could hear
it in his voice.
And now came the sound of police sirens, perhaps it was the
doorman who had called, and the man made a gesture where
he pointed his fingers at his own eyes and then at Zakaria, and
the gesture meant:
We've got our eyes on you.
And Zakaria understood that the weasel was dead and that
it was his fault—his big, monstrous body that had too much
power and always did, always destroyed
and lots of people had seen it,
and at least three would come after him
and he couldn't take it anymore
and what would it do to try to explain; he never managed to
explain, no one ever believed him, they always thought that a
body that looked like his had an agenda
and Zakaria simply shook his head and did what first came
to mind, the same thing he always did as a child when something similar happened:
he ran.

He took his bag, which contained a bottle of expensive gin he had received as a belated birthday gift from the bartender, and he ran.

He sat down on some steps several blocks away, where it was dark and there were no people, and there he sat and drank, and drank, and drank.

AAGNY
THAT SAME EVENING

Aagny had endured yet another unsatisfying evening. As usual, a glimmer of hope when she entered the venue, when the beer—two, no more, in case she had to drive home later, even though as usual she hoped she wouldn't have to—trickled down her gullet, when she bravely asked a man or two to dance, when she started talking to a whole group at the bar—

but for some reason, it always ended the same way.

And that way was Aagny all alone, staring at others who stood in pairs, as if everyone else had access to a rule book she lacked.

She went to the ladies' room. Swore at the mirror. *God dammit.* She tried speaking in a plummy Stockholm accent. *Gosh darnit.*

Maybe her voice was the problem? Maybe if she spoke like they did on TV? She looked at herself in the mirror. No, it was her posture. She walked slouching, like a sack of potatoes. She looked down at her body.

No, it was her belly.

Or her hands.

Or her legs.

From another stall, two women ran out; they had gone to the bathroom together, they wore stockings and lipstick and seemed dumb and happy. Their nail polish looked like it had been done by a professional. Aagny's nails looked like she had dipped her hands in a jam jar.

It must be her hands.

Aagny felt sad, so sad it was as if her heart was being squeezed, and even the thing she could usually use as a pick-me-up—the fact that, at home, a whole bunch of people were waiting who saw her as theirs, even a child and a young man who needed her—even this didn't help. Instead, she thought of József and Sara's unquestioned alliance; imagined how Ersmo, in a few years, would most likely leave her to seek out a love of his own; how little Låke, in even more years, would do the same. They were wonderful! Of course, they would find someone. Everyone usually found someone. Just not Aagny. She didn't usually do that.

She talked herself up. *Come on now, Aagny. It's just a matter of willpower. If you ask ten people, maybe the eleventh will say yes.*

So she made one last-ditch attempt—approaching a short and stocky man sitting alone on a chair by the exit, and said:

"Fun night?"

"Huh?" said the man.

"Having a fun night?"

"Huh?"

"I said . . . "

He looked up at Aagny, the difference in elevation naturally amplified by the fact that he was sitting and she was standing, but still, he flinched, looking genuinely scared.

"Yeah," was all he said, diverting his gaze further back into the venue so that the message couldn't be misinterpreted, and she moved on, out of the door, the whole city wide open like a daisy about to drop its petals. She walked into the alleyways, the backstreets, not knowing what she was looking for but perhaps trying to convince herself that she was in the city exploring, observing the life that was happening here from an outsider's perspective. Aagny had always felt like she was an artist who couldn't make art. She couldn't paint, sing, or write. Sensory impressions gathered inside her, piling up. When she saw a painting or heard a song, she could burst into tears, as though she so easily grasped what the painter or songwriter wanted to say, and she could identify new nuances. But she couldn't spell or anything. So maybe she wasn't artistic. At least, that's what they had said in school.

In one of the alleyways, there was a courtyard. It was completely silent there, so Aagny started when she heard a clink. And what was that, moving there? A cat? A rat? No, it was a human leg.

Aagny wasn't someone who shied away from physical pain, and so she immediately went to investigate—just like she had that time when she helped Sagne give birth.

Another sound, and her gaze turned towards the steps.

Sitting there was a marvellously handsome man, tall and strong, soft lips amidst his hair and cheekbones, Greek features perhaps? and Aagny's first impulse was to stop at a bit of a distance from where he crouched on the steps, drunk and bloody, desperate and crying; she just wanted to stand there and watch him, he looked like JAMES DEAN! and she thought it was a joy to stand there and watch him, the same way one thinks when seeing a sunset.

Aagny was barely afraid of anything, but this was one of the things that actually scared her—beautiful faces. She didn't dare talk to them; it feels unnatural, you feel faulty, like a pile of imperfection and humanity slithering through the streets; and when you see their glowing skin, you realize there must be something spiritual after all? there must be something greater?

—but the way he lay there, blood and snot and vomit, flabby posture, an empty gin bottle beside him, he nevertheless appeared vaguely relatable.

And, as mentioned, Aagny too was a bit drunk, and so she could overcome her fear and let out the caring part of her, and she sat down beside him and asked:

"How are you?"

The man looked directly at her and said, literally, his head hanging:

"Uaaagh. Uuugh . . . Uagh! Uugh."

Aagny grinned.

"*That* good, huh."

She looked around.

"We should get you some water. Clean you up a bit. Come, let's go to the burger joint I saw a couple of blocks back. They were open. You can lean on me."

The man was now yanked out of his extreme drunkenness and he stared at her, wide-eyed.

"But I CAN'T," he whispered.

His beautiful mouth with its drunken breath was so close to hers that she instinctively backed away; it was so wonderful that the impression was too overwhelming to process.

He looked around, and said now, still in a whisper but much too loudly, with his hand next to his mouth as if to ensure that no one would hear:

"I KILLED someone."

Here, Aagny looked at him closely.

His gaze and posture were kind through and through. They often are. But Aagny had very good instincts when it came to people. This also applied to the men she got involved with; on the occasions that she had met someone, it had almost always started with a bad feeling. She had simply gone ahead anyway.

But this man: drunk, yet kind. This she saw. A good person.

"You haven't killed anyone," said Aagny, trying to reason with him.

Now the man sobbed. "Yes, I diiiid," he cried. "I didn't mean to. He jumped me, and I reacted on impulse. That was my impulse. I have a mu-hu-hur-derous impulse."

"So why did he jump you?" Aagny asked interestedly.

"I don't knooow," the man wept. "Sometimes people jump

me. You'd think no one would jump someone who looks like this'—he ran his hand demonstratively down his long, broad torso—"but it's the o-ho-opposite. People want to gi-hi-hive it a go. I'm like one of those punching bags at the ca-ha-ha-harnival. Test your strength."

He suddenly looked determined.

"Yes. THAT's what it's like."

Now he paused his crying, wiped his arm under his nose to remove most of the snot, and looked at Aagny, as if he suddenly realized:

"I can't be here! I already have a record! I'll be convicted immediately! Murder!"

He cried:

"Mu-hu-hu-urder . . . "

Someone else might now have been scared. But not Aagny.

"It's not that bad," Aagny said.

"But I've ki-hi-hilled someone. I saw their FACE, and they were *dead*."

Aagny looked straight at the handsome one.

"Sometimes you need to get rid of someone. It's no worse than that."

It's no worse than that.

JÓZSEF
2012

Perhaps that was the day everything changed, the day when Aagny walked into the kitchen and it turned out she had brought someone home with her.

The man was in the shower, so Aagny quickly briefed them on the turn of events.

"He had nowhere to go, so I brought him here. He might want to become one of us. We'll see."

"Is it . . . have you . . . " József asked.

"Have they what?" Ersmo wondered curiously.

"Had sex," said Sara.

Aagny flinched, looking shocked but also flattered, stealing a glance at Ersmo to see if the question had bothered him. It hadn't.

"Most certainly not!" she said.

Her face was animated, and they only saw why once the newcomer emerged from the shower, wrapped in Aagny's bathrobe, with wet curls and an apologetic gaze, like a dog that knows it has done something wrong.

József had two immediate emotional reactions.

The first was, frankly, feeling curious about the person standing before him. His head tensed, became interested. Perhaps you always experience a slight physical reaction when faced with someone so evidently successful within the area of reproduction.

The second was looking over at Sara. He needed to see her reaction. And when he saw it, he swallowed.

On the other hand, he had reacted to the man's beauty, too.

Maybe it was only natural? Surely it wasn't such a big deal? Oh, József! Why did it always turn out like this for you. Why couldn't you sit with your own feelings without starting to defend everyone else in your mind.

He glanced around the room now: everyone looked silently fascinated. Everyone except Sagne, who looked the same as always, and Låke, who came running up to the newcomer, clinging to him, until Aagny had to carry him off. She did so with a kiss on the head.

Cautiously, the Newcomer sat down on a stool near the door. The others sat around the kitchen table. It was almost like a jury, or an interrogation, one which began with the accused himself saying, in a shy voice:

"So, who of you is it that lives here?"

József felt the question like a punch to the gut. Surely, only Aagny and Ersmo lived here? He and Sara, they were just visiting. For a little while. He needed to bring that up with Sara again.

"It's my house," said Ersmo. "Or my mum's. And then Aagny moved in. But it's also the others', if they want it to be."

He looked around questioningly.

"We live here, too," said Sara.

József's heart sank.

A pause, during which Sagne looked around, as if seeking approval.

"I live here, too?" she said.

No one objected.

"And him," said Aagny, pointing at Låke, who was playing in the living room now, with the door open.

"Is he yours?" Zakaria asked Sagne, based on his skin color.

"He's ours," Aagny said quickly. "Everyone's."

Sagne said nothing.

Zakaria was still in a haze. The haze seemed even thicker now. Where had he ended up.

He looked out of the window. Somewhere in the country-side, apparently. He had slept in the car all the way here. Who were they, this shady bunch who seemed so remarkably relaxed in each other's company? He looked around at torn shirts, old fleece sweaters, bare feet, and hair cut straight off, as if someone had gone around the whole house with a pair of kitchen scissors, cutting all the hair at a certain height regardless of whose head it belonged to.

He smiled to himself when he thought of the doorman. "Some people are so uncool that they go full circle and become cool," the latter had once explained when, among young blondes and buff hockey players, he had suddenly waved through a pale man with a bicycle helmet and a backpack. That's how it felt here. It was like entering a different world, where entirely different rules applied. Zakaria still didn't understand what they were, so he thought it best to keep quiet, at most responding when spoken to. He needed to lay low, and think.

"Who are you?" asked someone whom he would later call Sara, someone with long hair and a clear voice, and for some reason he immediately wanted to respond in a way she would like.

"My name is Daily . . . Mailer," he began, his gaze on an old newspaper, but realized that as usual he couldn't lie. "Zakaria," he said.

He paused.

"I had a bit too much to drink yesterday, and she"—he pointed to Aagny—"she was kind enough to bring me here and offer me a place to sleep."

Aagny blushed from the attention.

He paused.

"I mean, I have a place to sleep."

Pause.

"An apartment."

Pause.

"It's just, I can't be there right now."

Pause.

"I mean, it was just yesterday—that I had too much to drink. I don't do that, usually."

"He's one of us," Aagny explained. "He needs to lay low, too. He killed someone."

Zakaria flinched, as though offended:

"I mean, I don't do that, usually. Only yesterday."

Now it was the others' turn to flinch. Zakaria hurried to explain, about his job and the weasel and his criminal record—he'd had a friend when he was younger who had tricked him into things, he said, a friend who had wanted Zakaria to accompany him on various occasions. There had apparently been drug dealing involved, and Zakaria had unknowingly acted as a sort of bodyguard just by standing in the background looking massive.

"Other than that, I've never done anything, I swear. I'm not a criminal."

There was silence.

"Come, Zakaria," Aagny said, noticing the others' sceptical glances at the newcomer's broad shoulders. "Help me work on the potato cellar."

They had for some time been planning to dig a new potato cellar, but it had been such a daunting task; it was heavy work, for some reason there were lots of rocks in this particular area. First you had to remove the rocks, which they could only manage to do a few at a time—but now they all stood there, looking out of the window, watching the hungover newcomer carry away rock after rock, and it looked so effortless, like he was ladling up food with a spoon. And he whistled while doing it. There was a lightness about him, as if nothing would bite. That lightness had made its way into the kitchen, and now a fresh, new breeze was blowing.

József looked at Sara. Was it true, what he saw, the way she bit her lower lip,
    licking her mouth.

It took a few days. They kept a low profile. Sagne slept with a rifle. But Aagny vouched that the newcomer wouldn't harm anyone, and that she would be with him at all times, a knife in her pocket. "No offense," she said when she explained the plan to Zakaria himself. But soon, they relaxed; they sensed Zakaria's temperament, so light and bright and friendly—almost naive. They watched him tend to the chickens, pouring water into a large tub, bathing them just because he thought they would like it. He laughed out loud at everyone's jokes, listened to their stories with an open face. To have someone who looked like him, who spoke with his big-city dialect, see them and their lives, and say that he thought their way of living was right.

The Ant Colony
2012

Sagne did the math in her head. There were now three of them in the house evading the law: Aagny and Ersmo, who were living on benefits and working for a woman no longer alive—god knew how she had died, by the way. Sagne chose not to think about it.

Zakaria, who had killed a bar patron, and was possibly being chased by some sort of drug cartel.

There were Sara and József, who seemed to have simply stepped out of their ordinary lives.

And herself.

It felt strangely doable, to continue living like this.

In a different group constellation, someone might have demanded action from her. She kept hearing her mother's voice in her head. But she silenced it, trying not to think about her mother.

Come to think of it, perhaps Sagne had always been like this—longing to live outside of society, outside of how things "should be," outside of being married and having a job and going to meetings and having acquaintances to make small talk with.

She sometimes sent postcards to her family, so they would know she was alive and well. She had always thought that someday she would go visit them; they didn't live all that far away. But she just couldn't bring herself to do it. Today just didn't feel right. Nor yesterday, and probably not tomorrow either. She hesitated to go into town and shop; she might run into a relative, it wasn't impossible. They might ask questions, and Sagne would have to decide whether to tell them about Låke or not. If she *did*—tell them about Låke—her parents would be on her like glue. If she *didn't*, it would feel very wrong—to see her parents and not let them know they had a grandchild.

Just the thought made her nauseous, that she would phrase it like that, that she had a child, that it would be acknowledged through words spoken into the air.

So Sagne waited; just one more day, she waited.

In the beginning, Sara often went to visit her parents. Sometimes József came with her. But her parents had asked so many questions. *Where do you live,* they asked. *How do you support yourself. When will you go back to work.* Sara had given vague answers; she didn't want them to come visit, didn't want to be questioned. Maybe she sensed that the demands would start piling up again: *You have so much potential, Sara, you are so intelligent, you should work with people, you should be here among us so we can demand things of you.*

Sara had told the others—one of those evenings by the fire when they sat and talked—that it was impossible to explain to her parents. The truth about how they lived felt so right; it felt right in every pore, Sara said. But it would sound so dumb to an Outsider.

That they had given up their apartments, that pissed-off landlords had been forced to clean them out and send final bills that were never opened. That they lived with a woman Sara had met in prison. So she had told her parents that they lived in a village, that József wrote music there and Sara renovated the house. It was a real fixer-upper, but soon they would invite them for a visit. Soon.

When, her parents asked. *When.*

Won't you come to your aunt's funeral, Sara.

Won't you start studying.

Won't you come be a secretary at Dad's company.
Won't you get your life together.
Won't you be a normal person.
Won't you behave like an adult.
Sara stopped visiting.

József had no relatives in the country at all. He no longer had anything to live up to. It was as if, when his parents died, he could let out a long sigh after all those years of *pretending.* He had pretended to be happy, pretended to like swimming, pretended to be a normal person, pretended not to have anxiety. He wanted to leave, but there was also something here, something he was afraid to part with: how normal he was here, in all his strangeness. To socialize with a murderer, a bug-obsessed mother who didn't acknowledge her child, a dyslexic teenager who had showed him the joy of practical labor, a child you could tickle on the belly until it exploded with laughter, and the world's most beautiful and—József sometimes thought— *only* woman. A woman with as much anxiety as him. They all had anxiety.

He never felt *less than.*

They were all strange. They were all flawed. Together, they managed to survive. They each had something that benefited the others.

The Ant Colony
2013

I know you love the garden, Sagne," said József. It was a late afternoon in August; he sat on the porch with a cup of coffee, watching Sagne work tirelessly among the broad beans. "I like it, too. But I get the feeling that you love it even more than I do. Sometimes I see you out here for hours and hours, and I just wonder. It feels like you see something I don't. What is it you see?"

Sagne looked up from where she sat, squatting, with a small shovel. She barely had to think, answering clearly, right away.

"You know when you used to go to church," she said. "Why did you?"

"Well," he replied. "There were several reasons, I suppose. But one is that it brings together people who truly want to believe that the world is fundamentally good, and that everyone has a chance. Even if I'm not sure that I believe it myself, I wanted to be around others who do."

Sagne thought for a while.

"It's exactly the same, really," she said. "The garden makes me believe that the world is good. I've always had a feeling that people focus on the wrong things: on each other, or on the news. But just here at Ersmo's farm, in this climate zone, how many different crops do we grow? Thirty? In the natural landscape around us, many more grow wild. And out in the world, there are millions of species. Imagine the first time someone discovered potatoes, or the cocoa bean, or the coffee bean. Corn. That someone thought to heat the corn, to make popcorn.

Somewhere out there, maybe there's a plant so delicious that we can't even grasp it, better than coffee or chocolate. We don't know yet! And even if we don't discover something entirely new, just the fact that you can take a seed, put it in the ground, and it becomes a plant—I can't understand how people don't think about that all the time."

S ince Zakaria had arrived, things were different. They had been a group of people where two of them practised a sexuality and the rest did not—Sagne didn't want to, Aagny wanted to but couldn't find anyone to practise it on.

Ersmo's lack of self-esteem led him to assume that it was futile anyway. Before Sara and József had moved in, he had, on a couple of occasions, had sex with an older, bored girl from a neighboring village who looked away when he approached her in public, and eventually moved to Haparanda. Since then, nothing.

Sara and József had thus been the only ones with a sex life. It felt somehow logical within the group—like they were the parents who had an intimate relationship; the rest of the group were the children who did not. When you don't have sex for a long enough time, you rationalize it away to some extent; it becomes unnecessary, a luxury, you tell yourself, and especially if you are constantly occupied with chores—

but now Zakaria had entered the scene in his towel and reminded the group that *it existed*.

Sara said: "He must be allowed to stay. He won't hurt a fly. If he wants to, he must be allowed."

Aagny said: "I agree."

József said: "Aren't there enough of us already?"

He quickly realized his selfishness. He seemed so sympathetic, the young man, and he had nowhere to go. Would József's jealousy really be what hindered him—

"But I have no problem with him staying," József therefore added, meekly.

When Aagny barged into the large closet, where Zakaria had been sleeping the past few nights, and said that they had discussed it and he was welcome to stay if he wanted to—Zakaria felt more relieved than happy. Sure, he could hide out here for a time, while he figured out what to do. After all, he had nowhere else to go.

He felt glad, for a brief moment, not to have to play the Game—of who fit in where, who would be allowed in, who would sleep with whom. He thought it was a relief not to be hit on, or have to hit on anyone, for a while. And he felt right at home as soon as it became evident how many things he could help with here—building, holding up, digging, hunting. Everything his body seemed to be made for.

He didn't notice how they stalked his body. Every step, for different reasons. Aagny, Sara, József, and Ersmo. They watched him work.

* * *

Sometimes József had to walk away and clench his fists. It was when Aagny woke them up by being loud, standing outside the bakehouse yelling something to Ersmo, or when Zakaria never emptied the latrine bucket even though it was his job, or when they were all out of ground oats again and no one had bought more. Or when he was trying to say something and no one listened.

All this gave József a stomach-ache and a throbbing at the temple. His anger instantly turned to worry and extended not only to the things that actually were, but also to the things that potentially, possibly, could be.

So, he introduced the Circle, the same kind of circle he had used with the choir, where once a week they would all sit in a ring and share about the week that had passed.

"Naah," said Sagne.

But she complied.

In the Circle, József smothered any potential spark of conflict like a wet blanket.

So when Ersmo said:

"One could argue that some people should get better at cleaning up after themselves in the kitchen."

First József said:

"You think the rest of us should get better at cleaning up after ourselves in the kitchen."

He repeated what had been said. In this way, Ersmo felt seen.

Then József immediately added:

"I can definitely feel that I've been bad at cleaning up after myself."

He hadn't been.

"Are there more of us who feel the same way?"

József had thrown the first stone at himself, so he knew that the others would step forward—and as expected: now they all mumbled and nodded.

"Ersmo, we really need to get better at cleaning up after ourselves. Thanks for bringing it up."

Ersmo nodded graciously.

József then made a habit of always going into the kitchen to clean up, after someone else had cooked. He didn't think that Sara, or Zakaria, or Aagny, would ever get better at cleaning up after themselves. But this way, it wouldn't affect Ersmo again. Ersmo wouldn't be frustrated, and there wouldn't be any conflict.

Another time, he brought something up himself:

"Aagny, sometimes—I mean, it doesn't happen often—"

It did happen often.

"—sometimes, occasionally, you stand outside our window in the morning and talk quite loudly, and it wakes us up. It's probably just me being oversensitive. How typical of me! But IF it's not too much trouble, would you consider speaking a little quieter, just a little?"

"Sure," said Aagny.

Then she forgot all about it, and stood screaming outside the bakehouse as usual, and József never brought it up again.

There was almost never any fighting in the house. One person sniffed out all the causes of irritation before they blossomed, and used himself as a shield against conflict.

JÓZSEF

There were envelopes.

The envelopes were in a plastic bag. The bag was in a suitcase, in the top pocket, where you usually keep underwear.

There was also underwear there, on top of the bag, so you wouldn't see it.

József had had a feeling. The feeling was that he needed to bring the envelopes with him wherever he went. And so they had come with him to Sara's parents' place, and then to the farmhouse.

The feeling was also that the envelopes needed to be kept away from him. And so they stayed in the suitcase, which was in a wardrobe. He still had never looked inside them. They were hidden, from Sara and also from himself.

Perhaps he hoped he would forget about them? Other than this, Sara knew everything about him, every breath he had taken, it felt like; but she didn't know about the envelopes. It was because he knew that if she knew, she would prod him into action—some dramatic action in one way or another.

For example: opening the envelopes immediately, to find out what was inside.

Or the opposite: burning them, in some kind of ritual, to mark that he was free from his past.

József didn't want either of these options.

He wasn't free at all. He thought about the envelopes

THE COLONY · 263

several times a day. They appeared in his dreams. One night, he dreamed that the envelopes opened themselves, and out of them flew hundreds of bodies—dead bodies; they went from black-and-white to color. It was like the dream had a smell. It smelled musty, of decay. The bodies looked at him and cried out:

why are you free József why can you walk around in the sunshine without hiding why don't you have to wonder when someone will come and kill everyone you love

Mum's gaze and Dad's gaze

He felt a shame so deep it was hard to explain, while at the same time he knew this: that he wasn't free at all.

One night, it was winter and his anguish was particularly deep.

Sara came closer with her body, trying to breathe him down. It almost helped. Sara was good at breathwork; just how good, the others didn't know yet.

During their upbringing, most people see their parents perform actions, which they don't understand or can't relate to at all. Like József—his mother's scratching and screaming. But there should be a word for how, one day, you find yourself doing the same thing. You understand. The journey is different, but suddenly you find yourself there,

twitching in the night,

and you feel your mother within you and how she used to wake up and scream, and scratch.

He understood now, how it had felt for his mother. Part of it, he understood.

József hadn't even been through things, like she had.

He shouldn't be waking up screaming.

The envelopes bore his mother's name. *Márta Szilágyi.*

József had been shocked to see his surname spelled correctly, terrified—the "y" at the end and everything—like someone had ripped off a plaster and exposed a wound. He saw the handwriting before his eyes every day.

The handwriting the handwriting the handwriting, and he went out to the chicken coop and talked to a new chicken, who wasn't as good as Dr. Snuggles but all right.

She was the only one who knew.

"Cluck cluck," said the chicken, which had been given the name Therese.

"I don't know if I dare," said József.

THE ANT COLONY
2013

I t happened when Sara was cutting a raw potato in half, and she wasn't quite sure how, but the potato must have slipped a little to the side, causing the knife to slide as well, resulting in a fairly deep and bloody gash between her left thumb and index finger.

"Shit!" Sara screamed, sending an echo through the house.

She was alone in there; the others were outside.

Sara thought the following: that they had never, as far as she knew, bought any bandages in town. However, she seemed to recall that they had brought bandages with them when they first arrived here, from Stockholm. This was because József had thought they might get attacked by a wolf or something, and so it could be useful to pack some first aid items.

Sara had giggled at him.

"So you mean, if we were attacked by a wolf, the wolf would attack us, but only a little, so that three feet of gauze would fix it?"

"Laugh all you want," József had said, putting the gauze in his bag.

That's what Sara seemed to recall.

"József," she called out, but she saw that he was far away— they were all working on a new woodshed—so she went out to the bakehouse and found the suitcase he had brought, a soft mix between a bag and a duffel. The larger compartment was empty except for a ripped shirt, so she opened the smaller one. Some socks and underwear spilled out, which she paid no mind to. She dug around a little. She felt a resistance among the softness.

Her hand gripped and pulled. A plastic bag. Something harder underneath. Could it be a folded bandage in its packaging? Her hand in the bag, pulling up. A stack of letters. A photograph fell out. The photo was of a family. A laughing family, it was, in black and white, from a time when getting photographed was still a big deal, when you planned ahead, gathered the family, got all dressed up.

Two young adults, a woman and a man. Two elderly, both men: one with a big grin, the other more composed. Five children. The boys looked a lot like József.

Sara stared at the picture for a long time. She hadn't known about it.

In the evening, when they were going for a walk after dinner, she brought it up.

"I was trying to find the bandage," she began.

(Her hand was now wrapped in a tea towel embroidered with the initials F.L.—for Ersmo's deceased grandmother—and a bloodstain had seeped through.)

"I remembered you packing it in the bag—"

She didn't need to say more. József knew where the conversation was headed. Within the next hour, he would feel a pressure over his chest—his body would jump and twitch—

he would fall silent—

and then, finally, start speaking.

Just as he had anticipated, Sara would start prying, and she would extract what little he knew about the envelopes. (Where had they come from? His parents' apartment. Had he looked inside them? No. Why not? Because he was afraid of what it would bring up. What did he think was inside? Photos of his relatives, whose names he had never heard. Why was he so afraid of that? He didn't know, but maybe there would be photos of relatives whose names he had never heard. Maybe his parents' sorrow would then have a face.)

That evening, Sara called everyone together.

"There's something I've learned to do," she said. "I've wanted to show you, but I've hesitated. I didn't know if you would understand. But now I think it's time. It's something I learned in India."

Sagne flared her nostrils. She was sceptical of Sara's time in India.

"Think of it a bit like yoga," Sara said.

Sagne's nostrils again. She was also sceptical of yoga. Twenty people standing in a room wearing loose-fitting pants, panting, and talking about how close they felt to themselves.

Sara paused.

"You know I've had my demons," she said then.

Everyone nodded. There was nothing unusual about that in the farmhouse. They all had their demons. The demons didn't need to be talked about. They were there. Sometimes you could see it, in someone's eyes, that the demons were present. It wasn't a big thing.

Sara looked at everyone, but mostly at Sagne.

"Try to approach this with an open mind. Sometimes you don't need to understand everything. You can just accept that it works. If you don't like it, at least you've tried."

Sara made a fire in the fireplace. She had laid out mattresses on the floor, instructed everyone to pick a spot.

If it hadn't been her suggesting it, they would never.

But now they lay there next to each other.

"Breathe through your mouth," Sara said now. "Breathe to the rhythm. Breathe into your belly. Breathe into your heart. Breathe out. Into your belly. Into your heart. Breathe out."

She demonstrated the rhythm. *Ah-ah-aah. Ah-ah-aah.* It was quick, not slow.

"It might feel uncomfortable," Sara said. "Like you're on the verge of a panic attack. Don't be afraid of it. It's not dangerous. If your body starts to cramp, let it."

A few of them sighed a little. It's not like a bit of breathing could trigger a—

József lay there, feeling his body start to twitch within minutes. His head spun. His mouth began to contract. His nose felt dry.

"Keep breathing," Sara demanded. "Don't stop."

He felt afraid—afraid of his own body. The dizziness meant he no longer knew what was true or false. Ersmo next to him on one side, and Aagny on the other, twitching similarly.

Ah-ah-aah. Ah-ah-aah.

"Keep going," said Sara. "Even if it's uncomfortable. Breathe to the rhythm. Keep going. Keep going."

It was too much now. József felt himself nearly hyperventilating; it felt as though his body was detached from his mind. It was as if Sara was forcing his anxiety to the surface. After several nights of panic, why did she want to force it to the surface?

He stopped, looking at her questioningly. She looked back, suddenly stern, clear. Immediately, he obeyed.

Ah-ah-aah. Ah-ah-aah.

He heard the same across the room. *Ah-ah-aah.*

How long did they go on for? Half an hour?

"And now," said Sara. "Now we scream."

She screamed out loud. It made the others dare, too. They screamed now, pounding the floor, kicking. There was a boundary around them that suddenly expanded. Apparently, they were now doing this kind of thing in front of each other.

József heard someone crying. Zakaria?

"Keep breathing," said Sara. "Don't worry about anyone else."

Through their breathing, they heard her approaching Zakaria. His crying settled.

"And again," Sara said. "Scream now. Pound."

They were used to it now, no longer afraid. Everyone else was doing it, so it must be okay. They screamed and pounded. József heard his own voice through the group's. How angry it sounded. Did he have that in him? He felt scared when he heard it. In some ways, he thought, it was a bit like singing in a choir. In many ways, it was not.

"Keep going," said Sara. "A little longer. Breathe to the rhythm."

Ah-ah-aah.

How much time had passed now, an hour? Perhaps everyone thought someone else would question it, pull them out. Maybe Sagne? But she was in it now, too, just continuing. It was nice to have someone telling them what to do, like when you were little and an older sibling chose what game to play.

And then:

"Now," said Sara. "Release your breath. Breathe normally."

She went around, putting blankets over a couple of them. Put on a vinyl record, Joni Mitchell. The music took hold of them. József suddenly felt nothing—nothing at all.

I'm frightened by the devil
And I'm drawn to those ones that ain't afraid.

When he closed his eyes, he now saw a light behind his eyelids.

A calm settled. It was soft. It felt like the moment after sex, when two people lie panting in each other's arms, feeling completely and utterly relaxed. Entirely approved. You don't see any details, just the whole. You are a body and soul in one flow. All you need to do is exist.

Now he felt like that, with the whole room. With everyone lying there, he felt they were one. They didn't need to pretend. Just like he had always longed for the church to feel. Just like he had always longed for his parents to feel. That's how it felt now. Soft and warm. He felt safe in the world and secure in himself. And then he began to cry.

Tears flowed down his cheeks, so many that he momentarily wondered if he had burst something in his ears, for they filled with tears from his eyes. And around him, he noticed the same from Aagny and Ersmo and Zakaria, even Sagne?

József screamed again. Straight into the darkness, he screamed. He screamed out all his anxiety and fear, shame and sorrow. It was normal now. An hour ago, it hadn't been.

Sara was with him; she lay down beside him. She understood what he needed, how was it that she always did?

It just happened that way. But in the end, the whole group lay like that—like spoons they lay next to each other, first Sara, then József, Aagny, Ersmo, Zakaria, Sagne just a little further away.

They fell asleep like that. Slept deeply and didn't wake until the next morning, when Låke stepped over their bodies, trying to find Sagne but eventually settling in between Aagny and Ersmo.

Everything was the same, yet everything had changed.

From now on, they spoke even less. They didn't ask "Did you sleep well?" or "How are you?" There was a deeper calm between them. József's talking circle felt unnecessary. If there was something going on, they knew the others would say it. The others would wish them well. For they had shared something. For they had cried next to each other, all at the same time.

Their view of Sara had changed. They had thought they knew her. But apparently, she knew things others didn't—things that seemed almost unearthly. If she had known about that exercise without saying anything, what else might she know?

Sagne felt it worst. She was scared of how her body had responded to the exercise, of what came up. During the breathwork, she was back in the rape, not like she saw it in front of her,

but like her body recalled something in it. She had despised being in it, would have stopped, if it weren't for the moment when they screamed, which felt so incredibly liberating, like she was getting a tiny, tiny bit of restitution. She couldn't scream then, but she did now. The scream had been stored in her body. That's how it felt. Now it was out in the world. It didn't change anything, but she slept well that night; maybe for the first time in years, she slept quite well. She hadn't thought about it before, but now, as she fell into a deep sleep, she realized it had been a very long time since she had.

THE ANT COLONY
2013

In the evenings, they sat by the fire: if it was warm, outside around the firepit that Ersmo and Aagny had built just up from the water; if it was cold, around the tiled stove inside. Someone had started this, and now it was tradition. József had the guitar he had found in the attic, or if they were inside, the pump organ, and they sang together. At first, it was familiar songs with beautiful melodies—lullabies, "Moscow Nights," "*Tula Hem och Tula Vall*"—but as more evenings passed, the songs were replaced by various separate notes. Everyone chose the note they preferred. Then they held it, and took pleasure in the way their individual note felt together with the others'. Sometimes they switched, testing how a new note sounded against the others'. It felt like their voices and notes were needed.

Some of them liked talking—mainly Sara and Aagny. They went on long walks where all they did was talk. But as a group, they were mostly silent. When someone spoke, it was almost like a ceremony. On those occasions, they would tell stories to each other. These became like little films in the night. Zakaria might talk about the bar. Aagny about prison. Sara about India. But mostly it was Sagne who talked.

"Tell us something," Sara would sometimes ask Sagne when they sat around the fire.

Was it the way Sagne told the story? Or was it that Sara gave space and direction to Sagne's words? Perhaps both gave birth to each other. But Sagne knew so much. She talked about the insects, about the animals.

It felt good, reverential almost, to focus on them.

"We are not important in ourselves," Sara often said when Sagne had finished speaking. "We are merely *a part of.*"

József enjoyed hearing that—that he wasn't important. Often, the stories were about ants.

"Ants have two stomachs, one for themselves, and one to bring home food to the rest of the group," Sagne said, with a somewhat good-natured tone, like she was speaking to children. "When ants build their colonies, the soil loosens, and nutrients become available to other species. Without their digging, the soil would turn hard and compact, and rainwater wouldn't be able to penetrate the ground. It wouldn't reach the trees' roots. Ants kill insects that they eat and poop out, providing nutrients to others."

Everything Sagne explained seemed to imply that ants formed the basis of the entire ecosystem. Ants were ideal—the perfect creature.

"But that's how it is with most things," Sagne said. "We are all part of a perfect system. Everyone is needed." She pondered. "Except maybe humans. We are the only ones who take more than we give."

The group felt ashamed.

"But everyone eats each other," said Ersmo. "Surely humans must be allowed to eat animals, too."

"Maybe a single animal needed to fill your belly," Sara said. "Not thousands of animals in factories."

Here, some nodded, and others zoned out.

Through the stories, they reached conclusions. It happened gradually.

They concluded that, if humans wanted to live without taking up more space than the rest of the species on Earth, they should only kill what was directly in front of them, what they knew they could eat. Then the system wouldn't be upended.

"Perhaps you could do it politely," Zakaria said. "That would feel better."

"How do you mean, "politely"?" Sara asked.

"Well, maybe we could say *thank you* or something," Zakaria said. "Thank you to the animal, and thank you to nature in general."

"Thank you to all existence," said Sara.

She thought about it. The idea was so silly, yet at the same time it had a certain beauty. What she missed from her brief forays into religious experiences was a sense of *awareness*, that if one assumes there is a God, one also assumes there is someone who *gives* us something. The Big Bang, Sara thought, was like believing that a buffet had appeared out of nowhere and all you had to do was grab yourself a fork and eat before someone else gobbled it up. This led to a greedy way of thinking. If, instead, one assumed that nature itself is God hosting a feast, or that all species—including humans—are a kind of study group or housing cooperative hosting the party together, it inspires a humbler attitude. Thank you to nature/the housing cooperative/all existence.

"That's what we'll do," Sara said. "From now on, we'll say *thank you*."

"You do realize," Sagne interjected, "that if a wolf came and took one of the chickens, it wouldn't say thank you."

Sagne rolled her eyes at discussions like this. She didn't feel the need to say everything out loud. Surely everyone already knew to feel gratitude for the magnificence of nature and the bounty it provided.

But she didn't say anything more, for she enjoyed sitting there with them, and she had learned early on that most other people have a need to discuss obvious matters, and you should simply indulge them—you didn't have to listen.

And so it came to be that the group, which increasingly saw themselves as part of the ecosystem rather than individual humans, bought less processed meat, fished more, and when a perch found its way into their hands, they immediately said:

Thank you.

After a while, it felt wrong to go into town at all. They competed in gathering food from their local surroundings. A few times a year they would go in, to buy salt and pepper, flour and butter, and some ice cream. Other than that, nothing. Eggs and potatoes and fish were more than enough for them.

"It's best if we stay away," said Sara.

* * *

It was as if, without anyone saying it out loud, they turned into more and more of a flock. Anyone who has spent an extended period of time in a group knows that, eventually, language becomes simplified. You go from long, intricate sentences to single vowels and sighs—*ah!* when you sit down on the wooden steps, *mm!* when the potatoes are fresh.

And it happened here, too. Surely the birds didn't tell each other if one of them needed to land for a bit; they just landed wherever they pleased. If a certain person in the group was the one everyone listened to, then surely that person would be in charge, the alpha male—in this case *female*—and that's just the way it was. Why fight it?

There was an advantage to speaking less and coexisting more. The advantage was that it led to less bickering. Before they stopped making small talk, their days had been full of squabbles—who had forgotten to bring in water, who hadn't cleaned up after themselves—and József was busy trying to prevent every conflict. But now they made a point of being accommodating, not thinking too much. The chores took care of themselves. The one best suited for something did it.

Perhaps it was around this time they started calling themselves the "Colony". It started as a joke; Sagne was talking about ants as usual, about the way they coexisted, when Zakaria said:

"Like us. An ant colony!"

And he sounded so cheerful that no one could help but laugh. A colony of individuals, where everyone worked, where everyone had a different skill set. It felt good to say. Like there was a reason. Like it was natural.

They tried to stop thinking of themselves as individuals. Instead, each was a part. A part of the colony.

Every now and then, József would address the elephant in the room.

"Isn't it time for us to return to the city now?" he would say, maybe once a year, maybe twice.

"This *is* my real life," Sara might reply then. "I don't want it any other way. I'm sorry, József."

She would look soft, sympathizing.

But recently, she had started to add:

"If you really want to leave, we have a problem—then we can no longer be together."

He knew she wouldn't give in. She wasn't someone who gave in. If they were to continue together, there was only one possibility. That he would give in.

He stayed. Just a few more weeks, he would stay. Who knew what would happen next.

She might change her mind.

Another elephant was Låke. He was six years old now, an inquisitive child, and a little intrusive. He would always appear, asking what they were doing and if he could join.

"Not now," Sara would say when she was leading the breathwork.

"Not now," Sagne would say when she was working in the garden.

"Not now," Ersmo would say when he was wrenching on the car.

József saw Låke playing on his own, and it pained him. Perhaps he recognised himself. It was clear enough that they loved Låke—especially Aagny, and Ersmo, and himself—but he had no other children to interact with.

Good thing, thought József, that he would soon be starting school.

"What should we do about Låke, when he starts school?" József asked Sara one night. "We'll have to register him with the authorities."

"Mm," Sara murmured, and he gathered she was drifting off.

József knew that Sara should be the mother of his children. He had started longing for it more and more. Låke had grown bigger, and József had developed a liking for the feeling in his body, the feeling of holding a small child, smelling its head. The child's smile when you come near.

There was also something more. József was rootless. His parents were dead. If you really thought about it, he had no one else. Sometimes, when Sara or Sagne talked about their childhood—about their stable families that were still alive, about the houses they grew up in that still stood boasting of all the things that showed they had lived—he felt such a profound jealousy that he had to walk away and kick a root.

He only had Sara.

So far, there hadn't been any children. Sara didn't seem too worried about this. "If it happens, it happens," she would say. "We have to trust nature."

It's just that, so far, nature hadn't wanted to.

There must be something wrong with him, with his damaged, anxious sperm. Of course they didn't swim fast enough. Of course Sara's body didn't want them.

The Ant Colony
2013

If you are wondering what they did with their days, they lived. And if you have lived a certain way for long enough, it's hard to go back to anything else. They didn't want to be held accountable. If they re-entered regular society again, they would have to pay for the time they had spent here. They walked around with questions in their eyes—questions they let the others in the group answer, and the others always answered that what they did, the way they did it, was meaningful. The same way all people in all societies do. You look at one another and see others doing the same things in the same way and you think *ah, this seems to be a way of existing.*

Now they wanted Sara. They wanted what she knew, and her conviction that they should live here of all places, be themselves of all people.

She revealed that she had dreamed Aagny would deliver a child, long before Sagne or Låke moved in.

"But that's SICK!" Aagny roared then. "You dreamed that? Before?"

It must mean they were meant to be here.

"That same night, I dreamed that we are in the right place. This is right."

She fell silent.

"And that the more we share of ourselves with each other, the better."

In what way?

"In every way."

Oh, how they loved to hear Sara say this. No one in the Colony could manage life in the ordinariness. But when Sara spoke of their way of living as an ideal, it meant they were the winners, not the losers.

There was something so fragile about the Colony; they knew that at any moment it could crumble. That's why they cherished it so tenderly. Everyone accepted the positions assigned to them naturally, as the group desired. That Sara set the agenda, that József was the one to turn to with your burdens. That Sagne knew about nature, and that Ersmo and Aagny were the ones who knew how to farm it. That Zakaria was the light, the joyful one, the one who would burst out laughing, start humming a melody. That Låke was there but not really. There was no room to question this. Everyone assumed their role and played it. They were a part of the whole, and they were all needed.

* * *

József sat in the armchair, reading. He had picked a random book off the shelf: *Hash* by Torgny Lindgren. The book looked quite new, may never have been read before at all.

"I won it in some school lottery," Ersmo said. "Good that it's being put to use, by someone."

Ersmo himself didn't read.

József did read. The book, he thought, was quite good. Deceptively simple, or deceptively complex—it was hard to decide which. Possibly a bit obsessed with small towns and the way people talk in small towns; József never understood why this was so important to every author north of Gävle. "Read a little aloud," said Aagny, who stood washing the dishes.

There was a red and white striped hand-towel hanging from

the key of the pantry door. There were already several buds on the
Christmas cactus.
Eventually he said, "I've been looking for ages for a landscape
that would match my state of mind."
She stood up and took a couple of logs out of the wood-box. As
she pushed them into the stove, she said, "Yes, we should always
be ashamed of what goes on inside us."

József looked up across the room and noticed Aagny continuing to wash the dishes, listening with one ear, giggling a
little. Ersmo walked out of the door. But next to him stood
Låke, wide-eyed, taking a seat at József's foot. "More," said
Låke. "Read more."

They read the whole book. Then they read the other books
in the bookcase, most of which had belonged to Ersmo's grand-
parents and sprung out of a different era. A book like *Wuthering*
Heights shouldn't have appealed to a six-year-old, but József
made an effort to read it with as much suspense as possible,
giving the characters different voices: Catherine a feminine,
sensual flair; Heathcliff a low, booming voice that Sara thought
sounded more like Goofy. And Låke gaped, rolling around on
the floor when he heard the stories, started talking about the
places and Heathcliff on a daily basis. "Why does Hiskliss do
that?" he wondered. "Why is Hiskliss so angry?"

Soon, Låke started sitting next to József as he read—when
Sagne wasn't in the room, that is—and he stared at the pages,
so intently that it looked like his eyes might fall out of his
head.

* * *

One night, when Låke lay sleeping and the others were in
the kitchen doing various things, József brought it up: "I realized there's something we've never talked about. What do we

do when Låke starts school? We'll have to enroll him in some system, I suppose."

There was total silence.

"Surely, Låke shouldn't have to go to school," said Aagny. She and Ersmo had long agreed that school was a scourge, only meant for a type of person who enjoyed sitting still and being boring. She looked at Sara now, almost pleadingly; to her, it was entirely obvious that it would be problematic not only for the group but also for Låke himself—for him to have to go through the same experience as her and Ersmo, feeling bad and ugly and clumsy and restless and like his body needed to be restrained in a school desk.

József blinked. He didn't know what he had expected—perhaps that it would be a little awkward—but it sure wasn't this, the silence that unfurled. He had assumed it was a given, after all, that the boy would get an education.

József had, in some ways, loved school. He had loved having a desk and books and raising his hand and that everything had a clear plan and an agenda, and not having to be responsible for anyone but himself. And now they read and then it was break time and then it was math and this is exactly how things would go.

He looked at the one person around the table who he knew felt the same: a genuine love for knowledge. But Sagne got up and walked out of the door.

Sara's voice was light-hearted and a little weary; she sounded as if she were talking about a film maybe, or a dish. "I don't think he needs it," she said. "Låke is an inquisitive child, we can teach him everything he needs to know right here with us. Real knowledge, about life."

József looked around the room and saw the others nodding. He thought, maybe she is right. Everyone else seems to think she is right.

And thus fell the verdict, light as spring rain, regarding Låke's future, it fell over the dining table one night in February.

József went out and looked at Låke where he lay sleeping. A feeling in his gut.

So, in the end, it was József who taught Låke to read and write, and the hunger with which the child went about this task sliced through József like a hot knife through butter. All of Ersmo's old textbooks, he devoured.

"See," said Sara. "He's learning anyway, that one. He'll be fine."

Next year, József thought. Next year, I'll bring it up again. If I teach him enough, it will be easy for him to slip into a class. Besides, next year it's probably time to move.

* * *

Gradually, it came to be that Sagne's saved wages and József's money from selling his parents' apartment belonged to the Colony collectively. It was like the ants bringing half the food back to the group in their second stomach. Nothing strange about that.

And they harvested a tree here and there and sometimes bought materials, so they could build little cabins. The buildings were a motley crew, just like themselves. The big house, the old bakehouse, which had already been there since before. The first treehouse that Ersmo and Aagny had built, painstakingly. With each thing they built, they learned more and more. The details became more and more refined, the houses straighter and straighter.

Ersmo, Aagny, and Zakaria built and built, and József helped, too. Aagny's rushed style—*that* they were building was more important than what it looked like—paired with Ersmo's thoroughness.

It had started with Zakaria building himself a small shed to have somewhere to sleep. Sometimes he would fall silent, all of a sudden, and then he would say, to Aagny or anyone else:

"To think that it was possible to build my own house. My very own little house." And then he would laugh, such a joyful laugh.

It was the first thing he had done with his own two hands. They built more and more little cabins; like a game of Monopoly, these looked in the yard. One shed, and then another shed. No building permits were applied for, because no one heard them build, and no one saw the buildings. Sometimes they stood staring at the sheds, amazed at what their hands were capable of.

They built more sheds than they needed.

And Sagne worked in and organized the garden, and despite the barren inland soil, the farm and the home blossomed. But none of this could be seen from the road. From there, it looked like always. Boring. Nothing to catch the eye.

THE ANT COLONY
2014

In the summertime, they wanted to be out of the house, wanted to live under the open sky. They waited until the mosquitoes started to diminish. Sometimes Aagny stayed at the house; she often had back pain. But most of the time, they were all together. The goal was this: to live to the highest degree possible on what's out there. Like the other species did. Anything caught was shared. They were a collective organism, not individual beings. At their least, they were the people in the group; at their most, they were the whole Colony and maybe, just maybe, all of existence. They were the sun in the sky and the lakes and the bogs. They were the mosquitoes flying around and the willow tits and the Siberian jays. They were the reindeer and the wolverines and the beavers. They were the spruce needles and the lichen and they were the cloudberries, cloudberries, cloudberries. *Thank you. Thank you* echoed over the forest. *Thank you. Thank you* when a bird or a hare was caught and roasted over an open flame. *Thank you. Thank you* to the fire, for burning. *Thank you* to the branches, for allowing themselves to be burned. *Thank you* to the water, for allowing itself to be drunk. Just as the water allowed itself to be drunk by them, they let the mosquitoes drink the blood from their bodies. They tried hard not to swat at them on the bog. Just as all existence was available to them, they must be available to the rest of existence.

And time went by. After a while, they no longer asked questions. The questions had fallen silent, become neutral. This was life, neither more nor less.

JÓZSEF
2014

It had just started getting dark earlier in the evening. The blueberries were abundant in the forest, as were the cloudberries, and they had drunk their fill of blackcurrant wine and made an omelette in the pan. In late summer, it was good to be alive; life was like a pantry, a grand feast unfurling under the sky, and as a human you could simply go picking. *That old berry? Nah. This one looks tastier.* This József noticed himself thinking, and he felt ashamed for choosing the big, golden berries over the slightly shrivelled ones. But it was an instinct; in order not to pick the most beautiful ones, he had to think, use his brain, and eating berries, surely that was pure joy. Surely you had to allow yourself to pick the tastiest berry once in a while.

Around the Colony rose a constant *thank you. Thank you. Thank you* to the blueberries, *thank you* to the charr, *thank you* to the lingonberries and Arctic brambles and raspberries. They had made a fire down by the water, sat around it, and József had set the tone: *Ah—*

And the others had followed suit. Sagne and Zakaria both sang terribly, or so József had thought at first, before he realized that singing wasn't a destination but a constant doing, an action for the body to perform, just like sleeping or eating, and surely no one would tell another that they slept in an improper way? He had got used to it now, used to all the voices of the Colony—Sara's soft, Aagny's slightly hoarse, and Låke's clear child's voice from further away, approaching through the song. It was like he sensed that he could do this, Låke, that he had a talent for it, and so he dared to step forward, but also that singing always immediately invited a feeling of *belonging*, better than any speech or action. They sang notes, melodies, over each other, and József had learned to come in and connect the different voices, so they sounded like something harmonious. It wasn't necessary, but something he enjoyed. And he asked them now to transition into a hymn, an almost-gospel he used to sing with the choir, written to praise God, but now József thought perhaps it praised the Earth instead: *Thank you for today. Thank you for tomorrow. Thank you for all the gifts, you give us each day.* They sang it several times.

It had been a year or two since Zakaria had come to them, and it was in the middle of the song József noticed it: that Sara had turned her head so it was now facing only Zakaria, and she let her eyes glitter at him, like she was enchanted and shy at the same time. József remembered that gaze; it was the one she had given him when they first met, like József was utterly wonderful, like she couldn't take her eyes off him. And for József, that gaze had been a drug—so powerful he could have gone without eating and drinking forever, because all the voids inside him had been filled, and he had become new. And it was the reason he had ended up here, become part of a colony, for he would have followed that gaze anywhere. But now, the gaze fell on Zakaria, and Zakaria received it as if it were entirely natural; he barely reacted to it, like it was a given and normal for him to be seen this way, and this caused a pain in József so deep he was paralyzed.

That old berry? Nah. This one looks tastier.

There are some people who have the ability to act so naturally according to their own will that people around them lose their bearings—*well, I guess this is how it is from now on?*—and that's exactly what happened now, when Sara continued to hum along to József's song while placing her hand on Zakaria's thigh and kissing him softly.

Sara belonged to József, didn't she? Wasn't anyone going to say something?

Apparently not.

Zakaria looked around—he looked at József, and saw that József didn't react, and that no one else reacted—and he was perhaps so confused, and maybe a little aroused, that he kissed her back. Sara held his face, in both hands, and the ensuing kiss was so unabashed that within thirty seconds
   it completely redrew the map of the Colony's future.
Sara took Zakaria's hand, and led him over to Big Spruce, where she rolled out her sleeping bag and invited Zakaria to join her, and everyone else looked away, and continued singing. And József's voice was loud and desperate now.

Aagny was back at the house. *Good thing*, he thought for a moment. *She would have been so upset.*

The next morning, the sun rose, and Sara woke to see József sitting alone on a rock down by the lake. She was used to this. He wasn't a good sleeper. She snuck up behind him, sat down like a big spoon behind his little one. There was a battle inside his body now. How comfortable and happy he felt from feeling her next to him, both in general but also because ever since yesterday his whole being had been shaped like a question, which now had its answer. *She was still his*, the body responded now. *She's here and feels like usual. So she must be mine.* But József had learned that bodies could be deceptive; sometimes you had to override the body, listen more to your head, which even yesterday had warned him they needed to talk about what had happened. And he was glad that his face was turned away from hers, towards the lake, when he said:

"I saw you yesterday."

Sara's voice was light, genuinely curious.

"What did you see?"

"You and Zakaria."

"Oh, you mean—that we slept together?"

Her voice was so natural when she said it.

"Yes."

Sara shifted her body, so she could look József in the eyes. She put on a slightly giggly face.

"But, my love, surely you weren't jealous? Of *that*?"

József didn't respond.

"It's natural to seek different bodies. We're not made to be monogamous. It's not strange at all," said Sara. "I expected you to do the same. We share everything here."

József remained silent.

"The same way you talk to Sagne instead of me, sometimes. It's not strange. And you like Zakaria, too."

Different things screamed inside József. *It's precisely because I like him that it hurts. Because he's happy, young, beautiful. Because he has confidence. Because the things I can do are nothing compared to him.* He didn't say that. He said, glumly:

"It's not the same."

Sara lifted József's head.

"My love, you have to get used to this. Don't think so much. You're bigger than that. We all have things we need to work on to become one with all existence." She smiled. "Look at the ants over there. Sagne taught me the queen's role is to lay as many eggs as possible, with all the males in the colony."

She smiled her usual smile, but József noticed she was suddenly saying it out loud. That she was the queen. Everyone already knew it. But this was the first time she had said it.

"Perhaps you should look around, too?"

József looked around.

He saw Sagne, diligently rinsing a piece of cloth in the water. There was no living human exuding less sexuality.

He thought of Aagny, who was currently back at the house, unaware that the man she adored had slept with Sara.

He looked at Sara. There was no one he had loved more. When they had sex, he felt like all the evil in the world paused. Yes, that's everyone there was.

As if Sara had read his mind, she said: "You don't have to stick to just women, you know." She touched him again. "I would love it if you'd join us next time."

Then she stood up from the rock. József thought: *She's right, it's just me who's boring and stiff. Why am I so boring and stiff?*

She looked at him, smiled warmly and said:

"Think about it this way: there's also the possibility there'll be a child now."

Then she turned and walked back towards Big Spruce.

Did no one see the knife in his chest, how the blood gushed and flowed

* * *

Two weeks later, they were doing breathwork by the water. It was a need. A restlessness would sometimes set in. But the breathwork—which they did once a month—made any irritation fade, and the group always felt closer afterwards. They lay like a flower, their heads in a circle, feet in the middle, feeling each other's bodies inhale and exhale. As always during breathwork, József felt his anxiety bubble up, felt it pin him down; he was afraid of himself. But Sara's calm voice, *stay in it, stay in it, trust your breathing.* And finally, it came—the release, the crying. A few of them fell asleep afterwards. They lay in a heap.

Sara came to József, as she usually did in moments of calm and safety. He loved those moments more than anything. He was home now, not a worry in the world. He had Sara and he had the air and he had his friends. Right now, he didn't want to be anywhere else.

This time, Sara took József by the hand and signaled for him to stand up. He did. He looked at her and smiled. His body tired and light at the same time.

But she had one hand free. In that hand, she took Zakaria. The others had their eyes closed. And ever so silently, she led József and Zakaria to another spruce, not Big Spruce but another one a bit further away, where she had rolled out a sleeping pad. And there she said:

"Kiss each other."

Zakaria smiled in the evening light. He looked perhaps a bit shy. But he smiled at József with a questioning gaze. Zakaria wasn't against it, he showed, shrugging his shoulders.

József breathed.

It was a glorious late-summer evening; the mosquitoes were gone for the season and the sun was setting behind the mountain. Sara had a look on her face. It was expectant. She looked alive, as if everything were a game. He loved it when she had that look. She looked happy. He had an opportunity to make her happy. He couldn't not make her happy.

He felt soft after the breathwork. Doors had been opened that were otherwise closed. It was possible.

Yet it felt strange as he approached Zakaria. He only looked at Sara when Zakaria came closer and kissed him, first lightly, then more deeply. It felt strange to have another man's tongue in his mouth. It felt strange to feel stubble against his face. Not repulsive, just . . . different.

He stepped back a little, gazing at Zakaria. Zakaria looked like it was rather enjoyable and not too serious. Zakaria and Sara laughed. József's head was spinning.

Now Sara walked up to József, kissed him passionately. Everything was set right—

But then she turned away from his face, kissed Zakaria. It was awful and at the same time somehow arousing; József didn't understand his own reaction, his body responding positively when he saw that beautiful face kissing his Sara. He felt so bad again, seeing how they looked together—a beautiful, young couple, Zakaria smiling between kisses and Sara glowing. József was the weak link. József was the one who didn't fit in. József was the one who wasn't enough for Sara, which forced her to turn elsewhere.

If only he could be better. Then she would come back to him and him alone. If he changed his attitude. Then she would stay. Maybe he just needed to change his attitude.

Sara and Zakaria continued to kiss. Sara searched for József's hand, signalling that she wanted him to watch. He sat down and observed his young, beautiful friend move inside his beloved. They lay down under the spruce tree, Zakaria on top of Sara. József stood and watched with an erection and a deep, bottomless sorrow. If he had been an animal, either he wouldn't have cared, or he would have fought Zakaria for the female's favor. But he failed to be like that, like an animal. He was just sad.

Afterwards, all three of them hugged.

József said nothing.

Later, when Sara lay down beside him and fell asleep under Big Spruce as usual, he said nothing.

The others had seen, of course. Låke didn't understand, but he had seen. Ersmo had seen. Often, he didn't think about it, but sometimes, now, he thought that if he lived somewhere else, in some other context, there would be girls there. Other than these ones, who were much older than him. Girls with hair and smiles and arms, who might want to hold him.

They probably wouldn't want him.

But there was a possibility.

They were out there.

But everything became so complicated if he thought that way. Aagny was here, and she was all Ersmo had. He had no mother and no father. Besides, what would he do? He was

twenty-five years old and didn't even have a full education.
He wouldn't be able to get a job. No, he would have to deal
with that some other day. Besides, it seemed awful out there.
Murders and wars and fires.

Aagny was back at the house today. He wondered who
would tell her about Sara and Zakaria. He hoped it wouldn't
be him.

Another day, he and Zakaria went swimming. The water was
cold. Zakaria was beautiful and happy as he stood there, trying
to dive off a rock. It didn't feel too forward when he hugged
Ersmo and suddenly kissed him. He said: "I know you like
girls, but do you want to try this? It's okay if not."

Ersmo looked around. Aagny was still in the house, so she
wouldn't have to see Zakaria choosing him over her.

There was no one else he was more attracted to. So, why not.
Zakaria was perhaps ten years older than him but still handsome, so handsome that being attracted to him felt somewhat
genderless.

They jerked each other off. It felt like a practical solution.
Zakaria was so easy-going, Ersmo knew it would have been
okay if he had said no. The next time, he was the one who suggested it. It was a form of intimacy, nothing more or less.

THE ANT COLONY
2016

S ara had a suggestion. The suggestion was that they should become entirely self-sufficient.

"We need a cow," she said. "Two cows," she said then, and looked at Sagne. "And maybe pigs? More chickens?"

Aagny stared at her. "You're crazy," she said. "Do you know how good we have it here?"

Aagny saw all her lie-ins fly away across the sky, like migratory birds over the bog.

"We wouldn't have to depend on society at all. We would never have to go into town."

Ersmo shook his head anxiously. Town was the only place he could see people his own age. They already went so rarely, a few times a year. Going there gave him the feeling that he could do anything with his life. He just wasn't doing it right now.

"Sara," said Sagne. She sighed a little—did this discussion really have to come up again? "You don't know what it's like on a proper farm. You don't want to go there unless you're prepared to dedicate your life to it. You can't just leave for a few days and go sleep under Big Spruce. You have to get up every morning, muck out, milk, feed . . . And what would the cows eat? We would need to produce hay."

She didn't say what they were all thinking, namely that Sara was the only one who hardly did any practical work on the farm at all. But that was okay. Her role was to lead. They all knew it.

"And if an animal gets sick?" she said instead. "We'd need to bring in a vet."

That statement carried weight. They couldn't seek medical assistance at all, neither for humans nor animals. Then everything would fall apart.

Sara huffed. She didn't say anything more, which indicated that she hadn't been aware of the information just given to her. But she looked surly. József became nervous, tried to find a middle ground.

"Maybe just one pig?"

"It's not fair to have just one pig," Sagne pointed out immediately. "They are social animals."

József felt anger welling up. *For fuck's sake, Sagne, help me out here! If a pig is what it takes for us not to argue, then let's get a goddamn pig.*

That's what he thought to himself.

"We'll see," said Sara.

And in the future, she would talk about that potential pig often. "When we get the pig." As if to signal that the idea hadn't been dismissed, that they would someday have a pig, even if there was currently no pigsty on the farm and no specific pig was on the table.

And the others went along with it, in words:

"We shouldn't build there; when the pig comes, it'll need somewhere to live."

In this way, Sara's idea was cemented as a good one. Only, everyone knew it would never materialize in physical form.

The pig was talked about so often that everyone had a clear image of it, what it would look like.

"The pig will be small and ruddy," someone thought.

"No, big and dirty," said another.

"We'll eat it for Christmas," suggested a third.

"The pig will never be eaten," said a fourth.

The non-existent pig would come to hover like an invisible spirit over the farm. Everyone knew that at some point, there would be a change. When the pig comes.

The Ant Colony
2016

E very fourth or fifth year, something irksome happened. The irksome thing was that Society demanded Ersmo's mother see a doctor, and have it confirmed that she was still sick and in need of a personal assistant, which was Aagny.

Another irksome thing was that they didn't want to think about what had really happened, that time when she disappeared. Ersmo and Aagny spoke of it in vague terms. But the rest believed they knew: that Ersmo's mother had been an abuser who needed and deserved to kick the bucket.

"Oh well, maybe we should give up on this," Aagny said at some point, when the latest letter arrived in the mailbox. "We'll just say she's dead."

The others thought this might make things even more difficult. If she was dead, where was the body? Surely someone would demand to see it. The Swedish authorities were so tediously meticulous that a statement of someone's death would certainly require an actual dead body!

Sara, however, was fired up by the problem.

"Don't worry," she said and thus, every now and then, a theatrical performance was staged, with a script the actors were not allowed to read in advance but had to invent on the spot, under the guidance of a pushy director.

The first time, Ersmo showed up at the doctor's without his mother.

"We didn't think she needed to be here," Ersmo said, hanging his head.

The doctor, who came from the big city, sympathized with the obviously dull-witted country boy, who trembled with what she assumed to be fear of authority, but was actually stage fright. Hearing his dialect, she interpreted it as the boy being entirely helpless and utterly incapable of deception.

"A phone call is fine," the doctor said kindly.

At home, Sara sat ready, and played her part so brilliantly that an award nomination would have been in order. She had very thoroughly inquired about the symptoms of the brain injury and was now screaming a long list of obscenities and swear words into the receiver.

Ersmo was sweating. The doctor was struck by a certain gratitude that her *own* mother wasn't this crazy and that she didn't have to live almost alone with her in a house outside a tiny village. Poor Ersmo, the doctor thought. And what a hero she must be, that personal assistant, Aagny, who proceeded to grasp the phone and sounded so terribly resourceful.

Soon, the doctor's rotation came to an end and she moved on, as planned, to a bigger city.

That was one of those times.

THE ANT COLONY
2017

Zakaria and Ersmo were gathering firewood. They went to the woods right next to the house, spent a long time choosing the tree to be harvested.

"Thank you," Zakaria said, kneeling by the tree that gave itself to them. He looked like a knight.

"Thank you," said Ersmo, a little more aloof.

When the tree had been felled, they started sawing it into pieces. Putting their bodies to work.

Zakaria had gone through this routine many times since coming to the Colony—the approach when the saw would meet the wood. But what was it, that was different, this time? Because now, he managed to saw into his own leg. Afterwards, he could hardly explain how it had happened. He was sawing in a rhythm, and must have slipped, causing the rhythm to break and the approach to go wrong. It bled. Blood everywhere. The saw, red. The fabric of his pants, red. His boot, red.

"Blood! Blooood!" Zakaria shouted.

"Damn it," said Ersmo. He called out to Aagny, who was sitting on the steps in the sun, deboning fish: "Aagny! Zakaria cut himself! We need to go to the hospital!"

Aagny rushed towards them. She, who never raised an eyebrow, veritably shook when she saw Zakaria's leg, and how the blood behaved, *gushing* out of him.

"He needs to go to the hospital," she said too.

Zakaria said nothing.

Ersmo and Aagny held Zakaria on either side, heading

towards the car. His body was heavy to begin with, but heavier now that it was limp. They only had yards to go, maybe twenty, but it seemed so far away.

They struggled, sweat streaming down their bodies, the blood attracting mosquitoes.

Right-foot. Left-foot.

This Aagny shouted, as they walked with Zakaria's body. Her voice excessively loud.

Right-foot. Left-foot. Right-foot. Left-foot.

"Would you stop that?" Ersmo said after a while. "Having to listen to something makes it worse."

Aagny kept quiet for a while, but eventually she couldn't hold it in.

Right-foot, she whispered. *Left-foot.*

Ersmo heard, but couldn't bring himself to say something again.

They reached the car, somehow managed to get Zakaria inside, laying him down in the back seat. Aagny saw a T-shirt in the car, tied it over the wound. They were just about to drive off when Sagne shouted from the house:

"What happened?"

"He sawed his leg," Aagny said. "The blood is *gushing.* We really need to go to the hospital."

Sagne turned pale.

"You can't go to the hospital," she said. "He can't say his name. He'll end up in prison! We might all be in trouble! Everything will fall apart!"

József had an expression on his face.

"We have to leave *now,*" Aagny said. "He's losing too much blood."

Sara got to the car. She sounded calm.

"So he sawed his leg," she said. "People have done that throughout history. We don't need to give ourselves up over it."

She pointed.

"Aagny, go inside and get water, and clean the wound. Ersmo, get the bandage, and the alcohol. It's in the cupboard to the left of the stove.'"

She knew this because, in the end—after the incident with József and the envelopes—they had invested in a proper first-aid kit.

They all helped now, struggling to get Zakaria out of the car again, putting him on a mattress from one of the outdoor couches. There he lay in the sun, grimacing.

Aagny brought the water, gave it to Sara.

"You clean it," Sara said. "You're better at it than I am."

Aagny whimpered, but believed this to be true.

"I'll sing to you," Aagny whispered to Zakaria. "I'll sing to you."

First, Ersmo gave Zakaria a swig of the liquor. Then they cut open his pants. And while Aagny poured water on the wound, a whole gallon of it, she sang, the first song that came to her mind, all the while the blood kept flowing and flowing and flowing.

I want to know what love is.

I want you to show me.

This she hummed, softly and off-key, continuing as Ersmo now poured liquor over the wound, continuing as Zakaria roared out over the valley, continuing as the bandage was applied, continuing as Zakaria was laid in his bed with his leg elevated, two painkillers and even more liquor down his throat.

Sagne looked at Sara.

She looked at Zakaria's leg.

It didn't feel right. She couldn't quite put her finger on it. But it didn't feel entirely right.

József caught her gaze.

He said:

"This is probably what Zakaria wanted. He can't say his name. He could have ended up in prison for life."

He tried to speak the sentence as if it ended with a period, but it sounded to both of them like a question mark.

Zakaria lay in bed for days. A special tape from the first-aid kit had been carefully placed over the wound, which was cleaned daily and healing well. It looked the way it should, they thought, and Zakaria gradually regained the spark in his eye.

"It looks good," said Sara.

They all felt relieved to hear that.

Every evening, Aagny sat by Zakaria's bed, reading to him, feeding him soup and bread. He didn't particularly enjoy reading, though. So she would recount the plot of various films to him.

"*Pretty Woman*. There's a man, played by Richard Gere, who is incredibly rich. And he's staying at this hotel. That's when he finds a prostitute, with a heart of gold—"

Somewhere around this point, Zakaria usually fell back asleep.

Sometimes he would pat her knee.

After that, it felt as if her knee had a burn, a Zakaria's-hand-shaped burn, a sacred spot on her body.

Zakaria had a history.

That's what his mother and sister used to call it: "Your history."

The history was that he attracted bad company. They wanted him to "come along". A guy in the apartment below, who he used to play football with, would sometimes say:

"Wanna come along?"

"Where are we going?" Zakaria would ask.

"Just downtown. Catch a film."

Zakaria would be thrilled. He loved going to the cinema.

But once downtown, the neighbor would meet up with someone, and sometimes a fight broke out. Occasionally with weapons involved.

Zakaria had three upsides, the neighbor thought. The first was that he was tall and big, and looked like he could hurt people. The second was that he practised martial arts, so he actually *could* hurt people. The third was his bright personality, that he was loyal by nature. If you needed him, he would be there. He cared for you.

He also had two downsides, the neighbor thought. The first was that the last positive trait unfortunately applied to everyone: he cared for them. He didn't want to hurt anyone.

The second was that he had a very poor sense of direction. It was frankly a bit embarrassing. Once, a Dane had tried to steal some weed from the neighbor, and took off around a corner.

"I'll take this side, you take the other," the neighbor had said, and they went around the building to surround the Dane.

Only, Zakaria got confused. The building had all these different protrusions. He lost sight of them. It was like a labyrinth. Which direction was it he had come from? So the neighbor ended up alone with the Dane, who started throwing rocks to keep him away. If Zakaria had been there, too, the Dane would have given up immediately, which was the neighbor's plan. But now he was alone with the Dane. Amidst the rocks raining down, the neighbor could hear Zakaria holler:

"Julle? I got fucking lost! Julle? Julle?"

A couple of times, they got caught by the police. Another friend might have told the truth, namely that Julle had tricked Zakaria, who just wanted to go see *Space Jam* at the cinema. But Zakaria wasn't like that. He didn't blame anyone. He assumed no one would blame him either. He assumed no one wanted to hurt him. Julle probably hadn't planned to buy drugs, he thought. It just happened.

Zakaria's sister was the type who got straight A's. She wanted to become a doctor. She wanted to make money to send home to their mother, who was on her knees.

Their father had left a long time ago. They would see each other occasionally, brief awkward moments when Zakaria passed him in the street with the other junkies. They looked alike. Tall. Broad.

Once, his father said so.

"When you're built like we are," he said, "you have to behave better than everyone else."

Then he wondered if Zakaria had any spare change. Maybe even a couple of hundred kronor.

Zakaria gave him the money he had in his pocket.

The next time he heard anything about his father was the following day, when they called from the hospital. His father had gone into cardiac arrest from an overdose. It wasn't hard to figure out where the money for the overdose had come from.

Z akaria had, even before the incident with the weasel, harbored a feeling that wherever he went, trouble followed.

It seemed logical to stay away. In the house, they wanted from him only what he could give. Being strong, and kind, and happy. He wanted to give them everything he could. And now, as he lay there in bed, his wound healing, they ran around him, doting and soothing, Aagny worst of all with her soups and pillow changes and retelling old films he had already seen.

She was only ten years older than him, yet she felt like a mother—a really nice, slightly odd mother. He felt such love, such tenderness for Aagny. He missed his mother and sister so much; he didn't dare contact them, but he thought about them, all the time. How good it was to have another, temporary, mother figure stepping in.

LÅKE
2018

L åke had learned to take care of himself. It was for the best. Aagny would help sometimes—patch up a wound, comb his hair—but otherwise, he managed on his own. He stayed close by, so he could have food. It didn't always feel like a given.

József had taught him to read and write. There was an abundance of books at Ersmo's; before his mother went bonkers, she used to read every day, mostly detective stories and racy romance novels. Låke read all the books by Jackie Collins, and so he imagined life on the Outside like a Jackie Collins novel: full of opulence, but also a little frightening.

Falling in love is like getting hit by a large truck and yet not being mortally wounded. Just sick to your stomach, high one minute, low the next. Starving hungry but unable to eat. Hot, cold, forever horny, full of hope and enthusiasm, with momentary depressions that wipe you out, Låke read aloud from the Jackie Collins book.

"Maybe you shouldn't be reading that," József said.

Aagny said that surely it didn't matter. Children would come into contact with the world whether you wanted them to or not. It's not like the reindeer told their children not to watch other animals fucking or fighting.

So Låke took the book with him into his bedroom. In another Jackie Collins book, he read:

Your whole life is ahead of you. Don't you ever forget that.

He never did.

My whole life is ahead of me.

When he wasn't reading, he followed the others around. Or he was down by the lake. Ersmo had taught him to swim long ago. There was something about the water. It was so dangerous yet so inviting. There was a line of rocks, hidden beneath the surface like a string of pearls. If you believed in yourself, you could walk on the rocks a long way out. He had noticed that you didn't need to think about the whole way—you just needed to think about one rock at a time. When you stood on a rock, you almost always spotted a new rock from there. In this way, he amused himself. Stepping into the lake in different places. Finding a rock. Looking for a new rock. Stepping onto it. Seeing how far it would take him. Then he would throw himself into the lake, clothes and all, swim back to the shore. He hurried then, so the others wouldn't have gone anywhere without him, so he wouldn't be alone without food.

EMELIE
(THE NOTEBOOK, AUGUST 2023)

L ife is so fucking weird.
One moment you are buying a suit, trying to look like Diane Keaton in *Annie Hall*, hoping that others will catch the reference. You imagine that people look at you, searching for your shortcomings. "She didn't wash her hair today." "She really knows nothing about Foucault." That's what you imagine they are thinking, because that's what you think about others. You struggle to cover up the holes, patch over your shortcomings. Nothing must show. I must be complete.

You try to approach people with high status. It's not something you talk about, but it's true. You are drawn to them like a magnet, moving around in their wake at the club, like they are holding a leash. *Now they've gone to the bar, now I'll go there, too.* You go where they go, because wherever they are it'll be fun. You worry about your boyfriend—if he is really social enough, good-looking enough, for you. If you are smart enough, good-looking enough, for him. Should I have a kid with him? Should I have kids at all? There is always room for a little improvement. You lie awake at night, wondering if you have made the right decisions, comparing yourself. *The newspaper reached out to her about a permanent position. He proposed to her after two weeks. No one has proposed to me after two weeks. Why am I not the kind of person someone proposes to after two weeks?*

That's how it is one moment.

The next moment, you aren't socializing with anyone at all, except a teenage outcast who doesn't know any social rules whatsoever. Everything you thought you knew about life falls away completely. Turns out nothing really matters.

Låke took me under his wing after our meeting in the trailer. Now he comes to my tent every day, eats my provisions. The chips, the chocolate. He has emptied my little pantry completely; I keep driving to buy more all the time. I'll offer him a bag of peanut puffs. *Want some?* A little is what I'm imagining. A handful. But he takes the bag, empties the whole thing. He reminds me of an animal. You put out a bowl of food. It's not like the cat is going to ask if it's okay to eat the whole bowl. You gave me food, so I'll eat it.

Do you live here?

No, I live in the city. I'm a journalist. I write things.

Books?

Books? No, I write . . . articles. Mostly I like writing about people. I've actually done several long features for a national paper recently . . . Are you yawning?

Yes.

The last thing I published was an interview with a scientist. She studies people in group settings, how easily we are influenced. We do what others do. We're constantly relating to other people.

Isn't that obvious?

Sometimes you need to put a name to something for people to understand how important it is to think about, though. For example, have you heard of the bystander effect?

What's that?

There was this woman who was raped and murdered outside a high-rise. While it happened, there were probably a hundred people watching. But no one did anything, and it was because they all thought someone else would intervene. There were too many of them.

Ugh. That sounds horrible.

(Pause.)

But, you also think so? That it's horrible?

Yes, of course.

How many wars are there right now?

Well, there are a few—
Is Sweden winning?
Huh? We're not fighting any war.
Are we not?

* * *

Where do you guys live?
Nearby.
But where do you sleep?
Different places. At Ersmo's. Under Big Spruce. Sometimes
elsewhere.
Big spruce?
(Silence.)
So, when does school start again?
Yeah, I have to go now.

EMELIE
(THE NOTEBOOK, AUGUST 2023)

It's slowly dawning on me that this is a child who 1) may never have gone to school and 2) seems to be living completely outside of society. This realization has awakened a sense of concern in me—unfortunately not primarily for Låke, but rather over my own involvement. Should I do something here? Am I responsible now? I really don't have the energy to be responsible.

Today he turned around and said: "You can't tell anyone that we see each other. Do you promise?"

I pretended not to hear.

"Do you promise?"

He seems happy when we are together, but when I watch the group from up on the hill, he still keeps a distance from them. It's not a healthy relationship they have, and I know it; I can feel it in my whole body.

I really don't have the energy to deal with this.

Last time we spoke, he was eating a Snickers bar, brown spit flying as he talked. By the end, he was completely soaked in chocolate. He doesn't know that it's unbecoming to make a mess. I took the opportunity to ask him some questions of my own. I tried to sound casual; I notice that he gets defensive. A few times, he has mentioned that he isn't really supposed to talk to strangers. I asked how old he is; he doesn't know.

Don't you hang out with any other young people?
Other young people? You mean my own age? What does it matter?

Well, I don't know, maybe you'd have the same interests or something.

I have to go now. See you tomorrow, right?

We'll see each other tomorrow, won't we? We will, right? You won't have left?

I lay awake for a long time. This is what I was thinking. I have three choices, I thought.

1. Stay here and do nothing.
2. Stay here and try to understand Låke. When I do. If I do. Then maybe I'll tell the authorities. (Which authorities? Social Services? The police?)
3. Leave here, so I don't have to think about it anymore. Plus, I'll be able to have coffee and use a regular toilet again.

Just as I was about to go with option three, it started raining. The rain brought a soft pattering against the tent canvas, and I fell asleep. When I woke up, the sun lay on the mountain and Låke was already sitting outside, his peculiar face open, eyes curious. He seemed to have been waiting for me for hours.

He looked like a child. He was a child.

I knew what I had to do. After he left, I walked back to my car, drove along the gravel road until I got signal, picked up my Nokia, and dialed.

Ersmo
August 2023

Ersmo was home alone. There was a knock on the door
There was almost never a knock on the door.
Standing there was a man, in his forties.

"Excuse me, are you Ersmo Larsson?"

"Could be," said Ersmo. "Who are you?"

"I'm from Northern Woods," said the man. He looked friendly. "I was in the area. The owners of some of the forest here have decided to hire us to harvest their trees. We are about to get to work, and it's very exciting, for all of us. We were wondering—I mean—do you happen to own any forest here as well?"

"Possibly," said Ersmo.

"I see," said the man. "We have looked into—I mean—if we assumed that you owned some forest," said the man. "Theoretically. Then I just wanted to say that Northern Woods would be interested in helping you manage it. It might also solve any potential financial issues?

"If we assumed that you owned some forest," the man said again. "And it was a certain size, for example, this size."

He showed a piece of paper where he had written down an acreage, which happened to be the exact acreage of Ersmo's forest.

"Then you could make, for example, this much money."

He showed another piece of paper.

Ersmo had never had any money of his own, not a single day of his life. It wasn't something he thought about. He managed, after all. But it was a reason for things. A reason he never went anywhere, for example.

Because really, he could. He wasn't evading society, unlike some of the others. And they wouldn't have stopped him. But if you don't have any money, you can't go anywhere. This knowledge had brought a certain comfort to Ersmo—that there was no reason for him to long for elsewhere, because he couldn't get there anyway.

But now. The amount. What it could mean.

Ersmo's mother had worked in the forest her whole life. All his relatives had worked in sawmills, floated timber. This was in his DNA. Logging the forest seemed natural and reasonable and surely wouldn't hurt anyone. That's what he used to think.

But lately, he had noticed things. He had noticed that the deep forest suddenly seemed to be running out. He used to think that the forest where they lived was like Sæhrímnir—one of the few things he remembered from school. The boar from Norse mythology was slaughtered every night, but always resurrected the next evening, ready for another slaughter; you could take as much as you wanted.

But lately, it was different. Most of the forest was now planted. It wasn't all that bad, Ersmo thought, except that it was uglier and felt like a fake forest.

"We're facing a climate crisis," said the man. "We need forests to manage, so they can be utilised. We'd plant new trees—"

"Would you remove the old forest and what, plant those ugly little pines?"

"Lodge-pole pine is the fastest-growing—"

The man paused.

"More and more of your neighbors in the surrounding villages have, upon careful consideration, decided to sell their harvesting rights to us at Northern Woods. Now also a family from your village here. They explored many options, and then they chose us. I'd be happy to tell you more."

He could see that Ersmo wasn't ready to make a decision today.

"Here's my card," he said. "Feel free to get in touch."

Ersmo took the business card. He closed the door and breathed.

He had two things to think about.

On the one hand: his own forest and the money.

On the other: something else.

He stumbled down to the lake. It was rare for Ersmo to speak, so when he did, everyone listened.

"Now this must be big," Aagny said gaily, as Ersmo came pelting down. But Ersmo didn't grin.

"A man came by and wanted . . . " Ersmo said, pausing here; he didn't want to tell the others he had received an offer. So he swallowed and continued. "He came because he said another neighbor was selling their harvesting rights. And there's only one other house here that still has forest to sell," said Ersmo. "It's Old Man Mikaelsson. He died last year, remember. He would never have sold it himself. When he had his strength, when I was a kid, he used to potter about in the forest every day. But his children and grandchildren must have inherited it—they don't live here, and they probably sold without thinking much of it."

The others looked at him questioningly, as if to say: What does that have to do with us?

"Big Spruce," said Ersmo.

"And the Big Spruce Forest."

"And all the forest around us here."

József gazed towards Big Spruce. Suddenly it looked so lonely, sad, unprotected. It looked like a child with no one to turn to, a child with no rights at all. It had been betrayed. And he realized that what he had wanted from Big Spruce—that she would be completely unaffected by everything around her, that she would simply serve as a haven, a mother—wasn't true. She needed them, too.

There was so much forest he used to think of as just regular forest. *Here I am, walking around in the regular forest.* But this regular forest had turned out to be tree plantations. And he had learned this by comparing it to a single area where everything looked completely different.

At first, this latter patch of forest had almost stressed József out. Here, everything looked . . . *disorderly*. There were deciduous trees and conifers and dead trees and new trees, sparsely spaced, but all in a jumble, unlike the other forest, which was neatly arranged.

This was where the reindeer liked to go, he had noticed, when they passed through here; they were after the lichen.

The reindeer have less and less space to roam, Sagne had told him. The areas with planted pine give them nothing. The lodge-pole pine plantations are impassable for them, and there is nothing to eat there.

In the middle of the disorderly patch stood Big Spruce and Little Spruce, along with all the other trees that had grown to mean something to József. It suddenly felt logical that this was where the members of the Colony were drawn. Perhaps they felt more at home in this forest, where no tree was perfect and every species mattered to one another.

The days of Big Spruce were numbered. It was all too big and vague to comprehend, leaving a soft, sorrowful taste in his mouth.

Today was Monday. I had just got dressed when the damned machine started making noise again. It was strange to witness. I had started feeling at home among these trees. Now they were falling, one by one.

For a second, it felt a bit sad. Then my thoughts turned to other things.

I made coffee and stared. It was a new ritual. I no longer wanted to listen to podcasts. In the beginning, I'd had trouble relaxing without some sound. Now, my body had completely surrendered to the silence, and I felt very irritated by the din.

From above, I saw the little woman who I assumed was Låke's mother approach the orange men. The others in the group were nowhere to be seen. I couldn't hear what she was saying, but she looked furious. After a while, it seemed like the orange men couldn't be bothered with her anymore, so they started making a racket again. She stood there shouting.

The noise made it impossible for the woman to be heard. Eventually, she stepped aside.

I heard a pawing at the tent canvas. It was Låke, of course.

"Coffee?" I said.

I have started making a fire and brewing coffee now. If they see me, so be it.

Låke would love some coffee. He also found a pack of cookies in the cool corner of the tent where I keep my food—the one that's always in the shade. He didn't ask for permission. I have noticed that he thanks the ground for every ant, but he has never thanked me for anything, despite gobbling up most of the food I buy.

We sat there in silence for a while. Then I asked a question I had long been wondering about. I had practised in the tent beforehand, so it would seem casual.

"What do you want to do in the future?"

It was a risky question, for I knew I was knocking on a door to something bigger now, something that would ruin the previously jolly atmosphere where we pretended to have the same opportunities in life.

He didn't understand the question. "Today?" he said.

"No, in the future. When you're grown up. Do you want to study, or travel, or . . ."

The question had sounded good in my head, but now that it was specified and spoken out loud, it felt strangely wrong. It was as if, in the same moment I said the words, I realized the unlikelihood of Låke suddenly showing up to study engineering at Linköping University, or travelling to London to work in a bar.

Låke looked as if he had never thought about it. Now he gazed at me with amusement, and spoke the following sentence, which I will forever remember:

"You can't think that far ahead, you'll go crazy!"

He giggled loudly now.

I barely understood the comment at the time, but I saved it in the back of my mind, and later, in the evening, I would take it out and realize its mind-boggling core: *he lived only in the now.*

To be able to think only about today. It was something people talked about, but always in clichés, as a utopia—a bit like world peace. After all, everyone knew that no one could truly live only in the now!

I closed my eyes and tried to guess what it would mean.

And at first, I thought it sounded dumb, cruel—that he hadn't been taught how society works today, that you have to

think ahead if you want to get somewhere; you have to save up money, have a budget, apply to university, get an apartment—
But then I realized that his context had made possible what had always seemed like a utopia to me:
living just for today.

A task I had been given by my therapist: to reflect on my own thinking. If I were to put it into a percentage, she asked. What percent of my thoughts were focused on
a) the future, things that would happen or could happen
b) the past, things that had already happened, and
c) the here and now.
I estimated my percentages as 90/10. Ninety percent on the future, and ten percent on the present. The part about the present mostly revolved around things like my back hurting, or if I was hungry, or drunk, or in love.
Never the past. When would I find time to think about things that had already happened?
Mostly just the future. You have to stay one step ahead.

I have read that before trains existed, most people had little need for clocks. It wasn't until you had a train to catch that there was a reason to have a way of keeping time that applied to the whole country. Before that, it was enough to rely on the seasons and the weather. *Now* is the time to pick potatoes. *Now* the raspberries are ripe.
That's all anyone needed.

Låke
(The legal pad, August 2023)

I've started visiting the woman in the tent often maybe 1 time a day sometimes 2. Her name is Emelie She is NOT one of us! She is an Outsider!!!

No one must know!!! But I hope she stays.

She asks a lot of questions, at first I thought it felt strange & like she wanted something with them, maybe she is from the government I thought & she wants us to go to war and pay 50% of everything we have to the state!!

But now I trust her. She just listens & listens, PLUS she brings food from the shop that we never have

I wonder if the others would like her . . .

I also get a bit Curious to hear about her world like what young people do there. Cause I've heard that everyone has phones and technology that Enslaves them.

But surely they must also go swimming sometimes, right???

Well, it just happened. I'm writing this with a trembling pen, still full of adrenaline. So little happens here that when something DOES happen, it becomes gigantic. Låke and I decided to go for a walk. It was evening and astonishingly beautiful. The logging machines seem to have left for a bit. "Let's take this path, the others never go this way," said Låke and I followed him, onto overgrown trails and then up a mountain without any trails at all; we had to zigzag between the trees and blueberries and lingonberries, our eyes glued to our feet to avoid tripping over roots. We found a pair of sunglasses on a tree stump.

"Berry pickers," said Låke. "They come here, but not in the evenings."

I had seen them, too, in their cars, bumping along the gravel roads, often Thai people, sometimes in truck beds with large buckets. I had read that they got paid twenty kronor per liter of blueberries, and often thought about that when I was out picking on my own, my clumsy fingers, how long it would take to earn a measly twenty kronor.

But now there were no berry pickers in sight, only the sunglasses and the mountain we were hiking up, still quite a few mosquitoes but by this point I hardly noticed them at all. I followed Låke; he kept chattering, sometimes stopping and looking back at me with a worried expression, as though wondering if I was still there. It was a gesture that always pained me to see.

The same thing when he talked—like an eagerness to say as much as he could while he still had my attention, as if at any moment it might switch off. When he talked about those named Aagny, Ersmo, and József, he sounded like a normal person, which led me to assume these were the people in the group who treated him well. He spoke of Aagny almost like a mother, and I found myself liking her through his stories. But the one named Sagne, who seemed to be his real mother, sounded like a proper asshole, and I wondered about the story there, but I didn't dare ask, not yet. Once he referred to her as "Mum—well, she doesn't want me to call her that," and this physically hurt to hear. He spoke of both Sagne and the one named Sara in a subservient manner. I had dated a dedicated soccer fan for a while, and it struck me that Låke's gaze when he talked about Sara or Sagne was the same as when the soccer supporter once saw Jimmy Durmaz at the supermarket.

But here and now, Låke prattled on about this and that; like a strange mix between a child and an adult, he spoke, jumping conversationally between a hole he had dug and filled with water and made a channel down to the lake, and his stress over the roof needing to be fixed. I started to feel dizzy.

We reached the top of the mountain and stood there, gazing out at the vast magnificence, saw my tent and the water and even the spruce tree they sleep under, and I rested my head against Låke's. I wanted so badly for him to know that he was, perhaps not liked—more that he was *a person*. And he leaned his head against mine, and it struck me that we might look like friends.

And there we stood, heads leaning against each other,
and below us, coming from the left, the one named Sara suddenly appeared, and she saw us where we stood.

Initially, I felt a pang of fear; it felt as if I had done something illegal, and Låke veritably shook. But Sara came closer. I had imagined that she would be mean, maybe insane; based on Låke's talk, it had sounded like many of the group's stranger initiatives came from her. But now, as we stood there, eye to eye, she just looked sympathetic. She had a gaze that was both calm and curious but also somewhat *humorous*.

"Well, hello!" she said. (Surprised, cheerful.)

"Hi," I said. (Quietly, as though subdued.)

Låke said nothing now; he had turned into a stone. I remember using the same tactic as a child, when I was ashamed of something I had done. I froze, standing completely still.

"We've been wondering where Låke has been keeping lately," said Sara.

"Yeah, we've run into each other a few times now," I said. I didn't dare say anything that might imply we actively sought each other out.

"I'm shocked," said the one named Sara. "It's so rare to run into someone here!"

And then she broke into a belly laugh that was utterly disarming. You couldn't help but laugh along. And I did now, and after a while so did Låke. It immediately lifted my spirits.

Unfortunately, I tend to talk a lot when I'm nervous, and that's what I did now, telling her way too much—about my burnout and the tent and the calm I felt in the forest. But this time, it seemed to land well, for my rambling soothed both Låke and Sara.

"I can relate to that," she said. "Låke might have told you we're a group of friends living somewhat unconventionally. We sleep out in nature sometimes, precisely to find peace in our souls."

She was alluding to what I had said about burnout. It suddenly felt like we were similar, and I had to mentally remind myself that they were a group of lunatics who went around kissing the ground and thanking fish.

We talked for a while longer, and she looked me up and down.

"I have a good feeling about you," she suddenly said.

We had only been speaking for a few minutes.

Låke looked at Sara. He had a pleading expression. She looked at him and at me. Then back at Låke.

"I don't know what Låke has told you about us," she said, almost apologetically. "It might sound a bit strange."

"He hasn't said anything at all," I offered eagerly. I wanted to let Låke know that I was on his side, that I wouldn't disclose anything.

But she looked hesitant, as if she still thought he had said some things. Which he had, of course.

She looked at me, took a step back, like she wanted to see my whole body. The silence and her searching gaze made me nervous. But finally, she spoke:

"I feel that I would like to invite you to our place. We don't meet many new people. It's a bit sensitive, for various reasons. Nothing weird, of course. But we live somewhat alternatively. Many people don't understand us, they aren't . . . open."

She looked at me, and suddenly I felt that she assumed I was an open soul, and in the same breath I also felt that I definitely was—very open. I had many queer friends! An acquaintance who was polyamorous! Alternative ways of living were not new to me!

"You can trust me," I said. "I won't tell anyone. And I won't judge."

I shrugged my shoulders.

"I have no one to tell anyway."

I said all this because I wanted to reassure her, that Låke's associating with me wouldn't harm them in any way. But now, gradually, I also began to realize what she had actually said: that she wanted to invite me to their home.

Was I ready for this? I had indeed longed to actually speak to them, observe them up close, but now that I stood face to face with the opportunity, my head started scanning for dangers.

They might be a cult, said my head.

What if they are cannibals? They might eat you. Or drag you into some perverse sex game. Sacrifice you on a pyre. I composed myself. I looked at Låke, and his expectant gaze. I understood that he wanted to show me off to the others. And in the end, I was both bored and curious, so finally I said: "I'd love to come."

I shrugged my shoulders and chuckled a little—a laugh that Sara received and topped with her own guffaw, which once again was terribly contagious, and Låke joined in.

So there we stood, giggling, as the sun set behind us. "It's not a very good time right now," said Sara. "But tomorrow evening? Låke can show you the way. If the weather is nice, we'll probably be down by the water."

I nodded silently, and soon they were both on their way, bounding down the mountain as if it were a pedestrian street. I, on the other hand, spent at least an hour bushwacking down through the darkness and back to my tent, with my heart pounding, pounding, pounding.

* * *

I'm writing this at night. I have just returned from my meeting with the group. I'm jotting down what happened immediately, so I won't forget. The burnout means my memory is not what it used to be.

Låke came to get me. We went down to the water and followed it. I notice that my fitness is starting to improve; I could almost keep up with his pace.

For some reason, it felt like he was dressed up, even though he wore exactly the same clothes and hairstyle as usual. He looked jittery, running among the trees with his long, spindly legs.

"Where are we going?" I wondered, as I hadn't quite understood yet.

"Big Spruce," he said, as if it was obvious.

I imagined Big Spruce to be some kind of treehouse or maybe even a wind shelter, but it turned out to be nothing other than the big spruce tree where I had seen them gather. An unusually majestic spruce, I must admit, heavy and wide, with impressive branches. Spread beneath the tree were blankets and mats, and I understood this was often where they slept.

Big Spruce stands near the lake—so that's where the group seeks refuge when they suddenly disappear out of sight!—and down by the water they had made their usual fire. When we arrived, they sat in a circle around the flames, singing. It sounded surprisingly good, I thought from up close, multiple harmonies and everything, some singing, others humming. The smoke hung heavy over the evening's softness, and together they created an almost magical impression.

When I arrived, several of them jumped a little—even though they must have known I was coming. I had assumed we wouldn't shake hands, but the one named József immediately got up and extended his, and so we continued like that; I shook hands like it was an all-day conference. A bodily memory: *this is what my life used to be, shaking hands.*

Låke giggled nervously, as if an exotic dance was being performed.

Since I can't handle silence in a group, I started talking about the orange men.

"Whose land is this really?" I chattered.

"The land belongs to itself," said Sara.

"But someone must own it?"

Now everyone laughed. Låke laughed so hard he nearly fell backwards.

"This is one reason why you Outsiders are so bonkers!" he giggled. "You think you can own a tree, or a river! But the tree always belongs to itself!"

I felt like a circus animal showing up and saying silly things.

But the one named Ersmo, a man my age, looked at me calmly, and said there used to be an old man who owned the forest, but he had died, so the land was being sold.

He added:

"My mother used to work in the forest when I was little. Back then, it felt like scooping from an overflowing bowl. Now it's like the spoon is scraping the bottom."

He said this quietly, more directed at himself than anyone else. I didn't really have anything to say about the forest, but even I could see that Big Spruce was a truly remarkable tree. Perhaps the biggest I had seen up here. It looked almost kind. I must confess that I experienced the tree like the equivalent of a person with warm eyes.

A little about how they behaved in relation to my presence:

1. At first, when I arrived, they seemed excited, and a bit scared.

2. Then they looked hesitant.

3. Then Sara explained that I had sworn not to tell anyone about their existence, and they relaxed again.

As mentioned, I tend to talk even more than usual when I'm nervous. Even though I was sitting there with a completely unique group of people and should have been listening, I was the one who started blabbing. I talked about the city and my burnout, about fluorescent lights and apps. They just listened.

"It's hard," said Sara.

She said it with such empathy in her voice that I almost started crying. Now I felt it too. It *was* hard. It really was!

She continued:

"Those of us here are people who, for various reasons, don't appreciate modern life. We stepped away from it."

"Do you read the news?" I asked.

"Never," she said.

"Do you have a television?"

"No, not anymore," she replied.

"Radio?"

"No."

"Do you work?"

"No."

"But how do you survive, then?"

"We take it day by day," she said. "We complement each other. We don't believe that anyone has to be good at everything. But together, we can handle most things."

Låke's mother was there too, the short woman with glasses. I was prepared to dislike her, but face to face she barely made any impression on me at all. She looked out over the lake, while the others were all leaning in, like I was the most interesting thing to happen since the invention of the wheel.

The one named Ersmo looked shy; he sat in a corner and didn't say much after his interjection about the land being sold. But I had noticed he was usually the one who caught the fish and birds they ate. He would go around fixing things, and it was the same now. He replenished the fire with more logs.

My eyes often fell on the tall, handsome man with the smile. He looked out of place in this setting, like someone had left a diamond in a rubbish heap.

At first, it felt strange, to sit by this little lake with this group of people, but the more the night progressed, the more I got used to it. When they started singing again, two of them fell asleep: Låke and the one named Aagny. Låke on the ground, Aagny sitting. For a while, everyone was silent, and it struck me that I no longer felt the need to fill the silence with words. It had been a long time since I had felt so relaxed. I discovered that maybe I had been wrong in thinking that I needed solitude to feel calm. Instead, I realized, other people were the necessary condition for my body to truly unwind. But it couldn't be just any people; they had to be like these—people I had no actual need to be liked by. They seemed peculiar, like failures. I didn't need to seem normal in front of them.

I felt a sense of peace.

As it got colder, they leaned closer to the fire, and pressed their bodies together. Sara put her arm around me, and for a brief moment we all held each other in a circle. For two seconds, it felt unpleasant; I wasn't used to it, it was like we had jumped ahead too quickly. But very soon: something else. I felt the warmth from the others, oxytocin surging in my body. It was unforced; occasionally, someone would get up to go piss or drink water, and the one named Sagne soon chose to remove the arms around her. But the rest of us sat there, silent, our bodies pressed against each other. I felt my eyes start to twitch in a familiar way. I was relaxed, and so I started crying. That's how it was for me nowadays. I couldn't hold back the tears; it was futile. And now they were streaming down my cheeks, but as I looked around the circle I noticed that Sara pressed her arm against me just a little harder, as if to show that what I was experiencing right now was okay. Crying wasn't a big deal—and to the extent that it was, it was fine. And as I met József's gaze, I saw that he had tears in his eye, too, as if he were feeling my emotions through himself.

And I continued crying, continued until my body felt completely cleansed, and for a while longer we sat like that, in silence.

They said I was welcome to come back another day.

"Tomorrow, we're headed to the house," Sara said. "It's time to pick the potatoes. You're welcome to come and have dinner with us. If you're up to it."

The last part made me teary-eyed. *If I'm up to it.* That the thought was even allowed to exist. That it wasn't assumed I would be.

A long time ago, I studied photography at an adult education center. Back then, I came up with a theory I called the *desert island principle regarding romantic selection.* According to the desert island principle, humans above all crave love, or sex, and will find ways to make this happen regardless of the circumstances. This means that most of us change our perception of what is attractive based on the available options. If you were stranded on a desert island with only one man, you would be damned if you didn't start finding him looking decent after a while.

At the education center, there were about 120 students. At one point, we had forty-five couples. Outwardly, the couples had very peculiar compositions. I witnessed with my own eyes how a skinny communist from the north and a conservative blogger from a posh suburb found themselves falling in love— if not head over heels, then at least a little.

I remember the feeling when I came back to the city and introduced my new boyfriend—a short and compact computer programmer with an interest in World War II—to my feminist cultural circle. My new boyfriend had no training in how to communicate with this group at all. He cracked jokes about older women's vaginas. I saw my friends exchanging glances as we sat there, and I noticed I was moving further and further away from him. When we met his handball team, he moved further away from me. At the center, we felt like one, because we both thought that mac and cheese was tastier than regular boiled pasta, and that "Rhythm Is a Dancer" by Snap was an underrated song.

I know I should have focused on the handsome guy, the one named Zakaria. But that's not what happened.

I looked at Ersmo deboning the fish, how delicately he did it. His powerful, broad hands.

I looked at Ersmo who looked at me.

Zakaria and Låke also looked at me.

Aagny looked jealous.

Here, out in the mountains, fatter than ever, with dirty clothes and hormonal acne blossoming around my entire mouth area, I would reach peak popularity.

As I walked back to the tent, I heard myself laugh straight into the air. So uplifted by everything I had seen and felt.

Aagny's back complained more and more often. This annoyed her copiously. The joints in her body were bone stiff. Anything could cause pain—sitting for a few minutes in the wrong position, wearing rubber boots, chopping wood, sleeping on the wrong mattress, most certainly sleeping under Big Spruce. She also woke up at night in a sweat. Often, she couldn't fall back asleep.

She had heart palpitations, noticed that she started feeling intensely bad for short periods, like *bouts*. And she often felt angry, so terribly angry, snapping in every direction.

All of this transpired at the same time as she had started to realize that her period was becoming less and less frequent. Now, it hadn't come for, Aagny didn't know exactly, but maybe three months?

Aagny had read a women's magazine or two in her days. She wasn't stupid. She knew what was happening.

Entering menopause hadn't sounded so bad in itself. It was just something that happened to people.

But suddenly it had begun to dawn on Aagny what menopause meant.

It meant there would never be a child growing inside Aagny.

It meant that, presumably, there would continue to be no army of eager suitors fighting to be with Aagny.

It had been a long time since she had stopped going to dances—she'd stopped when Zakaria came—but the possibility had still lingered in the back of Aagny's mind, that if Zakaria didn't suddenly start taking an interest in her, she *could* still go into town, meet someone. Fall in love and maybe get pregnant.

When I think about it, Aagny said to herself while out on her usual morning walk, *I have given my life to the Colony.*

She took a few steps.

And it was totally worth it, she quickly added.

She dreamed about the bear again. It stood in the middle of the forest. A bald patch around its eye, just like in her previous dream.

Come, the female pointed. *Come here.*

I have something to tell you.

You have to find me, Sara. I need to tell you.

God, this anxiety. This immense, debilitating anxiety. I will admit that what happened yesterday could have been prevented, and it's all my fault.

How do I know? Because of my drunk personality. It's really not good. I know that.

Everyone has three personalities, minimum. One in real life. One on the internet. And one when you are drunk.

If I were to rank mine, my internet personality is the best. Objective, concrete. Quite funny! Scathing—but not too much. It's probably a matter of having time to read what I have written before posting.

My real-life personality comes in at a respectable second. I talk too much; I'm chatty by nature, insecure. But I mean well, and I often manage to suppress my worst tendencies.

Now to my drunk personality. It's terrible. Unfortunately, I become a truth-teller. I know this about myself. And I'm not talking about some universal truth, but rather purely personal opinions I have about people. Here, for some reason, I often feel the need to air these opinions out loud. My drunk personality is like a contestant on a reality show screaming, "I'm the type of person who speaks her mind," and then crying in secret because no one likes her.

I should thus have been more careful when Aagny first brought out the potato moonshine. What's more, the bottle was very large. I wondered if it had been a given for them, with their spartan lifestyle, to make moonshine of all things, but I didn't ask. I was happy to have a drink. It felt like it had been ages, and I was also a bit nervous.

So, I was going to the house where they lived. I had brought all the essentials in my backpack: my notebook, pen, Nokia phone, wallet, and car keys. Everything else was dispensable.

First, I took a detour with the car. It's a trick from my days in journalism. You want to anchor yourself in the geographical context, not just plop down at someone's coffee table. I drove around on the back roads for a long time, through little villages that had once flourished, now with only four or five inhabitants. Every other house cherished, every other abandoned. Closeddown shops and gas stations. Schools and chapels.

Eventually, I arrived at my grandma's village again. I drove a bit further, and here was a big, solitary house. Its wooden façade faced the road. The house looked friendly but needed a fresh coat of paint. It was surrounded by bushes, trees, and a fence, perched on top of a hill. The backyard lay below, impossible to see from the road, but when I parked next to it, I caught a glimpse of several small houses there, built almost like boxes. There was also a firepit. Below: slope, forest, and bog all blending together. I realized that, from here, you could walk straight down the path that eventually led to the water, without passing the road.

It was a house no one drove past. It was strange to realize how possible it all was. To disappear. I started wondering how many might have done the same as these people, letting themselves be swallowed up by the ground, vanishing completely without really hiding.

I remember my grandmother once saying: those who live up here depend on their neighbors. You need to be on a good footing with them, build friendships, look after each other. Because if you lived here without any friends and fell ill or something,

no one would happen to find you. You had to make sure someone would knock on your door every once in a while and ask
how things were going.

That's what I thought.

Perhaps it was actually the same in the city, I pondered further.

I wondered who I had, really. Who would check to see how
things were going.

I thought maybe it wasn't so much about the place as your
attitude. That people needed each other. It was like a penny
dropped; I could almost hear the clink.

I continued to think, as I sat in the car mustering up the
courage to get out. There was a way of thinking in the cities
that assumed all people wanted to be there—in the city—and
live according to the city's laws, and anyone who didn't lacked
a certain determination. Do you have what it takes to end up
in a big city? To be someone? That's how we think in the cities.

I reflected in the car that perhaps these were, rather, completely separate ways of living, sometimes so different they
couldn't be compared. And then there was Låke and the others'
way of existing beyond all this, a third way of living one's life.

I noticed I could no longer rank the different ways, and I had
an aha moment about myself: who is truly the loneliest, someone who lives far out in the middle of nowhere but is lumped
together with people, or someone who interacts with hundreds
of people every day but refuses to let anyone under their skin.

I looked down at myself, suddenly aware that I wore almost
the same clothes every day, changing my shirt only when I had
rinsed the other one in the lake. Today, I wore my dress, singu-
lar. Any clothes that were even slightly uncomfortable, I didn't
wear at all now. I had developed a certain body odor. It didn't
bother me. I remembered how I had previously been a person
who showered every day, using deodorant that I bought from

small boutiques, labeled with the names of the same herbs and flowers I now woke up among.

I was once again struck by a longing for the city. In many ways it was an easy life—a life where you got to meet people with social skills, who smelled good, who you could walk away from if they bothered you. You could eat whatever you wanted. You could find friends who wanted to talk about exactly the same things as you, who were the same age as you, with the same background.

Here, I had forced myself on a group that, just six months ago, I would have no doubt distanced myself from had I accidentally ended up sitting next to them in a bar.

I opened the car door, stepped out, and walked into the yard. It was even bigger than I had thought. A large potato field extended down towards the water and was surrounded by lettuce, strawberries, raspberries, zucchinis, sugar snaps, beans, dill, some kind of cabbage.

Chickens ran around freely. That part felt unsanitary. They have such scabby-looking feet.

The houses were red, simple. One big, one smaller. Several tiny ones. It bothered me that the paint had chipped on the big house, exposing the wood in lots of places.

Here came Låke. He had washed, I could tell; his hair was clean and thick, his bangs curly and defiant. I'm ashamed to admit that every time I saw him, I dreamed of giving him a makeover, bringing a jar of hair wax and showing how good that boy could look. My fingers itched. Every time we met, I thought of him like a thrift store find—*how nice this would look with a little care and color.* The thought sometimes crossed my mind to post about him on social media, to share what I had seen here, what I had experienced. That would be something. Ingunn at the newspaper was always boasting about letting some Roma family live for free in her garden cottage. Every time she went over there to donate some old puzzle, it had to go on Instagram. *I've found a whole cult here, Ingunn, and a beautiful boy who has never had wax in his hair.* I could write an article. Every day, the headline was rephrased in my mind: "Cult Living Outside Society: Leader Speaks Out'. The clicks would never end. They would give me a permanent position.

It's just a shame that as soon as my thoughts even touched on my place of work, or writing an article and receiving comments on it, my nervous system started firing on all cylinders again. I was genuinely *afraid* of the thought of working, as though a phobia had developed. That simply being there would be harmful to me.

Låke came rushing towards me, but it was like he stopped himself. He always did that. It was as if he instinctively wanted a hug, but there was a force field between him and other people that always kept him six feet away. He stood there scratching his downy cheek, unable to hide his gleeful smile. It struck me that maybe my Instagram instinct was universal—maybe it had nothing to do with social media at all: I could sense that he also wanted to show me off. I was his thrift store find, too.

Oh, Låke! What's happened to you? Why aren't you loved? From several feet away, I can sense how badly you want to be loved. I have spent fifteen years in the media industry; I can sense this with my eyes blindfolded.

Låke pointed towards the door of the main house. Just as I began to walk towards it, the door opened and Sara appeared. She floated down the steps in a simple navy-blue dress with leggings underneath and approached me, looking at me with a curious gaze. She held both of my hands.

"Can we trust you today?" was the first thing she said. When I write this down, it sounds completely ludicrous, maybe even threatening, but it didn't feel that way; it was more like an endearment—I was being let in, given access to something most people never got close to. I nodded, and she looked me square in the eye, striking me as both motherly and intriguing at the same time, two things I usually think of as polar opposites. She made no small talk; instead, she immediately began to speak about the chickens.

"We used to have two roosters here," she said. "Do you know about roosters?"

I shook my head. I knew nothing about roosters.

"They shouldn't be cuddled," she said. "It makes them mean when they're fully grown."

Everything she said sounded epic, wherefore I wondered if there was some deeper, vaguely feminist meaning behind it— but I actually think it was just information about roosters.

"The roosters conspired together," she said. "One was an alpha male, you could tell from a mile away. The other we thought might be a dreamer, but it turned out they were working together to rape the hens."

Then she said:

"We killed them both."

I won't go into detail; then I wouldn't be able to write it all down. But the others came, we sat down around the fire. I was served some kind of concoction of fried potatoes, beans, and carrots, which was unexpectedly delicious.

We had some shots. The moonshine trickled down my throat in a familiar way, and I remembered the last time I'd had alcohol, at a bar where someone was celebrating their birthday and serving vodka cranberry in special glasses.

I sat next to Ersmo. His leg was very close to mine. Every time I addressed someone sitting on his side, I took the opportunity to observe him in profile. Physically, he isn't all that attractive, not at all my type. His hair looks like it has never been combed; he has a round face and a rough-hewn body, patchy beard, and—despite living under a spruce—he has a way of nervously brushing his hair out of his face all the time, like he is being watched. It feels like a tic.

He is always doing something. He creates opportunities for the others. He puts food on the table. Before they even sit down, Ersmo has already made preparations, silently. I had watched him do it from a distance for a couple of weeks—watched him fish, shoot down birds, make fires—and now that I sat here next to him, it was even clearer. He doesn't talk much. But he keeps a constant eye on the group's survival. I compared him to Roy, whose every effort has to be dwelled upon and shared on Instagram. *Check out this campaign I created. Check out this award I received. Check out this compliment I got. Oh nothing, just a picture of me and a chair I painted #humblebrag. The salmon I sous vided turned out great.*

Now Aagny filled our glasses again, and Ersmo's chest rose and fell where it sat next to mine. He smelled of fire and fish.

They invited me to sing. Before the potato moonshine entered the picture, I probably would have backed away at such a request, but drunk me—with Ersmo's leg against mine—thought it was a great idea. I don't have much of a singing voice, but it sounded beautiful when we all sang together. Especially Låke, I noticed. And he sang from his toes where he sat, so that everyone would hear his powerful voice booming out over the hills. It vibrated, like a tenor.

I saw them all sitting there, their faces warmed by the fire. They seemed so calm, so close to each other, so soft in their bodies. The way they held each other every now and then, like it was natural. The way one of them would occasionally fall silent, walk away, come back, as if it were completely normal. Sometimes Sara would get up, lie down a bit further away, and breathe, looking up at the sky. The one named József would walk over to her, hold her for a while, help her breathe. Then they both returned. I realized that what I had just witnessed might be a panic attack, but in a setting where this was so normal that it seemed like blowing your nose, or putting on a plaster. I noticed that I leaned in, wanting to show with my body that I was *a part of*.

Aagny did most of the talking. She was a remarkable woman, full of stories she told as if with her whole body, getting up and demonstrating, *And then my old man said: Go to bed or I'll smack ya!* Followed by a belly laugh. Just like everyone else in the world, she seemed to view her life story as universal and relatable—something that didn't require further explanation. It didn't seem to occur to her that for someone like me, child abuse and prison time were things that raised eyebrows.

I wonder what she has been in the clink for.

The one named József came across as friendly and interested. I immediately found myself having two instincts towards him. One: to comfort him. The other: that he would comfort me.

And then there was Sara. Even though she didn't really say much, she was the one who laid down the law. I could see the others reading her reaction to things. Aagny's stories only became funny in Sara's ears, when Sara's laughter spilled out of her body. She intrigued me, and after a while I realised that I listened the most to Sara, that my body was following Sara's movements.

The more moonshine I imbibed, the more it felt right to confess that I had been observing them from a distance for several weeks. I said it casually at first: "I might have seen you on some occasion . . . "

After another drink, I said:

"You seem to have such a good time together. That's what I've thought when I've seen you."

A little later:

"I've seen you kiss the ground, could that be right? Why do you do that?"

"You always say *thank you* when you've shot an animal, why is that?"

And even later:

"But how did you END UP here?"

The others were drunk, too, all except the one named Sagne—and Låke, of course. Perhaps they appreciated having someone who saw them and was curious about the life they led. Maybe that's why they answered most of my questions. But they also asked some of their own, open-ended questions about life in the city. When I responded with something positive, they nodded faintly; when I said something negative, about the pressures and the stress, they shook their heads empathetically, *it's madness*. At first, it didn't bother me, but as the evening wore on it came to annoy me, that they—with their twisted way of life—actually thought they were right.

But back to the last question I had asked. The one that led to everything. Namely, how they had ended up here.

It was Sara who spoke. She answered simply:

"We're all people who have struggled to feel that anywhere else is okay. Here, we've created a life according to our own rules."

She continued. I'm writing here as best I can remember.

"As human beings, we make so many small choices every day that we forget we also have the ability to make big choices. We don't have to live where everyone else lives. We don't have to live like everyone else lives. We can sit down and ask ourselves: what do I truly believe in? And then you try to live that way, with people you actually want to live with."

The others nodded, with varying degrees of intensity.

I said:

"But what's it like living so close to each other? I have to admit, I've had a hard time living with just one person, or two."

My drunk personality added:

"You always end up hurting someone, or they hurt you. Usually both."

"I'—I noticed here that Sara used the word *I*, not we—"have felt that we can draw inspiration from the animal kingdom. Maybe we don't need to be on top of each other all the time. Maybe we can move like a herd of animals, drawing strength from other people, but not asking too much."

The one named József has a wide-open face, you can read him like a book, and here I saw him swallow. I wondered why.

Another swig, and my drunk personality now began to feel that the conversation was open and flowing—that there was room for some teasing and provocation.

"But," I therefore slurred, "I have to admit. I still struggle a little to . . . fully understand. What's so bloody great about it? You don't see anyone?"

I don't remember it all, for the potato moonshine had now seeped into every pore of my being. But I remember that they all seemed taken aback, and that Sara looked me in the eye and said something like:

"We also do it because we're ashamed of how most humans live. They've put themselves above all other living things."

"Yeah, sure," I continued, and held out my cup towards Aagny for a refill. They looked funny behind the flames; I giggled a little, tilting my head to one side, then the other. The smoke made it look as though Låke was wearing a hat!

"Let's face it," I said. "I'm sure it's nice and all, but there's no logic to what you're doing! You sleep under a spruce tree, but then you're suddenly living in houses. And what about the young ones? You older people sleep with each other all the time! What about Låke? Shouldn't he have the chance to find someone to sleep with?"

Here, I didn't stop to consider it might be perceived as intrusive to mention that I had seen them engaging in sexual intercourse. I remember putting my hand over my mouth, as if whispering a secret, and saying:

"Personally, I was *terribly* horny as a teenager."

I continued:

"And what's up with the way you hardly talk? I've seen you walking around. You don't say a word! You pretend you don't need to talk or experience new things, but here I am, a burnt-out city dweller who can't do anything, and you pounce on me like a . . . a chocolate praline! You're completely starved for company! COMPLETELY!"

I probably laughed out loud here, as I recall.

"And this one!"

I pointed at Låke.

"You think you're all so kind, but this poor guy has to walk several yards behind you, for some reason no one talks about."

Låke looked dumbfounded; now, when I think about it, I realize unfortunately his facial expression could better be described as *bulldozed*.

"Get out there," I bellowed, like an American president at a campaign rally. "Get out and see other people, go to restaurants, fall in love, sleep around, eat processed food, talk to other people. Play football, have a glass of cava instead of this—"

I raised my glass of moonshine.

"You've probably forgotten how good it tastes," I added. "A cold pint of BEER."

(Here, I'm afraid it's possible that I sang a short excerpt from a well-known comedy sketch.)

"Let Låke hang out with other teenagers. Leave the birds alone. Stop kneeling in front of anthills. They're INSECTS. Let them be. Live your lives."

I laughed, for I thought we were having a free-spirited, open conversation.

"The city," I said. "Granted, it's full of annoying people. But at least it's full of people. And life. And encounters. And things that happen."

Drunk me had missed that what I was doing was joking

freely and openly about the life they led, and what they lacked. It therefore came as a surprise when Sara suddenly stood up. I fell silent.

Like a dragon, she seemed, Sara, where she stood by the flames, the dress she wore cascading down her body, the bright summer night gentle against her face. She didn't look angry, more mildly amused, like a parent turning to a child.

"What you're forgetting," she said, poking around in the fire with a stick, "is that 'ordinary' life"—she emphasized the word by making air quotes—"isn't the least bit logical either."

"Why do you eat with a knife and fork, instead of your hands?

"Why don't you talk to people on the bus or metro? Why do you pretend they don't exist?

"Why do you celebrate Christmas if you don't believe in Jesus? Why have we collectively decided that Grandpa should dress up in red clothes and a hat and come knocking on our door once a year?

"Why don't we dance in Sweden, except in certain places, at night, when we've been drinking?

"Why do we speak when we could sing?

"Why do we act as if our minds are completely separate from our bodies?

"Why must we walk around pretending all the time—pretending to be normal, removing the parts of ourselves that stand out?"

And finally, she said this so quietly that you had to strain to listen, which we all did:

"Why do you work yourselves to death to earn money so you can become rich and have leisure time?"

She sat back down, but continued speaking.

"We're human beings," she said. "That applies to both us here and you over there. We carry on with our lives. We take the things we find rewarding, and continue with that. It could be Santa Claus, or being silent. We carry on with our little lives, whoever we are. There's no logic to it. We have no clue. We reach our hands up in the air and when something flies by that feels right we grab on to it. That's what humans do. "You can kill a deer—but if you kill a person, you'll go to prison. It feels right, but is it actually *logical*? No. Even in war, people die'—she looked at József—"and we establish rules, laws for how killing should happen. You can kill if you want, but only if you kill *these lives*, in *this way*. It's the same for us here, for you in Stockholm, or for the UN."

As mentioned, I was drunk, but I had started to find what Sara was saying to sound quite accurate. Humans do some very strange things. The Midsummer pole always struck me as the most peculiar. Thanking a blueberry wasn't so dumb when comparing these two things.

"I think you've forgotten," I said nonetheless, in some kind of attempt to regain my dignity. "That humans ARE stupid. No, there's no logic to us. But we need to be among others. We need that stupid life. Because we need something to look forward to. A trip. A nice dinner. The possibility of sex. That some-one might see us and like what they see. If we don't have that possibility—that something new could happen, that someday something might happen that we didn't expect. Well, then we might as well be dead."

That last sentence sounded harsher than I had intended. And now it was the one named Aagny who stood up. She looked furious, almost savage. It all happened so quickly when she walked up to me and shoved me, in the chest with both hands; I flew backwards, my body staggering, had to lean for-ward to regain my balance, fell awkwardly, on my knees.

"Shut UP!" she screamed. "Shut UP, shut UP, shut UP!"

Her eyes filled with rage.

Låke stared. Zakaria got up and grabbed Aagny. The move-ment felt strangely habitual, as did his voice, when he said:

"Calm down a little."

He pulled her away from me gently.

Where I lay on the ground, I had noticed the alcohol content in my body, and so I had started to see myself from the outside. I tried to get up, did a little stumble, fell again. "Oopsie daisy," I said here, adding a little laugh.

I think I expected a laugh in return, from someone—a sound that would confirm that my stumbling wasn't embarrassing but human—but it didn't come; there was total silence. I looked at the group, who all looked at Sara, and when I gazed towards her I noticed that her face was raised, her chin high, jaw clenched, eyes half-closed.

A shiver ran through my body, a feeling that I had done something wrong, that I was bad, that I had ruined everything.

The one named József cleared his throat:

"This is all so fascinating. People come from two different worlds, and then they meet . . . "

"Don't do that, József," said Sara. "Don't smooth it over. Let it be. Let it simmer."

I didn't know what to do. I looked around, and everyone in the group was staring into the flames. Eventually, I realized that I was alone, all alone and drunk on the ground. And so I said:

"I'm sorry . . . I don't know what I . . . "

I was too drunk to drive home; they showed me to a mattress in an empty room, one of the sheds. I vomited neatly by a root before going to bed. I fell asleep with anxiety and my feet on the pillow. I had behaved terribly. Especially towards Låke.

* * *

When I woke up, the sun had just begun to rise, and it was impossible to fall back asleep. The shame made it difficult to tolerate being inside my own skin. And my loneliness, once self-imposed, suddenly felt agonizing. My body itched all over. And it wasn't like I longed to go back home to the city or my old friends. I just wanted to get in, to the group. I wanted to sit around the fire again, the way it had been before I started harping on, the silence and the calm, the warmth of the flames, the feeling of being around people but without saying anything. How can I explain it? It was like there was a part of me I had forgotten existed. It was the part that fell asleep on the couch as Dad watched TV, my foot against his, the murmur of the TV in the background, my eyes beginning to fall shut, knowing that I could fall asleep if I wanted to because he would carry me to bed. It was windy outside, but he would carry me. I didn't need to be anything other than who I was; I didn't need to make an effort. There was no pull in any direction, just stillness.

Then came adolescence,
and the feeling was gone; I had forgotten that it ever existed. Until now.

I wondered how much of it had to do with the group and how much had to do with myself and what I had already come to realize over the past few weeks. I had found that what I used to consider a reasonable amount to do in a day now seemed utterly baroque; I used to *be busy* from morning until late at night, and what I had called free time and *relaxing* was actually just another form of *busyness*: doing yoga, having drinks, reaching out to people, seeing that new exhibition that was supposed to be so great. Sometimes we would get the urge to *really* do something and then we would go out to the bluffs, take a cold swim, grill salmon, drink cava. All at the same time. Because life had to be maximized—a meeting with a friend was never just seeing each other, it had to be as amazing as possible; we had to eat the most delicious food at the same time, maybe at a place where we could meet someone we were attracted to, maybe also see a band.

Now, all of this seemed to me both silly and self-torturous, and I thought the activities I now did in a day—check that the tent was pitched stráight, maybe go for a swim, possibly a walk, head into town to buy more chips and coffee—suddenly felt like full days.

All of this I had already felt, and what Sara said resonated within me as pure truth, and it struck me that the people I had initially seen as lunatics were holding up a mirror. I was the lunatic.

I must have spent an hour thinking about how to approach them again, whether I should apologize and how—especially to Låke.

* * *

By the time there was a knock on the door, it must have been seven o'clock. Or, it was more of a *rustling*, sounded closer to a dormouse than a human. I assumed it was Låke, and prepared to apologize.

It turned out to be neither Låke nor a dormouse. It was Ersmo, who looked as though he had just woken up, his hair pointing in all directions. Some kind of panic in his eyes.

"I saw you were awake," he said. "How are you?"

I found it touching that he was attempting small talk. It sounded very stuttery coming from his mouth. I shrugged, about to answer when he interrupted:

"I could hardly sleep. I've been thinking about what you said yesterday."

"Oh," I said. I felt ashamed. "I'm—I apologize—"

He interrupted me again:

"I mean, I don't agree," he added. "With what you said about us."

But it sounded like a question. It was as if his mouth said that he didn't agree, but maybe there was a part of him that wasn't sure—that had become curious about the things drunk me had said. He was here because he wanted to know more. All of this, I could guess from the tone of his voice.

"I don't know if I—" I said.

"That thing you said about Låke," he continued. "That, on the other hand, is true. I get that it looks weird from the outside. I think of Låke as a brother. It's strange that I haven't—"

I said nothing.

Now he looked up through his bangs and gazed straight at me. I took a breath.

"And maybe you were also right about some of the other things you said. Like meeting other people, for example."

Suddenly it crept into me. I realized that it wasn't just *me* who felt naked. It was some kind of double emperor's-new-clothes situation, where both I and the group felt that the pants had been pulled down on our respective societies. Both were naked, exposed in all their phoniness.

I looked up and noticed the hunger with which we gazed at each other. That's how I looked at Ersmo, and that's how Ersmo looked at me.

My hunger was partly intellectual; I wanted to enter his world, the group's world, but also: my body screamed with a longing to press up against another person again, to fill up on more of what I had experienced that first evening with them, to exist so easily with my body against others'. And especially Ersmo's.

God, I thought, how badly I wanted to kiss him. There he stood by the door, illuminated by the soft morning sun, his hair and his mouth, his hands and his arms; they looked so strong. I didn't really dare, of course, not at all; I had already embarrassed myself, and to bring my filthy mundane desires to this group of people who had a set of rules and a plan I still didn't fully know or understand—I didn't dare. I had also understood from what I had seen and what Låke once said, that Ersmo and Zakaria seemed to have some kind of sexual relationship;

I hadn't interpreted it as exclusive or that either of them was primarily homosexual—this was based solely on my sense of courtship from the men whenever I was with the group—rather that they were all bisexual, whether for natural or religious reasons was hard to say.

But maybe I had misunderstood the whole thing, maybe it was just friendliness, and excitement towards a new individual; I don't know.

At any rate, there we were, me wearing yesterday's dress with buttons down the front; I had taken off my bra in the night—and when I looked down, I noticed that the top button of my dress had come undone, exposing my breasts at least halfway. It didn't look indecent, but you could glimpse the outlines of my breasts in every way and how they wanted to escape the fabric.

In my ordinary life, I often felt ashamed of my breasts; it was like they were unplanned—the breasts you see in magazines are hard and firm and constant, but mine are *soft*, I can't trust them to behave—but here, in the morning sun, next to a man who hadn't seen a woman's body in years, I noticed that they were something in their own right. I could see them through his eyes. What they had wasn't about how they looked, but rather: that they existed.

I looked at him. I saw that he had seen that the button was undone. I saw that he had seen that I had seen the button. He saw that I had seen that he had seen the button.

He looked at me. His mouth slightly ajar. He breathed.

I looked towards his groin now, wanting to see if anything showed, if anything happened.

Nothing showed.

What did I dare do? I didn't want to ruin things further, the way I had yesterday. But I dared to hold his gaze. He looked down in a way that I interpreted as shyness.

"Sit down, if you want," I said, gesturing towards the

mattress, and he did, a bit away from me but close enough that I could smell him.

What did this mean? Did it signify something? How close or far away he sat. What did it mean in his world, under his norms?

Maybe it was the hangover, but I couldn't think; I barely reflected as I raised my stupid hand, brushed some hair out of his face. It was a gamble. It could lead to something, but it could also be dismissed as a friendly gesture—if that's what he preferred. I reminded myself that he hardly knew what was appropriate, and in this context neither did I. Perhaps, in a worst-case scenario, I could blame it on my society; that's how we did things where I was from.

The air stopped—

But then.

He took my hand, just as it was about to leave his face, held it firmly against his cheek, hard, but not so hard that I couldn't remove it if I wanted to, but rather clearly, tenderly.

One second.

Still—

We breathed.

He trembled.

I touched one of my fingers to his mouth now. Slowly, so that I could take it back if he objected. But my finger sensed his breathing, deeper now. My head was no longer part of the equation at all; I acted purely on instinct, as if his breathing had said it was okay; I inserted one of my fingers into his mouth, he sucked on it, still trembling.

I thought about what Sara had said yesterday. *What's truly logical, anyway.*

What is it that happens in moments like this? We have a set of rules for how to behave towards each other. Yet the second the premise changes and both have confirmed it—that we want to get close to each other—we completely change our movement patterns. How bizarre we become. We no longer speak at all; we grope, putting our hands in the very places where otherwise we aren't allowed to. We do things like sticking a finger in the other's mouth.

I like to think that for every expression, there is a moment when you realize the word actually has an origin. Here, the word was *attraction*. A force field arose between his eyes and mine, even though he occasionally looked down; he was nervous, which made me confident. I could have sketched the field between his body and mine, that's how clear it was.

Now it felt like the whole cabin was shaking. The curtains in the window blurred.

I undid the next button, and let my breasts fall out of the garment entirely.

It was so quiet, I heard him swallow. Then I took his hands and brought them to my chest.

He took my breasts in his hands, weighed them, pressed them against his palms, like they were pouring into his hands. The last button came undone on its own. And I moved my hands towards him, unbuttoned his shirt, too—his shabby, peculiar shirt, presumably from a previous generation. I gasped as I fiddled with the buttons, removed the garment, and found hair on his back, hair on his shoulders, more beautiful than any torso I had seen on those gymsharks and runners I had been with before, and then I moved closer to him, and kissed him; I was dizzy now, as though I might faint, my chest against his. Everything was so warm. His back was broad and the flesh almost soft, like he had both worked hard and eaten fries every day of his life. How pointedly he smelled, and new. Still like fish and fire, and strangely enough it didn't bother me. I noticed he was already coming now, he hadn't even taken off his trousers, and it made everything even better—how right it was that he came before he even got close to me; it made me feel more desired than I could tell you, and we went slower now, lay down, placed our hands where we wanted to place them, started all over again. I contributed a smell of hangover and sweat. "Should we close the curtains?" I asked. "Why?" he wondered. Yes, why. What did it matter if someone saw this, just as I had seen them having sex with each other from up on the hill, just as I had seen the moose and the reindeer and the hares. "Låke," I said.

It was as if Ersmo realized that yes, maybe it was good for a teenager not to have to see their adults sleeping with each other, so I got up and closed the curtains.

It ached in my groin just seeing him, standing by the window and seeing him on the mattress; I needed to go to him, hold his hips, notice the softly embedded angles of his hip bones against my hands.

The curtains wouldn't fully close and the morning light painted different parts of us.

Later, I would realize that what had ruined all other sexual encounters I'd had before were two things:

it was the stress—I had never been fully *there*, I'd had a pattern that I followed that usually worked, but I was never *there*-there,

and it was all the other people, all the magazines, all the billboards, all the hairdressers and skin therapists and personal trainers standing there screaming *be better be better*,

and I had never before been able to completely shut them out—no matter how amazing the sex was, they had always been there at the same time, a part of the event—it was as if the act actually consisted of thousands of people and all of capitalism. A small performance for an audience of one, where the result hadn't been to build desire but doing it right, being enough.

But now, just once, I had captured something pure. Because

all of a sudden I was the only woman roughly the right age for miles around, and he was the only man, and it wasn't about living up to anything;

instead, we were two individuals with a single shared goal that was clearly coming from within both of us.

I was on all fours and screamed out loud as he entered me.

And we were animals.

Afterwards, Ersmo immediately became tired. I thought perhaps it wasn't so strange, if he had waited fifteen years to be inside a woman. Though I had a similar experience I had also waited a long time to get inside myself.

I, on the other hand, became wide awake, lying there staring at his wavy hair and square torso moving up and down in heavy breaths. He apparently had no need to say anything, and—when it became clear that this was an option—I realised I didn't either. I had the feeling that I hadn't known I was searching, but I had found. Partly it was Ersmo, but even more so: everything else.

I dozed off, and when I woke up he was gone.

* * *

The second time I stirred that morning, I felt considerably more alert. I wondered if what had just happened really did transpire—maybe it was a dream? But the bed still had a wet spot, and the pillow smelled faintly of another person. For an hour or so, I lay on the mattress, rolling around in the memories of the morning.

I got up, put all my clothes on right, downed a glass of water that someone had thoughtfully placed beside my bed. Then there was another knock on the door. It was Låke. I was so happy to see him, it felt like my heart stopped. He wasn't angry with me. Or maybe he was, but he still wanted to see me. I had such a strong urge to apologize that I shouted it out almost before he had even entered the room.

"I'm sorry, Låke, I'm sorry! I'm an idiot, sorry for everything I said."

Låke looked happy. There was something different about him today, a new spring in his step.

"What are you apologising for? Getting so drunk? You were *really* wasted! You fell! You couldn't walk!"

He looked happy, full of piss and vinegar.

"No, but . . . saying those things . . . that I said. About you. About thinking you weren't . . . that you weren't really allowed as deeply into the group as the others."

"Oh, *that*. Well, that's true." He fell silent. "So, do you want to go fishing?"

I nodded wordlessly.

I would love to go fishing.

* * *

I knew what needed to be done. It was shameful, but my drunk personality has embarrassed me more times than I can remember, and so apologising had become a learned behavior. I shuffled out into the yard, where the others were having breakfast, and I walked with my head bent and stood right in front of them. I looked especially at Sara, since I understood that the path to the group's forgiveness went through her, and I said:

"I'm so sorry. I'm so very, very sorry."

I continued to specify how, yesterday, I had felt so envious of their incredible company and wonderful home that I—this broken, sick woman—had felt compelled to burst their bubble, just to defend my own vapid life in the city.

I only partially agreed with what I was saying here, but I have learned that in successful apologies it's best to exaggerate both the recipient's virtues and one's own idiocy.

I immediately realized that Sara saw right through me, but she still seemed to appreciate the gesture. To show this, she said:

"It's not easy being sick. We here have been without the rest of society for so long that we almost forget what it's like. But in meeting you, we remember again."

Then she smiled, warmly.

I swallowed, both some actual vomit and my own pride, but I also noticed that the heavy atmosphere around the table dissolved, postures relaxed, József lifted his legs off a chair and asked me to sit.

"Would you like some breakfast?" Aagny said now. "Or do you need another slap?"

She grinned, and I understood that it was all water under the bridge.

I grinned back, and sat down on the chair. She fetched me a glass, and indicated with her hand that I was welcome to help myself to the sandwiches and the eggs, small and various faint shades of pastel, presumably collected from the chickens whose constant cackling I had now grown accustomed to.

Ersmo alternated between looking down at the ground and smiling at me—a secret, bashful smile that ran the gauntlet straight into my heart. And Låke stood waiting by one of the sheds, looking downright jittery, with two fishing rods in his hand.

It so happened that I stayed another night. And then another. And so it went on.

E rsmo was like a bear after a long, long winter's hibernation, when suddenly spring arrives.
That's how it felt.
It was just that spring was so difficult to handle and know what to think about.

In the beginning, it had been simple.
He didn't have anything, nothing at all, or so it felt, and then Aagny came. And Aagny had saved him from his mother, and she had cared for him, and she had told him he was good.
It had felt like the calm after the storm, and he hadn't needed anything else but Aagny and to live without fear. Without fear of his mother, without fear of school when lower secondary school was over. Aagny didn't think upper secondary school was something he needed to bother with, which was an opinion he shared.
And then came Sara and József, and with them giggles and safety. And József and Ersmo had built things together, and Sara had come and said that what they were doing was important, and Ersmo had felt almost happy.
And then little Låke and Sagne came, and later Zakaria too, and there were so many people to like. He thought then that he had more than he'd ever dreamed of: so many who accepted him.

Back then, they still went to the shops often, in town.

Sometimes he even popped over to see a neighbor. There was no clear boundary to the outside world. Ersmo probably thought he would eventually meet someone, but it's not like there was a rush.

Over the years, things happened. The trips into town became fewer and farther between. The atmosphere in the group changed from what it had been in the beginning. Ersmo could almost touch it:

Sagne's attitude towards Låke, which hadn't become warmer over time, rather the opposite.

Aagny's embarrassing infatuation with Zakaria.

József's heavy gaze on Sara.

Zakaria and Sara's sleeping together, which crushed both Aagny and József.

Ersmo's own strange sexual relationship with Zakaria, which felt less like sex and more like . . . something to do? A bit like eating, or cleaning the chicken coop, or dancing. Jerking each other off in the water, or in the morning if they were bored.

There was a longing.

Every time he drank, it rose to the surface—the longing to set off, to see what was out there. Right there and then, it felt possible.

Then he woke up, and there was always something to build, or harvest, or a dance to dance, and the longing faded. And Aagny. If he left. Would he lose her then?

But now the rules had changed completely. Now there was suddenly a woman his own age, in the shed on his farm. She said exactly the things he had felt but couldn't find the words for, and with those words his thoughts took flight. So, there *was* something. People could feel that way. He wasn't just making it up.

And in the forest, there was suddenly an opportunity to make money.

Sagne
August 2023

Sagne felt tired. She was shivery.

She had read that snakes, when they shed their skin, withdraw and hide until the skin is off. There was a metaphor in this that Sagne could appreciate. It was scary to show yourself during a period of change, when you yourself were a question—all soft, no protection.

She withdrew.

Sagne could tolerate a lot. She had a trick. The trick was to completely shut out everything that went on outside her field of vision. And to fix her gaze on something beautiful.

To her, most things were beautiful.

She could go out and sit on the front steps and look towards the yard. There, regular wasps and tree bumblebees flew around in peace—the wasps more focused, the bumblebees restful. If she brought out a glass of lemonade, they instantly came up to say hello. The bumblebees' incredible bodies, like tiny comedians; you would think they couldn't get anywhere at all with such a big rump, but they did!!! They flew and flew. And now was the best time; now it was late summer, time to mate. The bumblebees had a system with queens and workers, too; now the males flew around looking for queens to mate with, and when the mating was over the males immediately died, while the queens withdrew, hibernating, preserving the sperm.

Sagne was so proud of the garden. It had grown tall, full of flowers and herbs that bumblebees and butterflies loved. They loved the thyme, rosemary, sage, not least the redcurrant bushes. Here were several different species of bumblebees. Here, they lived and thrived. She had created a home for them, a loving home where they wanted to live, and the others in the Colony indulged her and accepted getting stung a couple of times each summer.

Over by the fence, some of the forest was more deciduous. Here were plenty of dead trees and stumps. Sagne had asked Zakaria and Ersmo, when they felled the occasional tree there, every now and then: to mainly take spruce trees, to let the deciduous forest stand tall and free. And wouldn't you believe it: that one day, what she thought was a *white-backed woodpecker* had been sitting there in the flesh—such a rare species—she wasn't entirely sure but maybe it was so, that a *white-backed woodpecker* had decided it wanted to be outside the farmhouse, of all places, right where Sagne lived. That's where it wanted to be. The white-backed woodpecker could barely be found in Sweden anymore; it needed deciduous forest and dead trees to exist.

Sagne wasn't inclined towards magical thinking, but she had at some point decided on this: that if she saw the possibly white-backed woodpecker again one morning, if she heard it— well, then it would be a good day.

She looked towards the birch tree.

The woodpecker wasn't there.

Her brain was, in some ways, unstimulated. It longed to learn things. It thought a fair deal about the internet, about missing that immense knowledge base, all the people around the world who knew things, who were interested in the same things as her. Her brain had read every book in the house a hundred times, but it wanted more. To cover this up, she started making long lists, categorizing, taking notes, and sketching every insect she saw, their movement patterns—just like she did as a child. But her brain wanted more.

When she panicked over this, she closed herself off.

That usually worked.

But suddenly it was like she could hardly even sleep. She used to feel irritated, restless maybe. But now, it gnawed at her. She tried to shut off the gnawing, but apparently she couldn't.

This was what she saw in her mind when she tried to sleep: Låke. She saw Låke's embarrassing, unmasked joy; his restless legs; his exaggerated enthusiasm; and his face, which was so completely open every time he saw her, just waiting for love— and this made Sagne so stressed and even more closed off.

But when she wasn't near him, she could sometimes think about him in theory.

The others said he was a good kid.

They appeared to laugh in his presence. Like he was funny.

She had understood that it seemed to be her fault he kept a bit of a distance. How silly! She had never said he couldn't be there?

Perhaps she had been a bit gruff whenever he approached, walking away, but that's not against the law, is it?

A new thing had started to show in Låke's face. She had thought about it at times. In the beginning, it was so clear, that thing with the Cupid's bow.

But now also: something new.

That he resembled her, too.

She saw herself in his cheekbones and his eyes.

Sometimes it made her gag reflex kick in again—her eyes and that creep's mouth together, in the same face—but occasionally she would pause and realize that, since she was adopted, she had never before seen her own features in another person. The feeling was dizzying. He actually existed. He was actually her child.

Then it was daytime again and he came out into the garden with that mouth and that demanding gaze that followed her, and she had to walk away.

EMELIE
(THE NOTEBOOK, SEPTEMBER 2023)

A few days have been calm. But this morning, as I stepped into the house, I was met with full activity. There is always someone moving about, but today: suddenly everyone at once. They carried water in and out as usual, but they also came with buckets and bags.

"It almost dipped below freezing last night," I had heard one of them say the day before. "It's time."

I had understood that this meant something but hadn't asked what. Maybe I hadn't been interested.

"We're going mushroom picking," Ersmo said now as an explanation, while rummaging around for five old plastic buckets that once held jam.

"Ooh," I said. "I'll join you!"

I imagined a peaceful day, maybe filling up the stores of chanterelles or horse mushrooms. A plentiful stock had already been gathered and dried, but I supposed there could always be more. We set off, everyone except Låke, walking in a line with buckets in hand, a short distance along the gravel road, then onto a path that veered off. We walked for a mile or two. There was a house that had clearly been abandoned by its owner—presumably, the former owner's relatives—and in front of the house there had once been some sort of pasture. Now there was tall grass instead and the ground was undulating, with hillocks but also holes where rainwater had pooled. Shabby tufts.

That's where the whole group went now.

I followed.

"What are you doing?" I wondered, seeing them suddenly focus very intently on the tufts instead of heading into the woods where the chanterelles were likely to grow.

They started picking from the tufts, a kind of mushroom I had never seen before.

Everyone filled their buckets with the thin little mushroom. It must be a very tasty mushroom, I thought, probably envisioning a soup being served towards evening, but this mushroom turned out to be of a completely different variety.

The liberty cap.

Aagny had dried most of the mushrooms, but a few bags lay fresh in the refrigerator.

Sara handed them out. Låke was in the other room. He wasn't allowed to participate. Sara wouldn't be taking any either. It was apparently important that someone kept an eye on the others.

"Emelie?" she asked, looking at me.

I suddenly felt so moved, so happy to be invited, that I noticed my mouth responding: "I'd love some!" Ersmo's hand brushed against mine. I felt tingly. There were lots of mushrooms to eat, but the group started chewing frenetically, and so did I. They weren't tasty at all, but not stomach-churning either. Swedish mushrooms, I thought. From a shabby pasture. It's not like much can happen.

A warmth spread in my belly.

That was the first thing.

The second was that I saw their faces.

Their eyes. A softness. It was like we were interconnected, the same person possibly, I don't know. Maybe one's own body wasn't constant, maybe the boundaries were blurred; perhaps I was the same as Aagny, perhaps she was the same as me. And Ersmo, and Sara, and Sagne—

but suddenly, even more: the flowers in the window, the ones someone had picked. They weren't a bouquet; they were one petal, another petal, a third, a fourth. The petals were so fascinating I almost swooned. The fact that they even existed. The lamp in the room, its light, broken into prisms. I had to sit down. It would have been terrible if it weren't so wonderful.

I looked at my hand, for the first time truly *seeing* it. It had five fingers, and skin. The fingers could bend at several places. My eyes welled up with tears.

I sat like that for a while, I don't know how long. Looking around and thinking how amazing everything was. And now I realized again who was in the room. Ersmo. I could see our attraction before me, physically. It was a band of light encircling the two of us. An incredible band of light. Suddenly he went outside, down towards the water, stretching the band to its breaking point. DON'T GO, ERSMO! I shouted. STAY HERE WITH ME! At least I thought I was shouting in my head, but I wasn't. My mouth didn't follow suit. Only my head. It felt terrible.

Suddenly so much felt terrible!! Now everything rose to the surface. Now I felt it. Those nagging demands. Nothing was true. You started something, then you were stuck. You were one way and then you had to be that way forever.

And besides, there were so many bubbles floating around among the stars, and everyone expected ME to be the one to pop them. I had to pop them all! It was up to me! I flew up from my chair and ran around, trying to get to them all, to pop them with my hand. Pop, pop! But I couldn't reach them all; there were always more, more everywhere.

I have a recurring nightmare. In the nightmare, I don't have a driver's license. Suddenly, something happens! An accident. Someone needs to go to the hospital.

You have to drive, someone says.

But I can't, I say. I don't know how.

Drive anyway, they say.

And so I drive the car, because I dare not say no. I don't know how the steering wheel works; I don't understand the clutch, so the car jumps and stalls intermittently. It's slick outside and I slide between lanes, always so close to crashing; I don't even know if I'm in the right lane or where to turn or what any of the signs mean, and the line behind me honks furiously, HOOONK HOOOOOOONK, and the ones in front of me honk, too, and I scream out loud:

BUT I DON'T KNOW HOW!

And one time, the dream continued with all the drivers in all the other cars looking in my direction, before speaking with one voice:

WE DON'T KNOW EITHER!

Now I screamed, and cried, and I shook, and my body twitched. BUT I DON'T KNOW HOW! I screamed. And then Sara came. She looked at me, and I saw that she understood. She held me in her gaze; we spoke to each other without words. She comforted me with her eyes. I don't know how, I sobbed. I don't know how.

And now Zakaria came over, too. He also understood. We don't know how, none of us know.

I looked at Sara and thought:

She knows.

I zoomed in on her eye, looking at it slowly and for a long time. It seemed gigantic.

It's truly amazing that eyes even exist.

I found myself in the yard. Zakaria ran down to the river,

where the others seemed to be, and I was about to follow, but then I changed my mind.

Suddenly, I saw what's important in life. Now I knew. It's eyes, and it's NATURE.

And I flew towards a birch tree that stood by the side of the house.

I ran my hands along the trunk, feeling its rough yet soft skin—rough and smooth, rough and smooth. That I didn't usually see the trees like this. It was terrible. Now I knew better.

I stood there, embracing the tree. Then a car pulled up and stopped on the road. The car door slammed so loudly; they trampled so heavily on the grass. Two people got out. Something didn't feel right. They brought a different energy.

"We're from Social Services," they said to Sara.

I had forgotten that I'd called them. It was at least a week ago. It felt like several years.

Sara went off with the Social Services. A while later, they came up to me and stared. They asked if I was Emelie Beritsdotter, and I said I was. I needed to salvage this, show that I could be trusted. So I asked politely if they wanted to smell the tree trunk, but they did not. I panicked then and really needed to get away. I excused myself and went to sit on a distant rock, which I later realized was only fifteen feet from the tree. Here, I felt great satisfaction at making my escape.

After a while, they took off.

LÅKE
(THE LEGAL PAD, SEPTEMBER 2023)

I was inside the house when it happened since I have to be when they are eating Mushrooms. I don't mind because then I can read as much as I want & be alone in almost every Room. & besides it's always fun afterwards when we talk about all the strange things they did & everything they felt.

But now what happened this time was that a lady & a Man came and said they were from Social Services. Sara met them. I heard them talking.

We've heard there's a Teenager here who's not attending school, they said or something like it, sounding very Serious.

Wha-wha-wha-what said Sara then & she sounded totally shocked. Then she said No, we are only adults here and my fiancé & I are visiting our friends.

She didn't mention Mum or Zakaria & that's probably because they are Secret.

Here's my fiancé. He's got a bit of a headache & is taking a nap she said.

I'm guessing she was pointing at József & he had fallen asleep somewhere maybe in the hammock because he often does when they take mushrooms I don't think he takes much.

Sara is good at stuff like this. She talked & talked and I could hear in the Social ones' voices they were changing their minds.

Then Sara finished by saying I'm assuming the call came from Emelie! & I want you to meet her.

Then I saw through the window how they went up to Emelie & she was standing there hugging the Birch Tree looking all

Blissful and a little Mad. & then they talked and it sounded like this:

Are you Emelie Beritsdotter? Am I? Yes, I am. I am her. & she is me. But do you know what matters in this world? Trees & their Bark. Yes that's what's important. Do you hear? Do you hear the song of the trees? Go on, smell it.

Here she pressed the Social Services' woman's head against the birch tree.

Wonderful, isn't it said Emelie.

The Social Services said: Yes, we've seen a tree & heard bird song before, we're from Arvidsjaur.

Then there was some talking & not a very long time, & it turned out that Sara had been neighbors or something with one of their's Girlfriend, & then they left.

We can do that too.

Not much happened for Ersmo on the mushroom trip. Sometimes it didn't. He stood down by the water, trying to summon the same enthusiasm as the others, but it just wasn't happening.

He thought of Emelie.

He thought of Emelie's hips, Emelie's mouth, Emelie's eyes, Emelie's breasts, and Emelie's knees. She had a birthmark on her arm and light downy hairs on one side of her upper lip.

Then he thought of what it was like to be inside Emelie.

He turned around and walked back towards the house.

This is what he saw:

Sara, who stood talking to two people he had never seen before.

They very rarely had people visiting, so Ersmo's heart started pounding; his instinct was to keep away, to stand behind the wall of the house and eavesdrop.

The woman said: "We've been informed that a group of adults live here with a child who is kept out of the system and hasn't been allowed to attend school."

Sara said: "What?"

She managed to look both shocked and amused, like it was the most absurd thing she had ever heard.

The woman said: "If that's the case, the child wouldn't be registered anywhere. If it's true, that's serious and goes against the Care of Young Persons Act."

The man said: "You can't keep a child out of society. They have a right to education and care and healthcare."

Ersmo thought of Låke. He thought of Emelie, who wasn't foolish and enslaved at all but quick-witted and kind—and brave. He thought of the man and the woman from Social Services who looked serious, like they cared. He thought of the young men cutting down trees; neither of them had seemed evil or insane.

He thought of Låke. He wondered what it would be like for Låke to learn things. Personally, he had hated school, as he struggled with reading and couldn't sit still. But Låke was different. He might have liked it, sitting with a book and writing and doing math.

Ersmo could envision it. Låke in school. Raising his hand.

He thought about the time Låke sprained his foot. The whole thing had turned blue. They should have had it checked. It turned out fine anyway. But Låke still walked with a limp sometimes.

He tried to imagine Låke with a group of peers his own age.

He tried to imagine himself with a group of peers his own age.

He imagined himself and Emelie, sitting in a café or pizza place, the kind of café or pizza place he and Aagny used to go to in the past. He could have his arm around Emelie's shoulders. They could buy a Coke.

Ove had had the problem that he was losing weight. It wasn't good at all.

It happened by chance. He was struggling with lower back pain, and the doctor said it was up to Ove himself to fix it. The back pain, he said, was due to a lack of activity and ergonomics.

"How much physical activity do you usually get in a day?" the doctor asked, and Ove said, well, I guess it's into the car and then out of the car and into the kitchen to grab a sandwich and onto the couch.

"I'm physically active at work, though," Ove said.

"What do you do for work?" the doctor asked.

"Car mechanic," Ove responded.

"So it's mainly static muscle work," the doctor said.

"Huh?" said Ove.

"You're standing in the same position for long stretches of time," the doctor explained.

"Yes," said Ove. "Or lying down. Sometimes I'm under the car."

"You need to start jogging," the doctor said. "There's nothing like jogging to loosen up the body."

Aagny was initially very supportive. She went to the shops and bought him running shoes, watching through the window as Ove set off along the trails. She imagined he would return cussing and blistered. Running was new to Ove—to him, the forest was a place for working and logging, maybe riding a snowmobile, certainly not somewhere to go and run around for fun. He would die of shame if anyone saw him. But he was also a person who didn't reflect much, so if he must run then run he would. He was a machine that way, Ove. Just like the time he realized he needed a woman to take care of the home, someone young and strong; he had gone dancing and come back with Aagny. Problem—solution.

Now he took up running, Ove, and something happened. He didn't even notice that his back got softer and the pounds fell away as he soared along the paths he used to walk as a child. It was like there had always been something unredeemed in Ove, and suddenly he found it. Despite not being exactly young anymore, he turned out to have an incredible talent for running. Apparently, he was a runner. After only a few months, he was running thirty to forty miles, then fifty to sixty. Turns out, there was no end to how far he could run. And his body never said no or protested. Instead, it became alert and ready to face the day.

While he ran, he began to think. What did he really want out of life. Was this what he had dreamed of.

Aagny watched her ugly, sweaty husband become fit, start showering. He had to buy new clothes. He no longer wanted the greasy sauces Aagny served him. Instead, he started making minced moose meat without butter, and omelettes. He drifted further and further away from her.

The other woman was named Maria; she'd had a broken-down Volvo 240 that Ove repaired. This was the only information Aagny really had.

Yet there was no lack of details. The details were created in Aagny's own mind. Maria, Aagny's mind decided, was five foot five—eight inches shorter than Aagny—with long, blonde hair that shimmered in the sun. Maria had a sparkly laugh. She had smooth skin. She was truly feminine! And petite and delicate, almost girly, yet with a warm gaze! She didn't speak too much, but also not too little—just the right amount. She had a sense for aesthetics, knew which clothes matched and so on. She was a dancer, or a gymnast, with a naturally limber body. She had done well in school, had no difficulty reading, and found it easy and enjoyable to learn new things. She was the kind of person you wanted to have children with. She never had to beg a man to want children with her; the man would say it voluntarily. "You know, I would really like to start a family with you. Even though I have three grown children, I want to start fresh with you." That's how much fertility she exuded. And once they started trying— well, then it worked right away! Healthy, round babies.

And worst of all: Maria had a whole background, present parents with jobs who loved both Maria and each other. No more than one sibling, or two. There was enough love for everyone in the family.

In this way, Aagny's mind created her rival.

Ove felt angry. He was annoyed with Aagny, for he needed to get her out of the way, out of the house, and at the same time he felt ashamed—sweet, faithful Aagny. He didn't want to walk around feeling shame every time he saw her, so he needed her gone, out of the house. Suddenly she seemed to always be in the way, with her sad eyes. She started wearing lingerie and walking around in nothing but a towel. It didn't suit her at all. Ove got more and more annoyed.

"You need to pack your things now," he said finally.

Aagny stood there in a lace bra and lace panties with freshly washed hair. She had tried to make it look natural—here I am, just walking around, just had a shower, I just need to walk down the hall here to get to my clothes, now I'm standing here by the dresser looking for a shirt, sucking my belly in, sticking out my butt–

She turned to ice.

Aagny was a loyal person. Whomever she ended up with, she loved. She'd had that instinct since childhood. If I'm the best I can be, if I do everything right. Then they won't leave me. But it had never worked before, and it wasn't working now either.

Aagny looked down at her belly and the lingerie. She noticed her own posture, how tense it was, how hard she was trying. What she felt was humiliation. She had tried her hardest, and failed. And before that, she had moved in with the ugliest, most irksome man in all of Norrbotten just to be sure he wouldn't leave her. And now the ugliest, most irksome man in all of Norrbotten stood here saying he didn't want her. After she had done everything. She couldn't do any better. It wasn't like she had another gear to shift into. She was all out of gears.

Ove looked away. He went to fetch a bathrobe. His own filthy old bathrobe, that smelled of Ove.

"Cover yourself," he said.

Aagny had nothing left. Nothing at all.

Suddenly Aagny remembered a time when she was seven years old. Her mother had been sitting there with her younger siblings when Aagny came home from school with some news. The news was that Aagny had received a "Good" from her teacher when she could identify the calls of three different birds.

"Mum," Aagny had shouted from the front door.

Her mother didn't respond at all. When Aagny came bursting in, announcing her news, her mother kissed her little sister on the head without interest.

"Start peeling the potatoes, would you," she said. "Go help out instead of standing there bragging."

It was Ove's eldest who had found the body at the bottom of the stairs.

"What happened that time with Ove, Aagny?" Sara had asked at some point.

At the time, Aagny hadn't mentioned anything about Maria. Instead, she may have let Sara believe that Ove abused her, and that Aagny acted in self-defence. It didn't feel entirely incorrect—only, the attack had been on her soul rather than her body. She didn't feel like she was lying.

AAGNY
SEPTEMBER 2023

Aagny stood there, staring down into the water. She watched the waves.

The water waved here.

Then it waved there.

Here.

There.

Yes, it was incredible.

She continued to follow the wave.

Here, here, here.

There, there, there.

For maybe two hours she stood like that.

Life was truly wonderful, when you thought about it.

She turned around, and saw Zakaria lying in the sand, soaking up the sun's beams. In just the same way, he beamed, too.

Zakaria had never shown any sexual interest in Aagny. This was a detail she had always been aware of, but which she had rationalized away. It could change in the future, she had thought. Maybe he was shy. She was older than him, after all; maybe he felt respect for her. Everyone knew they belonged together. Surely they did? She had saved him. He had once said that she was unlike anyone he had ever met. She didn't know what that meant. In the evenings, she would lie awake weighing up the sentence, playing it back with positive and negative undertones.

You're unlike anyone I've ever met.

But now, as her body relaxed, yet with all her senses turned up to ten, it happened.

She looked at Zakaria and now she saw.

There was an energy flowing from her to him, but it wasn't flowing back.

He lay there so beautiful, and he was never going to want her. His body wasn't turned towards her, she noticed. He wasn't looking at her. He had asked Ersmo for sex, but never Aagny.

She could only guess at the softness of his lips, his stubble grazing her cheek. The strength of his upper arms—how she had dreamed of touching them.

She would never get to touch them.

First came the pain. It stabbed at her heart and unfurled in her body, turning into a nausea that slowly wandered through her veins, penetrating into every nook and cranny.

Aagny gasped for breath. She felt sick.

It wasn't just that Zakaria didn't want her; it was that she had put all her eggs in one basket, and now the eggs were gone.

Grief consumed her; she saw it physically before her eyes. She breathed. The mushroom trip was coming to an end. Aagny couldn't bear grief, so she managed to transform it into another feeling—one more familiar and comfortable to her.

She suddenly understood whose fault it all was.

It was Sara. If Sara hadn't been there with her body, pressing herself against Zakaria right from the start.

This thing between Ersmo and Zakaria meant nothing. It was just men jerking each other off. That's what men had always done, Aagny believed. All the boys in her class used to play "soggy biscuit" every Friday night. It wasn't sexual. Men were just funny that way. It wasn't about true love.

But Sara.

Aagny had always been loyal to Sara. She had placed all her faith in Sara. And how had Sara rewarded her? With nothing, nothing at all. Zakaria should have been hers—Aagny's. Surely it was her turn to have someone.

JÓZSEF
SEPTEMBER 2023

One thing about József: he could sense what others were feeling from miles away, but struggled to sense what he was feeling himself.

Occasionally he had gone almost a whole day without eating. He watched his legs tremble and suddenly realized through a purely mental process:

Why are my legs shaking? What could be the reason?

I haven't eaten anything all day. Maybe I'm hungry.

Now it was the same. He suffered from anxiety every night and parts of the day. When he held Sara, his body wanted both to get closer and to move away.

What could be the reason?

And then the answer, which emerged:

I don't want to be here.

I don't believe in what we're doing.

Did I ever

It's remarkable how long a person can dither. As long as you are standing on one side, you can rationalize anything to support the side you are on. *The reason that politician said that thing is probably because she was misquoted. The reason my husband is beating me is probably because I'm so annoying.* But as soon as you have taken the step over to the other side, everything crumbles, and that was what happened now. József had for many years been storing situations inside him. He realized it now. And now they unfolded before him, like the pages of a book.

*

He had taken it easy, only eating a few mushrooms for appearances' sake, mini-tripping mostly to keep the peace—if one of them backed out of eating mushrooms, it unsettled the mood; it had to be all or none—but he didn't actually feel like taking mushrooms today. He didn't feel like taking mushrooms any day, to be entirely honest, but especially not today, when there was so much to figure out and he was already in a state of total confusion. At the same time: clarity—suddenly some kind of clarity.

He lay in the hammock and heard what was happening. He heard the man and the woman who arrived in the car, heard Sara, how elegantly she lied, how kindly she spoke to them, how she showed them Emelie by the tree. He felt sick.

Emelie's drunk words had detonated inside him like a bomb. She had articulated what he had been feeling for so long, but no one wanted to deal with. It was the stuff about Låke.

He saw:

That Låke hadn't been allowed to be a child, since it was most convenient for the group if Låke didn't have the needs of a child. It was most convenient for the group if Låke didn't go to school; didn't receive healthcare; didn't have friends; didn't even have an adult fighting for him, challenging Sagne when she put her foot down.

How could it have come to this. He brooded. *How did it come to this.*

József had an image of himself as a good person. He had this image of himself because others had often told him so. He never got angry; he always tried to make peace, always tried to understand the other side. He comforted and listened.

Surely that made him a good person?

Suddenly he realised that he wasn't at all.

He began thinking of an experiment he had read about, where test subjects administered electric shocks to people they didn't know. It was ordinary students delivering the shocks, and they did so because the leader of the experiment asked them to. It was often mentioned in relation to World War II, as an attempt to understand how so many ordinary, well-adjusted people had, so seamlessly, transitioned to killing and harming the innocent. *Someone else told me to*; it's someone else's responsibility.

Now he could see it, József—see himself as one of the test subjects, pressing the button, Låke in the other room with a pane of glass between them. József looking questioningly at Sara, and Sara giving the order: *Continue, continue.*

It wasn't just him, either. He could see it in the others, too, that they had started behaving differently since Emelie came and delivered her drunken speech. An uncertainty had begun to spread. He had noticed it first in Ersmo. Then Zakaria. Now maybe Sagne, too. There was something in their gaze, their movements. How they approached Låke. How they approached Sara.

And suddenly the thought struck him, crystal clear.

I no longer believe in Sara. I think she has gained too much power. We wanted so badly for her to lead us. We encouraged her too much. Suddenly we live completely outside of society and none of us really wanted it to be this way.

The thought was uncomfortable, unsettling. He would very much have liked to return to the way he used to think—that things would work out in the end; that Sara was good; that he was good, too.

But now he saw, and he couldn't go back.

I love Låke, he also realised. Why has Låke been straggling behind us. Why haven't I stopped it. Even worse: Maybe I have seen it, but chosen not to do anything.

He saw Sara sit down at the picnic table with a plate of potato salad left over from yesterday, pleased at having duped the Social Services.

And he also realized: I have been a very bad partner. I haven't stopped her.

"Sara, we need to talk."

He covered his eyes, partly because it was sunny out, but partly also because he couldn't bring himself to meet her gaze.

One thing about Sara: she never reacted as you would expect. Perhaps it was part of her greatness. You could never predict how she would react, and it made you obsessed with her reactions.

Now József had expected Sara to be upset, maybe worried, possibly cold and haughty. But instead, she turned to him with her soft voice and soft eyes—the Sara he had known from the beginning.

"Sure, I'll just finish up. Want to go for a walk afterwards?"

He sat at the table and watched as she finished her potatoes. Then she left the plate on the table, for someone else to clear away.

She placed her hand in his and he didn't know how to navigate. He wanted so badly to have it there and he wanted to remove it. *You have to stick to your guns now, József. You have to stick to your guns.*

"I want to say something serious," he said.

He felt silly.

They walked out onto the gravel road. They rarely went there. Sometimes cars would pass by, the occasional motorcycle, sometimes even trucks. People raising their arm in greeting as they drove past. You could be seen by others. He didn't know how they ended up there. Maybe his legs unconsciously guided them to where there might be other people. A sense that he might need witnesses.

And now he stared straight down at the ground as they walked, so careful not to look directly at her and even more careful not to touch her; he had let go of her hand; he walked at a bit of a distance, not far but a bit, a little bit. Usually, he would walk so close that his body brushed against hers with every step they took.

"Sara," he said. "I heard . . . over there, with the people from Social Services."

She unleashed her laughter.

"I know! Wasn't that insane? I knew we were taking a risk by letting Emelie in, but on the other hand she wasn't very difficult to explain away today!"

She imitated Emelie tripping by the tree, and was very funny. She laughed. *Damn, that laugh!* He felt himself being pulled into it. Meatballs, he thought. Meatballs, meatballs. He picked a word, any word, to focus on so he wouldn't start laughing along. A giggle bubbled up from his belly, wanting out. But he wouldn't let it.

He stopped, and said simply: "It didn't feel right."

She opened her mouth, about to say something, but he continued speaking, eager to say what he wanted before she would take over.

"That stuff Emelie talked about that evening. Sure, she was drunk and said some stupid things, but a couple of them I thought she was right about."

He emphasized *I thought she was right*, speaking those words so loudly and clearly that they couldn't be misunderstood. He had an opinion, and now he was expressing it.

He went on:

"And the two things I mean she was right about are, firstly, that there is a life out there we haven't been a part of for the past, what is it? My god, the past eighteen years."

He had to pause and take in this number, before continuing:

"And the other thing is that we haven't treated Låke right. We have kept him away from society, too, from school and friends—Lord, even healthcare, his foot! And on top of that, we've gone along with this strange situation with Sagne being unable to handle him and so we've all kept him at a distance."

His voice sounded so small and foolish, his breathing shallow, like a child suddenly being allowed to speak in the classroom.

Now he wanted her either to
1) say he was right
or maybe
2) convince him that he was wrong, that they had done right by Låke. By extension: that József hadn't made a mistake.

He hoped for either of these options, where the latter would be preferable right here and now, but the former would most likely be decidedly better in the long run.

But she didn't say any of that. Instead, she looked at him calmly.

"Why are you saying this to me, and in this way?"

"Because I . . . Because you're the one in charge."

"Am I?"

"You are." He stamped his foot and repeated: "You are."

"You're just as involved in this as I am. Everyone is as involved in this as I am."

"That's not true, Sara. We've done what you wanted. We've always done what you wanted."

"Is that so?"

She smiled. "If you and everyone else think that Låke should have gone to school, then why didn't he?"

"It's not possible. We're not strong enough to . . . "

"Oh, but listen to yourself, József! You're five grown people. Not exactly idiots, either. If I have led anything, it's because you've asked me to. And I have probably felt compelled to do so. If I've been silent, no one else has spoken."

"It's not been possible. Sara. We can't. It's something you emit. People become weak in your presence."

At first, she laughed, a short little sound. Then fell silent, suddenly looking almost small.

Then said:

"If you say something, nothing comes of it. If I say something, it's what happens. Do you understand what that's like? What a burden that is?"

Here, Sara looked at József, and something resembling sorrow flickered in her eyes. Just fleetingly, it flickered. He swallowed, feeling the instinct to move closer, to hold her. And now he put his hand on her arm.

"We can start over, Sara. We can leave this place. We can contact the authorities, sort everything out. It's possible. I promise."

He dared to look at her now. Expectant.

But the Sara looking back at him was different now. She regrouped, attacking when she had his gaze.

"One could have thought that you, of all people, would have had the courage to do something if a person gained too much power."

"What's that supposed to mean?"

"What I mean? Your entire personality revolves around a trauma you weren't even a part of. You're so focused on your parents that it prevents you from growing up. You're over fifty, yet you still haven't grown up."

"That's not fair."

He stared up into the air.

"You've never been happy here, József! You've walked around like a sour lump of dough, asking to be shaped but turning surly when you're not satisfied with the form. The only reason you've loved me is that you have wanted to follow me, for me to tell you what to do, so you won't have to take charge of anything yourself."

This stung. For József, the moment suddenly felt like they were in the middle of a boxing match, delivering blows that—if enough were thrown—would knock the opponent to the ground. This blow hit hard. Maybe she was right.

He couldn't think of anything to say in response, but now she had gained momentum.

"You've trapped me, József. You've sat there staring at me, asking me to take us somewhere. And I'm sorry, but I can't make you happy and I can't erase your scars. No one can. I'm just a person. I'm not your God or your leader. I know you want me to be, but I'm just a small, rotten person, like the rest of you, doing the best I can."

Sara looked as if she were standing on a stage now, a proud actor in a Shakespeare play, or a politician, dressed in dirty hiking trousers and a tattered shirt, her hair tousled, yet so eloquent that it scared him, the power in her person. He would never be able to catch hold of her.

"We need to change, Sara. I can't do this. I can't anymore."

His voice sounded disheartened, small and hopeless. It pleaded for her compassion.

It didn't get it.

She drew breath before continuing. Now soothing, almost well-meaning.

"You need to confront yourself, József. This isn't about me or the Colony. It's you. This isn't working, my love. You're a grown man. You're getting older now. Start by opening those envelopes you're so afraid of."

Those words, *You're getting older now*, how smoothly she slipped them into what she said, how succinctly and elegantly. They both knew what it meant—that she didn't hesitate to aim a knife at the sore spot on his Achilles' heel: that he had always feared being older and lesser than her, that he wasn't man enough for her, that she needed others to cope.

He no longer knew what to say and he also felt that she was right. He hadn't taken charge of his own life. He loved her clarity. He should dare to open those envelopes. He was a grown man.

Sometimes there comes a moment when you are so tired that you can't bring yourself to think about the words you choose. You just speak. Precisely what's on your mind, you speak it.

"I don't know what to say, Sara. You're probably right about some things. But I'm afraid of you, Sara. Do you see that I have to cover my eyes when we talk? That's the power you hold over me. I understand that you didn't choose it yourself. You're right about everything you say about me. But I must also dare to believe that what I say can be true. It might be true just because I feel it. Because the others feel it. For Låke's sake."

And now he said:

"I think we need to move out. At least, I'm moving out."

And with that he walked back towards the house, still with his hand over his eyes. He walked alone; directly after saying this, he turned around and started walking, for he knew he didn't have any strength left. One more blow, and he would fall to the ground and remain there forever.

The trip was starting to fade. I felt soft and happy, like my whole person was grinning, and I walked into the kitchen, hoping someone had prepared food. I was very hungry.

Sitting there was Sara. At first, I was overjoyed to see her, remembering our meeting of souls just a few hours ago, but I paused mid-step. There was something about her. She looked tense, and she stared at me in a new way.

"What a day," I said light-heartedly, wanting to return to the connection we'd had, to confirm the incredible thing that had just happened—that the group had tripped together. I had never taken mushrooms before. Now I had done this brave new thing, and it had gone so well.

A quick flashback to the woman and the man by the tree. Perhaps not everything had gone well. But we had fixed it.

"Sara—" I said.

She stared at me.

"You promised," she said. "You promised you wouldn't tell anyone about us. And the first thing you do is alert the authorities."

"But that was before, before I got to know all of you," I said. Surely she must understand? I still felt happy and soft. "When I had only met Låke, I found it strange—that he couldn't go to school, for example."

"I had almost forgotten, what it's like to be among ordinary people," Sara said—she spat the word *ordinary*, and I felt just like that: pale, dull. "You have to be like everyone else. Exactly like everyone else."

She looked at me with disappointment. I remembered what it was like to be in middle school. Dad's gaze. *I'm not angry, just disappointed.* The tough girls at school. Ugh. *You're so immature.* A combination of these two gazes and the emotions they evoked gathered in me now.

Sometimes I feel myself being physically swept along by other people's waves. I can't resist. It's like my body longs to be a part of, to join in, to follow, to be involved. I know this about myself. My mother had certain narcissistic traits; I've had more therapy than the rest of the population combined. So I've also developed strategies, for everything. One of them is for resisting powerful individuals when I need to.

The strategy is as follows: In my mind, I convert what Sara is saying into plain text, written on a piece of paper. There, the words are neutral, not colored by the person who speaks them. It's the words I respond to, not the way they are spoken. I often become emotional in such situations, standing up for myself. And so my words become shaky and forceful.

"I'm sorry it turned out this way," I said, choking back tears. "I didn't fully understand the good things you have here. But I still maintain that you have done wrong by Låke. You have let your system stand in his way. He doesn't know anyone his own age. He hasn't been allowed to go to school. You need to change. Please, change.

"He's an amazing person. He's funny, good-natured, energetic. Kind. He's creative. And he wants to learn, Sara. He really wants to learn. He will be able to accomplish great things."

I heard a sound behind me, and turned around. And now I saw him standing there, Låke. He looked like at any moment he might burst into tears. Wide open and fragile, he looked, and

I wanted to weep, too—weep at how important the words just spoken appeared to be to him. I meant them, but they were also just *words*, swiftly spoken words.

Now I saw there were others standing behind him; they came in through the kitchen door. Ersmo, Sagne, and Zakaria. And after them, József.

Ersmo said now: "I agree with Emelie."

And Zakaria said: "Me, too."

And now it happened, that Sagne looked up, with her sharp gaze, and she said: "Me, too."

She took a few steps towards the stove, spoke, staring straight ahead as if stating a fact:

"This shouldn't be directed at Sara. It's me. It was always me. I made a mistake, Låke."

A sound came from Låke's throat.

They rearranged themselves. Now they were all standing on the kitchen floor, in a circle. In the center of the circle now was Låke. József walked up to him, and held him. And Zakaria placed his hand on Låke's back. He was surrounded by hands.

Sara stood up and left. Without a word, she left.

S ara walked into the forest now, at a furious pace. She
didn't know where she was going. Perhaps she just
wanted to get away. Perhaps she wanted to show that she
wanted to get away.

She did a breathing exercise on her own as she walked. It
helped a little. She noticed her pulse slowing slightly.

She wished she could have bounced her thoughts off someone. But there was no one to bounce them off. Her mind felt
too full. She felt so angry, and so sad. Betrayed, even. They
stood gathered: Zakaria, Ersmo, Låke, even Sagne.

And József—

They had wanted her. They had asked for her. She had felt
safe with them. She had sacrificed everything for them—all the
places she could have traveled to, all the flings she could have
had, all the job offers, all the animals she could have saved—
just to care for this group of lost souls.

They were grateful. That's what she had thought.

But apparently not.

She grasped at another feeling. It was almost fearful.
What if—
That was the feeling.
What if they were right
She brushed it aside.
Marched angrily along the trails, her feet stomping against
roots and her arms pressed tightly against her body.

*

She had walked for a couple of hours when she saw it. It was in the middle of the forest. The sunset was filtering through the spruce trees. It was remarkably beautiful where it sat, with the evening sun on its fur.

The bear.

At first, she only saw: a bear. That was something in itself.

But then she froze—

It had a bald patch around its eye.

It looked just like in her dream.

Here it was, finally, the bear. Her guide.

That's how life worked. If you just kept your eyes open, the answers were everywhere to be found.

She stood at a bit of a distance. The bear hadn't seen her yet, but she saw the bear. She knew how you were supposed to behave: turn around slowly and walk away. Bears weren't hostile by nature, but still, that's what you were supposed to do.

Yet she knew, though. She'd had a dream. She knew the bear was her friend, knew it deep in her soul, in every pore of her being.

That's why she moved closer, creeping. Ten feet away, she stopped. Peering at the bear from behind a tree.

She gasped.

Up close. How big it was.

Slowly.

She stepped on a spruce twig.

The bear looked up. Saw her now.

Sara thought they were the same.

The bear.

A woman, just like Sara.

A leader.

It, too, hadn't chosen its peculiar power. It simply possessed it.

Then she saw: there was something wrong with the bear.
Its gaze.
It wasn't stable.
Now she saw,
Hidden behind the bear—
A cub.

One thing Sara remembered that Sagne had said about
bears. They are peaceful animals,
unless you happen upon them when they have a cub to protect.

Aagny had walked into the kitchen and turned around, seen them all sitting there, Låke suddenly at the dining table, not on the chair by the stove. It looked strange, the others overly friendly towards him: *have more jam, Låke, what do you think about this, Låke . . .*

She avoided looking at Zakaria.

"Where's Sara?" she roared, with that gaze, the one they had only seen once or twice, the dangerous one, the one that had glimmered in her eyes that night at Max's house, and by the fire that evening when she pushed Emelie. But hardly any other time. She was often angry, even surly. But this Aagny— this Aagny wasn't the same.

So the others mostly just gaped, not saying anything, simply pointing towards the edge of the forest.

And so Aagny chugged a glass of water, grabbed a head-lamp—for it was getting dark now—and then immediately headed out the door, into the woods.

It wasn't like she really needed the headlamp. Dark or not, Aagny had been walking these woods for almost twenty years now, talking to herself.

At first, she didn't say anything. She just thought.

She thought about Zakaria's face when Sara kissed it.

Then she thought about Sara's face when it kissed Zakaria.

Right-foot! Left-foot! she said. Ever since she was a child, she had used her voice to keep the rhythm in her step. It had started when she was little and her father came home drunk and screaming. They used to go to a relative's house, all the kids, so they wouldn't have to watch as Dad hit Mum. Aagny needed to block out Dad's voice from her head. So they walked, all the siblings, and none of them must think about Dad. *Just keep walking. Right-foot. Left-foot.* Just say those words, and you won't think about it. *Right-foot. Left-foot.* That's how they walked.

Aagny, the soldier. She walked along the trails but constantly made detours. She had got to know this forest like the back of her hand.

Now she called out.

Sara, Sara!

Where was she?

Slowly, as she walked, Aagny noticed her mind clearing.

She kept walking.

* * *

She had been walking for hours, had just started thinking about turning back.

But as she veered onto one of the paths leading back to the house, she suddenly saw: a foot. In the middle of the spruce twigs. It was a foot she knew. A familiar shoe from the hallway. Sara's foot. She recognised the dirty fabric, and the end of the pant leg.

The foot led to a body. Sara lay facing the ground, her legs like a ragdoll's. And she was bleeding everywhere; the blood seemed to come from her back. Blood on her upper body, blood on her lower body; perhaps she had crawled a bit but didn't get very far. Now she lay there, still breathing.

Aagny had had so much anger in her body. She'd had a thought, and a plan.

The plan was going better than planned. Here lay Sara, already completely neutralized.

But suddenly, it appeared

a feeling,
an image
in her mind.
What she saw:
Ersmo, and Låke.

Their friendly faces.
Their bodies against hers.

Adolescent Ersmo, who had sometimes made sure to accidentally walk close to her, fuelling up on physical contact, as though no one would notice.
Låke straggling behind.
Aagny waiting for him.
Giving him something to eat.

A joy, when she realized:
She had. She might never have Zakaria nor any other man, but in the darkness the thought of Ersmo and Låke lit her up from within.
They turned to her. Not to Sara. They had never turned to Sara. Now she saw that.
And as soon as that thought settled in her, spreading through her body like a warm drink,
Aagny suddenly saw who lay there, bloody and broken.
Her best friend.

So Aagny picked her up. Gently, she picked her up. As fast as she could, she walked along the trail, her legs high over the roots; she mustn't stumble, never stumble. She tilted her head in a certain way so that the bright light from her headlamp wouldn't shine into Sara's eyes but on the ground. And Sara's breathing in her ear, and the blood dripping from her body. And Aagny started singing, the first song that came into her head, which turned out to be "Gå och Fiska" by Per Gessle.

I'm going fishing, ooo. And taking a quiet moment.
And as she sang, she noticed Sara's body relaxing. It relaxed in the wrong way, as though becoming completely calm, giving up.

Aagny stopped, gently laid Sara against a spruce tree. She sat down opposite her friend. Removed the headlamp, placed it on the ground, still on. It turned into a spotlight shining straight up at the trees. Like in a haze, she saw what was about to happen.

"Sara," she said. "Say something. Come on, say something." Sara's eyes were almost closed, but her mouth breathed out: "Remember me." That's what she said. "Remember me."

"Remember me," Sara said again.

Then she exhaled, a final sigh. And her head slumped heavily against her chest.

Aagny sat there on the damp moss for a while. Then she lifted the lifeless body and carried it ever so gently back to the house.

And the queen was dead.

* * *

In the kitchen, everyone was gathered. Sagne, staring straight ahead. Låke, at the table next to Ersmo, who was holding Emelie's hand.

It was pitch dark outside, but suddenly: sounds, and the bright glow of a headlamp.

Zakaria was the first to see the body.

"Fuck!" he screamed. It echoed over the field. He went out into the yard and continued screaming, pounding on walls, kicking the ground. Aagny would later run after him, and they would walk down to the water and feel the September winds blowing in, and they would talk, and he would hold her like a friend.

Sagne said nothing. She went out onto the front steps. In the darkness she sat there, trying to peer towards the birch tree.

And József. It was as if all the blood drained from his body, which turned into a thin shadow, collapsing. He looked down at the ground.
Grief finds its way through the body. It has no clear agenda. It only notices that something is different. It settles in as a back-ache or a chafing angst or a need for movement. And József hadn't found it yet, where his grief wanted to go. And so he sat there now, apathetic. Soon, his body would start twitching again, as it had done nineteen years ago when his mother passed, and now there was no one left who knew how he needed to be held.

"Did she say anything," József asked, just before the sun started to rise again. "Before she died."
Aagny took a breath.
"She said she loved you," she offered then. "That she had never loved anyone else more than you.
"She said she loved us all,
"and that we were ready for life."

Låke
(The legal pad, September 2023)

The next day Mum came up to me & said Låke can I talk to you & she has never done that before.

I brought my breakfast but I couldn't eat for she was Pacing so verily around me & it was like she couldn't sit down. I had some zucchini & boiled potatoes left over from yesterday

Mum looked wearily at me & then towards the wall & she said this:

I wasn't well when you were born but it wasn't your Fault.

That's what she said.

You shouldn't walk behind us said Mum it's I who should walk behind the rest of you.

There's nothing wrong with you.

Isn't my Dad the one who there is something wrong with I said. He who took without asking.

Yes that's true said Mummy Sagne.

She swallowed now & said.

I haven't been able to tell you this because it's so terrible that. But you see you look a bit like him & that's why I couldn't look at you or be in the same room.

I swallowed for I didn't know what to do with this information.

I'm sorry I said.

No I'm the one who should apologize. I'm sorry for not being a good mother. I'm sorry Låke.

Then she left.

Now there was a ringing in my head, like a whisper. I didn't really know what I had been searching for in life but now I understood what it was that it was this among other things.

She patted my arm which felt Strange. Then Aagny came in & hugged me. She always grabs onto me tightly when we hug so I can't move. Which I like. & then a little later Ersmo came in with tously hair? I wondered where he had been. But he held me too & the three of us hugged until I had to take a piss.

Emelie. Apparently they're not all bad those Outsiders.

My whole Life lies Ahead of Me.

The Ant Colony
September 2023

No one said it out loud, but they all knew it anyway—that it was over. They started gradually. They no longer had a landline, but someone borrowed Emelie's phone, called the police, and reported Sara's death. Someone else went to the gas station and bought a bag of Cheez Doodles. Another came along for the ride, said hello to passers-by.

Ersmo went into town. Sat there staring. Went into the supermarket, bought a chocolate bar: nougat crisp. Ate the whole thing on a bench outside the shop. Watched people walk by, living their normal lives.

Zakaria went on long walks. Asked Aagny about life in prison. Maybe he could take it. Maybe the penalty would be ten to fifteen years, and after that he would be out. Maybe then he could live some kind of life.

Sagne thought about her parents. How worried they must be. She thought about her mother. Her warm, wonderful, worried mother. The shame of having stayed away was so great, she hadn't been able to bear thinking about it. She wondered what it would be like if she suddenly showed up one day. Would they be angry, saying *oh now is a good time, is it?*

Or. Might they even be happy.

They took the remains of Ersmo's mother, who lay buried in the yard, under the redcurrant bush. They put the bones inside one of the sheds. Aagny doused it with lighter fluid and threw in a match. She insisted on standing alone, watching the shed burn to the ground. She did it while Ersmo was at the shops.

Then she borrowed Emelie's phone again and called the police, reported Ersmo's mother as dead, saying that in her confusion she had accidentally set fire to a sleeping cabin with a cigarette, so she no longer needed Aagny's assistance.

They might examine the bones and notice that she had been dead for a long time, Sagne pointed out.

Oh well, Aagny said and shrugged. If that happened, she would take the blame herself. She did well in prison. Ersmo wouldn't last a day.

* * *

József brought the envelopes down to the river. There he sat now, opening them.

The letter was written in Hungarian. József understood the language approximately, and he sounded out the words as best he could.

Budapest, 23 July 2001

Dear sister,
I'll keep writing even without a reply. I believe the reason you haven't replied yet is that it rips open such deep wounds in you, just as it has in the rest of us. It took a long time before I could think about it. Our generation has frozen into statues. But I go out into the street and see young people living as if it never happened. They laugh. Sometimes it makes me happy, sometimes angry. For so long, I couldn't sleep at night. Eventually, I started talking about it, and after many years I now dare to remember, to look back in time, to before all this happened, when we were children—Éva and Péter and Bela and you and me. One by one, they were taken away, just like Mum and Dad. Did you know I

*ended up in the same place as Bela? He died in my arms, Márta.
I console myself with this knowledge, that for a brief time he got
to be with me.*

*Márta, it's just you and me left now. I would so love to see you
again. Reply if you read this. Do you have children? I want them
to get to know mine.*

*I met Dad's brother. He had somehow gotten hold of a few
pictures from when we were little. I have made copies and am
sending them to you now, Márta. I'm not the same as I was then,
but I know that if I get to embrace you, some of the wounds will
heal. Please reply, Márta.*

Your sister, Nina

At the bottom: an address.

József took the photos out of the envelope and studied them
again. Five children, two parents, all lined up. They looked solemn. His own mother's gaze stared back at him, but it was open,
happy. As if life awaited. Like it had been towards the end, when
her dementia had progressed and she once again didn't know the
evil in this world. The names were written neatly on the back of
the photo. Nina seemed a little younger than his mother. At the
far end, the youngest. Bela. How old might he be in the picture?
One, maybe two years old. He held on to his father's leg.

He felt lonely, so very lonely. It was autumning now, and
cold winds blew in from every direction.

He had a family, the letter said.

They could talk about it, the letter said.

All of life was a blank space now. The letter didn't say that,
but that's what it said inside József. That's what it said on the
day when his mother died, before Sara immediately replaced
her. He had never lived a life without adapting to someone else.

There was too much space, too many paths to take.

He searched within himself.

Carefully, József put the letter and the photographs back into the envelope. He thought about Sara.

He spoke to the sky.

God, if you're there. Take care of Sara. Tell her to wait for me.

He looked out over the scenery. The water and the bog. The trails and the trees. All the times he had walked here. All the times he had slept here—slept well for being him, quite well after all.

Then he went back to the others.

"Could we sit in a circle?" he asked.

In the circle, everyone got to speak their mind.

"There's one thing left that we have to do," József said.

They understood what it was.

* * *

Aside from the mushroom episode, the Colony had mostly been staying up at the farmhouse lately. Therefore, they had missed it.

A road had been ploughed straight through the forest where they used to visit. Torn-up underbrush everywhere. Logs without limbs, needles, and leaves neatly stacked in a pile. In another, branches and greenery. Half the forest cleared. Half still there.

It was Monday morning and the work was about to start again soon.

They walked around drowsily. It looked peculiar, like when your uncle shaves off the beard he has had your whole life. Naked, wrong. Random trees rose up among stumps and sticks.

"The birch tree that stood here," said Ersmo. "It was my pissing tree."

"The pine tree that stood here," said Aagny. "It was always my favorite. It's where I went when things felt crappy."

She sniffled.

"Well, my *second* favorite."

Right next to them the forest stood untouched, but anyone could figure out that this section was next in line. They stood there now, by Big Spruce. Their sleeping bags still under there. The tree's thick, thick trunk, sturdy as life itself. Under her, they had huddled together on all those cold nights, and all the warm. They had hidden their secrets in her, whispering into the bark, and she had kept them, faithfully. Through all the nights and days, she had stood here. When the outside world had failed them, Big Spruce stood firm. She had stood here before their time, before the previous generation, before the generation previous to that. She was still alive; she could still stand here, be something—for future generations, too.

It was time for them to give back.

Behind them, sounds could now be heard. The machine was coming.

EMELIE
(THE NOTEBOOK, SEPTEMBER 2023)

I woke up late. Looked around. Ersmo wasn't there. I stretched, put on the clothes I now wore every day: an old shirt that smelled of Ersmo, and a pair of baggy old jeans that had belonged to Sara and were so soft now they felt like sweatpants.

I was about to go into the big house when I realized it was eerily quiet everywhere. I checked the time. Damn it. I had forgotten. I had to hurry. They might not know if I wanted to come.

I wanted to come.

I grabbed a carrot and ran downhill. As I ran, I heard the black woodpecker. I ran past the wilting red clover and the ants, ants, ants. Now nature was changing color, tinged with yellow, red, orange. It was misty over the slope. My legs ran as if of their own accord.

I threw myself down the hill, flung myself. I stumbled, got up, kept running. My voice shouted and screamed. Stop, my voice screamed. Stop, stop.

The others were already there, embracing Big Spruce, holding her. I went and stood there too, in front of Big Spruce, my body arced like the figurehead on a ship. I didn't have a strong connection to the tree myself, yet I watched myself hugging it, like a mad person, embracing the trunk. It wasn't trippy Emelie who had stood by the birch tree that time when the Social Services came, I realized. It was regular Emelie. There was a fire burning in my body, something I noticed as I stood across from and compared myself to the orange young man sitting in the harvester; he looked confused, like he had just woken up. He didn't seem angry or stressed, and it struck me that he probably didn't have an agenda of his own at all—he was just an employee. That's what I had been, too, when I sat in the newsroom conducting interviews as I was told to. But all the worthless things I had done in my life hitherto, everything that hadn't led anywhere, everything that had only revolved around myself. This was the moment when I would step forward, I would *take action*; if I ever had grandchildren, they would be proud of me.

The orange guy backed away a bit, scratching his chin.

"Okay," he said, a little slowly, like he had seen a lunatic.

When he walked back towards the car, I saw him raise his phone. He was filming.

* * *

Ánne Helena called the very next morning. "What the hell," she said. Her voice a mix of amused, concerned, and—I thought—a bit impressed. She had seen the clip; it had been picked up by the algorithm.

"What are you doing," she said, interested. "And what the hell are you wearing. I didn't recognise you. That's not a designer dress!"

"Now I know, Ánne Helena," I said. "Now I understand . . . "

I started prattling on, my voice feverish, about my close connection to nature and how I now considered myself one with it, that we were all the same.

I heard Ánne Helena cough impatiently.

"You forget where I'm from," she said. "This is what my people have always done. You should ask, not lecture."

I fell silent.

"How are you," she said. "Isn't it time for you to come home now? The old man at the kiosk has put away the outdoor seating. It's getting to be autumn."

Home. I looked around at the expanse, heard the agitated cackle of the new chickens. Aagny was sleeping in a chair, and there was Ersmo, Ersmo. Låke and József digging up potatoes a bit further away. Sagne sat in a chair, reading.

God, I longed for the city.

* * *

Something I haven't told the others is that, during her last week, one day Sara and I stayed up all night. The evenings had been getting colder. We had been drinking wine. I don't know what the others were doing, but they weren't in the big house, at least. Perhaps they lay sleeping in their sheds. The candles grew shorter and shorter. Sara's voice echoed in the kitchen, her contours softened by the light. She was completely and utterly captivating.

"I would like to interview you," I said suddenly. I had always wanted to, but the wine made me bold. I felt a need to get closer to her.

"Interview me? About what?"

"Anything."

She laughed.

"Okay then, go ahead."

There is a voice memo function on my Nokia, and I hit *rec.*

I typed up the interview one night when I couldn't sleep. I remember lying there, staring at Ersmo as he snored. His shoulder in the moonlight resembled a freshly baked bun. I wanted sharp canines so I could sink them into his soft flesh.

Sara's voice is calm and light on the recording, mine grating and eager. But her words feel different to read than what it was like to hear them. Her mannerisms become peculiar in written text: she has to deliver the words herself for you to understand.

Me: "So, what do you want to talk about?"

Sara: "I don't know, you tell me?"

Me: "I want to talk about the Colony. How things turned out the way they did. How you guys ended up here."

I hadn't had time to prepare any questions, of course, but it didn't matter. My head was already full of the questions I'd had since I arrived here. And besides, after years as a journalist, I have learned to pare down my questions to an absolute minimum. A good question shouldn't contain anything about your own preconceptions—if so, the interview stops there, never goes further. The interviewee closes themselves off. Ideally, a question should be just one word.

Of course, I forgot all about this after a while.

Excerpt 1.

Me: "What were you like as a child?"

Sara: "In my own world. I drew a lot. I guess I was trying to escape, maybe. The horses were one way."

She grinned.

"Would you like to see a photo?"

I nodded. She went to fetch it. It looked creased, like it had been stored in a wallet for a very long time.

I wish I had taken a picture of the photo. It showed a young Sara, sitting on a horse. She looked completely and utterly happy on the horse's back. But there was something more: it was like she was uncertain, and soft. Indistinct. In the photo, her eyes were closed. Her grin wide.

Sara: "I've always wanted to get back there."

Me: "To the horses?"

Sara: "No, to that feeling."

Me: "So what happened then?"

Sara: "Adolescence."

Excerpt 2.
Me: "How was your time in India?"
Sara: "It was pretty lousy. I had to get up and meditate in the middle of the night, and sleep with some old guy." (Laugh.)
Me: (Laughs, too.) "Mm, you've told me about that. But . . . why did you? Sleep with the old guy?"
Sara: "I don't know, I think I . . . I felt so annoyed about taking up so much space everywhere, and then he showed up and took up even more space. So I got curious. But then it turned out he was a fraud. He said things, but they didn't mean anything. He wanted to speak, but he had nothing to say. I learned things there, though."
Me: "What did you learn?"
Sara: "I learned that people *want* to be led. That it's an act of service to lead them. Otherwise, so many people don't get anywhere. And I started to feel I've been given this gift, to speak in a way that makes people want to listen."
Me: "What responsibility does a leader have?"
Sara: "Responsibility? There's no responsibility. Yes, well, maybe if you're elected, by a populace. Like a politician, or a manager with a high salary."
Me: "But what if you have power simply by your way of being?"
Sara: "Well, then the others can speak up."
Me: "But can they really?"
Here she laughs, as if I have a twisted mind, and then I laugh, too, a silly laugh that I'm embarrassed to hear.

Excerpt 3.
Sara: "It was also in India that I started to develop an interest in Gandhi and eventually the idea of letting everything in nature take its course."

Me: "I've noticed that you have a book by Pentti Linkola next to Gandhi and *Walden*. I wrote an article about him once, I know a bit about him."

Sara: "Yes?"

Me: "What do you think of Linkola?"

Sara: "I think he has some valid points. Humanity needs to be stopped from destroying other species. We should live in a way that respects everything else. We're moving more and more towards everything being about growth. He wants to bring back agricultural society. I can see what he means."

Me: "Linkola also wants a totalitarian society where people are monitored around the clock by the state, and sentenced to death for crimes against nature."

Sara: "We're moving towards increasingly extreme times. It may require extreme solutions."

Me: "But you're aware that Linkola has said a third world war would be a good thing, killing off as many people as possible? Because it would be better for the planet?"

Sara: "It would be a good thing for the world and other species if overpopulation was curbed, yes."

Me: "He believed that a dictatorship was necessary, to stop industrialisation."

Sara: "Yes?"

Me: "He thought Nazi Germany had its upsides, that so many people died."

Sara: "Yes."

Me: "The Unabomber and Charles Manson are two other people who believed the fight for the environment was a good reason to kill. How does all this relate to Gandhi?"

Sara: "Don't play dumb now, Emelie. You know what I mean."

Me: (Laughs nervously.)

Excerpt 4.

Sara: "I had three abortions when I was young. I didn't want to do that again. And I don't believe in populating the Earth even more. So I got sterilized. Don't tell József, he would be devastated."

Me: "But why haven't you told him?"

Sara: "Oh, you know. It would make everything so complicated."

Me: (Laughs.)

Here we take a break; both Sara and I go out to pee. We chat, have more wine, talk about Ersmo. I hear myself trying to build bridges to Sara by joking at Ersmo's expense, nothing major, more like little jabs—that he hasn't cleaned up after himself in the kitchen, that he's always working on something. It's strange, I thought as I listened through the recording and saw Ersmo lying there sleeping. I think I love him. But here, I used him. Through the jokes, it seems I was trying to show Sara that he and I were close enough for me to make jokes about him, but also that I was one of them now.

Me: "God, it's so dirty here. Must have been Ersmo tracking in all the mud again."

One of the things I dislike most about being a journalist is how unforgiving it is to be transcribing recorded interviews. You are forced to listen to your own voice, hear it trying, coaxing and flattering the interviewee to extract as much information as possible; you hear yourself choosing the words, *umm*, you say, *what was I going to ask.*

Here, you can sense that I'm gearing up to ask the core question. I do this by slowing down, building up to it, speaking admiringly of things I watched them do from up on the hill. You can hear that I have an agenda.

Excerpt 5.

Me: "I remember the first few times I saw you guys. You were dancing, you were thanking the campfire bread, Zakaria lay flat with his face down into the ground. And I remember thinking it was the most amazing thing I had ever seen."

Sara: "Mm."

Me: "And I suppose . . . I mean . . . I think that . . . "

Here, I go for it.

"I have to ask. I've never really understood. What's actually your whole . . . thing?"

Sara: "Thing?"

Me: "Yes . . . what do you want? What's the reason you do what you do? What's the plan? Is it what you said earlier—letting everything in nature take its course? *Walden*? Linkola?"

Sara: (Smiling with her voice.) "Ha ha, what are you saying, Emelie? We don't have a thing. There's no plan."

(I'm desperate, you can hear it.)

Me: "But what does the dancing mean?"

Sara: "The dancing? We just like to dance."

Me: "But what does it *mean*?"

Sara: "It just means that one of us started dancing down by the water one day, and someone else joined in. Then it became a common thing, that we dance."

Me: "So you mean that the way you live, that things just happened that way, by chance?"

Sara: "Yes, or because of the people who are here, and the things that have happened to us. And what we like."

Me: "What you like? But the animals, and the thanking, and the breathwork, and your sense of unity, and living outside of society . . . "

Sara: "Some of it is probably based on our beliefs. I believe in the equality of species. Sagne is a bug nerd. József likes to talk things out as a group. Is that what you mean? Well, mostly it just happened that way."

(There is a panic in my voice now.)

Me: "And then you've built some kind of religion around it?"

Sara: "There is no religion. We just did."

Me: "Everything based on what you, or the group, felt like?"

Sara: "Isn't that always the case, Emelie? Isn't that always how it works? Is there any society where it's not like that. People do things. Some of it feels good. Then they do those things again. That's how traditions form."

She yawned, bored now.

"I just need to go get something."

She never came back. I sat there alone, waiting, and the next time I saw her it was morning and she was in the kitchen with József. I felt that I loved her.

THE ANT COLONY
SEPTEMBER 2023

Aagny sat leaning against the house in the evening sun, a newly purchased beer in her hand. She looked down towards the firepit. Sitting there was Ersmo, and Låke. Ersmo was holding a guitar—József had taught him a few chords—and Låke piped along. They sat across from each other, equals now, like brothers.

But they weren't brothers.

They weren't her sons.

She had no genetic link to them.

She had no right to celebrate Christmas with them, to be around when their children were born.

She looked at them, and couldn't bring herself to think anything other than that it had been worth it.

Even though she would never be able to have any children of her own and had missed that window by living here and taking care of these ones.

Surely, it had been worth it.

She walked inside, preparing to do the dishes. She spun a lap through the house and outside, gathering the glasses and plates she found along the way, by habit. They had left it all, knowing she would clean up. Almost tenderly, she gathered the dishes. She knew whose plate was whose; Sagne's plate always with some scraps left, Zakaria's licked clean. A hand landed on her shoulder. It was Ersmo's.

"I just wanted to say," said Ersmo.

"Whassat," said Aagny.

"This probably goes without saying. But I thought it best to say anyway. If everyone is going to leave here for a while."

"What," said Aagny.

"That this house, that it's as much yours as mine."

"That's kind of you," said Aagny. "You're kind, Ersmo. But it's not true. It belongs to you. To your family."

"But you are my family," said Ersmo, almost surprised. "When I think of you, I'—" he looked uncomfortable, he wasn't used to talking like this, but apparently this thing with Emelie had loosened his tongue—"think of you as my parent. You're all I have."

He looked away as he said it; the words felt clunky as he spoke, but he wanted to say them.

"If you want to be, then you are. My family."

Suddenly he felt insecure; what if she didn't want to. Maybe he had misunderstood. But now he saw tears on her face, and he grinned.

"Surely you knew that, Aagny. Why are you bawling."

* * *

"You're practically grown up now," Aagny said to Låke. "Fifteen or so. You can do whatever you want."

"Maybe I want to be here with you," said Låke.

"I take back what I just said," Aagny corrected herself. "You can do whatever you want, but you can't stay here. You have everything ahead of you. You have to see things. Find out who you are. Find someone to love."

They stood in front of the house; evening was falling. The sky was red, and the air smelled of earth and straw. It had just rained. It was as though the ground beckoned with its finest.

"But what about you," said Låke. "What will you do."

"I'll probably stay for a while," said Aagny. "I don't like being out in the world much. But why don't you send me a postcard. We'll meet up somewhere."

"I might get a phone," said Låke. "Then I can call you."

"Then maybe I'll get a phone too," said Aagny. "In case you call."

The next day, they went into town and got phones. They had signal if they walked out to the gravel road. Emelie had recommended an app and helped her download it. Aagny stared in fascination when she saw the little logo with the flame, and the word written in white:

tinder.

* * *

Zakaria took the car to the local police station.

"Hello," he said. "I would like to report myself for a murder."

"What murder?" said the woman behind the counter.

"I don't know," Zakaria said. "But I'm probably reported anyway. I might be in some register."

He stated his name, and she typed it into her computer.

"Was it outside Beijing Bar? Eleven years ago?"

Eleven years ago.

"Yes."

Zakaria held his breath.

The woman started laughing, which felt both unprofessional and wonderful all at once.

"He's not murdered," the woman said. "His name is in here, and he's still in the register. He's in prison for dealing drugs. But there is a report on you for minor assault, and you might be looking at a fine or some jail time for not showing up."

* * *

József lay on the train. It was a sleeper car. Here he lay all alone, listening to the sound of the rails.

He found himself beside no one.

With a gaping mouth, he had watched as the others—at least seemingly—were able to shrug it off, move on, not dwell on the past.

Personally, he felt dirty, so incredibly dirty.

He had a hundred feelings about what had happened. Ninety-five of them had to do with Sara, and the remaining five with himself.

A child who hadn't been allowed to go to school.

A mentally ill woman who had been killed.

A rapist who'd had his leg broken.

A system they had defrauded for money.

He had loved a woman. In hindsight, it seemed so unbelievably, painfully clear the way he had humiliated himself for her. He didn't know how it had happened, but he had crossed every line, every boundary he had set for himself. Everything he thought was important, he had experimented with.

Had he understood it at the time? Possibly.

He carried it close to his body, trying every day to do something to atone,

but it stayed with him, like a mosquito bite that never stopped itching. And some of the others walked straight out into life without carrying it at all. Even though the same acts had been committed—or rather, not committed. He envied them, yet at the same time not. He had understood not only what a small person he was, but also: how small everyone has the potential to become. That's what he carried now. Precisely that.

He fingered the note in his hand. Kornélia's address—his cousin. He had never met her. She lived in Berlin. He was on his way to visit her.

From there, he would travel to Auschwitz.

He thought of Sara, wishing she was with him.

* * *

Sagne was in the far north, in Padjelanta National Park. It was the first thing she did after leaving the Colony. Later, she would reach out to her family. She sat down on a rock, gazing out over the massif. Its beauty made her stomach drop; she felt dizzy, experiencing all this newness, observing, being curious, seeing a new place, discovering its secrets.

A movement beside her in the air; she looked over.

It was a dragonfly. But—

She got out her camera and magnifying glass. Went about it methodically, taking photos, studying its details. Tried not to jump to conclusions.

Compared the observations with what she knew.

A tingle ran through her.

She saw: one cross vein, not two.

Very angled appendages.

Incredibly angled.

She gaped.

It was a treeline emerald.

* * *

Låke had packed a bag and walked along the big road to the bus stop. He waited for hours until a bus came, heaped out coins for the driver, who sighed and sorted through the ones that were still in use until he gave up and just pointed back into the bus. Låke took a seat somewhere in the middle, a window seat, passing houses and people and land. He stepped off in town, and from there he took another bus. On the seat lay a newspaper. "Potato pickers wanted," it said. "Accommodation available."

The ad was illustrated with a picture of happy youths in a potato field.

He would take one step at a time, walking onto a rock and seeing from there if the next rock appeared. In this way, he might not go anywhere extraordinary, but at least he would *go*, and even if the rocks turned out to lead him back home, at least he would have been somewhere. At least he would have seen things.

A novel is not a solo venture. I would like to thank the following people, who have helped me in various ways throughout the writing process.

These people have read through the manuscript and provided valuable comments:

Monika Fagerholm, Therése Granwald, Anders Gunnarsson, Erik Hansson, Kalle Lundin, Bengt Norlin, Hugo Sundkvist, and Jonas Teglund.

Some have patiently answered questions on topics they are knowledgeable about. Above all, they have helped me understand what *not* to write. If, God forbid, any facts in the book are nevertheless incorrect, it is of course my fault, and mine alone. Malin Gustafsson, Kjell Gunnarsson, Maret Sofia Jannok, Lars Östlund, Maria Östlund.

Most of all, thanks to Anton Gustavsson and Tove Larsmo at my Swedish publisher, Weyler förlag, whose readings and suggestions have greatly improved the book.

The psychiatrist and professor who commented on the invention of the lightbulb and its consequences is Marie Åsberg.

The quote by Torgny Lindgren on pages 279-280 is borrowed from Tom Geddes's translation of *Hash: a novel* (Gerald Duckworth & Co., 2004). The quote by Jackie Collins on page 305 is borrowed from her book *Lucky* (Simon & Schuster, 1985). The lyrics by Joni Mitchell on page 269 are from "A Case of You" (Composer: J. Mitchell; Reservoir Media Management/Mushroom Music).

Annika Norlin, June 2023

About the Author

Annika Norlin is a Swedish author, songwriter, and artist. Her music is released under her own name and as part of the the projects Säkert! and Hello Saferide. Her short story collection, *I See Everything You Do*, was nominated for numerous awards. *The Colony* is her first novel.